Bloomsbury Publishing, London, Oxford, New York, New Delhi and Sydney

First published in Great Britain in May 2017 by Bloomsbury Publishing Plc
50 Bedford Square, London WC1B 3DP

www.bloomsbury.com

BLOOMSBURY is a registered trademark of Bloomsbury Publishing Plc

ISBN 978 1 4088 6661 0

MIX
Paper from
responsible sources
FSC® C020471

Typeset by Integra Software Services Pvt. Ltd.
Printed and bound in Great Britain by CPI Group (UK) Ltd, Croydon CR0 4YY

1 3 5 7 9 10 8 6 4 2

For Helen
Time and change shall not avail
to break the friendships formed

O, my love's like a red, red rose,
that's newly sprung in June;
O, my love's like the melody
that's sweetly play'd in tune.

As fair art thou, my bonnie lass,
so deep in love am I,
and I will love thee still, my dear,
till a' the seas gang dry.

Till a' the seas gang dry, my dear,
and the rocks melt wi' the sun:
I will love thee still, my dear,
while the sands o' life shall run.

And fare thee well, my only love!
And fare thee well awhile!
And I will come again, my love,
tho' it were ten thousand mile.

Robert Burns, 'A Red, Red Rose'

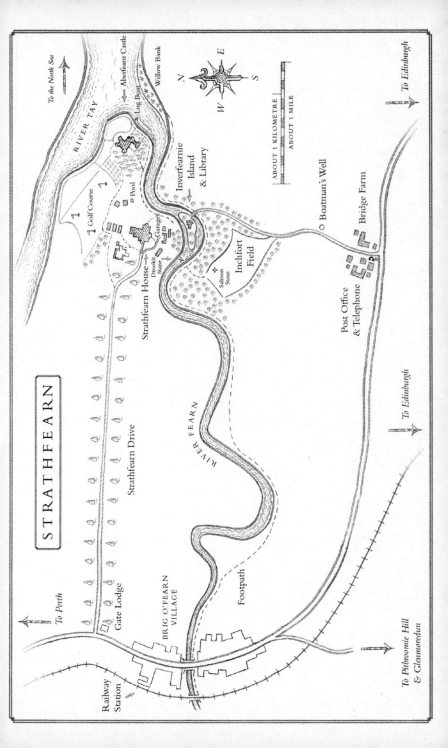

PART

1

WHAT HAPPENED
15TH–28TH JUNE 1938

1

AN ASSORTMENT OF THINGS GONE MISSING

'You're a brave lassie.'

That's what my grandfather told me as he gave me his shotgun.

'Stand fast and guard me,' he instructed. 'If this fellow tries to fight, you give him another dose.'

Grandad turned back to the moaning man he'd just wounded. The villain was lying half-sunk in the mud on the edge of the riverbank, clutching his leg where a cartridge-ful of lead pellets had emptied into his thigh. It was a late summer evening, my last with Grandad before I went off to boarding school for the first time, and we'd not expected to shoot anything bigger than a rabbit. But here I was aiming a shotgun at a living man while Grandad waded into the burn, which is what we called the River Fearn where it flowed through his estate, so he could tie the evildoer's hands behind his back with the strap of his shotgun.

'Rape a burn, would you!' Grandad railed at him while he worked. 'I've never seen the like! You've destroyed that shell bed completely. Two hundred river mussels round about, piled there like a midden heap! And you've not found a single pearl, have you? Because you don't know a pearl mussel from your own backside! You're like a bank robber that's never cracked a safe or seen a banknote!'

It was true – the man had torn through dozens of river mussels, methodically splitting the shells open one by one in the hope of finding a rare and beautiful Scottish river pearl. The flat rock at the edge of the riverbank was littered with the broken and dying remains.

Grandad's shotgun was almost too heavy for me to hold steady. I kept it jammed against my shoulder with increasingly aching arms. I swear by my glorious ancestors, that man was twice Grandad's size. Of course Grandad was not a very big man – none of us Murrays is very big. And he was in his seventies, even though he wasn't yet ill. The villain had a pistol – he'd dropped it when he'd been hurt, but it wasn't out of reach. Without me there to guard Grandad as he bound the other man, they might have ended up in a duel. *Brave!* I felt like William Wallace, Guardian of Scotland.

The wounded man was both pathetic and vengeful. 'I'll see you in Sheriff Court,' he told my grandfather, whining and groaning. 'I'm not after salmon and there's no law against pearl fishing, but it's illegal to shoot a man.'

Grandad wasn't scared. 'This is a private river.'

'Those tinker folk take pearls here all the time. They come in their tents and bide a week like gypsies, and go away with their pockets full!'

'No tinker I know would ever rape a burn like this! And they've the decency to ask permission on my private land! There's laws and laws. Respect for a river and its creatures goes unwritten. And the written law says that I can haul you in for poaching on my beat, whether it's salmon or pearls or anything else.'

'I didn't – I wasnae –'

'Whisht. Never mind what you were doing in the water: you pointed your own gun at my wee granddaughter.' Grandad now confiscated the pistol that was lying in the mud, and tucked it into his willow-weave fisherman's creel. 'That's excuse enough for me. I'm the Earl of Strathfearn. Whose word will the law take, laddie, yours or mine?'

Grandad owned all of Strathfearn then, and the salmon and trout fishing rights that went with it. It was a perfect little Scottish estate, with a ruined castle and a baronial manor, nestled in woodland just where the River Fearn meets the River Tay. It's true it's not illegal for anyone to fish for pearls there, but it's still private land. You can't just wade in and destroy someone else's river. I remember how shocking Grandad's accusation sounded: *Rape a burn, would you!*

Was that only three years ago? It feels like Grandad was ill for twice that long. And now he's been dead for months. And the estate was sold and changed hands even while my poor grandmother was still living in it. Grandad was so *alive* then. We'd worked together.

'Steady, lass,' he'd said, seeing my arms trembling. I held on while Grandad dragged the unfortunate mussel-bed destroyer to his feet and helped him out of the burn and on to the riverbank, trailing forget-me-nots and muck and blood. I flinched out of his way in distaste.

He'd aimed a pistol at me earlier. I'd been ahead of Grandad on the river path and the strange man had snarled at me, *'One step closer and you're asking for trouble.'* I'd hesitated, not wanting to turn my back on his gun. But Grandad had taken the law into his own hands and fired first.

Now, as the bound, bleeding prisoner struggled past me so he could pull himself over to the flat rock and rest amid the broken mussel shells, our eyes met for a moment in mutual hatred. I wondered if he really would have shot at me.

'Now see here,' Grandad lectured him, getting out his hip flask and allowing the wounded man to take a taste of the Water of Life. 'See the chimneys rising above the birches at the river's bend? That's the County Council's old library on Inverfearnie Island, and there's a telephone there. You and I are going to wait here while the lassie goes to ring the police.' He turned to me. 'Julie, tell them to send the Water Bailiff out here. He's the one to deal with a poacher. And then I want you to stay there with the librarian until I come and fetch you. Her name is Mary Kinnaird.'

I gave an internal sigh of relief – not a visible one, because being called 'brave' by my grandad was the highest praise I'd ever aspired to, but relief nevertheless. Ringing the police from the Inverfearnie Library was a mission I felt much more capable of completing than shooting a trespasser. I gave Grandad back his shotgun ceremoniously. Then I sprinted for the library, stung by nettles on the river path and streaking my shins with mud. I skidded over the mossy stones on the humpbacked bridge that connects Inverfearnie Island to the east bank of the Fearn, and came to a breathless halt before the stout oak door of the seventeenth-century library building, churning up the gravel of the drive with my canvas shoes as if I were the messenger at the Battle of Marathon.

It was past six and the library was closed. I knew that Mary Kinnaird, the new librarian and custodian who lived there all alone, had only just finished university, but I'd never met her, and it certainly never occurred to me that she wouldn't be able to hear the bell. When nobody came, not even after I gave a series of pounding kicks to the door, I decided the situation was desperate enough to warrant breaking in and climbing through a window. They were casement windows that opened outward – if I broke a pane near a latch it would be easy to get in. I snatched up a handful of stones from the gravel drive and hurled them hard at one of the leaded windowpanes nearest the ground. The glass smashed explosively, and I could hear the rocks hitting the floor inside like hailstones.

That brought the young librarian running with a shotgun of her own. She threw open the door.

She was bold as a crow. I stared at her openly, not because of the flat, skewed features of her face, but because she was aiming at my head. The library window I'd smashed was public property.

Nothing for it but to plunge in. 'Miss Kinnaird?' I panted, out of breath after my marathon. 'My grandad has caught a poacher and I – I need to use your telephone – to ring the police.'

Her smooth, broad brow crinkled into the tiniest of irritated frowns. She'd sensed the importance of what I'd said, but she hadn't heard all of it. Now she lowered her gun and I could see that around her neck hung two items essential to her work: a gold mechanical pencil on a slender rope of braided silk, and a peculiar curled brass horn, about the size of a fist, on a thick gold chain. She'd lowered the gun so she could hold the beautiful horn to her ear.

'Your grandad needs help?' she said tartly. 'Speak up, please.'

'STRATHFEARN HAS CAUGHT A THIEF AND I NEED TO USE YOUR TELEPHONE,' I bellowed into the ear trumpet.

The poor astonished young woman gasped. 'Oh! Strathfearn is your grandfather?'

'Aye, Sandy Murray, Earl of Strathfearn,' I said with pride.

'Well, you'd better come in,' she told me briskly. 'I'll ring the police for you.'

I wondered how she managed the telephone if she couldn't hear, but I didn't dare to ask.

'Grandad said to send Sergeant Angus Henderson,' I said. 'He's the Water Bailiff for the Strathfearn Estate. He polices the riverbank.'

'Oh, aye, I know Angus Henderson.'

She shepherded me past the wood and glass display cases on the ground floor and into her study. But I poked my head around the door to watch her sitting at the telephone in its dark little nook of a cupboard under the winding stairs. I listened as she asked the switchboard operator to put her through to the police station in the village at Brig O'Fearn. There was a sort of Bakelite ear trumpet attached to the telephone receiver. So that answered my question.

I went and sat down in the big red leather reading chair in Mary Kinnaird's study, feeling rather stunned and exhausted, and after a few minutes she came in with a tray of tea and shortbread.

'I expect Grandad will pay for your window,' I told her straight away. I assumed his wealth was limitless, three years ago. I hoped he wouldn't be angry, and I wondered how he was getting on, waiting alone with the vicious and miserable prisoner. 'I'm very sorry I had to break the glass.'

'And I am very sorry I pointed my gun at you.' Mary knelt on the floor beside me, there being no other chair but the one behind her desk.

She offered the shortbread. I found I was ravenous.

'Oh, I knew you wouldn't hurt me,' I told her. 'You are too bonny.'

'You wee sook!' she scolded. 'Bonny?'

'Not beautiful,' I told her truthfully. 'Your face is kind. You're sort of fluttery and quiet, like a pigeon.'

She threw her head back and laughed.

'*Prrrrrt*,' she said in pigeon-talk, and this made me laugh too. Suddenly I liked her very much.

'What's your name?' she asked me.

'Lady Julia Lindsay MacKenzie Wallace Beaufort-Stuart,' I reeled off glibly.

'Oh my, that is quite a name. Must I call you Lady Julia?'

'Grandad calls me Julie.'

'I will compromise with Julia. Beaufort and Stuart are both the names of Scottish queens; I can't quite lower myself to Julie.' She smiled serenely. 'Not Murray? Isn't that your grandfather's name?'

'Some of my brothers have Murray as a family name.'

'You know the Murrays were in favour with Mary Stuart. There's a bracelet on display in the library that belonged to her when she was a child. She gave it to your grandfather's people because she was their patron, four hundred years ago.'

'Scottish river pearls – I know! Grandad showed me when I was little. They're the only thing I remember about the display cases. All those dull old books along with this beautiful wee bracelet that belonged to Mary Queen of Scots! And I'm related to her on the Stuart side.'

Mary laughed. 'Those books are first editions of Robert Burns's poems! I don't find them dull. But the pearls are everybody's favourite.'

My hidden criminal inner self noted what an idiot the wounded trespasser was, stripping young mussels from the river when this perfect treasure lay in plain sight of the general public every day.

But perhaps the river seemed easier prey than Mary Kinnaird.

She said to me then, 'So I'm a Mary and you're a Stuart. And I have the keys to the case. Would you like to try on Mary Queen of Scots' pearl bracelet while you wait for your grandad to come back for you?'

Mary Kinnaird suddenly became my favourite person in the entire world.

I noticed something. 'How can you hear me without your trumpet?'

'I'm watching your mouth move. It helps a great deal to see your mouth straight on. I don't like the trumpet much.'

'The trumpet is *splendid*.'

She twisted her mouth again. It wasn't a smile. 'But the trumpet makes me different from everyone else. And I am already a bit different.'

'No one's *exactly* alike,' I said blithely. 'I can find my mother in a candlelit hall full of dancers by the scent she wears. Everybody's different.'

It was very easy for me to say, flush with the fear and triumph of my last summer afternoon with my grandfather, the Earl of Strathfearn. I was safe now, eating shortbread in the Inverfearnie Library, and looking forward to trying on pearls that had once been worn by Mary Queen of Scots. *Everybody's different*: it was easy for me to say.

★

'You're a brave lassie!'

It was a perfect echo of Grandad, but of course now it wasn't Grandad and there wasn't a life at stake. It was only the taxi driver congratulating me.

'A lass like you, taking the train alone across Europe! Times have changed.'

'I had my own berth on the Night Ferry,' I told him modestly. 'Men and women are separated.'

I didn't tell him I was coming home from my Swiss *boarding school* for the summer holidays – I'd spent the entire trip carefully trying to disguise myself as being closer to twenty than to sixteen. I'd put my hair up in a chignon and hidden my ridiculously babyish panama school hat in a big paper bag. With my childish socks and school blazer crammed into my overnight case and the collar of my blouse undone, and the help of a lipstick bought in the rail station in Paris, I thought I pulled off a believable imitation of someone old enough to have left school.

'But I did arrange the journey myself,' I couldn't help boasting. 'My people aren't expecting me for another three days. It may be my own fault I've lost my luggage though. I think it is having its own little secret holiday in a hidden corner of the port at Dunkirk.'

The taxi driver laughed. Now we were on the Perth Road on our way to Strathfearn House. Nearly there – nearly! Scotland, summer, the river, Grandad …

And then that moment when I realised all over again that Grandad was gone forever, and this was the *last* summer at Strathfearn.

'My grandfather died earlier this year and my grandmother's selling their house,' I told the taxi driver. 'My mother and I are going to help her with the packing up.'

'Oh, aye, Strathfearn House – he was a good man, Sandy Murray, Earl of Strathfearn. I saw in the *Perth Mercury* that the Glenfearn School bought the estate. They've been working like Trojans to get the house and grounds ready for the students to move in next term. Lucky lads! Your grandad had a nine-hole golf course out there, didn't he? Good deal of debt though …'

Bother the *Mercury*. I hoped they hadn't published an amount, although I supposed they must have printed some number when the estate went up for sale, including the house and everything in it that my grandmother hadn't brought with her from France in 1885. She must have been so ashamed. Grandad left tens of thousands of pounds' worth of debt. Originally he lost a great deal of money when the stock market collapsed in 1929, but then he added to it by borrowing to put a new roof on Strathfearn

House; then he'd had to sell parts of the estate to pay back the loan; and then he'd been struck with bone cancer. And the treatment, and the visits to specialists in Europe and America, and the alterations to the house so he could go on living in it, and the private nurses ...

And suddenly I was longing to be at Strathfearn, even if it wasn't ours any more; longing to see my mother and grandmother and my friend Mary Kinnaird, longing for one last summer of childish freedom on the River Fearn; but also full of grown-up excitement about being included as someone sensible enough to help settle the Murray Estate, when any one of my five big brothers could have done it. I didn't want the summer to begin. I didn't want it to end.

The taxi could not go right up to the house because a digger and a steamroller were engaged in widening the drive. I had to put the fare on my mother's account, but the driver just laughed and said he knew where to find us. I got out to walk the last third of a mile.

The first person I recognised was Sergeant Angus Henderson, the Water Bailiff whom Grandad sent for to take custody of the pearl thief we caught. Henderson was there with his bicycle, with his tall cromach across the bars as if he were about to do a high-wire act and needed a long stick to balance him. He was having a row with the driver of the steamroller.

'I've told you before to keep your men off the path by the Fearn when they're ditch-digging!' the Water Bailiff roared. 'Bad enough the place crawling with those dirty tinker folk camped up in Inchfort Field, in and out the water looking for pearls. That river path to the Inverfearnie Library is off limits to your men.'

'Those men are digging the pipeline for the new swimming pool – how d'you expect them to stay off the river path?' steamed the roller driver. 'All the work is downstream of Inverfearnie. I dinnae want them mixed up with those sleekit tinkers anyway. Bloody light-fingered sneaks. You'd not believe how many tools go missing, spades and whatnot.'

I did not want to get caught in the crossfire of this battle. The Water Bailiff is a terrifyingly tall and gaunt ex-Black Watch policeman. Grandad told us that in the heat of the Great War, Henderson allegedly shot one of his own men in the back for running away from a battle, and then strangled a German officer, an enemy Hun, with his bare hands.

'I'm off down the Fearn path now, and if I catch any of your men there …' Henderson let the threat hang, but gave his cromach staff a shake.

The Water Bailiff had been known to thrash every single one of my five brothers for some reason or other in the past – guddling for rainbow trout out of the brown trout season, or swimming in the Fearn when the salmon were running, or just for getting in his way as he patrolled the narrow path along the burn on his bicycle.

I stepped back so I was well out of his way as he set off along the drive ahead of me. When he'd become nothing but a dark beetling shape among the bright green beeches, I held tight to my small overnight case and set off after him, considerably more slowly. I was looking forward to getting out of my modified school uniform if I could. But the dark skirt and white blouse did give me a smart official air, like a post office clerk or a prospective stenographer for the Glenfearn School, and the men working on the drive paid no attention to me.

My grandmother's roses in the French forecourt garden in front of Strathfearn House were blooming in a glorious blazing riot of June colour, oblivious to the chaos through-out the rest of the grounds. There were people all about, hard at work building new dormitories and classrooms and playing fields. None of them I recognised. I let myself into the house – the doors were wide open.

The whole of the baronial reception hall had been emptied of its rosewood furniture and stripped of the ances-tral paintings. I felt as though I had never been there before in my life.

I went straight to my grandmother's favourite sitting room and discovered it was also in disarray; and my remaining family members were nowhere to be found. I hadn't told anyone I was coming three days earlier than expected. So, like a hunted fox bolting to the safety of its den, I sought out the nursery bathroom high in the back of the east wing, and drew myself a bath because I had been travelling for three days and the hot water seemed to be working as usual.

I didn't have any clean clothes of my own to change into, but it is a good big bathroom, and in addition to a six-foot-long tub and painted commode there is a tall chest full of children's cast-offs. I put on a mothy tennis pullover which left my arms daringly bare and a kilt that must have been forgotten some time ago by one of my big brothers (probably Sandy, who was Grandad's favourite, his namesake and his heir, and who had spent more time there than the rest of us).

I was David Balfour from *Kidnapped* again, the way I'd been the whole summer I was thirteen, to my brothers' amusement and my nanny Solange's despair. I plaited my hair and stuffed it up under a shapeless faded wool tam-o'-shanter to get it out of my face, and wove my way through the passages back to the central oak staircase.

The banisters were covered with dust sheets because the walls had just been painted a modern cool pale blue –

not horrible, but so *different* from the heraldic Victorian wallpaper. Light in shades of lemon and sapphire and scarlet spilled through the tall stained-glass window on the landing. As I turned the corner, the telephone in the hall below me started to ring.

I swithered on the landing, wondering if I should answer it. But then I heard footsteps and a click and the ringing stopped, and a harassed man's voice said, 'Yes, this is he … No, they're not gypsies, they're tinkers. Scottish Travellers. It's tiresome, but they're allowed to stay in that field till the end of this summer.' The voice took a sudden change of tone and continued brightly, 'Oh, you've sent the Water Bailiff up there *now*? My foreman thinks they're pretty bold thieves – wants him to check all their gear for missing tools … Jolly good!' His footsteps thumped smartly back the way they'd come.

Goodness, everyone seemed to have it in for the Travelling folk.

This Scottish traveller didn't bother anybody. If the ditch-diggers were all downstream and the Water Bailiff was off bothering the campers at Inchfort Field, I could count on having the river path to the library on Inverfearnie Island all to myself. I thought I would go to say hello to Mary Kinnaird, who would not care if I was wearing only a kilt and a tennis pullover.

I crossed the broad lawn, broken by men smoothing earth and digging pits and laying paths. In the distance by the edge of the River Tay, over the tops of the birch trees, I could see the ruinous towers of Aberfearn Castle. The Big House is new by comparison; it was built in 1840, before Grandad was born. Before the railway came through. It was hard to believe that none of this was ours any more.

I passed into the dapple of sunlight and shade in the birch wood by the river.

An otter slid into the burn as I started along the path, and I saw a kingfisher darting among the low branches trailing in the water on the opposite bank. For a moment I stood still, watching and breathing it in. The smell of the Tay and the Fearn! Oh, how I'd missed it, and how I would miss it after this last summer!

See me, kilted and barefoot on the native soil of my ancestors, declaiming Allan Cunningham in dramatic rhapsody:

'O hame, hame, hame, to my ain countree!
When the flower is i' the bud and the leaf is on the tree,
The larks shall sing me hame in my ain countree!'

I crossed from the west bank of the Fearn to Inverfearnie Island by the footbridge. It is a creaky old iron suspension bridge so narrow you can't pass two abreast, erected in the year of Queen Victoria's Jubilee. I jumped along its span to make it sway, the way my brothers and I had always done when we were little.

The library stood proud on the unnatural mound of Inverfearnie Island, which Grandad always told us might hide a Bronze Age burial beneath it. The oak front door of the library was locked, just as it had been three years ago.

This time, knowing Mary much better than I did then, I went round to the kitchen door. It was standing ajar.

'MARY?'

I let myself in, hollering, because she can never hear you.

The kitchen was tidy and empty. I went through to her study, yelling my friend's name. She wasn't there, either, and it was also tidy and empty, as if she hadn't been in all day.

I glanced into the telephone cupboard with its red velvet stool, in the dark little nook under the winding stairs. No one.

I went through to the library.

The library is two rooms on top of each other, the walls surrounded by shelves and scarcely a single book newer than before the Great War, apart from recent volumes of antiquarian journals and almanacs. But they still lend books to anglers and Scots language scholars and farmers trying to solve boundary disputes, and there is almost always someone or other studying in the Upper Reading Room.

I spared a reverent glance for the pearl bracelet. It lay locked under glass on its bed of black velvet, on permanent loan to the Perthshire and Kinross-shire Council for display in the library here. I couldn't quite believe Mary had let me try those pearls on. They were beautiful fat Tay river pearls, so pale a grey they shone nearly like silver, the size of small marbles. Staring into the glass until it began to get fogged by my own breath, I could remember exactly how they'd felt against my wrist, cool and heavy with the magic of having been worn by Mary Stuart herself, whose surname I shared, as young as me and already Queen of Scotland.

I wiped the glass and turned away to continue the hunt for my own living Mary. I took the narrow winding steps to the Upper Reading Room of the library two at a time.

'AHOY, MARY!'

And the Upper Reading Room was empty too.

But here was a strange thing. The Upper Reading Room was empty, but unlike the rest of Mary Kinnaird's domain, it was not tidy. The great big chestnut table was covered end to end in ephemera and artefacts. I identified these as what my brothers and I called 'the Murray Hoard': intriguing archaeological finds that our grandfather used to keep on display in the tower room at Strathfearn House. I guessed

22

that this must be a grand sorting job, with Mary called upon to catalogue the priceless ancient pieces before they went to auction. Iron and bronze spear tips, all different sizes and shapes, lay in rows, with more waiting in cigar boxes; I recognised an iridescent Roman glass vial shaped like a leaping fish which was, Grandad told me, nearly two thousand years old; and the dark polished stone axe heads were eerily three times that.

And there was my favourite item, a small round cup made of blackened wood set in silver filigree. I could picture it sitting in a back corner of a dusty glass case in the tower of the Big House, full to the brim with loose pearls like the ones on the bracelet downstairs. I had never been allowed to touch the cup, but Grandad had let me play with the pearls when I was very small.

'My mother's mother's mother's …' he'd said they were. I can't remember how many mothers back they went. All those pearls were found in Scottish rivers. I'd loved the way out of all the ancient artefacts in his collection, only the pearls didn't look old. Like the royal pearls downstairs, they were as beautiful and ageless as the rivers where they'd been grown.

Now the cup was empty. The pearls were gone. Another wave of sadness washed over me. I'd felt instinctively that they belonged in that cup. Grandad must have sold them, as he'd sold so many of his heirlooms and so much of his land, to keep the estate going during his illness.

I was surprised that Mary would have gone out leaving a door open with all this valuable stuff lying about. She takes her job as the Inverfearnie Library custodian very seriously.

I poked my nose into the other rooms, her bedroom and the bathroom, but Mary was nowhere to be found.

I decided to leave her a note. I went back up to where she'd been working. There was paper everywhere, but all covered with lists and descriptions of artefacts. Finally I settled on an empty brown envelope addressed to my grandfather and postmarked *Oxford* from two years ago. The back was engraved with the name of a scholar I'd never heard of at the Ashmolean Museum. The envelope had been slit open with a knife or letter opener long ago, and whatever message it had once contained was not lying about in an obvious place. It didn't seem important in any way, so I wrote to Mary on the back quickly to say that I was home in Scotland and staying at Strathfearn House for the next few weeks, and that I would stop in again to visit.

Here was another odd thing. When I went to prop my message against a chipped clay pot of unknown origin, in front of the pushed-back chair where Mary would be sure to see it when she came back, a pearl fell out of the envelope.

I thought it dropped off *me* at first – as if I'd been wearing it in my hair, or as an earring! It was the palest rose-petal pink, the size of a barley grain and perfectly round. It hit the green baize table cover with a sound like *pip* and lay still. It was intact and beautiful.

I picked it up – it was so round I had to wedge it beneath my fingernail to get hold of it. It must have been part of the collection. I thought of dropping it into the black wooden cup. But afraid of disturbing the cataloguing system, I put it back inside the envelope it had fallen out of. I folded the envelope over so the pearl couldn't fall out again and propped it against one of the jam jars.

I went back outside, leaving the kitchen door a little open behind me, the way I'd found it.

The hammering and drilling and tractoring going on at the Big House and further downstream was no more than a faint hum. I didn't feel like going back to the Big House. I thought I'd go to look at the Drookit Stane and the Salmon Stane, the standing stones in the river and Inchfort Field, just to make sure the builders hadn't knocked them down to make an access road or boat ramp or something. Maybe I'd just peek at the one in Inchfort Field without leaving the birch wood. I didn't want to get mixed up with the Water Bailiff.

I went down the gravel driveway, and crossed the humped bridge of moss-covered stone, as old as the seventeenth-century library itself, that leads to the opposite bank of the Fearn. Then I continued along the path on the other side of the river.

Where the burn bends it has scooped out a little shingle beach on one bank, where we used to swim. There was a heron standing midstream near the tall Drookit Stane, absolutely still, focused on fishing. Its shadow was dark against the stone and its reflection rippled in the water. I stopped still too – but not still enough. It heard me and lifted off awkwardly, heading downstream with long, slow wing beats.

I sat down on the flat sun-dappled rock slab where the wounded poacher had rested, and where Grandad had taught me and my brothers to guddle for trout. I wondered if I could still catch a fish using only my hands. No one was about, not even the heron, and I was overcome with a wave of sadness over my grandfather and his house and his things that weren't ours any more, and all the summers that would never come back.

So I lay down and slid my bare arm into the clear brown water.

There. I was minding my own business, waiting for a fish to tickle. I suppose I didn't really have any right to fish there because it wasn't our land any longer. Julie the poacher!

I thought about the pearls that I'd never see again, and all my grandmother had lost. I thought about picking an armful of her own roses for her. The plan improved: I would dig some up so she could take them with her when she had to leave the house for good.

I'd not slept well on the trains across Europe. I'd been travelling for three days. I was lying in the sun and lulled by the sound of running water, and I fell asleep thinking about roses.

I remember what it looked like when my head exploded with light and darkness, but I didn't remember anything else until the moment I found myself in St John's Infirmary in Perth three days later.

2

NO MODESTY AT ALL

I don't think I am capable of describing the headache with which I woke up.

For a long time I lay very still, not daring to move, and wishing I would lose consciousness again. When it became clear that this was not going to happen, I opened my eyes.

My friend Mary Kinnaird was sitting beside me, reading a book.

She was wearing her usual tweed skirt and a powder-blue blouse and a dreadful prickly cardigan like the sheepskin in the story of Jacob and Esau. I had no idea where I was or how I'd got there. But if Mary Kinnaird was sitting next to me calmly reading, I knew I was perfectly safe.

I said, 'Hullo, Mary.'

She didn't hear me. I waved.

She was so startled she dropped the book. Her smooth, broad brow crinkled with distress. Then she leaped out of her chair and landed on her knees next to me by the bed in which I'd been laid out, and grabbed my hands and exclaimed, 'Oh, *Julia*! Julia, do you know me?'

'Of course I know you, Mary,' I said peevishly.

'I'm sorry, darling, you're speaking into my bad ear.' Flustered, she dropped my hands to hold up the beautiful brass horn. 'Can you see? Can you hear me properly? What *happened?* Oh dear, now that you're awake I really should go and ring your mother. Julia, can you speak? How do you feel?'

I wanted to tell her to shut up or her blethering was going to kill me. I wanted to tell her it didn't matter whether I could see or speak and that I didn't care if she wanted to go and ring the King. I couldn't possibly tell her what had happened because not only did I not know, but due to my fearsome headache I never even wanted to find out.

I knew she could read my lips if I was facing her. I turned towards her on the pillow and said clearly, gazing into her eyes, 'Please cut my head off.'

'Oh, darling,' Mary Kinnaird said, and kissed me. 'I don't think anyone but me knows you're here! The ward sister was rather run off her feet when I came in, and I haven't had a chance to explain to her who you are. You were brought in here to the hospital two days ago by a family of travelling tinker folk, and they didn't know who you are, either. Everyone thought you were one of them! There was a story about it on the front page of the *Perth Mercury* – "Tinker Lass Left for Dead on Riverbank"! Why aren't your people worried about you?'

'I came home early without telling them … I'm not supposed to get here till Saturday. Two days, you said? It's *Friday*?'

'Saturday. The tinkers kept you with them overnight when they found you. They brought you here the next day.'

'*Saturday!*' I gasped in disbelief.

I'd been unconscious since Wednesday.

It was the most tremendous thing that had ever happened to me.

'But how did you know the person in the *Mercury* was me?'

'Of course you'd left me a note, darling. Only I didn't find it till this morning. The library's shut all day on Wednesdays, so I can get the messages in the morning before early closing in the village, and I was out when you came in. And then when I found your note I guessed that the girl left unconscious on the riverbank might be you, and I was *dreadfully* worried – especially as it was a lad that found you, lying at the edge of Inchfort Field with a great dunt on your head. Did he … did he *do something* to you, darling?'

'What kind of something?'

'Oh, well … *anything*. You know. Any *thing*.'

I was still too dazed to be alarmed at this subtle innuendo, though obviously I'd nearly had my head smashed in. Surely not by the same person who said he'd found me unconscious? Who'd be stupid enough to ambush someone and then deliver her to the hospital?

I began to take an inventory of my working parts as Mary spoke. Impossible to move my head without being sick. Crikey! Did someone actually hit me, or did I somehow crack my skull on the slab of rock I'd been sitting on? My tongue caught on the jagged edge of a tooth – it was chipped. I poked gingerly at the snaggly enamel with a fingertip, then moved my hand so my friend could see my mouth shape these words:

'Oh, Mary! Do I look like a hag?'

She answered a little briskly, 'You're quite as lovely as ever.'

It was probably the most thoughtless thing I'd ever said to her.

I wished I'd never woken up. I wished I could start all over again and never have let her see vain, coquettish Julie whose first thought in the *world* is always for the way people see her. Mary Kinnaird lives like a hermit most of the time because people who don't treat her like a cretin are *scared* of her. She has the kindest face in the world but it is not a face like everyone else's.

When you say something that hurtful it only draws attention to it if you try to take it back. So I didn't. I reached further up my head to explore the bump and the bandages, and discovered what was left of my hair.

I am ashamed to put down here what happened next, but I shall, as a sort of penance for being so utterly shallow.

'Oh, Mary, how *could* you! "Quite as lovely as ever." Oh, what happened? Who did this to me – *why*?'

I sobbed pitiably. You could say like a three-year-old, except that I would not have howled about my hair when I was three.

It was *all gone*.

I could feel the different lengths all around my head – much shorter near the great big bump than on the sides. I think the doctor sawed it off tidily at the back of my head first, to get at the wound, and then that – that *witch* of a nurse took the rest off to even it up.

'What will everyone say when I go back to school?' I wailed. 'That cat Nancy Brooke will laugh her head off. And *just* when I'm *finally* old enough to wear it up for dances – and my sixteenth birthday coming …'

Well, I am embarrassed. But that is what I said, and more besides.

'Darling, don't cry over your hair, for goodness' sake,' Mary scolded. 'That's not the brave lassie I know at all!'

Her voice was warmer now. I think she must have attributed my excess of vanity to the dunt on my head, because she hastened on to more important things.

'Now, I'll say it again, because I'm afraid you're a bit woozy – you said your people are expecting you back today, but they've no idea you're here, so I must tell them now. I suppose I should have rung someone *before* I came to see if it was really you, but the papers this morning said you hadn't woken up yet and I thought, if it *was* you, it was more important someone should be with you when you *did* wake up ...' She trailed off.

I think it is lack of company in general that makes her so loquacious with people she trusts. Just now it left me rather breathless with emotion and confusion.

'Anyway I *must* go and tell your lady mother!' she finished with great purpose.

'Please warn my mother's companion Solange about my hair,' I said selflessly. 'She was my nanny and she will be just as upset as I am.'

Mary Kinnaird got up and hurried off back to Strathfearn.

I managed to roll over on my side and was able to get a better view of the rest of the ward. The explosive headache began to subside and I grew increasingly aware that my mouth felt like it was full of sandpaper. I hadn't eaten or drunk anything for three days – apparently I'd been given fluid injections while I was unconscious, but I was desperate for a glass of water. I had no idea how to get anyone's attention, and I thought I could help myself to a drink from the jug on the trolley at the end of the bed next to mine.

Gravity helped me to topple out of my own bed. They had dressed me in a hospital gown that felt like it was made out of newspaper, tied at the neck and waist and otherwise completely open to the elements. It did not cover my backside as I crawled to the trolley.

It all took a lot longer than I expected it to, and when I got there I couldn't stand up or lift the jug.

Defeated, I crawled indecently back to my own bed – getting into it was like scaling Mont Blanc. All the exercise combined to set upon my skewed equilibrium as if I were at sea in a Tay coble in a tempest. I had to stop and close my eyes and take some deep breaths before I attempted the battle to get back under the covers.

I heard somebody say, 'Dirty wee besom. You saw that? Bold as brass. Asking for trouble.'

And a voice that answered, 'That's their kind. *No modesty at all.*'

I seem to be good at asking for trouble.

I was not so successful at asking for water. Although I finally had the attention of the nurse on the ward and spoke politely, she downright refused me.

'Not if you put on airs, you sleekit Lady Muck,' she told me in tones of Cairngorm mountain granite. 'I'll not be mocked by your kind.' She took hold of the trolley that held the water jug and wheeled it away.

I was left gaping. What had I *done*? How could she think I was mocking her? Was it because I'd said 'please'? Surely I was *expected* to say 'please'?

She passed me twice more in the next hour and both times I asked her again, taking care to keep it simple and polite:

'Please may I have a glass of water?'

How could I be putting on airs? I'd never felt so pathetic in my life. It is true you can hear Landed Gentry in my ordinary accent, but I'd never had anybody take *offence* at it before.

'That's their kind,' the horrid woman had sneered at my lack of discretion on the floor. 'I'll not be mocked by your kind.'

Whose kind? Truant finishing-school girls home for the summer? Did she somehow scent my grandmother's French blood in me? Had I raved in my sleep about the unchaperoned skiing holiday last winter? Who did she think I was? One of the 'tinker folk' whom Mary said had brought me in?

Of course. The headline Mary had quoted from the front page of the *Mercury* explained it all: 'Tinker Lass Left for Dead'. The adjectives the nurse had used on me already – *dirty, bold, sleekit* – were all implied in that one damning word, *tinker*. *Their kind.* Angus Henderson, and the steam-roller driver and the man on the telephone in the hall at Strathfearn House had all used the same words.

The nurse thought I was a Traveller, like the people who brought me here. That's why she thought I was dirty. That's why she thought I was indiscreet. That's why she thought I was making fun of her by putting on airs.

I suppose my bare feet and bare arms and cast-off clothes hadn't helped my case much when I first arrived.

Whoever they were, the folk who brought me here had gone out of their way to *help* me. They were charitable. They were good and decent people. No one should be sneering at them.

It *made me mad*.

At which point I was sitting there seething quite help-lessly, when two more visitors came in to see me.

They were a girl and a boy, about my own age. They appeared to be twins. The boy was fully one foot taller than me, and they both had glorious ginger hair like Mary

Queen of Scots (or how I imagine Mary Queen of Scots, anyway), and the pale clear skin to match. The girl walked like the goddess Athena, head high, looking neither left nor right. The boy came in furtively behind her, moving in absolute silence, as though with every step he was expecting to be shouted at to leave. There were curtained screens at the foot of some of the beds in the ward, and he stepped cautiously between them, not daring to catch the eye of any of the other patients. Both the girl and the boy wore much-mended clothes, patched at the elbows and let down at the hems. The girl had a small closed basket like Grandad's fisherman's creel slung on a strap over her shoulder.

She stopped next to my bed. She fixed me with stony eyes the dark blue of descending storm clouds, and continued to hold my gaze while she beckoned her brother with a shake of her head. He came to stand next to her, saw consciousness in my face and smiled.

'Well now, Davie Balfour!' he said warmly.

Even if I did once spend three months demanding that everyone in the household call me Davie (they might have been more indulgent if it had not also been my eldest brother's name), I don't expect to be recognised when I'm in drag as one of my favourite literary obsessions. Astonishment and joy made me want to laugh, only I couldn't because my head still felt like it was being gently but methodically drubbed with a mallet. I tried weakly to manage a responsive grin.

'You're awake,' the girl observed.

'Only just,' I said.

The boy padded silently to my side and knelt there. 'Better than you were. We came again later after we brought you, the first day, to see if you'd wakened yet. We came yesterday too, and you were still away wi' the fairies.'

'What happened to me? Do you know what happened to me?'

He shook his head.

'Do you not know yourself?' the girl asked coolly from the foot of my bed.

'Who are you?' I asked. She was so self-assured, so *queenly*, that I thought I ought to recognise her, and I was worried she would be offended that I didn't.

'We found you,' she answered.

They were the dirty bold sleekit tinkers.

They were not dirty, did not appear to be all that bold, and it remained to be seen how sneaky they were. In fact, I was floored by the girl's beauty. She was quite Mary Kinnaird's opposite: no kindness in her face at all, but oh, what loveliness of form in everything about her – tall and lithe with the long legs of a ballet dancer, a tiny v of ivory showing between her collarbones just above the top button

38

of her blue and green gingham blouse, and her long hair like a flaming cloud spilling down her shoulders. Could Mary possibly feel like this looking at *me*, this mixture of worship and envy?

'I found you lying on the path that leads from the burn up to Inchfort Field, wearing a lad's kilt, your hair and tam all matted with blood,' said the boy. 'You started up and told me your name was Davie Balfour, then tumbled over out cold, on your face, at my feet. So I carried you over to our camping place. When you slept on, my mam tucked you in with my sister for the night. And then the next day when you *still* didn't wake we brought you here in our cousin's van.'

I couldn't believe I'd spent a night sleeping beside that goddess-like creature and didn't remember her.

She was still gazing down at me with the cold stare of an intrigued scientist. 'What's your real name?' she asked.

I was faintly, irrationally disappointed.

'You don't believe I'm David Balfour?'

The boy gave a comical grimace and shook his head. 'Nor did I believe you the first time, either,' he said. 'But then you fell over before you could change your story.'

I decided to change my story *a little*. I was wary of being accused again of putting on airs and really didn't want to make the wrong impression.

'I'm Julie Stuart.'

Julie Stuart *is* my name. Just not all of it.

'How are you the day?' the boy asked, with genuine concern.

'Shipshape, I suppose,' I said. 'I would sell my soul for a glass of water.'

'*Whisht!*' he said, frowning. 'What a way to speak! You would never.'

His imperial sister eyed me coolly. 'You talk like gentry,' she accused.

Her tone rang alarm bells in my head. She sounded like the miserable nurse. I'd never had anyone hold my accent against me before that day.

'I'm a filthy sleekit tinker lass who doesnae deserve a glass of water,' I told her.

Neither of them answered right away. The girl and I stared at each other in sudden hostility, like cats about to fight.

Then: 'Who says?' she challenged.

'Everyone on this floor says!' I glanced at the lump in the next bed – every fibre of her being and all her bedclothes appeared to be listening.

And then, with a deep breath and in spite of the villain-ous headache, I changed how I was talking. Because I can.

I grew up sharing my summers with Travellers. The Perthshire Stewarts, when they are up in Aberdeenshire, are old friends of my father's, who is a Stuart … likely we are all related regardless of the Gallic spelling of our name. They come every year to Craig Castle, my real home, and camp there. They come in July to thin the turnips and they come back in October for the tatties. I can give you an earful in the peculiar patois code they call cant. The Stewarts laugh at me for trying, but it makes them think twice about me.

I said to my visitors now, 'If you brought me here, I'm likely one of your kind, aye? If I'm bingin' wi' Nawkens, I am no barry scaldy dilly.'

For the first time, the girl at the foot of my bed looked away from me. She and her brother exchanged sharp, unspoken glances of warning and caution. I'd shaken her. I felt better.

The boy said abruptly, 'Now you do sound like a Stewart.'

My turn to be shaken. That was canny.

'I *am* a Stuart,' I said rebelliously.

The girl made a dismissive little sigh, as if she were growing bored. 'You're not one of those Highland Gaelic-speaking folk. Who are you really?'

I was still mad. I was a bit mad at everything, now. I rubbed my temples. I countered fiercely, 'I told you my name! I told you *two* names. Who are *you*?'

'My real name?' The boy grinned.

'Any old name!'

The girl spoke for him. 'He's called Euan McEwen.'

'She's Ellen,' Euan said.

Ellen suddenly gasped and laughed. 'I ken who you are! You're Strathfearn's granddaughter. Julie Stuart, is it? Och aye, Lady Julia! Well then, Lady Julia, tell me – why don't you deserve a glass of water?'

It was like playing tennis, and we'd both won a point. We stared hard at each other. She wasn't angry with me. She really wanted to know.

'The nurses don't know who I am,' I said. 'They think I'm one of you because you brought me here. One of them thought I was poking fun at her because of the way I talk.'

Euan stood up. He padded silently to the foot of my bed, where he peered up and down the ward as if he expected the police to come along and arrest him. Finally he crept deliberately to the other end of the floor. Ellen and I watched, she standing with her arms folded and me leaning up on my elbows against my pillow. Euan picked up a glass from a tray next to someone's bed – I saw him nodding in a friendly way as he spoke a quiet word or two to the bed's occupant, and nobody seemed to object. Then he went to the back wall where there were worktops and a basin with running water, and he came back with the glass full.

It was such a simple kindness.

I drank like a person rescued from dying in a desert. I was absolutely parched. When I'd finished he took the glass and went to fill it up again.

He filled it three times for me but I couldn't drink the third. Ellen watched indifferently.

Euan sat back on his heels by my bed, holding the glass. 'Better?' he asked.

I nodded. 'Thank you.'

'Nae bother.'

Ellen beckoned her brother with another nod of her head. 'We'd best be off. You'll have everyone's attention the now, Euan, after parading up and down the ward like a soldier. And that librarian might come back.'

I found I didn't want them to leave. 'Oh, at least do stay until she comes! Mary won't mind if you're here –'

'You think?' Ellen gave a quiet little snort of scorn. 'I'm not staying for the librarian.'

'But –'

I'd somehow managed to tap into a wellspring of intolerance I hadn't at all expected from the McEwens.

'I hate that librarian!' Ellen vowed vehemently. '*Shaness!* She doesn't speak to you if you greet her. She stares and then she turns her back. You always feel she's laying a curse on you.'

Euan picked up where Ellen left off. 'She carries a gun. She shoots into the night if she hears so much as a twig snap!'

'She can't hear a twig snap,' I said. 'She's mostly deaf. It would have to be a thundering great tree limb falling before she'd hear it! I bet that's why she doesn't return your greeting, either. If you were a young lady living all by yourself on an island in a burn in the middle of a wood, I bet you'd carry a gun too!'

'She's skittery as a haunt,' said Ellen. 'She looks like a goblin. God pity her.'

Now this was making me cross.

'She has a medical thing. She was born with it. It's called ...' My brain stretched. Yes, it still worked. '...Treacher Collins syndrome,' I pronounced triumphantly. My elder brother Sandy had explained it to me. 'The bones in her head didn't get made properly before she was born. That's why her face is so peculiar. And why she can't hear. She is the kindest person I know.'

'Not to "filthy tinker folk" she isn't,' said Ellen. '*Every year* when she sees Dad fishing in the burn for pearls she calls out the river watcher after him. She doesn't even speak to Dad, just rings for the law straight away. She knows full well he's not after salmon and that he has a right to be there. Sergeant Henderson puts up with him because they were both in the Black Watch together during the war, but *every year* when we come back she makes out like she's never seen our dad before. Last year he thought he'd knock at the library door, polite, to warn her, and she told him it was Council land and he'd no right of way to cross the Inverfearnie Island bridges. She threatened him with her shotgun! *And* –'

Euan took over the story. 'And this year, Ellen went and borrowed a book from the library. She wore a tweed skirt and the librarian thought she was country hantle from Brig O'Fearn village. But when the librarian realised after a bit that Ellen was a Traveller lass, didn't she ring the hornies straight away *again*! She sent a policeman out to us to collect a *library book*.'

'What was the book?' I asked.

Ellen was silent for a moment.

'Last year's *Proceedings of the Society of Antiquaries of Scotland*.'

Somehow even *Proceedings of the Society of Antiquaries of Scotland* sounded like a challenge when those words got spat out by Ellen McEwen.

My brother Sandy, who is a curator at the British Museum in London, has got an article published in that volume. I wondered what Ellen wanted it for.

At this dreadful moment the officious nurse came back.

'*What* is going on here?' she thundered.

And then she asked me what the blazes I thought I was doing, helping myself to the King's own medical equipment, and how dare I? I told her the King didn't own the city supply of drinking water, which I am not sure is technically true, but it is the principle of the thing – you can't expect public infirmary patients not to drink. She accused me of cheek and of putting on airs again. Then she directed her venomous gaze on my visitors.

Euan, still holding the drinking glass, turned magenta and shrank into his brown garments in fear and embarrassment under her blazing ire; Ellen blanched and stood fast with her arms crossed over her chest, gripping her sleeves.

'*And what do you mean by bringing these creatures into the women's ward?*' the nurse bellowed at me. '*How dare you keep your meetings here, you dirty fast wee midden!*'

With that, she seized the glass from the quivering hand of Euan McEwen and dashed the last unconsumed stolen King's water straight into his blushing face. For a moment, he knelt by my bedside absolutely and damply astonished.

'*Get out!*' the nurse raged at him. She swung round to face Ellen, who was holding herself so tightly she'd torn a hole in the thin fabric of one sleeve. I thought Ellen was going to explode with rage.

But she didn't. She stepped past the nurse without a word, and wiped Euan's face with the back of one hand. He stood up. Together they walked with dignity back the way they'd come in, with every patient watching the show. Euan held the door for his sister.

She hesitated. Then she turned around and called to me defiantly, 'We're away to Blairgowrie for the berry picking. We'll be back at the Strathfearn Estate for the flax at Bridge Farm. Get well and come to see us at Inchfort Field!'

'*I will!*' I vowed to her from across the ward.

My mother arrived eventually, but I was asleep again by then and she did not want to waken me. She arranged for my discharge the following morning, and I was assigned a different nurse for the duration of my stay. The ward sister in charge was extremely grovelly and apologetic for her subordinate's behaviour, concerned when I couldn't bear to finish my breakfast porridge, and called me 'Lady Julia'. I used my new-found power to demand coffee, but couldn't finish that, either.

I left St John's on a spring tide of obsequious kowtowing. The noted surgeon who had last year coaxed an extra five months of life out of my dying and bedridden grandfather came out to the car to see me off.

(It was my mother's little two-seater Magnette which she drives herself – Grandad's landaulet had already been sold and the driver dismissed. Mother's car is a cracking red sporty thing with glittering chrome knobs all over and it is utterly impractical, apart from her occasionally giving me a driving lesson in it when she is in one of her more Bolshevik moods. Driving like a man is one of her few foibles.)

The surgeon held the door while Mother tucked me in with pillows and a blanket, as the car has no top. 'Lady Craigie, I do apologise your daughter wasn't given a private room.'

'Of course you couldn't have known who she was!' Mother said. 'How lucky we are that the Travellers were so kind to her. That was Jean McEwen and her folk, wasn't it? To think Jean and I used to play together along the Fearn! It's my own fault she's never met my daughter and couldn't recognise her!'

She didn't say, *You can't be blamed for the occasional small-minded pig-headed idiot turning up on your nursing staff – it is hard to cure people of ingrained cultural platitudes.* But I knew that, like me, she was thinking it hard.

And like her, I didn't say anything. I was sheerly grateful that the headache had subsided, and that I was out of the newspaper nightgown. Mother had brought me sensible clothes of her own (my trunk *still* had not arrived). I dared to ask, 'Can I drive?'

'Do not be *ridiculous*, Julia.' But she laughed.

As we headed out of Perth on the Edinburgh Road I shook off the blanket and managed to kneel backward on the seat, sticking half my body out of the car like a dog, enjoying the fingers of wind rumpling the tufts of leftover hair.

'Darling, I cannot bear to watch,' Mother shouted.

'Slow down, then, Mummy! You're supposed to be watching the road, not me.'

The concentration it took to hold myself up made me seasick again, however, so I was forced to behave myself and sit properly.

3

LES LIAISONS DANGEREUSES

My grandmother, the Dowager Countess of Strathfearn, whom my brothers and I call by the French pet name Mémère, had been reduced to three rooms in her late husband's ancestral mansion – four if you counted the bathroom. (Not the nursery bathroom – it gave everyone vapours to think I was lounging blissfully unclothed in that enormous bathtub, which was also used by the workmen in the east wing.) Four little iron beds had been brought down to Mémère's big bedroom from the abandoned staff rooms in the attic; two of these beds had been installed side by side in Mémère's dressing room for Mother and Solange, with just enough room to walk between them, and another was lined up at the foot of Mémère's four-poster for her lady's companion Colette. Mine was shoved against Mémère's tall French windows. This was really the nicest place to be because I got to decide for myself whether the windows were open or shut. Also we still had the little morning room downstairs to ourselves, with big notices saying NO ENTRY posted on the terrace and in the corridor to keep the workmen out. We had use of the kitchen, but so did everybody else.

For my first two days out of hospital, I couldn't go downstairs to the morning room anyway. Standing at the top of the stairs was like being on the edge of a sea cliff, only worse – the vertigo actually made me want to be sick. I had to sit down on the top stair with my head between my knees before I managed to creep back to bed. The days that followed were *interminable*. I couldn't do anything – I couldn't focus my mind sharply enough to do a crossword or read or even be read to, though Mother and Solange and Mary Kinnaird all did try.

Solange also fussed with my hair and filled my surroundings with roses, and brought me tall drinks full of mint leaves and lemon peel. Eventually I wanted to strangle her. I'd never known her to be so nervous.

'*Please* go away, Nanny. I don't want to be read to,' I told her petulantly, a small child all over again with my grown-up self-sufficiency completely destroyed, and felt instantly, hideously guilty as she tiptoed out of the room to continue her never-ending quest for something to distract me with.

Bored nearly to weeping, I sat at my grandmother's dressing table – used by all four of the older women in turn each morning, very quietly so as not to awaken me unnecessarily – and I methodically removed and replaced the lids of every single jar of cold cream and face powder again and again. There was something mesmerising and comforting about this, possibly because it proved to me that I was still able to coordinate my brain with my body. The clink of the glass stoppers in Solange's scent bottles was as soothing as birdsong. Nosy, idle, with the prying right of an indulged and pampered baby, I was delighted to find a jewel case from MacGregor's of Perth pushed against the mirror stand at the back corner of the table.

'Mémère, has *all* your jewellery been sold?' I asked my grandmother wistfully, in French, because although she'd been living in Scotland for over fifty years, she and Colette and Solange are French-born and ordinarily we all chatter to each other in their native language.

'The Murray jewellery has been gone for years,' Mémère said dismissively, as if she'd never liked it anyway. She and Colette were sitting at opposite sides of an octagonal card table covered with green baize, folding about a million lace-edged napkins and packing them into an enormous woven willow hamper. 'What's left of my own jewels is locked up in my great-grandfather's sea chest over there, beneath still more of my mother's linen. There's too much of *that.*' My grandmother tossed another pile of napkins unceremoniously into the basket.

I pried open the jewel box I'd found as if it were a mussel shell. Inside it lay a pair of pearl earrings. They were tear-shaped Scottish river pearls like grey raindrops, like a sky heavy with cloud, perfectly matched.

'Whose are these, then?'

I unfastened one earring from its blue silk bed and tried to dangle it from my ear.

'*Julia!*'

That was Mother. All in an instant, she and Solange were both hovering over me like crows mobbing a thieving magpie. When I lowered my hands, Solange tweaked the little jewel away from me as though she thought I were about to pop it in my mouth and choke myself to death.

'Are these pearls from the Murray Hoard?' I asked.

'They belong to Solange,' my grandmother said, shrugging. 'They were a gift.'

Solange packed them smartly back into their case.

Which amount of circumnavigating my question did nothing to slake my curiosity.

'Who –'

My mother and my nanny exchanged sharp looks over my head.

'She's old enough to know,' Mother said. 'She *should* know.'

'You may tell her, Madame,' Solange said miserably.

'You must do the telling,' Mother said coolly. 'I won't speak for you.'

Solange, the jewel case still held between her hands, one on top of the other, walked to the tall French windows and sat down on my narrow bed, as far away as she could get from the rest of us, and gazed out over the tractors and wheelbarrows bumping back and forth over the lawn. She sat quietly for a moment, steeling herself. She took so long to continue that I found myself holding my own breath in apprehension, and let it out sharply when all of a sudden she began to speak.

'I have made the acquaintance of a special friend,' Solange said carefully. 'An *intimate* friend.'

She was still speaking French, and the euphemism 'special friend' didn't sound as coy as it does in English. *En français* it is quite ordinary to call your sweetheart your '*bon ami*', your good friend.

'He is called Dr Hugh Housman,' my grandmother expanded drily on Solange's behalf. 'He is the scholar who has been cataloguing the Murray Collection of Antiquities.'

'I thought Mary Kinnaird was doing that at the Inverfearnie Library,' I said.

Mother corrected gently, 'It's being done at the library because everything is so chaotic here. There's room to spread things out there in peace and quiet. But it's Dr Housman's work, not Mary Kinnaird's.'

Solange, distracted, now didn't go on.

Colette bent in embarrassment over the old linen.

After another agonising long moment of silence, Mother and Mémère in unison gave little cat sighs, a sharp sniff that always indicates either one of them is losing patience with you, and Solange started talking again all in a rush.

'Something has happened to him. I *think*. It was the day you hit your head, Julia. I argued with him – bitterly, *bitterly* – the same morning. I refused his ... I refused his affections ... and then I watched him from this very window as he crossed the lawn and entered the wood where the river path is, but I had locked myself in this room and did not come out again until your lady mother and your grandmother returned from the solicitor's that afternoon –'

Here Mother did interrupt. 'Jean McEwen's man found Dr Housman's cap in the river not far from the standing stone that very afternoon. None of us has seen him since.'

Dear Solange – what cracking melodrama! No wonder she seemed so skittish. I rubbed at my temples.

'He gave you those earrings?' I queried.

'We'd been very intimate,' Solange sniffed. 'He found the pearls himself –'

'From the cup in the Murray Hoard?' I interrupted. 'Grandad used to have a pile of pearls in that wood-and-silver cup in his artefact collection.'

All the older women looked at me strangely.

'I don't remember that,' said Mother.

'Dr Housman found Solange's pearls in the river,' Mémère explained. 'Fishing for pearls is a hobby. He was a colleague of your grandfather's, and interested in many of the same things.'

Mother sat down again in the overstuffed wing chair where she'd been curled for most of the morning. 'Dr Housman was an admirer of your grandfather's anti-quarian and archaeological work,' she explained. 'That's why your grandmother recommended he be the one to catalogue the artefacts you call the Murray Hoard.'

'So Grandad and this Housman chap both collected pearls?'

'Goodness, Julia, do stop going on about pearls,' Mémère said crossly. 'I told you the jewellery was sold.'

Mother was gentler. 'We are quite concerned for Dr Housman. And more so for *you*: what happened to you that morning? Did you slip and fall, or did someone hit you? Did you and Dr Housman cross paths, perhaps without seeing each other? I'm anxious to ask him if he saw what happened to you. But I'm increasingly concerned that some-one else attacked *both* of you – a poacher, perhaps – and that Housman didn't have the narrow escape you did.'

I tried to shift my mind from Grandad's pearls, which I remembered, to Dr Hugh Housman, whom I'd never heard of, and it was like trying to play the trumpet without know-ing which end you were supposed to blow into. Colette looked disapproving. Mother and Mémère and Solange all leaned forward breathlessly, expectant.

'Was this Housman chap staying here?' I asked. 'Isn't there anyone he reports to who you could ask about him?'

Solange gave a sniff. Obviously she felt he ought to be reporting to *her*.

'He reports to the solicitors of the Murray Estate in Edinburgh,' Mémère said. 'And his people at the Ashmolean Museum in Oxford.'

'But no one seems to have any idea where he is.' Solange sniffed again.

As before, the most useful information came from Mother. 'And his job isn't being done. I've put a call through to Sandy to see if he can take over the archaeological catalogue until …' My mother, the resolute Lady Craigie, couldn't work out how to best finish her thought without sounding ominous – she couldn't say 'until Dr Housman comes back' if he wasn't going to, or if he was going to be fired when he did. She fumbled, 'Sandy can do an adequate job as long as he's needed. He'd love to do it. Initially the Murray Estate felt he wasn't experi-enced enough, as well as him having an interest in the estate. But he's the new Earl of Strathfearn – it's *right* he do it. Mary can help him just as she's been helping Dr Housman.'

Mother took a deep breath, and soldiered on. 'We've notified the police about Dr Housman's absence too, and they've been talking to the builders on the estate here. I'm surprised the chief contractor for the Glenfearn School hasn't seen him. Solange, you said that Dr Housman and the contractor Mr Dunbar sometimes share their meals –'

'What about Mary?' I interrupted. 'Wouldn't this Housman fellow normally ring the library, or leave her a note to say when he's coming and going?'

'Julia, please do wait until I've finished speaking,' Mother corrected automatically. She is used to running her own household and likes to have everyone's full attention.

I shrugged.

There was a silence.

'*Well?*'

'I spoke to Mary this morning,' Mother said. 'She hasn't noticed anything unusual at the library, except that Housman had left her back door open on the day you arrived. But he doesn't always work at the Inverfearnie Library; some days he's here, or in Perth, or even at the National Library in Edinburgh, so Mary didn't think anything was amiss until I mentioned it to her.'

'He might have left her a note. I did.'

'She hasn't found one. That leaves Solange as the last person who communicated with him. She'd been putting fresh roses in his room, and went up earlier today to change them; she didn't see anything that suggested he'd slept there.'

Poor Solange gave another miserable sniff. 'But he hadn't taken anything away with him, either, Madame! It was the same as always. Oh, how can I speak to the project manager – to Mr Dunbar – about Dr Housman? How can I admit I go in and out of his *bedroom*? It would not be *correct.*'

'Well, I can speak to the project manager. I'll go to ask him now. I don't like it that Julia should be mixed up in something as nasty as this. The man might have been *murdered.*' Mother got up again, with an air of determination.

'Perhaps I'm a witness!' I said, relishing the idea.

No one else relished it.

'Everything is so unpleasant,' Mémère said unhappily. 'I detest having policemen in my house. And they stop at nothing. They will question Julia. What a thing for the front page of the *Mercury.*'

I laughed, improvising an appropriate headline. '"Injured Tinker Lass Saw Nobody."'

This time Mother scolded swiftly in a tone of iron: '*Julia.*'

Her voice was low and sharp. 'Just because you can't remember what happened doesn't mean you had any less of a narrow escape! And don't you dare forget that the Beauforts have been raked through muck before. Your

59

grandmother had to fend off a household full of policemen after her sister's husband died, and it's an invasion
not to be borne when someone you love has lost a battle
against cancer. *Not more than once.* It may be that it was
in France and it was before you were born, but that
should not make you too young to understand nor care.'

I was ashamed of being so callow and thoughtless. I
looked over at my grandmother, sitting frail and unhappy
and bravely elegant in her slim Murray tartan skirt, with her
white hair coiled so that not a strand was out of place, and
I wanted to *be* like her, moving into a terrible unknown
future without showing any fear; also I wanted to leap up
and run to her to take her in my arms, but I still wasn't able
to make any sudden moves, and I was too craven to displace
my equilibrium.

I bit my lip. 'Mémère. I do understand. I'm sorry.'

'It's not a game,' said my mother. 'If you ever remember
anything that happened to you that day, you might really be
a witness.'

She added as she got to the door, 'Do try to be kind to
your grandmother, Julia, darling. And to Solange. And don't
toy with those pearls!'

I could see why Mémère would have put Grandad's
pearls out of her head – out of sight, out of mind – but
it irritated me that Mother didn't remember them.

Grandad had said they were his 'mother's mother's mother's'. How could everyone have just *forgotten* about them like this?

I tried to rationalise it. My mother grew up in Strathfearn House: perhaps she wasn't fascinated by the little tower room museum the way my brothers and I were. It had been her father's private place and she wasn't allowed in on her own. I, on the other hand, had been his spoilt only grand-daughter. How strange it is that everybody remembers things so *differently*.

I wondered what had happened to those pearls.

On the third day after my release I was able to make it down the stairs to the little morning room. This cheered every-body up very much, so much so that they finally dared press on cautiously with their administrative tasks. Solange was hopelessly gloomy, which was having its effect on me as well, so Mother insisted that Solange come out with her and Mémère, and they left me alone with Colette while the rest of them visited the offices of Sweet's in Perth with an eye to arranging the auction of the Strathfearn House furnishings. The Murray Hoard was to be auctioned separately by one of the big London houses. Mother said the most valuable pieces in it were potentially of National Interest.

'Mary Queen of Scots' bracelet?' I asked.

'The Glenfearn School trustees are going to allow that to stay in the Inverfearnie Library.'

I was glad of that, even if it wasn't ours any more.

Clad in a blue serge skirt belonging to my mother, wearing the remaining wisps of hair teased back over my forehead with a steel hairgrip (put there by Solange trying to work a miracle, probably with more success than I credited her for – she is a creature of taste and elegance), I sat in the morning room with the doors to the terrace open because the air was nice, trying to pull my brain back together. I felt a great deal better. But I couldn't manage words on a page yet. I couldn't read. I thought maybe I could write. I ended up doodling.

I wasn't happy about the lid of my jam jar – I couldn't decide what I wanted it to look like. The picture in my *head*

was fuzzy. And I stared at the specs for the longest time, trying to work out what was wrong with them.

Someone knocked at the door to the passage, and I jumped and dropped my pen. I was the only one in the room, as a few minutes before I'd managed to convince Colette that it would be all right to put down her endless knitting of winter stockings and leave me alone for the time it took to go and prepare some tea and sandwiches for lunch. Colette is fully ten years younger than my recently widowed grandmother, so only sixty-nine, but she is much more of an old woman, all timid fuss and flutter. No matter how strenuous the task, Mémère usually insists, 'I could if I had to.' But it always takes a firm hand to stop Colette fretting, and she was reluctant to leave me alone.

Now her worst fears were realised, ha–hah! At the sound of the knock, a false feeling of wild freedom swept over me. I realised it could be the first time since the day of my injury that I'd had any whiff of contact with the outside world, and I got up to open the door full of eager anticipation, hoping vaguely it was going to be somebody I'd never seen before with a special problem that only I would be able to solve.

Well, it was only a little problem, but *such* a somebody I'd never seen before.

I opened the door and found myself facing the most splendidly attractive man I had ever met. It is true I am not terribly experienced, but he had all the devil-may-care athleticism of a certain ski instructor my school chums swooned over last winter, coupled with considerably more age and sense, which I liked. Clean-shaven, in smart office clothes but without his jacket and with his tie and collar loose, he looked as if he'd spent the morning trying to work and had been constantly interrupted. His hair was brown and wavy and threaded with silver, as if someone had lightly sprinkled Christmas tinsel over it. He was so much taller than me I had to tilt my head back a little to look at his face, and that made me feel rather childish, so I stepped away from him.

He stepped away from me as well, backing a foot or two into the corridor. He opened his mouth as if he'd been about to say something and made a mistake, then shut it. For a moment I thought he was going to dash off in the other direction.

I made a guess about who he might be.

'Dr Housman?'

'I … *no!*' he said explosively. Then pulling himself together very suddenly, he offered a hand for me to shake. 'Miss Murray?' he addressed me.

Unfortunately this made me laugh. I am acquiring aliases by the barrow-load! Alexander Murray is my *maternal* grandfather, so even though I consider myself a Murray, it is not my name.

Unoffended by my laughter, he still held out the offered hand, and I took it. His clasp was firm and warm and strong. He held on a moment longer than I expected him to, gazing down at me assessingly, and I waited for him to let go first, not wanting to show any signs of backing away again. His eyes were the grey-green of a winter sea.

'Is it Miss Murray?' he asked, and then, without waiting for an answer, he introduced himself, a bit nervously. 'I'm Francis Dunbar. I'm the chief contractor for the building work that's to be done to Strathfearn House on behalf of the Glenfearn School.' He let go of me and quickly put his hands in his pockets, as if he were banishing them in disgrace for being so forward. 'I organised the recent alterations to this house, the ramps and handrails, for the late Earl of Strathfearn, and his widow ...' He hesitated, and added, 'That's your grand-mother, I believe? She recommended me to the Glenfearn School trustees to manage the current renovation.'

I should have corrected my name *straight away*, but no, I was so smitten with his physical beauty and his communist approach to speaking to me as his equal that I just launched into conversation with him. He appeared to have forgotten why he was here, and seemed to need prodding.

'Can I help you with something?' I enquired politely.

'Oh! Yes. I've been trying for weeks to get the terrace doors in my office to open. The heat is asphyxiating in the morning when the sun's shining in. It's the room adjoining this one. I … I hoped that someone who knows the house better than I do might help. Is there a trick?'

'Probably!' I said cheerfully, hoping he'd let me do it myself rather than change his mind and wait for one of the adults to come back. 'Shall I come through and see?' I was charmed by the vulnerability of a 'chief contractor' who couldn't work out how to open his office windows.

'Thank you.'

He gestured me politely ahead of him down the passage with an open hand. His office was a twin to the morning room, a mirror image, the two being divided by a partition of oak panels that folded up like an accordion to make it into one large reception space opening on to the terrace above the lawn. Francis Dunbar crossed to the French doors of his half of the twin rooms and twitched back the heavy curtains in irritation, trying to let in more light through smudged glass panes that hadn't been opened or cleaned for a good long while.

'Sorry about the dust in here,' he said. 'This room was closed off for some time when I took it over in May.'

That must have been barely a month after my grandfather's funeral. I didn't want to create more awkwardness by mentioning how quickly the property had been sold; I just launched into an attack on the doors.

'There's a third catch – bolts at top and bottom and then others there between the panels.' I pointed; I couldn't reach the upper catch. In the morning room next door we never bothered to fasten it. I stood back so Mr Dunbar could get at the high bolts himself, again self-consciously aware of the difference in our height and how young it could make me look if I drew attention to it.

'Ah!' He threw the hidden bolt. Light and air flooded into the room, as next door.

Francis Dunbar put his hands in his pockets again, gazing out over the disrupted and busy lawn for a moment, then turned to look at me standing there, frail and boyish with my chopped hair, wearing my mother's serge. His face was a little shadowed; mine was in the light. I considered how to prolong the moment. He did it for me, taking a hand out of a pocket and holding out his cigarette case to me.

'I should have offered earlier,' he said.

My heart swooped. He hadn't taken me for a child.

Probably I ought to have refused, having only on *one occasion* let tobacco pass my lips, on that same highly educational skiing holiday last winter. But I'd learned to make smoking look natural by the end of that evening, and now I just couldn't resist being treated with such sophistication. Also, Francis Dunbar was so very beautiful, and I liked him, and I wanted to see how much I could get away with. I was beginning to *hate* being treated like porcelain.

I took a cigarette and let him light it.

That is a terrifically intimate thing, you know? Letting a stranger light your cigarette. Leaning forward so he can hold a flame to your lips. Pausing to breathe in before you pull back again.

It was *so good* to be flirting with someone a little, and to feel more like myself again.

Thank goodness Colette wasn't around. I wondered how much time I had.

I stood back carefully, trying to keep the cigarette casual. *Don't think about it too hard, Julie.*

Francis Dunbar lit his own cigarette. He flicked the match into a curious carved soapstone ashtray on his desk, turning away from me. He drew a long, slow, contemplative breath on the cigarette before he turned to me and said, 'Thanks for your help, Miss Murray – I'm sorry. You're Strathfearn's granddaughter – Julia? Should I be saying Lady Julia?'

'Julie. Julie Beaufort-Stuart. Lady Julia is correct, or Miss Beaufort-Stuart, but my name's not Murray. Murray is my mother's maiden name – Beaufort-Murray, actually. We keep the Beaufort. That's from my grandmother, the Dowager Countess of Strathfearn. She was Juliette Beaufort. She's French.'

He continued to gaze at me intently. I felt like a boring little animated edition of *Debrett's Peerage*.

I said, 'It's all right for you to call me Julie.'

He shook his head – not saying no, exactly, but with an expression of bemusement, as if he couldn't believe his luck. 'Only in this office,' he agreed. 'And only if you'll call me Frank.'

'Oh. Should I?' I nodded, thinking about it. Then I repeated it, trying it out. 'Frank.' I gave him a little crooked smile. It was like tasting an alcoholic drink – and more intimate than the lighting of a cigarette. I hadn't realised that using his given name – his nickname, even – would be more daring than giving him mine.

I probably didn't have any longer with him than the time it took to smoke the illicit cigarette. I gazed at the disorder of his office, trying to discover a little more about him. There was the curious ashtray; and he'd got what looked like a miniature Ludo game board over on a back corner of his desk, shell playing pieces in place on dark and polished wood with intricate paisley designs set into it. Propped on the fixed shelves against the wall, along with piles of paper and bottles of ink, was a framed display of medals and service ribbons.

He wouldn't have those there unless he was proud of them. He'd had to bring them with him from wherever he normally worked.

'You did your training in the military?' I asked. 'In India?'

He stared at me, startled. I pointed at the souvenirs, and the medals behind him. 'Good God, I took you for a clairvoyant!' he exclaimed.

'Just nosy.' I laughed.

'Canny though! Yes, I was an officer and an engineer in India with the Black Watch all through my twenties. It's only been three years since I've been back, but it feels very far away now.'

'You weren't in the Black Watch at the same time as Angus Henderson, were you? The Strathfearn Water Bailiff marched with them in the Great War.'

'Have the tropics aged me so much?' Frank Dunbar exclaimed, running a distraught hand through his silver-shot hair. 'I was in primary school when the Great War started!'

Now we both laughed. Oh, I loved this game. I was trying to make myself look older; he was trying to make himself look younger. I'd played this all the way across Europe and I'd got *good* at it. I felt it was safest to add only two years to my age instead of three this time.

'Well, you have my sympathies. I won't be eighteen until August, but it's dreadful what they did to my hair in the hospital. It makes me look like *I've* only just finished primary school.'

Take that.

70

And then among the piles of paper on his desk I was startled to see something I recognised.

It was the brown envelope on which I'd written my note to Mary. It was face down so that the engraved return address was showing, and I realised that of course Francis Dunbar couldn't possibly have any reason to be interested in my note to Mary. It was the scholar at the Ashmolean Museum he must have been trying to track down.

My rattled brain, focused on navigating stairs and the state of my hair, had shoved the missing Dr Hugh Housman aside. But Mother had started to say that 'the contractor Mr Dunbar' shared his meals with Dr Housman, so I did exactly what Frank had just done, and used a slow drag on the cigarette to give me time to think.

I suddenly had a lot of questions I wanted to ask him and I'd already confessed I was nosy. Also, if Colette came back and I was sitting there in the sun, she might think I'd wandered in here out of boredom and be more forgiving of Frank Dunbar than if she thought he'd lured me into his office himself.

'Do you mind if I sit down?' I said, waving my cigarette in the direction of his leather armchair.

'Oh, please do. I should have offered.' He scurried to pull the chair forward for me so I could sit in it and reach the ashtray on his desk. 'I'm a terrible bachelor and I forget

71

how to be polite sometimes. And you – you're only just out of hospital. I'm so sorry.'

The contrite sincerity in his voice made me a bit embarrassed. I really hadn't been meaning to play the fragile convalescent. I arranged myself on the edge of the chair, knees and feet tucked together demurely. Better not give Colette anything to worry about if she *did* find me here. I thought I could get rid of the damning cigarette pretty quickly.

'Are you actually living here?' I asked.

'Aye, in one of the guest rooms in the east wing.'

'Is that where the visiting scholar stays too?'

'Dr Housman? Yes. But you've … you've never met him yourself, have you? You called me Housman when you answered the door.'

'No, I've never met him. But my mother is worried about him because no one's seen him for the past week. She was going to ask you if you know where he's been.'

Frank shook his head. I didn't know if he meant he didn't know where Housman was, or if my mother hadn't asked, or if he couldn't say anything because his mouth was full of smoke.

'I *am* just being nosy. I don't know a thing about him except that he's supposed to be cataloguing my grandfather's archaeological collection,' I confessed. 'But look …'

I reached across the desk and picked up the envelope with Housman's name engraved on the back, and flipped it over.

'This is the note I left for Mary Kinnaird on the morning I arrived here,' I said. 'It startled me to see it on your desk.'

'You *are* canny,' he said again, breathing out. 'That's got Housman's work address in Oxford on it. I couldn't find anything in his room; all his paperwork is over at the library. Miss Kinnaird passed this on to me so I could write to his people at the museum where he's employed. And they've given me the address of a sister, his ... Well, this is unpleasant, but she's his next of kin. Your mother and the police – at least, the Strathfearn Water Bailiff – came to see me, both hoping I might have seen Dr Housman this week. But his room and mine are at opposite ends of the east wing, so I rarely run into him coming and going. We do sometimes eat together in the evening. I have so much space in this office, and he likes to talk; he gets excited about things – he's excited about –'

Here Dunbar checked himself and took a drag on his cigarette. Then he laughed.

'He thinks your grandfather's Bronze and Iron Age assemblies of spear tips and arrowheads are exceptional – "of British Museum level importance to typological dating," he said. He's a man who loves his work. It made me a little envious, actually.' He glanced away, suddenly boyishly and appealingly shy.

'Haven't you *missed* him?' I asked. 'If you'd become friends, and you haven't seen him for nearly a week, aren't you lonely?'

The contractor laughed. 'With this job?' He waved an arm around him, taking in the pile of blueprints on his desk, the churning cement mixer and wheelbarrow-loads of stone which men were hauling up and down the garden, and distant hammering somewhere in the bowels of the house itself. 'I'm too busy to get lonely. Sometimes I don't go up to my own room until well past midnight, and Dr Housman isn't even in this building most of the time.' He paused. 'He might have run into trouble with the Travellers, I suppose.'

'They really don't go around causing trouble,' I said. 'Not any more than anyone else does, anyway. Not on purpose.'

Frank was finished with his cigarette. I'd neglected mine for so long it had gone out, and I didn't want to draw attention to my inefficiency by asking him to light it again, so I discreetly stubbed it to pieces. Then I realised I was still holding the brown envelope with Dr Housman's Oxford address on it, so I stretched out my hand to put it back on Frank's desk.

And a little pearl dropped out into my lap. Frank, still standing, didn't notice it, and neither did I until I looked down.

I thought it dropped off *me* at first — as if I'd been wearing it in my hair, or as an earring. It was the size of a barley grain and perfectly round. It lay there in the cradle of woollen skirt between my knees. It was beautiful and perfect.

Why was it in that envelope anyway? Had Grandad sent it to Dr Housman? Or just put it in there for safekeeping? Or had Dr Housman put it there himself — had he found it in the Murray Collection? The last of the Murray pearls?

I picked it up — it was so smooth I had to wedge it beneath my fingernail to get hold of it.

And I remembered.

I remembered leaving the library. I remembered walking to the beachy place in the burn, and lying on the rock there with my arm in the water, and falling asleep. And I remembered the splashing that woke me.

When I opened my eyes there was a man standing in the burn. He hadn't been there when I lay down, but I had been dozing and dreaming and feeling sorry for Mémère for having to leave Strathfearn at the end of the summer, and for Mother who'd grown up there, and a little sorry for myself perhaps; and I'd been looking up at the sky, and he must have worked his way downstream. The beachy place is at a bend, and you can't see around it when you are lying on the rocks hidden by hazel shoots, like I was.

I looked up and saw him standing over by the tall Drookit Stane in the middle of the stream. He was in water up to his waist. He was bearded, with wiry whiskery sideburns the exact same horse-chestnut colour as the clear river depths. He had a soft wool cap. That's the only thing I remembered about his clothes – not their colour, not their pattern, not if they were tweed or tartan or oilcloth. It was his face that startled me most. One eye was swollen shut and his lip was split – fresh, red blood oozing beneath his nose. But the reason I noticed his face wasn't because it was so battered but because of how discs of light played over it, dappling his pink, shining skin with moving spangles of brightness, as if some-one were sitting on the bank throwing gold coins at his head.

I thought: *He's not stealing salmon. He doesn't know what he's doing. He's not* hard *enough to be a poacher.*

Then I realised he was fishing for pearls. But he wasn't a proper pearl fisher, either. He had all the kit for pearl fish-ing – glass-bottomed jug, shoulder satchel, pearl stick – but he carried it awkwardly, as if it were getting in his way, as if he were in costume. He was as ignorant as the man I'd caught with Grandad, but unlike the one who'd pointed the gun at me, this man was *comical*.

He took a deep breath, bent over and put his battered face in the water for a good long half a minute. Then he stood up, gasped and did it again. His head went the whole way under. His cap came off, and he splashed about as he tried to grab it back. It drifted away downstream.

I sat up, snickering behind one hand, and dabbled my feet off my rock to watch the show. He looked up when he heard me. We stared at each other in astonishment.

And then the explosion in my head.

'Julie?'

Francis Dunbar was on his knees beside me, holding my hand. The wave of memory had submerged me for a whole minute, while I'd just sat staring and let it all come flooding back. Now I looked down at our hands clasped together, and then at Frank's face. He wasn't being forward – he was concerned and, I think, a bit frightened.

'Oh!' I said, pulling my hand back.

He let go of it instantly. 'I'm sorry – I …'

I knew. There was no question in my mind that the bloodied man I'd seen in the river had been Hugh Housman.

I needed to tell Mother, but I couldn't share this tremendous strange vision, like a remembered dream, with someone I scarcely knew. Not that moment.

'It's my head.' I swallowed. 'Every now and then the headache starts up and I get dizzy.'

He stood up quickly. 'Your maid's just come back. I'll go next door and get her.'

'She's not a maid. She's my grandmother's companion.' I stood up. I was fine – physically, I was all right. 'She's been making lunch for me. I'd better go and let her know I'm here.'

'Thank you for helping me with the terrace door,' Frank said.

'It was my pleasure,' I answered, smiling up at him as he ushered me out.

He was careful not to touch me again.

The pearl was still stuck beneath my fingernail, invisible.

No one knew it was there but me.

This time I thought I'd keep it.

4

MY JANGLED BRAIN AND THE YELLOW DOG

Of course as soon as my returning memory offered up an actual picture of the missing Dr Hugh Housman, *after* he was last seen by anyone else, I was required to add an account of what I knew to the official police report that was being maintained by the Perthshire and Kinross-shire Constabulary.

They sent a person called Inspector Duncan Milne out to Strathfearn House to interview me. They made Frank Dunbar relinquish his office for an hour to accommodate the interview. My *school uniform* was still the most present-able thing I had to wear, and Mother was there to make sure I wore it properly, so it was jolly difficult to take on the persona of a grown and sensible woman. Mother was settled in the leather chair across from Frank's desk when Colette ushered me in; she'd been speaking to Inspector Milne herself. There was another chair waiting for me.

Inspector Milne had a neat beard and thin salt-and-pepper hair cropped short beneath his peaked cap. He was scribbling away at his notes in a tiny cleared rectangle of space on Frank's desk, looking down through reading glasses, and kept scribbling as I hesitated in the doorway. I wondered if it was correct to wait to be told to sit or if I could just do it without being told, or if being Strathfearn's youngest grandchild put me too far down the pecking order to act so boldly in the presence of authority. I wouldn't have dared sit in my headmistress's office, or a solicitor's or something like that, without being invited to. I glanced at Mother and she shook her head ever so slightly. So I waited.

Inspector Milne didn't look up even when he became aware of me. He just said, at last, 'You may sit.'

So I did, feeling a bit foolish, as if what I had to say couldn't possibly be as important as I'd thought it was going to be.

I sat, and waited another while. I noticed that Francis Dunbar kept a pillow and blanket folded under the wing chair Mother was seated in. I thought, *Poor Frank must nap here when he's working late*.

Eventually Inspector Milne did look up, presumably to make sure it really was me and not an impostor. He didn't change his expression or say hello or ask me how I was getting on after my dunt to the head.

When he did speak, he plunged right in.

'You observed Dr Housman fishing for pearls in the River Fearn at about midday on the fifteenth of June?'

I answered cautiously, 'I don't know if it was him. I don't know him – I'd never seen him before. It could have been anybody.'

'Your description does match.'

'Oh – thank you,' I said ridiculously, as if he'd complimented me.

'Did you speak to him?'

'I don't know.' Another ridiculous answer! How could I *not know* what had happened between us? I felt I had to do better.

'I don't think he knew I was there. He didn't look angry or startled. He didn't even look *interested*. I suppose he might be the one who hit me, but perhaps he saw me fall and hit my head and tried to help me, and got into trouble because he couldn't swim, or slipped and drowned and ...'

And then his death would be my fault.

I shut up quickly, appalled. *Buckets of blood!* I hadn't considered *that*. If I was the last person to see him alive, I might also be the one who'd killed him.

'I *didn't*. I *couldn't!* Could I? But ...'

Of course I couldn't remember anything that had happened. Could I have harmed him somehow? Maybe I *could*. What if he'd attacked me for some reason – perhaps he'd taken me for one of the Travellers that everyone was so suspicious of, and I'd fought back, hit him perhaps, tripped him, made him lose his balance in the river and … What if all this time he'd been dead and it was *my* fault?

'What if you never find him? What if I have to go *all my life* wondering if I killed him? What if I remember that I *did*?'

'Julia, darling, leave the what-if-ing to Inspector Milne.' Mother suddenly spoke up. 'Perhaps Dr Housman got into trouble himself and you tried to help him and then slipped and hit your head.'

Inspector Duncan Milne shuffled pages. 'Those are considerations,' he said. 'But at the moment …'

He peered at his notes and then looked up at me over the top of his glasses.

'There's no need to jump to conclusions. We've no reason to believe the man is dead. In any case, as your mother Lady Craigie has suggested, we think it more likely that you were both assaulted by the same attacker. I'd like to ask you about the young man who brought you to the hospital.' He changed tack abruptly. 'You know Euan McEwen?'

It took me a moment to remember why I knew the name.

Of course, that was the Traveller lad who'd found me. The one who'd brought me to the hospital; who'd come back every day to see if I'd woken up yet; who'd quietly conjured me a glass of water.

A moment later, I remembered Ellen, and my heart surged with pleasure and anticipation at the thought that I might get to meet her again. How could my wandering thoughts have put aside the challenge and mystery that was *Ellen McEwen*? It made me a bit more sympathetic towards my mother for forgetting her ancestral pearls.

I wondered if the Travellers were back at Inchfort Field yet. I wondered if I was capable of walking there on my own.

'Lady Julia?' Inspector Milne prompted.

'Yes,' I said. 'I met Euan when I was in hospital. He came to see me.'

'Why did he visit you in hospital?'

I couldn't imagine what Euan visiting me in hospital had to do with *anything*. I exclaimed, 'You *just said yourself* you know he brought me there after I'd hit my head!'

Mother gave a short, sharp sniff, which I knew to be scolding.

The policeman glanced up at me over his glasses again. 'Perhaps you've remembered something else about your time in the tinkers' camp, as you were with them for nearly a full day? Young McEwen was known to be out and about on the river that morning. I believe the tinkers fish for pearls as well?'

I don't know where this man's suspicious mind was leading him, but I could see he was following a familiar map.

Frank had suggested the same thing. Maybe the tinker lad had attacked the scholar. Or fought with him. Or surprised him. Maybe the boy was a thief, stealing shells or pearls from an amateur. Shiftless. Homeless. Penniless. Heartless; *lawless*.

Whatever had happened, it should be easy to pin the blame, if there was blame to be pinned, on a Traveller.

I wasn't going to gratify Inspector Milne by even acknowledging that I understood what he was driving at.

'Do you remember anything about your first meeting with Euan McEwen?' Milne pressed.

'No,' I said, making a supreme effort to be polite rather than coldly hostile. 'He probably saved my life. But I don't remember him doing it.'

I began to have the uncomfortable feeling that it might be up to me to make sure Euan McEwen didn't get blamed for whatever had actually happened that morning. And until we knew what that was, neither one of us was free of suspicion.

To my frustration, Mother was still irritatingly cautious about letting me walk by myself on the river path. But once I was on my feet again I was allowed to go and visit Mary if she came to fetch me. The prolonged loss of independence would have driven me quite mad otherwise.

It was a dull, chilly day when I arrived back at the Inverfearnie Library for the first time after my injury. I was decently dressed in Mother's skirt still, but had bundled myself up in a nursery-bathroom sweater that smelled exactly like a sheep. It was wonderful to be out of the house. As Mary and I crossed the swaying iron footbridge I was surprised to see Sergeant Angus Henderson striding down the slope of the unnatural mound of Inverfearnie Island towards us in his intimidating waterproof cape and high boots, stumping along with his ram's-horn-hook-topped cromach staff.

As he came towards us Mary waved.

The river watcher stopped short. His iron-grey eyebrows drew together ferociously. His face was very white.

'Miss Kinnaird …' He spoke as though he wasn't sure. 'Lady Julia?'

I couldn't remember him ever having *noticed* me before, let alone called me by name. Being Mary's companion must have made me special.

'Hope you're well,' he said gruffly, doffing his tweed hat at me with military sharpness.

As we came off the bridge he gave Mary a very cordial bow and a kindly pat on the shoulder.

'No harm done here the day,' Sergeant Henderson bellowed at her.

'Oh heavens, I should hope not!' she said.

'Aye, well, it's quiet now those mucky tinks are away.'

'They'll be back for the flax at Bridge Farm no doubt, if not before,' Mary said. 'I'll be glad when the Glenfearn School opens and they're gone for good.'

'I'm counting the days,' the Water Bailiff growled. 'If that young lad gives you any trouble this summer, be sure to put a call through to the Brig O'Fearn police. I'll have his teeth on a string.'

'Thank you, Sergeant Henderson, you're a dear. You always take good care of me.'

They shook hands and off he went to pull teeth somewhere else along his patrol.

Well! That was a surprise. Apparently the Water Bailiff had a soft spot in his heart for Mary, who acted as a sort of loyal unofficial river watcher on the front lines.

'Which "young lad" did he mean?' I asked Mary as she unlocked the heavy oak front door to let us in, guessing perfectly well whom he'd meant. 'Not Euan McEwen, surely, the one who took me to the hospital? I can't *imagine* him giving you any trouble.'

She didn't hear me. I'd have asked again, but when she turned towards me she'd already moved on.

'Now, darling, I'm often busy with library patrons and the running of the place, and I won't be able to be with you all the time you're here. But you can help me with the Murray Collection. I'll show you what we have to do.'

Mary led me up the winding staircase.

'My little library's been commandeered,' she said as we emerged in the Upper Reading Room.

It was exactly as I'd left it the day I arrived at Strathfearn, with the great chestnut library table covered with artefacts. There were the spear tips spread all over the place; there was the beautiful black wooden cup in its silver filigree setting.

'Who moved the collection here?' I asked. 'Did you help?'

'Dr Housman packed the boxes. I believe the chief contractor came along to keep an eye on the workers who brought them here.'

'Did they bring all of it? Is this the whole thing, the whole of the Murray archaeological collection?' I was still thinking about the pearls that no one remembered.

'It's all here, but it's not all unpacked. I've to make sure no one moves anything that's on the main reading table, because that's what Dr Housman left there. The police were round looking at it and I had such a hard time stopping them touching things.'

'Shouldn't they have put a barrier round it or something?' I asked, impressed.

Mary gave a little laugh. 'You've been reading too many Harriet Vane novels!'

'That's true.'

'Imagine there's an invisible barrier. These folding tables are for Sandy to use when he comes.' She brightened as she spoke my brother's name: Mary visibly *brightened*. 'He's working on a project in London that he can't get out of till the middle of July, and I suppose Dr Housman might come back before then, but I thought I'd try to get things ready for Sandy just in case.'

She paused, still a little bit flushed, and it dawned on me that she called me 'Julia' and she called the missing antiquarian 'Dr Housman' and the 'dear' Water Bailiff got called by his military rank. But when Mary spoke of my big brother, Grandad's heir, who has always been 'the Honourable Alexander Lawson Murray Wallace Beaufort-Stuart' and is now by Special Remainder 'Alexander Beaufort-Stuart, Earl of Strathfearn', she simply called him 'Sandy'. And he wasn't even here yet.

'Mary, you have given yourself away,' I said, and she knew exactly what I was talking about, because her smooth and shapeless cheeks went even pinker. 'You and Sandy?'

'No, no! We're friends. I read his article and wrote to him about it, and he wrote back. We write to each other all the time now, by return post sometimes. He visited in the spring to see your grandfather just before he died, and … and Sandy and I went walking.'

'Just walking?' I said, disbelieving. I wasn't trying to be coy. I really wanted to know.

'Well, no! *Not* just walking. But not what you think. He sat here after your grandfather's funeral and drank such a quantity of whisky that I thought he'd drown himself – in the River Fearn, properly, not metaphorically in drink – if he tried to make his way back to the Big House alone in the dark. I let him stay here, which was perhaps not the correct thing to do, but he'd fallen asleep at last in the chair in my study and I didn't have the heart to wake him.'

'Nor would I!'

'*Exactly.*'

Mary knew she was blushing, and turned her face away from mine in embarrassment. 'I know he would never – well, Julia, you see me for what I am. But I like him more than anyone I know, and I don't have many friends. Sergeant Henderson is a *dear*, you know, but he's not really a *friend*. I am concerned for Dr Housman, but I am selfishly glad his disappearance means I am to work with Sandy ...' Mary hesitated all of a sudden. 'I wouldn't confess this to anyone but you, Julia.'

'I *do* understand, Mary! And I don't spill secrets.'

I obviously didn't know her *any bit* as well as I thought I did.

Because –

Mary and Sandy! I couldn't imagine it. I couldn't imagine Mary with *anyone*. But was that because I thought she was not ... not, say, *ordinary* enough to have ordinary desires and ambitions? Perhaps my feeling that she had a 'kind' face was as unthinking and shallow as Euan and Ellen calling her a goblin.

What Sandy thought was another story. A story I didn't know.

Mary became brisk again all of a sudden. 'Now, darling, I don't want you sitting about here idly, so you can help me set up the card tables and unpack the boxes. The tables are going to go around the edges of the room in front of the shelves. It'll make it very tight, so be sure to leave a gap for people to get through. And if you could make a note of *everything* you take out of the boxes and which table you put it on, that would be most useful.'

I couldn't believe my luck, really. Perhaps I would come across Grandad's pearls myself. Taking an inventory of the Murray Hoard would be a fabulous way to spend my convalescence. And maybe I'd find some clue as to what had happened to Housman.

After nearly a fortnight of being treated with the fearful gentleness one might use to handle a treasured pet budgerigar with a broken wing, it was a shock to be awakened one morning with the mattress beneath my feet bouncing so hard it made the iron bed frame squeak. I raised my head and shoulders, leaning back on my elbows. And there was my favourite brother Jamie. He is only a year older than me.

'You are going to give me concussion again,' I told him.

He stopped bouncing, took one look at me and clapped a hand over his mouth in an attempt to suffocate himself so he could not laugh. His shoulders shook.

'*Stow it!*' I said.

'Sluggard!' he accused. Then he added, rather chokingly, 'I think I shall call you *Feathers*.'

'Don't be unkind!' I was very pleased to see him. 'They cut my hair while I was insensible in hospital and I've only just been allowed to wash it.'

'It's very modern. Very gamine. You look like a jazz singer.'

'Shut up.'

'Actually, you look more like that doll you used to carry around by its hair, Donalda. Do you remember? Till most of it fell out except that wiry ashy tuft on the very top that you used for a handle –'

I threw my pillow. He nearly threw it back, instinctively, but checked himself just in time. Instead he tucked it behind his head against the French window. I pulled my knees up so there was more room for him.

'How are you feeling?' he asked.

'Much, much better.'

'I thought you might need cheering up. Invalids need cheering, don't they? I'd only just got home from school myself, and I overheard Father speaking to Mother on the 'phone. You know how he echoes back everything you say to show he's being attentive? "She spent a night with the Travellers! A man standing in the river! That's all she remembers! The scholar's still AWOL!" I couldn't hear what Mother was telling him – just all the intrigue he was repeating. So here I am. I took the milk train from Aberdeen.'

'You have cheered me up enormously already,' I said. 'Now that you're here to look after me I'll be able to go somewhere other than the library day after day! I want to retrace my steps. I want to know what happened to me.'

'Let's get started,' Jamie answered, grinning.

He provided me with clothes. This is the sort of thing that makes him my favourite. No other brother would have thought of it. He was patient with me eating the tea and toast he'd carried up from the kitchen, and then with me getting dressed in Mother and Solange's little room (in Mother's clothes again because although Jamie had brought me several of my favourite garments, it cannot be said he'd included anything *practical*). He got bored waiting for me to finish fussing with my hair at Mémère's dressing table.

'Let me,' he said, leaning over my shoulder to take hold of the comb. 'We did *HMS Pinafore* this spring and they made me be Josephine because I'm so scrawny. I've become rather good at primping.'

He was standing behind me and we could see each other in the mirror. With my hair short we looked very much alike, except that he was grinning and I was scowling.

'I should think you made a lovely Josephine,' I said. 'You are quite as pretty as me. I'll bet you wore a wig though. Yellow curls.'

'True, but not for rehearsals.'

'I wish you'd brought it down with you. I could have used it.'

Jamie laughed. He was deft and sure with the comb and hairgrips. 'It would not have suited you at all. Anyway we had a ritual burning of it after the last performance, carrying it down to the river on a pike like a beheaded aristocrat.'

'You seem to have a great deal more fun at school than I do,' I grumbled.

Jamie stood back, lifting his hands. 'There.'

He'd really done as good a job as Solange. He held a hand mirror to the back of my head so I could see how he'd hidden the stubble.

I said, 'You should leave off bothering with Eton and become a ladies' –'

'Stop being such a miserable cat, Julie,' Jamie said hastily, going a little pink. 'Now. Where do you want to go?'

'I'm burning to go to Inchfort Field!' I answered. 'I want to see how far I got between hitting my head and falling over. I want to see if we can find any trace of Dr Housman. And maybe the lad who rescued me has come back. The Traveller folk who took me to the hospital told me to come and see them. Everyone is so *suspicious* of them and as far as I can tell they haven't done a thing to deserve it. I want to tell them thank you.'

FREEDOM!

We left the house through the terrace doors of the morning room and stood for a moment surveying the building works.

'They're putting down paths,' I observed, and was struck with melancholy over my grandfather not being around to appreciate this improvement. 'We could have pushed Grandad about in his chair if there'd been paths last summer.'

'I remember him wishing for a smooth path down to the river. He didn't have the money for it,' Jamie said soberly. 'Cheer up. Let's see what they're up to over by the tennis lawn – it looks like they're digging a swimming bath. Tell me what it was like to sleep in a Travellers' camp!'

'I can't remember,' I said crossly. 'I was asleep the whole time.'

'Perhaps they'd let me stay with them tonight, if they're there,' Jamie said. 'Better than sleeping all by myself in one of those servants' rooms in the attic. Or I could build a camp tent on the terrace. I wonder how deep they've gone with that swimming hole.'

He was doing his best to distract me – although I knew, based on his fascination for hydromechanics (or as our eldest brother Davie calls it, 'Jamie's obsession with drains'), that he was serious about wanting to look at the pool project.

We didn't get too close, but it *was* interesting. There was a hole in the lawn as big as a cottage, and the invasion into the riverbank was a miniature geological history lesson if you knew how to read it, slices of different coloured earth piled neatly one on top of the other like a giant layer cake with green grass icing on top. The layer they were currently digging into looked like Black Forest gateau.

'Peat,' Jamie commented. 'I wonder if they'll find anything interesting in it. Remember the log boat, under the water near the river gate by Aberfearn Castle? That's three thousand years old. They can tell because the peat's laid down into it, all around it.'

'Show-off. You only know that because you've read it in Sandy's antiquarian article.'

'We could go to see if they've uncovered it. It's still there. They must be digging nearby if they're laying pipes beneath the riverbed for this pool.'

'*Drains*,' I exclaimed in disgust. 'What about the Traveller folk camping at Inchfort?'

'I'll go to look at the pipes on my own later,' Jamie conceded generously.

We carried on down to the river path, just as I'd done two weeks earlier, and turned upstream along the Fearn. I watched my brother's face change as he gazed around him at the birch wood. I knew he was feeling exactly as I'd felt that first day here; all the sadness and joy.

Jamie spoke quietly. 'I can't believe this isn't Murray land any more. And to think I wouldn't even be here if it hadn't been for your sore head! I felt like Grandad's funeral was the end. I'm glad I came.'

We walked for a little while without talking. But when we got to Inverfearnie Island we both jumped along the iron foot-bridge to make it bounce, and ended up laughing. We passed the open door of the old library, crossed the mossy stone bridge to the other side of the burn and took the path towards Brig O'Fearn by way of Inchfort Field. The river wood hadn't changed in the least bit since the first day I'd arrived.

We'd nearly reached the bend in the river where the beachy place and the big stones are when the yellow dog came bounding out of the undergrowth along the path as if it had been waiting for us.

It really did come straight towards us as if we were old friends. It saw us, scampered around us both in a circle of excitement, then made a rash decision and plunged into the clear brown waters of the Fearn.

Something tugged at my brain.

The dog found its footing and scrambled out again, bounding through the tangle of nettles and forget-me-nots on the riverbank. It shook itself gloriously and was suddenly transformed from a dripping rag to a golden powder puff, like a pantomime Cinderella under her fairy godmother's wand. She was a very beautiful tan Border collie. She chose me to leap upon in greeting.

And I knew her.

This dog – this sodden whirlwind of golden fluff – was one of those terribly sweet, terribly brainless characters that you can't take anywhere if you want to work: she barks at sheep, she'll scare the grouse before your gun is loaded, she leaps at strange girls to give them kisses. That's what she was doing now, and I knew that's what she'd done the day I met her, the day I'd fallen.

'Pinkie! You silly, silly girl! Down, love. Good girl, Pinkie.'

You see, I even knew her name.

Jamie helped to drag her off me before she knocked me down. She shook herself again, splattering us with river water.

'I *do* remember you.' I fondled her ears. 'Pinkie, love, where are your people?'

She pranced away from me towards the river's bend. She knew where her people were, and she was going to take me to meet them.

They were standing in the burn by the flat rock, fishing for pearls with glass-bottomed jugs and pronged sticks, just like the man I'd seen before my head exploded. Unlike him, they knew what they were doing.

One of them looked up at us and waved. It was Euan McEwen. He was so clearly a younger copy of his tall and ginger-haired companion that it took me one glance to guess the older man was Euan and Ellen's father.

'That's the Traveller lad who found me,' I told Jamie. 'And his dad, I think.'

They were both wearing waders, but the water scarcely came to their knees. When Euan saw us, he pulled the tin-and-glass jug of his trade out of the water and slung it over his shoulder.

'You're looking bonny, Davie Balfour!' he shouted.

The dog ran to meet him. She took a flying leap off the flat rock and into the water. The older man winced away from the splash with a strangled noise that was half groan, half laughter. She was obviously not a working dog.

'You're here! Hurrah!' I cried in answer to Euan. 'I remember your dog – the daftie! She jumped all over me!'

'This is my dad, Alan McEwen,' Euan said. 'Dad, here's our Davie Balfour come back from the dead.'

Funny things, names. Funny how it felt easy and natural for me to call Euan by his first name, and daring and grown-up to call Frank by his. I suppose I would never call Mother by her given name either, though she is Mummy in fondness.

I liked it that Euan kept calling me Davie. It felt special and friendly, though I think he did it partly to avoid having to call me Lady Julia.

'This is my brother Jamie,' I said. I was trying to make it clear I didn't want the dreadful formality of a title – especially since it was only me, as the Earl of Craigie's daughter, who had this dilemma; Jamie, a younger son, isn't saddled with a courtesy title in everyday speech. I added firmly, 'And I'm Julie.'

Alan McEwen whipped off his cap and flashed us a McEwen grin. 'You're looking braw, lass! Hello, Jamie.'

Jamie knelt on the flat rock and held out a hand. Alan McEwen gave it a wet shake. Pinkie sloshed about around the McEwen men's legs, struggling a little against the current.

'I wanted to thank you for taking me to Perth the other week,' I told him. 'And Mrs McEwen too.'

Alan McEwen smiled warmly. 'Mrs McEwen will be glad to know you're on your feet again.'

'Have you found anything?' Jamie asked.

Alan McEwen grimaced a little. 'We've five fat fiddle-bellied crooks for Mrs McEwen to open. But I dinnae like to see so much rubbish chucked in the burn – glass target balls and tins and jam jars and whatnot. Washing downstream frae the village, I suppose, but it saddens me, folk using the burn as a midden. Not like the old days.'

'You can get a penny for a jam jar,' Euan said.

'I'm no' divin' for rubbish.'

'I say, can I see?' Jamie asked, as eager as the dog. 'Could I take a look through your glass jug?'

Mr McEwen smiled. 'Aye, but you'll have to get wet.'

'Go on,' I told Jamie enthusiastically, anticipating an excellent variety performance. 'The water's pretty low. The chap I saw fishing here two weeks ago was up to his waist!'

'The Fearn's tidal right the way past Brig O'Fearn village,' explained Alan McEwen. 'It's coming up on a spring tide just now. Makes the high tides extra high and the low tides extra low.'

Jamie undid a couple of buttons at his throat and shrugged out of his shirt. He handed it to me for safekeeping and, just like Pinkie, slid off the flat rock and sloshed into the burn. Euan passed his pearl-fishing glass across to Jamie so he could look below the surface of the water.

Jamie's arms and shoulders were fair as flax, as though he'd spent the last ten years in a dungeon. He bent over by the flat rock, and as he leaned down, light from the river caught his face and light from the sky gleamed on his bare back, and – *incredible*. Incredible the way it comes back. Just like that. It happened in a flash, in an instant of clarity – sparked by another pale body standing in the River Fearn.

The man in the river on the day I'd fallen – there was a reason I'd thought he was comical. There was a reason I hadn't been able to remember his clothes.

He hadn't been wearing any.

That man had been stark naked. Seeing Jamie with his back stripped bare, with the reflected light off the water on his face, made me remember.

I could see the other man perfectly now, splashing about when he lost his cap, the lenses of his glasses spangled with drops of water after he submerged his face. Those shifting dots of light on his skin like gold coins – I'd seen those because he'd been wearing glasses. The lenses had reflected in the river as he moved. I hadn't been able to see his eyes, focused on something below the surface of the water.

I stood quite still, remembering. It was a bit like being hit on the head all over again. It made me go quiet for a moment.

But then Pinkie came crashing out of the stream, romping up devotedly to keep me company, since everyone else was in the water. I took a deep breath. Jamie peered intently at his feet, or something, through the glass jug. I wondered what he could see. The McEwens stood by watching, indulging him.

'What happened after Euan brought me up to your camp?' I asked. 'Did you try to find where I'd come from? I was *here* when I hit my head. There was a man – I saw someone in the burn here, over by the Drookit Stane in the middle of the stream. We think it was the scholar who was working at the library, and no one's seen him since that day, either.'

'Aye, the police have been sniffing around here looking for him,' said Alan McEwen. 'We knew him because he'd been in about the place last month, wanting to know the good fishing spots for Fearn pearls. Nice enough gadgie and a friend of Strathfearn's, but none of our business.'

'How did I get up the path to Inchfort Field before you found me, Euan – did Dr Housman carry me?'

'He might have,' Euan answered. 'It was Pinkie found you. Your scholar might have been frighted by the dog, and put you down, and gone away again.'

Alan McEwen laughed. 'Frighted by *that*!'

'Well, Dad, some people don't like dogs. And Pinkie was with her when I found her.'

'Did you *see* the other man?' I asked.

Jamie straightened up to listen, intrigued.

Euan shook his head.

'We found that cap, lad,' Mr McEwen said. 'The Water Bailiff took it away with him for the police to look at, remember?'

'So we did.'

'What did he look like, your man in the stream?' Jamie asked suddenly. 'Was he wearing gold wire-rimmed specs?'

My mouth dropped open. Because he had been.

'*Why?*'

Jamie bent over, using the jug to pinpoint something at his feet, and reached into the water with his free hand. He came up dripping, holding something that glinted gold between his fingers.

It was a thin metallic wand, slender as a stem of wheat and about as long as Jamie's hand. It curled at the end like a giant fish hook. It was a shape that made no sense, a thing that had no business being in the river, and yet there was also something perfectly ordinary and familiar about it.

'It's a temple,' Jamie said.

'It's a what?' said Euan.

'It's one side of a pair of spectacles. It's a temple. You know, the arm thing that holds your glasses on your head – it hooks over your ear.'

'There's all sorts rubbish in the burn,' said Mr McEwen. 'Folk are careless.'

I didn't consciously remember that Dr Housman had been wearing broken glasses. But when I'd doodled that pair of spectacles, they'd been missing one side.

Jamie's small gold twist of wire was the piece that had come off – the piece I hadn't seen.

It had to be a trace of Dr Housman. But it didn't tell me a damned thing more than I already knew.

'This sun is burning me already – I can feel it,' Jamie said, hauling himself wet and gleaming as a selkie on to the flat rock. 'Give me back my shirt before I am entirely grilled.' He looked up at me. 'Are you all right?'

I nodded. I didn't quite trust myself to speak.

'I expect we'll have to hand that in to the police to go with the chap's cap,' Jamie said.

'We'll let you do that,' said Alan McEwen. 'They've been round here twice already poking their nebs in about, and they dinnae like us. No point in looking for trouble.'

'Well, the Water Bailiff is a terrifying man and no mistake,' said Jamie. 'He's thrashed me and every one of my brothers at some time or other – our Sandy used to dive to look at the log boat sticking out of the peat near the mouth of the Fearn, and the Water Bailiff hauled him out of the river once and thrashed him with a birch switch without even letting him get dressed first. I'll take this in to the police and leave you out of it.'

Mr McEwen strode through the water and waded out on to the little beach, where I was standing with Pinkie. 'Come along up to the camp and meet Mrs McEwen,' he invited. 'You can thank her yourself for the care she gave you; she'll be happy to see you well again, lass. And now that we know you're one of Strathfearn's – well, I knew your grandad, and he'd have done the same for any of my bairns. A fine man, Strathfearn. The finest.'

'And maybe we'll find a pearl or two inside the crooks we've got for Mammy,' Euan said. 'Come and watch her open them.'

5

WHAT'S YOUR PROPER WORK?

You know what I was expecting to find at the McEwens' camping place? A community of twenty families, a nomadic village of tents, each with its own cooking fire, filling Inchfort Field like a ghost of the Roman military outpost it is named for. But the McEwens had got a most modest set-up, in a high, sunny corner of the field sheltered by the beech hedge of the estate boundary. They'd parked themselves as far away as possible from the queer old standing stone at the bottom of the field, covered with lichened carvings of starey-eyed fish, and I didn't blame 'em. Grandad always told us that stone walks down the path to join the tall Drookit Stane in the river on Lammas Night and swim with the salmon in the dark. Antiquarians are all secretly pagan heretics.

There weren't twenty people, let alone twenty families camped at Inchfort Field, and a third of those were little.

'Gosh, I thought there were more of you here!' I said as we crossed the field. 'Everybody makes it sound like –'

'– the place is crawling with tinks?' Euan made *tinks* sound like *bedbugs*. Suddenly he reminded me very much of his twin sister. My heart leaped again, thinking Ellen might be there.

'Well, I didn't say it.'

'There's three families here. Daddy's and his brother's. And Mammy's best friend and her daughter and her man. Lots of weans – you'll see! And Daddy's old Auntie Bessie, who's got no family but ours.'

Ellen *was* there. She and Mrs McEwen and the very old Auntie Bessie were the only grown-ups about, though there were a handful of wee lassies skipping rope lower down the field; everyone else was out thinning turnips at Bridge Farm. Ellen was busy though, stripping bark from whippy willow branches. The old woman fed bits of bark to a fire over glowing coals, and Mrs McEwen was deftly weaving a willow basket with the supple wands that Ellen gave her. They were looking after the wee-est of the bairns while they worked – Ellen had a baby tied cuddled against her chest in a shawl, its downy hair just brushing against her chin. Her own hair was a glory of copper fire that morning, shining like a whisky still, long and loose in gentle flames down her back.

'Mammy, we've brought our lucky lass for you to meet,' Euan called out as we came close. 'She's awake and walking.'

Their mother, Jean McEwen, laughed. 'Looks like our Pinkie's found a new best friend!'

Their mother wasn't like the other McEwens at all. She was little and merry and good-natured. Instantly I wished I'd thought to bring her a gift, and wanted to kick myself for not having anything to offer.

I knelt abruptly in front of her. When she put aside the willow withies she'd been weaving, I snatched up her hands, held them close together in mine, and kissed them. 'Hello, Mrs McEwen! I think I owe you my life.'

She shook her head and laughed. 'Och, Lady Julia, no such thing. I only kept the rain off you for a night!'

'And isn't that a woman's proper work, sheltering bairns?' Ellen remarked coolly.

Mrs McEwen still grasped my hands – I'd instinctively done the right thing to greet her so warmly – but Ellen McEwen held my gaze with chilly challenge, menacing and stony-faced.

I wanted very much for her to like me.

'Well, somebody has to look after bairns,' I said.

I swear, it was as though I could read Ellen's mind. She was practically daring me to ask her: 'Is that *your* baby, Ellen McEwen?'

In the same instant I was certain that it wasn't. She was just waiting for me to jump to conclusions about her, in exactly the same way the St John's Infirmary staff had jumped to conclusions about me.

'What's your proper work?' I asked her.

'What's yours, wee primsie toffee-nose?'

'Whisht, Nellie!' the very old woman scolded her.

'I'm still in school,' I said. 'So's Jamie.'

'I'm a willow basket weaver,' Ellen said in a voice that made it sound like she'd made it up on the spot.

'Oh, aye?' Jamie flung himself down on the grass by her side, artless and winning. 'Did you cut all this lot yourself? Do you make your own creels?' He patted her small fisherman's basket on the ground next to her. 'There were always *piles* of baskets in the Big House – they use 'em for everything from sandwiches to guns. We used to see people cutting willows on the far bank where the Fearn meets the Tay.'

Ellen looked down her nose at him, the tiniest of smiles curled in the corner of her mouth.

'Aye, Jamie Stuart, that's us. That's *our* willow bank. We own it, by ancient deed. Since before the new house was built. Since the Murrays lived in the castle.'

The 'new' house, Strathfearn House, replaced a Georgian mansion destroyed by fire. The castle is five hundred years old and nobody has lived in it since the eighteenth century. 'Since the Murrays lived in the castle' is a very long time ago however you look at it.

'And that's us banned after your gran moves out,' Ellen added grimly, and the rudimentary smile disappeared.

'But why, if it's yours?' Jamie asked.

'There's no place to camp after this year. You can't camp on the riverbank because of the mud and the tide. So that's us done with those willows. Forever. The camping green by Bridge Farm's been closed down by the County Council, and Inchfort Field will be closed off when the Glenfearn School opens. *Shaness!* We've always done casual work for the Strathfearn Estate – working the fields, gardening, helping with the grouse shooting. But those scaldy builders aren't interested in giving us work, and I ken the Glenfearn School won't want *filthy tinkers* anywhere near their boys. And the pearl fishing – we won't be able to do that here either. Do you know what Fearn pearls are worth? *Ten pound* Daddy got for one last year.'

Cripes. At that rate, twenty-five pearls would pay Jamie's school fees at Eton for a year. And there was me ten years ago as a little girl playing with Grandad's pearls like marbles, and me now feeling sentimental that my pretty toys were gone.

It makes you very uncomfortable to realise that your emotional attachment to something is an indulgence.

'Neither did our gran want to have to sell the estate,' I said hotly.

Ellen gave a snort. 'Your poor gran. Hungry, is she?'

Ellen's mother apologised firmly. 'Never mind our Ellen. She's angered about the big changes and she's still mourning your grandad. His passing's a great sorrow to all of us. Your mother Esmé and I were playmates when we were half your age.'

The old woman added, 'See, Nell, she's got her grandad's eyes – hazel as autumn leaves turning, clear as Cairngorm mountain amber.'

I couldn't help smiling at her. 'Thank you! I loved Grandad's eyes.'

Ellen gave an undisguised snort of disgust. I could hear her thinking at me: *FATHEAD*. I was not making a good impression.

'I've five fine mussels for you to open, Jean,' Mr McEwen said briskly to his wife. 'We'll let the lucky lass try one as well, aye? Give her a sup of tea and I'll crack these crooks the while.'

'Bessie, put the tea can on,' said Ellen's mother.

'Julie take it off again,' I misquoted on purpose, and they all laughed, except crabbit Ellen, and I felt warm. *This* was more like it, this was what was missing in the stifling, strained atmosphere back at Strathfearn House – ordinary cups of tea with people laughing and chatting over them. I hadn't realised how tense and worried my people were until I was away from them, or how much it was weighing on me.

While the big black tea can boiled, I had time to make good sense of the small campsite. There was a cooking fire in an old sheep-dip tin, standing on flat stones on the bare earth where they'd cut away the turf so it could be filled in when they left. A handful of chickens scavenged together under the hedges, and there were a couple of placid ponies and a couple of fine-looking horses cropping grass in the sun, and a wagon and a smaller cart by the gate. There was a long bow tent snugly made of hazel wands and sacking; there was also an old military tent. Clean washing hung discreetly on poles behind the tents. All the shelters looked sturdy but could be easily dismantled when they decided to move on; nothing wasted.

'Where do you draw water?' Jamie asked.

'From the burn for washing,' said Mrs McEwen. 'From Boatman's Well for drinking.'

'But it's so browny yellowish!' I protested.

'Och, that's just peat,' Mrs McEwen answered. 'Peat never hurt anyone.'

'Gives flavour to the tea,' said Ellen slyly as Bessie set out tin cups, one of which would be mine in a moment or two.

I answered boldly, 'I cannot wait to try some.' I had not ever drunk from the Boatman's Well before but I am not afraid of PEAT, Miss Ellen McEwen.

'Here you are, Davie.' Euan knelt beside me and handed me the first mussel.

Scottish river mussels are not like the little ones you get in the sea, or find scoured as blue and white shells along the tide line. The five mussels that Alan McEwen had brought back for his wife were as long as my hand, and nearly as wide, narrowed in the middle like fiddles.

'That's maybe a good hundred year old,' said Mr McEwen, indicating the one I held. 'Older than the Big House. Go on, open her up.'

It was smooth and brown as a leather wallet and it opened like a hymnal. I couldn't see anything that looked like a pearl, though the inside of the shell was beautiful. I held the two halves spread wide on my palms while Mrs McEwen slid her thumbs underneath the shell's luckless inhabitant – but there was nothing in it but a grey blob of dying mussel.

I felt sad, all of a sudden – not about there being no pearl, but about us having killed a wild thing that had been minding its own business in the River Fearn for a hundred years or more. A little violation.

'Ah well, there's four more here!' McEwen Snr said cheerfully.

'What do you do with them after?' I asked. 'Can you eat them?'

'Eh, no, lass,' Mrs McEwen said. 'Too big and tough. You're thinking of sea mussels. Pinkie can have the insides.'

She took the next and used the edge of the first shell to prise the new one open.

'Ah!'

We all crowded closer to see what she'd found.

She laid the shell on her lap. There was a small deformity in the blob of mussel there, a little membrane bag, and she pinched it between her fingers and squeezed out the pearl.

'Well, this is a bonny wee thing, but will MacGregor's buy it without a match?'

She dropped it into the palm of her other hand so we could see it. It was shaped like a teardrop, and the palest salmon colour, like a cool sunset. It was beautiful and strange.

She held the shell up to me. 'Run your thumbs beneath the meat. There may be more.'

I copied what she'd done earlier. An inch of smooth slime, then sudden rolling grains like barley beneath my thumbs. It surprised me. 'Oh!'

They all laughed at me.

'It's full of them!' I gasped.

Mrs McEwen took the shell from me. She slipped half a dozen peachy pearls into the palm of her hand to show me. 'Luck's with us now!' she said, and gave me the next mussel.

114

There was nothing in that one, either, nor the fourth. They handed me the fifth.

'Ellen, you've not had a shot,' I said.

She shrugged. 'You're the lucky one.'

'Well, no, I haven't actually found anything. That was your mum's shell that had all the pink pearls in it. You have this one. Then it's on me if it's a dud, and it's on you if it isn't.'

Ellen stared at me over the silky hair of the sleeping baby tied against her chest. Then, unexpectedly, she laughed. 'I like those odds. Give it me.' She paused, then said with exaggerated politeness, 'Pass the crook here, *Lady Julia*.'

What's my proper work, Ellen McEwen? I am going to make you call me Julie.

I gave her the crook. She opened it.

Inside, in its membrane sac, there was a perfect creamy pale-pink pearl nearly the size of a marble. It must have been worth a packet.

'Lady Julia, ye're a fairy,' said old Bessie.

Jamie laughed. 'Don't give her ideas.'

But my mind was working, it's true. I was thinking about the villainous man Grandad had caught, who'd torn through all the young mussels on the riverbed in nearly exactly the same place where the McEwens had been fishing, and how he'd found nothing; how if he'd known where to look, all along, these hundred-year-old shells full of pearls were just sitting there for the taking. They'd been there the entire time.

And I wondered how many Dr Housman had found. He'd had those beautiful earrings made for Solange. Maybe he'd found an ancient river pearl that was absolutely extraordinary, or more than one, and he'd gone off to get them valued, or to sell them and bank the proceeds; maybe he was trying to do it quietly because Grandad was dead and the house was sold, and he wasn't really sure whether those pearls belonged to him or to the Glenfearn School or to the King himself.

Ellen gave her pearl to her mother.

I offered to help with the tidying-up, still trying to win her over – with willing friendliness if nothing else, much like Pinkie.

'Off you go back to your granny's,' said Mrs McEwen. 'She needs your help with the packing more than we do.'

'Actually, I've been *unpacking*,' I laughed. 'Since Dr Housman's not around, I've been helping Mary Kinnaird sort out the Murray Collection at the Inverfearnie Library. Our brother Sandy's going to do the cataloguing when he gets here. I keep hoping I'll find treasure that everyone else has forgotten about.'

'And to think folk call us sleekit, you spoilt wee galoot of a schoolgirl!' exclaimed Ellen. 'But say, can you take me to see the Murray Collection?'

'Well, of course!' I'd have thrown myself under a *bus* to get her to thaw a little. But I should have guessed the Murray Hoard might interest her. Euan had said she'd gone to the library to borrow the *Proceedings of the Society of Antiquaries* annual in which Sandy had published that article about the log boat.

'Our Nell worked on the drawings for Strathfearn's collection two years ago, when it got so hard for him to see,' Jean McEwen explained.

'I measured and drew all his spear tips,' said Ellen, not without pride. 'Could we go and look at it *now*? I want to see the Reliquary again.'

'Now? Why not?' I said. 'The library's open ...'

All unexpectedly, with quick and efficient hands, Ellen untied the shawl that held the sleeping baby cuddled against her chest. The small person opened her eyes and yawned and blinked and crinkled up her face, and I could see the little fists opening and closing. Jean McEwen reached out welcoming arms and Ellen gave her the baby.

Jamie bounded to his feet to offer Ellen a gallant hand to help her get up. He really was layering it on. I suppose I was too.

'What's the Reliquary?' Jamie asked.

'A reliquary's a wee pot you keep a saint's finger bone in, or something,' said Ellen. 'Your grandad's one looks like a cup.'

'Black wood?' I asked. 'Set in silver, spiralling around it like the fish on the Salmon Stane? That is my favourite thing in the collection.'

'Aye, and it's special to Strathfearn,' Ellen told us. 'We gave it to the Murrays to pay for the willow bank.' She made it sound as though the transaction had happened yesterday, not four hundred years ago or whatever it had been. 'Your grandad was worried it would be sold when he died, and one of the things I did for him was to write to the National Museum of Antiquities about it. He wanted them to be able to bid on it first.'

'Oh!' I gasped. I realised that here was someone who might actually know, who might remember. 'Were there pearls in it?'

Ellen dropped Jamie's hand. For a moment she stood staring at me strangely.

'No.'

She held my gaze, just as she'd done when I'd first seen her in the hospital. She fixed me in the disintegrator-ray of her stony blue eyes. 'There weren't any pearls in it that I've ever seen. But there were pearls in it when we gave it to the Murrays. That was part of the price for the land. It was a long time ago.'

'That's the way the tale is told,' said Alan McEwen gently.

And then I wondered if maybe I'd just *imagined* the pearls. I wondered if Grandad had told me the same tale, and in my head I'd been so taken with the wonderful image of the immeasurably ancient black and silver cup filled to the brim with pearls, that I'd put them there myself without ever having really seen them.

It made sense. In the past two weeks I'd learned that memory is a strange and unreliable thing.

And yet … I thought I could still remember *playing* with those pearls.

Ellen reached down to pick up her creel basket and sling it over her shoulder. 'I didn't think I'd get to see the Reliquary again,' she said. 'You come too, Euan. You've never seen it. You should see it before it's sold.'

The library was officially open, with a card posted in the window to let you know, and the great oak door was propped wide, welcoming. Pinkie, still damp from her swim, was too enthusiastic about coming in with us.

'Euan spoilt her when she was a pup,' Ellen said. 'Bitches are useless anyway, but he had to go and carry her about in a bucket everywhere we went.'

Ellen paused, waiting, as if something in what she'd said had been a test.

Jamie figured her out ahead of me. 'So that's why she's called Pinkie,' he laughed. '*Pinkie*'s your word for *bucket*, aye?'

119

I felt that I'd not passed. I was a bit meanly glad that it was *me* the enthusiastic dog didn't want to leave. We finally had to shut the door on her. We could hear her mourning sadly outside, presumably lying pressed against the doorstep.

I led the way through the library. We crossed the downstairs room with the glass cases, Euan silently following the rest of us in a heightened state of reluctant stealth.

'Hallo the library!' I yelled.

Mary didn't hear me. We made our way up the spiral stair to the Upper Reading Room. It was empty; Mary must have been in her study downstairs. Ellen looked around the room with an odd expression, for the first few seconds not taking in the collection spread across the tables, but just taking in the *library*: the smell of ink and foxy paper and old wood, the green view of the river beyond the leaded casement window propped open just an inch. As if she loved it, but was a little scared to be there.

And then her gaze swept over the Murray Hoard. Her lips parted as if she were inhaling it like smoke.

'We're not supposed to touch anything on the central table,' I felt obliged to point out. '*Jamie.*'

'I shall put it back exactly where I picked it up,' he said, reaching for the Reliquary.

He held it out to Ellen.

She hesitated for a moment, then took it gingerly, using both hands to cup it on the tips of her fingers. Just the way she held it made it seem more special.

'It's smaller than the one the National Museum have already,' she told us. 'So your grandad said. But maybe even older.'

'Beautiful Celtic craftsmanship,' said Jamie. 'Were they interested?'

'I don't know. Strathfearn had a secretary read his correspondence, not me. Also, he'd crack away on the 'phone and make folk confirm what they'd said to him in writing, but then he'd often not bother to open the letter when it came! The Reliquary's still here, anyway. Euan, you have a shot. You've never held it.'

She passed the cup reverently to her brother.

And then Mary popped up the stairs behind us.

She and Euan found themselves gazing into each other's faces over my shoulder.

'God pity us all,' I heard Euan mutter.

'Oh!' Mary cried. She stamped her foot. '*Put that down this instant!* How dare you come in here!'

I had not ever seen her angry before.

There wasn't any space between the crowded folding tables and the big permanent chestnut one for Euan to back away. He gave the cup to Jamie, who put it back down hastily, in exactly the spot where it had been when we came in. Nothing else was disturbed in the least.

'We brought the McEwens.' I tried to make an excuse for them. 'Please don't be angry with Euan. He came with me and Jamie.'

I didn't say any of it loudly enough and Mary wasn't looking at me to see my mouth move. I bawled at her good ear, 'He's with us! Euan and Ellen came with us!'

Mary hesitated, watching my face and waiting for me to elaborate.

'It was Jamie – it was me, poking around here, showing off. Please don't –'

Mary faced me with blazing eyes and railed as if Ellen and Euan weren't within hearing distance, or as if they were incapable of taking instruction themselves.

'How *dare* you allow *those people* to lay even a finger on the Murray Collection! If you brought them here, you tell them to get out, this minute, and wait for you outside! I won't have them in here! After all you've been through, to *think* of going about with *their kind*!' She paused for breath. 'You tell them to get out.'

Of course I didn't need to tell Euan. By the time Mary had finished, Euan had already scuttled back down the stairs. I heard the clunk and crash of the heavy front door being opened hastily.

For a long moment, Ellen held my gaze with a look of bleak frost in her smoky eyes. Then she drew herself up to her full height – not as tall as her brother, but nevertheless queenly among us slight Murrays – and said to Mary clearly, 'It's a public library. It's Council property. Nobody need get your permission to come in when it's open.'

Mary turned around and galloped downstairs. Jamie and Ellen and I stood in the Upper Reading Room feeling rather stunned at how quickly the librarian had come and gone.

'I'm sorry,' Jamie said quietly. 'That was my fault.'

'It's you with the damp trousers,' Ellen said bitterly. 'And us the librarian chucks out.'

But she didn't go. She walked defiantly around the long chestnut table, her hands carefully locked behind her back so she couldn't possibly touch anything. She was just *looking*.

At last she stopped by the spear points. 'See those drawings?' she said, with a nod of her head at a sheaf of paper in the middle of the green baize table cover. 'Those are mine.'

She amended bitterly, 'I mean, they're not *mine*. But I made them.'

She finished her tour of the room.

'Well, I expect Euan's waiting.'

She would have gone down just then, I think; but now Mary, having left us alone with the Murray Collection for what seemed an unnaturally long time, came back up, pink and panting with exertion. It was silly to pretend I didn't know what she objected to in the McEwens. But I'd never imagined Mary to be capable of such – well, of such *meanness*.

Of course she must really be just as capable of meanness as anybody else. As capable of it as I am, for example.

'I've spoken to you before,' she said coldly to Ellen.

'I'm *away*,' said Ellen fiercely, and bolted down the stairs.

Mary turned on me. 'How could you bring them in here, Julia!' she exclaimed. 'And they were *picking up the artefacts*. I can tell that boy had just come from the river – his sleeves were still wet! My goodness. I do understand they can be good people – they did look after you when they found you in difficulty – but to bring that lad in here and let him touch things! And the way those folk mutter under their breath, blessing themselves and whatnot when they see me, as if I were a magpie sent to foretell a death. It's not civil- ised. Those people are careless as can be, and I've to be so particular with this room now –'

'Excuse me,' Jamie said, squeezing past her towards the stairs. 'I'm sorry, Miss Kinnaird – I've just come from the river also.'

Mary and I were left staring at each other.

I moved my mouth silently, saying words I couldn't quite bear to speak aloud because I didn't quite mean them.

I'm sorry too.

Then I ran down the stairs after the others.

They were gathered at the iron footbridge. Jamie and Euan, with his cap pulled low over his eyes, were perched on dangerously sagging rails opposite each other with Pinkie lying subdued at their feet – someone must have given her a severe talking-to. The heron was fishing under the bridge beneath them.

Euan slid off his perch as I came out. I saw the bridge shudder, dipping closer to the rushing water, as he came down hard on his feet. The heron took off, heading downstream with long, slow wing beats. Euan tipped up the peak of his cap so he could see me, but didn't take it off.

'She likes me,' he said briefly, and with a perfectly straight face, when I got close enough that he could say it without raising his voice.

'Look, *we* like you,' said Jamie. 'I just didn't realise. I wouldn't have –' He shut up abruptly. It was an embarrassing, *excruciating* apology for all of us, mostly because it didn't do any good and never would.

I caught hold of one of the cables fastening the bridge to the ground, gripping hard with both hands. Euan and Jamie jumped to attention at my elbows, concerned, as if they thought I was about to catapult myself over the cable and into the burn.

'I'm *fine*. I'm *just so angry*.'

Ellen watched me with something like disdain. 'Not used to it, are you?'

She opened her fisherman's creel and drew out a little white clay pipe, which she filled from a leather tobacco pouch worn dark and soft before clamping the pipe between her teeth like a sailor.

'Block the wind for me and I'll give you a draw,' she said to Euan. She dug out a box of matches and she and Euan worked together with cupped hands around the little flame. When they'd got the pipe alight Ellen had the first shot at smoking it; then, puffing out smoke like a steam engine, she handed it over to Euan.

They passed it back and forth, sharing, but not with me and Jamie.

The silence was heavy and awkward. Jamie threw me a querying look: *Should we go?*

As we hesitated, they finished the pipe. Ellen leaned down to knock out the tobacco residue against the base of the bridge. She was just packing the pipe back into her creel when Sergeant Angus Henderson came barrelling along the drive at a terrific pace on his bicycle, his long cromach staff under his arm like a jousting lance.

He came to a tearing halt before us, the bicycle tyres spewing up gravel almost as if he were reining in a galloping horse. He threw the bicycle aside.

'Well now, young McEwen,' the river watcher growled.

Euan took a step backward and Pinkie cowered, the craven thing.

Ellen stood with her fists clenched, the tendons standing out along her wrists, her face drained of blood.

For a wild moment I imagined Sergeant Henderson was challenging Euan to a duel, perhaps with quarterstaffs like Little John and Robin Hood. He clapped his tweed hat squarely against the back of his head before thumping the cromach against the ground between him and Euan with a crack that would have broken Euan's foot if he'd meant it to. Ellen jumped back and crashed into Jamie, who steadied her with a quick light touch of one hand on her shoulder.

'Ye dare, lad!' the river watcher said in that quiet, laden, tense tone – as if he were reining in passion. 'Ye dare fright that good woman Mary Kinnaird – ye dare set foot in the house she lives in and watches over, ye dare touch any of the treasures she keeps there! She was fair weeping when she rang!'

That was why it had taken Mary so long to come back to the Upper Reading Room after she'd chased Euan downstairs. She'd telephoned Angus Henderson to come and clear away the riff-raff.

Euan's face, like Ellen's, was drained of colour. He was on the balls of his feet in their worn tackety boots, poised for flight. But there were too many of us crowded at the base of the narrow, swaying bridge for him to run that way, so he was cornered.

Henderson's staff rose and fell.

Ellen reached out – instinctively, I think – to grab hold of the person nearest in front of her, and it was me. Jamie tried to shove past us, but Ellen was digging her fingers into my forearm so fiercely they left little round black bruises there later. At the time I didn't feel it. I'd grabbed hold of her too. It all happened so suddenly.

The cromach crashed across Euan's shins. He stumbled, and Henderson hooked him by the ankle with his staff and hauled him back against his broad chest, so that he and Euan were nearly cheek to cheek over Euan's shoulder. The river watcher held Euan fast.

'Next time Mary Kinnaird tells me you've set foot on Inverfearnie Island I'll throw you into prison for attempted theft.'

Euan nodded understanding, his eyes clenched shut.

Jamie managed to put me and Ellen behind him and boldly took hold of Sergeant Henderson's staff. But he underestimated the force he'd need to wrestle it from Henderson's grasp. The Water Bailiff lashed out to give him a warning whack across one shin as well.

'You keep out of this, lad.'

'*Buckets of blood!*' Jamie swore, grabbing at a bridge cable and hopping on the other foot.

Henderson turned his attention back to Euan. 'Speak so I can hear ye, ye mucky tink,' he growled.

'I ken. I won't set foot on Inverfearnie! I won't use the bridges here!'

Henderson glanced up at Ellen. 'You see that he doesn't, girl.'

She nodded without speaking, still clutching me.

Henderson threw his prey to his knees. I heard Euan gasp. Pinkie whined and shrank – heavens, what a useless dog. The river watcher cracked two more fearsome blows over the back of Euan's shoulders with his cromach, and when Euan slumped forward, Henderson gave him a kick in the ribs for good measure.

'Remember it, wee man. I'll arrest you *and* I'll knock your teeth in if I get another call from the librarian about you.'

Sergeant Angus Henderson straightened up, resurrected his bicycle and pointed it back in the direction of Brig O'Fearn village.

Ellen let go of me quickly.

I couldn't *believe* how fast this had happened, and how disorganised we'd been – how *helpless* in the face of authority and violence.

With a grunt of effort, Euan suddenly dragged himself erect to avoid the humiliation of me, or his sister, swooping down on him in concern.

The Water Bailiff tucked his staff under one arm and did an odd little balancing act as he turned back to us and doffed his hat, the way he'd done when I'd met him with Mary.

He didn't look at me but reproached Jamie gruffly, 'I've warned you before about running wild, young Jamie, and I've a mind to have a word with your lady mother about the company you keep.'

Then off he went.

Ellen leaped to Euan's side. I wanted to touch him too. I wanted to see he was all right. If Jamie had taken a beating like that he'd have let me peel off his shirt and mop his broken skin with clear burn water, but I couldn't do that for Euan McEwen; and Ellen wouldn't do it with us watching. I stood clenching and unclenching my fists in frustration as they inefficiently checked the damage.

'Och, it's nae bother,' Euan said breathlessly. 'I can walk. Friend of my dad's was beaten so bad by the police he lay in a ditch for a day before anyone found him. He couldn't work for two months. He hadn't even done anything – just made a racket singing on his way back to camp after a night in the pub.'

'You haven't done anything either!' I exclaimed.

'I'm lucky.' Euan winced and shrugged.

'Come along back to Mammy,' Ellen said to him, and Jamie and I watched them go, Ellen with a supporting arm around her brother's waist; just as Jamie and I would have been if it had happened to us.

But of course it wouldn't happen to us.

The Water Bailiff had told Jamie to stay out of it. He hadn't even dared to look in my direction.

6

FINDING OUT WHAT A PRECOGNITION IS

Late in the afternoon I dived into Frank's study, without knocking, because otherwise I'd have had to hang about in the passage and the older people would have been sure to tell me off for unchaperoned mixing with the contractor. But I had an idea for doing Euan a good turn and I thought Frank could help. My God! You have to be cunning as a vixen to get anything out of *anyone*. I am afraid it is going to be like this for the rest of my life; I thought I might as well continue as I've begun. Davie Balfour wasn't going to get me anywhere, but the coquettishly eccentric Lady Julia might.

'I'm so sorry to interrupt …'

He jumped up from behind his desk with a smile like sunlight breaking through cloud: winning, warm, swift and honest. He was glad to see me. He could have been annoyed, but he was obviously delighted, and made me a spontaneous bow. It was elegant and natural and made my heart leap in a perfectly embarrassing way.

But the heat rising to my cheeks also warned me to be careful. I knew I was smitten with him, and that we were already more intimate than anyone in the house was aware, and I knew I had to hide it. I really couldn't imagine how Mother and Solange would have reacted just then if they felt I was flirting with an older man.

He remembered my public name, tentatively formal. 'Miss Beaufort-Stuart! Can I help you?'

'You absolutely can,' I said. 'At least, I think you can. Do you need any more casual labourers? Only I wondered if you'd be able to offer work to the Traveller lad who took me to the hospital. Just for a few weeks, perhaps on an hourly wage? Helping to dig the pool or something like that? He's camped at Inchfort Field and I rather owe him a favour. And Grandad always gave the Travellers jobs when they stopped here.'

Francis Dunbar leaned against the edge of his desk. He folded his arms and considered, not looking at me. 'There's plenty of digging to be done on the pipeline out to the Tay. I can certainly make it happen. But I'm afraid my foreman won't be very welcoming. Those Traveller folk don't use clocks – just turn up when it suits them. And things have already gone missing from the building site.'

'Yes, I know your foreman thinks the Travellers are light-fingered. But you can give Euan a *chance*, can't you?'

Frank nodded absently. It seemed to me that every move Francis Dunbar made was a little absent, as if he were pre-occupied with a burden of work and worry that constantly pressed on his brain like concussion. I hated to give him more to think about.

And all the time I was fearfully aware of how striking was his silhouette against the long midsummer evening's warm light in the open window.

He turned to look at me at last.

'Canny *and* kind,' he said. 'I'll have a word with Mr Munro.'

'Kind yourself,' I said. And because he was perched there on the edge of the desk, closer to my level than when he was on his feet, I dared, spontaneously, to give him a little kiss on the cheek. 'Thank you.'

He didn't move or say a thing. When I stood back we looked at each other eye to eye.

What's your proper work, Julie? I would like to be a theatrical escape artist, I think, like Houdini, or a circus owner like Bertram Mills. I want to dazzle people and be applauded for it. I am good at it, and it is thrilling. Walking a tightrope when you've had too much to drink – dangerous and wonderful.

So I gave him another kiss, on the mouth this time, and he let me. I could feel his lips moving beneath mine as he responded very gently, just for a moment.

Then I felt myself reddening.

So I stopped.

I really shouldn't have done it.

But … but I felt I'd restored both my authority and my feminine charm. How powerful it made me feel. It reminded me, actually, of my very first driving lesson in Mother's sports car – the thrill of holding all that energy in my feet, of knowing that my small person was harnessing all that magnificent strength – that is how I felt now. How quick-witted and alluring and powerful!

'You'd better go,' he said gently.

'So I had.'

He didn't tell me I shouldn't have done it though.

Our suppers were all cold now unless it was soup or we dined out, because it was so much easier to prepare and tidy up a cold meal ourselves from the distant kitchen. Solange had been doing the running, as the youngest of the grown-ups, but now that I was better I was able to help. In a couple of the overstuffed Queen Anne chairs ruined by jubilant Victorian upholstery, Mémère and Jamie sat tight doing nothing – Mémère because she is the Dowager Countess of Strathfearn and Jamie because he is a boy. But as the morning room faces east and is dull in the evening, even during the long light of midsummer with the tall windows open, Jamie got up to switch on a lamp.

It was just as I was coming back into the room after a trip made to sweep away the remains of our supper. When the light went on as I crossed the threshold, I noticed a corner of brown paper peeping out from under the edge of the faded Persian carpet close to the door to the passage.

I set down the tea tray I'd been carrying and slid the paper out from under the carpet. For a moment I found myself staring in bewilderment at what I thought was the same brown envelope that had been haunting me ever since I arrived at Strathfearn House: there on the back was the engraved name and address, Dr Hugh Housman of the Ashmolean Museum.

But this was a different envelope. It was sealed and had never been opened.

I turned it over. It was addressed to 'Mlle Solange Lavergne'.

He must have pushed it underneath the door while it had been closed, but hadn't realised that his note had slipped beneath the carpet on the other side. If it hadn't been for the switched-on lamp suddenly spotlighting it as I walked in, we might never have seen the corner peeking out.

But now everyone saw me kneeling there staring at it. So there wasn't anything to do apart from hand it over to Solange.

I think we all felt the same feeling of dread in our stomachs as we watched her open it. Jamie actually shoved one of the chairs behind her to act as a sort of aerial artiste's safety net, expecting a collapse when she got to the end of whatever she was reading.

It came as expected.

'*Mon dieu!*' Solange exclaimed, and fell into the chair in tears with her face in her hands, the crumpled letter pressed against her cheek as if it were a handkerchief.

Mother leaped to her side.

'Solange, darling, whatever is it?'

'It's my fault,' Solange sobbed in French. '*All my fault.*'

'What's your fault?' Mother gasped.

'Monsieur Housman has taken his own life, killed himself! I–I told you we fought, but not – not *how* we fought. I struggled with him – I struck him in the face, I broke his spectacles.'

Well. Solange confessing to the broken spectacles explained and confirmed a great deal.

She didn't give anyone a chance to respond though; just tore on with guilty and miserable sobs. 'And because I was sulking upstairs I was not here to meet Julia when she came home from school, so perhaps it is my fault she was hurt as well – oh! *I should be arrested.*'

Needless to say, the rest of us were now quite helpless with astonishment.

My nanny raised large and beautiful dark tear-filled eyes, despairing, and I tried desperately to comfort her.

'You know I saw him, Solange,' I said. 'I saw him standing in the burn and his glasses *were* broken, but he was fine. So you had already struck him then …' I remembered his swollen eye – yes, it had had time to swell, some time must have passed between when she hit him and when I saw him. But not much, because he hadn't cleaned the blood from his upper lip … or maybe his nose had started to bleed afresh. At any rate … 'He wasn't trying to kill himself! He was fishing for pearls. Whatever happened to him after that, it couldn't have been your fault!'

'He was not himself – he might have been passing the time until the Tay tide came up, waiting to let the river take him! He says so right here! He says the river is more constant than any lover – that he is returning to the river because …' She bent her head, sobbing, and then read aloud: '"The river's gifts are more eternal than the fleeting gifts of the flesh –"' Another sob. 'He begs me to forgive him.'

I wanted very much to twitch the letter out of her hand and read it myself, but I didn't dare.

'*Nanny.*' I put my arms around her.

I don't know if I was more shocked at her confession that *she'd struck a man*, or that she'd been so entangled with a man that she'd had to strike him. Dear *Solange*? A man who'd then been so distraught he'd gone and *drowned himself*?

Mother was not so sympathetic as I might have expected.

'Suicides must be reported *properly* to the police. The Procurator Fiscal must be notified; he's supposed to investigate sudden deaths. There may be an inquiry. It won't be a matter of poking about on the riverbank or writing to the man's colleagues and family. There will be proper police interviews all round – yourself included. Are you *sure*, Solange?'

Solange handed her the note. Mother waved me and Jamie away in irritation as we crowded in on both sides of her to try to read along. Colette stood behind our grandmother with her hands on Mémère's shoulders; we all knew how much Mémère dreaded a thorough police investigation in her house. But she just sat like a statue beneath the electric lamp, stoic and calm.

There were too many of us in the room. Mother told us sharply, 'Go outside, the pair of you.'

Jamie stepped out through the open French doors and crossed the terrace to lean against the stone railing, waiting for the storm to calm. I followed him. We felt terrible for Solange, but also I think we were both a little embarrassed.

'It's so still when the work stops,' Jamie said irrelevantly, looking out over the lawn. 'Makes it feel a bit like it's summer ten years ago.'

'But not really. Because the grounds weren't covered with diggers and wheelbarrows and tips full of concrete when we were little.'

I sat down on the terrace railing.

'I suppose we'd better not show Nanny the piece of Dr Housman's specs you found this morning,' I said. 'It would just cause more hysterics.'

'We'll have to show the police though.'

Something occurred to me.

'What happened to the rest of his clothes?' I asked.

'What do you mean?'

'Hugh Housman wasn't wearing any clothes when I saw him. The McEwens found his cap; and I saw him lose it, so that makes sense. Where are the clothes he was wearing when he left the door open at the Inverfearnie Library? Why'd he take them off to drown himself, anyway?'

Jamie thought for a moment. Finally, he said quietly, 'Don't tinkers collect old clothes? Sheep's wool and coal and old clothes?'

'*You're not the least bit funny!*'

'I wasn't trying to be funny.'

We looked at each other, and I knew what he was thinking. The McEwens were in for it.

Now began a time of protracted gloom and torrential rain. It was heralded by Inspector Duncan Milne, the policeman who'd been appointed by the Procurator Fiscal to grill us all about Housman's declaration of intent to drown himself.

This time he didn't warn us he was coming. When he turned up at Strathfearn House no one answered the wide-open door, and no one heard him when he shouted. He stomped back out to his car and sat leaning over the driver and blasting on the horn until Jamie and I came tearing out to see what was going on.

The police took their time getting out of the car, the driver opening the door for Inspector Duncan Milne and for Angus Henderson, whom they'd brought along in the back. Then they all lined up facing me and Jamie, as though we were about to begin a football match. Both other men were rather dwarfed by Sergeant Henderson. They looked faintly absurd lined up against the dripping roses in the French garden.

Inspector Milne stepped forward. He raised his peaked cap and nodded to me. But it was Jamie he addressed, in a cool, dry voice: 'Mr Beaufort-Stuart? Your mother Lady Craigie is in, I hope? I've been appointed to make a precognition for the Procurator Fiscal.'

'What's that?' Jamie drawled amiably, hands in his pockets, every inch the Earl of Craigie's son. 'The precognition, I mean.'

The dry, thin man looked him up and down indifferently. 'Mere gathering of facts,' he explained. 'At this time, we're interviewing known witnesses. No formal statement is needed yet. The Procurator Fiscal may refer to the precognition to make a ruling as to cause of death, or to determine if a hearing is necessary.' He paused patiently, as if this were an explanation he gave on a regular basis and he knew he had to wait a moment or two before it stuck. Then he finished, 'It's principally Lady Craigie and her maid with whom I'd like to speak today, though I understand Lady Julia has remembered a few more details. There will be an interview with Miss Kinnaird tomorrow. Mr Dunbar was kind enough to come in to our premises this morning.'

'Julie, can you get Mother? And Solange,' Jamie suggested neutrally. 'I'll show these gentlemen in.'

Inspector Duncan Milne of the Perthshire and Kinross-shire Constabulary established himself in Frank Dunbar's study.

My own session with him went very quickly; all he wanted was for me to add a description of Dr Housman's state of undress to my original interview.

Jamie, of course, had nothing to say except that he'd found the piece of Housman's spectacles. He hadn't even been at Strathfearn when Dr Housman first went missing.

While the interviews were going on, Sergeant Henderson stood guard to prevent anyone trying to eavesdrop through the door in the corridor. Mémère posted Colette to stand guard outside our door, next along the corridor, so that no one could eavesdrop there, either, and after Milne had finished with me and Jamie, this arrangement of course allowed us to eavesdrop through the folding wall in the morning room. Mémère provided us with the glass tumblers necessary to amplify the sound through the panelling. Mother sat *like Patience on a monument* staring out over the wet terrace, trying to pretend the eavesdropping wasn't happening.

It was nearly as good as listening to a BBC radio play on the wireless. We couldn't quite hear the police inspector's questions, but to begin with he had his assistant read aloud the whole of Housman's pathetic letter to Solange. The policeman's halting matter-of-fact voice uttering this tragic statement gave it the faintest taste of farce, and as Jamie and I listened, I could see my own astonishment mirrored in his face. In our wildest dreams I don't think we could have ever imagined our dear nanny entangled with *anyone* – and *what* a splendid entanglement this had been!

"'My sweet Solange,'" the officer read. "'It has broken my heart that you are so im–'" he coughed in embarrassment, "'*immovable,* that you have so little belief in me. I swear I can give you no answers, no details, no measure of my worth. I can only give you my promise. How I long to be able to offer more than mere promise! But if you cannot take my hand on trust alone, there is no other woman ...'" another choke of embarrassment, "'... no other woman alive to whom I would ever turn.'"

The officer plunged on, "'I so longed for a new life with you. I cannot bear to think it cannot be …'"

Here Mémère, growing impatient at our enraptured listening faces when she couldn't hear what was going on herself, hissed, 'What are they saying?'

And Jamie actually shushed her.

"'… What new worlds we could have known together! How different, how empty my own new world will be when I enter it alone …'" (And so forth.) "'And now, I return to the river I know so well, where you know you can find me, the river whose gifts are …'"

I thought the poor constable fellow was going to choke himself with the clearing of his throat it took to gird his loins for reading the end of the letter.

"'… the river whose gifts are more eternal than the fleeting gifts of the flesh. I beg you to forgive me …'" harrumph, "'my darling.'"

Dr Housman had signed it *Your Hugh*.

Nanny put on an excellent performance.

She was as chilly and poised and regal as Mary Queen of Scots on trial. Though Inspector Milne was irritatingly low-voiced, we were able to judge by Solange's answers that he asked her all the expected questions about where and when we'd found the note, and if she recognised Hugh Housman's cap and the broken piece of his spectacles, and whether she had reason to believe Housman was of volatile character. But it was when Milne started prying into the nature of her, ah, *friendship* with the scholar that she truly shone like a star.

SOLANGE [frostily]: I am offended at your suggestion that our liaison was not proper. We are not children, Inspector Milne, exchanging sordid kisses in the darkness of the cinema! [Sound of nose-blowing into presumably lace-edged imported French handkerchief.] Dr Housman was a fluent speaker of the French language.

INSPECTOR DUNCAN MILNE: [mutter, mutter, snort]

SOLANGE: [sulking silence]

INSPECTOR MILNE [in loud tones apologetic]: Perhaps, Mademoiselle Lavergne, you do not understand the significance of your friendship with Dr Housman in the event there need be a hearing at Sheriff Court as to the nature of his death.

SOLANGE [loudly]: I understand its significance perfectly. I could not hear your question.

INSPECTOR MILNE [just as loudly]: Was there an exchange of physical affection between you?

SOLANGE [with queenly chill]: It would have been a poor affair if there had not.

('One for the French!' Jamie hissed in my ear, and I had to smack him because he made me snigger inappropriately and miss Milne's response. Mémère threatened in a stage whisper that she would not let us be her spies if we couldn't do it quietly.)

SOLANGE: ... Between us, yes, not secretly, but in private. And the physical exchange of affection does not prove itself only in the touch of bodies, Inspector Milne. There are other small kindnesses a person can do to show affection. I saw to it there were always fresh flowers in his room at the day's end. He made me a gift of a pair of earrings, pearls he'd found himself in the river here – he had them set at MacGregor's.

(Of course all of this took place before I arrived at Strathfearn. I feel sure that if I'd been there I would have sniffed out the romantic hanky-panky sooner than Mummy, possibly preventing the fatal tiff.)

'And yet you feel Dr Housman may have had reason to end his life, as this letter to you suggests?' came the dry, relentless voice of the interviewing police inspector.

'We fought,' Solange said simply. 'And I do not mind saying why. He tried to turn me against my dear Lady Craigie. He also made remarks about her mother, Lady

Strathfearn, which I found coarse and tasteless; about her age and her sanity, criticising the way she has run the estate since her husband's death ...'

Jamie and I, face-to-face as we listened through the folding wall, caught each other's eye at exactly the same moment in silent agreement not to pass this insulting gossip on to our grandmother.

'I was angry and did not speak to him for several days. When he approached me he made no apology and I found his physical advances ...' She struggled for a word and came up with, '*inappropriate*. After more rebuffs than I can count he took my lack of response for coyness and when he would not stop, I struck him.'

She paused, then added remorsefully, 'I struck him quite hard.'

'How hard?'

'I broke his spectacles.'

'Ah. That was the last you saw of him, was it?'

At this point Solange lost control of her carefully maintained hauteur, and burst into loud tears, and began theorising rather hysterically as to what might have happened to *me*, which really did not count as factual information pertinent to a precognition. And her interview came to an end.

Then it was Mother's turn.

She was queenly in a different way to Solange. She had none of Solange's frost or magnificence; Mother was simply in control. She stood up and let Sergeant Henderson escort her next door without the least fuss or drama. Jamie and I had our ears pressed to the glass tumblers against the wood panelling the second the door to the passage had closed behind her.

'Please sit, Lady Craigie.' Inspector Milne was as dry as ever. This time, irritatingly, it was Mother who spoke in such a low voice that we couldn't make out her answers. Of course that was because she was wise to us. After quite a lot of unintelligible mumbling from them both, Jamie rolled his eyes at me and put his tumbler down on the floor.

So I was the only one who was listening when the inspector, quite clearly, asked my mother an absolutely outrageous question.

'Is your daughter intact?'

It was like being brutally smacked across the face. I felt myself burning with indignation. Just the asking of it made me feel filthy, and I wasn't even in the room.

Mother's voice went up too. 'Really, Inspector Milne, I fail to see what such a thing has to do with Housman's *death*.'

'Your daughter was the last to see him alive. She recalls that he was fully unclothed when she met him, alone on the riverbank, and she can remember nothing of the night she

148

then spent in the company of the travelling tinkers. What happened to her in those hours, or *what she did*, is surely of relevance to this investigation. I want to know if you are aware of any misfortune she may have encountered that is not yet on record. Was she not examined in the hospital?'

Mother didn't say anything for a moment.

She thought Jamie was listening, which was partly why she was embarrassed about answering the question.

But something in her absolute silence made me aware that yes, medical staff had checked me over very carefully in the two days I'd been unconscious, and Mother knew what they'd been looking for and what they'd found, and hadn't told me.

I tried to imagine my senseless anonymous stripped self in that hospital bed behind the rail curtain, being *examined* for signs of *assault*. And felt violated even though I hadn't been.

'It's a delicate question,' the dry man acknowledged, prompting her. 'Was there evidence of an attack of a sexual nature?'

Mother spoke with the presence of an advocate defending a case. 'Notwithstanding his courtship with Mam'selle Lavergne, Dr Housman was a respectable and temperate man and I have no reason to believe he would have assaulted my daughter.'

'I was not thinking of him. I was thinking of the tinker family with whom she spent the night.'

I felt my face go incandescent with embarrassment, and no small amount of horror at how the inspector's mind was painting the McEwens.

But Mother never lost her sangfroid.

After a moment, she said loudly and clearly, in a voice of frost pitched for me to hear because she *knew* I was listening, 'Whatever *Housman* may have had in mind when he removed his clothes for the last time, Inspector Milne, you will never hear me speak ill of Jean McEwen's people.'

'It's possible that young Euan is the one who struck her,' said the policeman.

'I positively don't believe it,' Mother said firmly.

Inspector Milne went back to muttering and mumbling, finishing with: 'Perhaps your daughter interrupted a rendez-vous.'

The next thing I heard was Mother saying explosively, 'Of course it wasn't Solange who struck her!'

Milne raised his voice in response. 'We have to take into account that your lady's maid admits to relations with Dr Housman, and to doing him violence,' Milne pointed out drily. 'And she has no alibi.'

PART

2

WHAT HAPPENED
11TH–23RD JULY 1938

7

WE DON'T KEN HALF WHAT'S BURIED IN THE PEAT

The rain continued, rather unbelievably, for some two weeks. Solange was not arrested for anything but she was sure she was going to be, and spent so much time sniffing into Mémère's endless supply of lace-edged handkerchiefs that she spread a cloud of gloom everywhere she went. The uncertainty was hard to live with.

Jamie attempted escape.

He first went back to Inchfort Field to deliver Frank Dunbar's (or rather, my) offer of a digging job to Euan McEwen, but Mother wouldn't let me out with the river running so high and fast and the path so muddy and slippery.

Then Jamie went every day.

He'd always surreptitiously primp a bit before he set off, suddenly cleaning his teeth or running his fingers through his hair with a quick glance in Mémère's dressing-table mirror.

'What do you *do* up at Inchfort Field all day?' I asked crossly. 'Crouch in a tent in the rain weaving willow baskets?'

'I talk to Ellen.'

I was very jealous.

But all I could do was sit with Mémère and Colette and the miserable Solange in the torrential gloom of the morning room, sorting china and table linen and three generations' worth of French novels.

My blasted trunk still wasn't here, and the Schiaparelli blouse Jamie brought from home wasn't really suitable for such dusty work, so I got him to fetch me all the frayed and faded summer clothing abandoned in the nursery bathroom. Sandy's outgrown athletic shorts came down to my knees; his kilt had to be double lapped and pinned around my waist. I was quite desperate not to let Frank catch sight of me in drag as Davie Balfour – with my shorn hair I looked very like a Bohemian thirteen-year-old boy, and to be seen as such would have ruined all my credibility as an aspiring debutante.

Jamie went back and forth to Inchfort so often that he and Ellen *missed each other* when she came to the Big House herself one morning.

She first came to the front door, which would have been entirely inappropriate a year ago, but this year nobody even bothered to answer the bell. So then she came around to the terrace at the back – even less appropriate – and knocked on the French windows of the morning room.

I leaped to meet her. 'Come in! Oh –'

She shook her head. She wouldn't come in.

I stepped outside into the drizzle. I hadn't seen her, or any of the McEwens, since the terrible day at the library.

We stood about a yard apart, looking at each other.

'I'm sorry about Mary Kinnaird,' I said. I hadn't seen Mary since that day either; I didn't know how to face Mary.

'You've got your grandad's eyes but not his say in matters,' Ellen commented drily.

'Is Euan all right?'

'"Aye, nae bother" – so he says. He's going to take the work you've offered him, helping to dig that pipeline in the riverbed for the Glenfearn School. But they've told him not to come till it stops raining.'

'Come in and talk to me,' I begged. 'You talk to my brother all the time.'

'I'm drookit. I'll drip all over your gran's fine carpet.'

'I'll go around to the front with you and you can go in there. It's all painters and dust cloths in every room but this one. No one will care if you drip.'

We walked around to the front of the house in silence. I wondered why she'd come.

'Looking for Jamie, are you?' I asked as we entered the reception hall.

Out of the rain now, she pushed the damp hair back from her face and straightened her skirt. She gave a little laugh.

'Are you jealous of your brother?'

I frowned. I was, a little – of his healthy independence and maybe, a little, of his being able to sit and do nothing while I ran the supper dishes to the kitchen. But something about the way she'd asked the question gave a different twist to her meaning.

'Well, *are* you looking for him?' I asked impatiently.

She gave a dismissive shrug. 'Any of you will do. I wondered if you could mend things with the librarian a bit. Euan promised the Water Bailiff not to set foot on Inverfearnie Island, but that means he has to go round by the village at Brig O'Fearn to get here to the Big House for the work you've offered him.'

'It's ten miles by road that way!'

'Isn't it! I don't suppose you thought of that when you were playing Lady of the Manor, finding him work?'

'Look, he doesn't have to do it,' I said hotly. 'I thought it might help. Why are you stopping here anyway? You won't harvest the flax for another three weeks at least. Didn't you all go to Blairgowrie for the strawberry picking while I was in the hospital? There are berries all over Perthshire just now. You could go away and come again in August.

Maybe you *should* go away. Otherwise everyone will just work out a way to blame you for Dr Housman's suicide somehow.'

'You've mucked it up with your bountiful job offer. It's not as easy to move on as it was: the Council authorities keep closing off old camping greens. You turn up and it's all posted *Keep Out* with barbed wire all over. So Mammy wants Euan to do the work here. He'll get three times as much as he would at a day's berry picking. And that gives Dad one long last chance at Fearn river pearls.'

Then Ellen made a sound like *hnnph* that rather stopped me being able to respond. I sat down on the bottom step of the old oak staircase.

Ellen didn't sit. She gazed down at me with that look of cold challenge and asked, 'So how shall you mend it? I expect you'll send your chauffeur round to collect Euan first thing the morning the rain stops.'

I knew that was Traveller sarcasm, but I still found myself retorting defensively, 'There isn't a chauffeur at Strathfearn any longer. You know my grandmother had to let her staff go.'

'And have you found other work for them too? No, that's no' your business. Or even hers. And why would she need a chauffeur when your mother drives her own car?'

Her face suddenly lit with amusement.

'Ask your lady mother to bring Euan round here when the rain stops,' Ellen said. 'Tell her it's because of you he needs the ride and see what she says.'

Blast her! She knew I couldn't do that.

Or … I *could*, of course. And Mummy would likely do it, quite graciously, out of obligation and apology. But it was blackmail. It wasn't as if Mother hadn't anything to do all day other than work on a matching set of needlework cushion covers for the twenty-four eighteenth-century dining-room chairs that were being auctioned at Sweet's. She was closing down a country estate for her nearly-eighty-year-old mother, in the swift aftermath of her father's lingering and debt-ridden illness.

'It's nothing to do with my mother,' I said.

'That's true,' Ellen agreed. 'Well, then, *you* do it. You bring Euan round in your mother's car.'

I sat silent, glowering at her. She returned my stare coolly. Of course the simplest thing to do would be to go and try to make peace with Mary. I wished that didn't also feel like the *hardest* thing to do.

Then Ellen said, 'I expect you dinnae ken how to drive.'

'*I can drive*,' I said.

Mummy *had* given me a handful of useful lessons in her racy little Magnette, but the last time was at Christmas.

'She'll test me before she lets me take it on my own. I'd need to practise …' I spoke through my teeth, trying to piece together a plan that would put me behind the driving wheel of Mummy's car – preferably without having to steal it – the next morning if necessary. 'I haven't been allowed out this week.'

Ellen rolled her eyes. 'You're like a flipping princess.'

I sat pouting, torn between feeling affronted and rebellious. Ellen got out her tobacco pouch and lit her pipe while she waited for me to come to a decision. There was no one about at that moment but it felt very clandestine. I watched her with envy – not at the pipe's existence, but at her sure and casual confidence in lighting it. She wasn't thinking about it, what it would look like as she smoked, or whether or not anyone would care. She was just being *herself*.

'I'll do it,' I said.

Ellen blew out a slow stream of smoke and then laughed. 'Just for a wee while, till we find some other way for him to get here. Our uncle has a pushbike he can borrow maybe. Or our cousins the Camerons might help; they're coming to Bridge Farm to help with the flax, and they have a van. That's how we got you to the hospital.'

She smoked calmly, finishing her pipe.

'Has your dad found any more trace of Dr Housman?' I asked. 'His clothes?'

'Not a thing.'

'And the police – have they been round again since Solange found that note?'

'Oh yes. Wanting to poke through every piece of rag we have with us.'

'I'm worried they'll try to arrest somebody.'

'*Somebody?* Euan? Aye. Mammy and Daddy have been raging about whether we should get away from that. But the police have no reason to arrest anybody – they stood right in front of us trying to find a reason, and they couldn't. Mammy told 'em she'd haul the Water Bailiff into Sheriff Court herself for beating Euan. Of course she *won't* – I dinnae think she *could*. But Euan bothering the librarian a wee while has nothing to do with the missing scholar, and that beating makes the hornies look bad. And if we pack up and leave the day, it'll look like Euan *did* do something, when none of us has done a thing. And …' She put the pipe away. 'And Strathfearn will defend us. Your gran. Your mam. You and your Lady Bountiful play-acting. Mammy thinks we're safer here than running.'

'Well, my brother Sandy will defend you too. He'll be here soon – you'll like him.'

'He's the one got thrashed for nosing about the log boat, aye?' Ellen said. 'Runs in the family! You know, your grandad tried to dig that log boat out of the riverbank when he was a young man – my own grandad helped him. They had a team of men and horses working on it. But it goes too far into the peat and they were damaging it. So he left it there for the tide to work at.'

She knew the damnedest things about Strathfearn.

'I bet Sandy will want to look at the log boat again before we leave for good,' I said. 'Like you looking at the Reliquary. One last time. Just to make sure it's still there.'

'Och, there's sure to be something else for him to find some day,' Ellen said. 'We don't ken half what's buried in the peat.'

And as we spoke, it occurred to me that *right now* she knew more about the Murray Collection than anyone else in the house.

I stood up. 'It's raining anyway and you're not doing much, are you? Come with me and let's see if they left anything behind when they moved the Murray Hoard to the Inverfearnie Library.'

Ellen laughed. 'Oh, aye, Lady Julia. Show off your estate.'

'Oh, *come on.*'

I was starting to see that she laughed and poked fun when she was actually quite interested.

Selfishly pleased to have her to myself, I took Ellen all over Strathfearn House, nosing into every single room that we found wasn't locked. It was a good deal more freedom than I'd ever had there before; of course my brothers and I hadn't ever been allowed to nose into the guest bedrooms and the gunroom and the billiard room. There wasn't anything of interest in any of them now; mostly bare except for the furniture and paintings marshalled together in unappealing ranks in the former drawing room and the Long Hall, all labelled for auction.

We lingered in the tower room where Grandad's museum had been. All his glass cabinets stood there empty, gathering dust and dead flies.

By sheer coincidence Ellen and I spoke together, and we both said the exact same thing.

'This makes me sad.'

We turned to look at each other. After a moment Ellen gave a single nod.

We peered out of the cobwebbed windows. From this high room, there was a clear view of the ruined towers of Aberfearn Castle, soaring above the birches where the Fearn meets the Tay.

'Did you work with Grandad here, in this room?' I asked.

'We mostly worked in his study when I was drawing. But I went up and down the stairs for him, fetching things from the cabinets sometimes.'

'He gave you the *keys*?'

'Aye, he did that,' Ellen said with straightforward pride.

'Gosh. You *are* lucky. Did he pay you?'

'Och, I wouldn't have taken money from him. He taught me all about typological dating. And he gave me Pinkie.'

Ellen walked over to the cabinet that used to hold the wonderful little black and silver cup.

'You asked about the pearls in the Reliquary,' Ellen said. 'Look here.'

She knelt on the floor by the empty cabinet. The boards were old, wide planks of smooth dark wood. They didn't quite lie flat against each other; in one or two places the cracks between them were nearly half an inch wide. Ellen laid her index finger against one of the gaps, pointing.

'You can only see from here,' she said, moving over to let me kneel beside her. 'Get close to the floor and look along the gap where I'm pointing.'

I bent over, pressed against Ellen's thigh, and saw the hidden pearl.

It looked like a little lost moon, wedged tight in the gap. It must have dropped in and rolled into place. I could just poke the tip of my pinkie finger in and feel its cool smooth-ness there. But it was stuck fast.

'Strathfearn showed me,' Ellen said. 'It's the last of the Reliquary pearls. I tried to pick it out with hairpins and whatnot, but it wants to stay.'

'Did he tell you how it got there? Or what happened to the rest of them?'

'He didn't like to talk about them. They made him sad; I think he'd sold them, or was thinking about selling them … and then regretted not keeping them together with the Reliquary. I never saw the rest.'

She turned her head to look at me.

'This one …' Her tone was matter of fact, but her voice was quiet. 'Your grandad said it was put there long ago by a wee girl playing about with them like marbles.'

'*Oh.*'

I stared back at her in amazement.

'He must have meant *me.*'

'Likely he did,' she said drily. She didn't ever seem to get excited about *anything*.

But I hadn't made those pearls up. I hadn't imagined them. They'd been real.

I closed my eyes, my finger resting on the cool surface of the pearl I could never play marbles with again. And even though I knew now that the Reliquary pearls had been real, it was still like an image from a dream: the black cup brimming with milky pearls, dove-grey and dove-pink, all different sizes, a little galaxy of gleaming planets in a small shadowy celestial sphere.

★

I woke up in the middle of that night feeling haunted. The clouds had temporarily cleared and there was a round silver moon sailing high in a bottle-blue sky and bathing everything with otherworldly light. The moonlight fell right across my face and once I was awake I couldn't go back to sleep. I padded very silently to Mémère's dressing table and found a nail file, and then sat on my bed in the fairy glow of the moon for a while, giving myself a manicure and thinking of all the people who had lived and died in that house in its hundred years. Grandad was born and died in that very room.

But I wasn't feeling haunted by Grandad – or even by the miserable Dr Housman. I was suddenly, sharply, overwhelmingly aware of all Strathfearn's quiet, hidden, ancient past: my vanished medieval great-grandparents who left behind the empty, towering halls of Aberfearn Castle, and *their* vanished great-grandparents, who carved the starey-eyed fish on the standing stones that were already old; and the folk before them who left nothing but strange green mounds and iron blades; and those who built the buried boat and raised the walking stones.

I thought: *Their blood runs in my veins. They are alive in me.*

But that made me feel even creepier, as though my very self were part ghost. I could just imagine how Ferdinand felt, shipwrecked in The Tempest, where *the isle is full of noises.*

All those people who lived here before us – their ghosts belong here. But Hugh Housman's doesn't. It is surely an unquiet ghost.

Full fathom five thy father lies;
Of his bones are coral made;
Those are pearls that were his eyes –

Mémère interrupted my rhapsody by asking me crossly, in French, to stop filling the isle with noise (the very quiet noise of buffing my nails), so I put on my school blazer over my nightgown and went downstairs.

I opened the French doors to the glorious moon. But I also switched on the lamp to banish the ghosts, and after a while it started to get buggy. The moths battering against the lampshade were both annoying and a bit spooky. I put out the light and sat in the dark for a while longer with the doors open, to give the insects a chance to leave. Then I closed the doors and went back upstairs.

And then I lay awake for another twenty minutes wondering whether or not I'd bolted the doors.

This was wholly irrational. What in the world was I worrying about? Bolts don't keep out ghosts, and dead men won't come in on their own!

If you're scared, do *something, Julie,* I told myself. *Go back down and check the bolts if you think it matters!*

So, back into my school blazer and back down the staircase bloodied by the strange dark wines and indigos of moonlit stained glass, back along the inky oak-panelled corridor to the morning room. It was entirely still apart from one imprisoned moth fluttering vainly against an upper windowpane. I stepped into the room.

The French doors suddenly shuddered as if they'd been caught in a tempest.

It would have been startling even if my nerves hadn't already been stretched to snapping. I didn't scream – I dived under the legs of the Queen Anne settee and cowered there in absolute mindless terror like a rabbit in the shadow of a hawk.

The door handle rattled with the sound of a skeleton dancing on a tile floor.

I had my brain back, though my heart was galloping, and I knew it wasn't a ghost. *But what in the world –*

The noise scared me nearly out of my skin. I'd thrown myself on the floor as if I'd been caught on the moor in a hail of gunshot. Now I didn't dare stand up. It was *that* kind of instinct: *protect yourself, Julie.*

I peeked out under the settee between its legs and I could see the shadow at the door – bulky and shapeless – and the door handle rattled again, but indeed I had bolted it after all and it didn't open.

The dark silhouette stood there, just quiet, not moving, for another minute. I counted how long and it seemed to take forever. Then I saw it put up a hand and scratch its head. It reached towards the door again, then changed its mind and edged away.

I let out a little strangled laugh. There was something so very ordinary about the way this terrifying shadow had moved.

I heard the rattle of the door to Frank's office. Then there was no more noise.

It couldn't have been a burglar – he didn't try to break in. It was somebody checking the doors to see if they would open or not, but I didn't know why.

If you're scared, do something! I gave myself another fierce lecture.

All in a rush, I ran at our door, unbolted it and threw it open.

There was no one on the terrace. I stomped out into the moonlight and stood there defiantly in my nightgown and school blazer with bare feet cold against the damp stone, listening. I seemed to stand there for ages and heard nothing. Where on earth had he gone so quickly? Was he hiding below the steps to the lawn?

I didn't have the confidence to look. Words leaped into my head and I sang aloud, quavering and ridiculous:

'My castle is aye my ain,
An' harried it never shall be,
For I'll fall ere it's ta'en –
An' wha dare meddle wi' me?'
'Julia!'

Mother had the French doors open in the room above. She was kneeling on my bed and leaning out of the window to scold me.

'*For goodness' sake*, Julia, stop that racket and come to bed!'

'There was someone rattling the door out here!'

'There are watchmen all over the estate! You were down there with the lights on and the house wide open at two o'clock in the morning, waking your grandmother and all the rest of us right above you – of course they're checking the doors!'

'Well, it scared me,' I said petulantly. 'I thought he might still be about. I didn't see him go.'

'He'll have gone around to the front of the house. You won't frighten off intruders singing Border ballads! *Come to bed!*'

I wished quite suddenly I was tucked up in my narrow iron cot in the crowded room my grandfather was born and died in.

'But when I go back to the reception hall so I can come upstairs, whoever it is will be testing the front door …'

My voice was still quavering a little. Thank goodness Jamie was upstairs in his servant's garret; otherwise I'd never live down his mockery of my lack of fighting spirit.

'I'll come and get you,' my mother said with resignation, as if I were ten years younger.

'I'll come myself,' I said with dignity, bearing in mind the bold reputation of my glorious ancestors.

What a thing to be afraid of, I scolded myself; but I stood on a chair to bolt the terrace doors behind me at the top too, when I came in. I didn't hear anybody try the front door.

I didn't think the shadow I'd seen had the look of a nightwatchman. He'd been missing something watchman-like. Where was the torch, the inevitable cigarette, the peaked cap?

But that wasn't what was nagging at me; it had been something more fleeting.

Where was the *confidence*?

8

RATHER A LOT OF GIVING AND TAKING

The car conversation went something like this:

ME: Mother, would you let me drive your car, like you did at Christmas?

MUMMY: I expect so. But I haven't a great deal of time to teach you.

ME: I could go around the grounds, like Jamie and I do at home in the big car.

MUMMY: *I expect so* …

ME: And if you thought I wasn't too bad, I could take Euan to work. The Water Bailiff …

(Here I inserted a list of unfounded grievances against the McEwens in general and Euan in particular.)

ME: I wouldn't be going far. Just back and forth on the Perth Road between here and Inchfort Field, through Brig O'Fearn.

MUMMY: Hmmnn … you haven't got a licence for being on the road, darling.

ME: It's only one road and almost all through country. It's wide and flat all the way except the last bit of lane that leads down to the library, but that's never got traffic on it. And it would save the McEwens ever so much time and trouble.

MUMMY: I shall make you change the oil in it *yourself* to prove your commitment to the safety of my motor.

So I twisted Mother's arm enough to let me take her sedately up and down the drive in the Magnette the next day, in and out among the new dormitories, proving I was not a reckless idiot. It was still raining and we did not stay out for long, hurrying to get the open-topped car back under cover.

The grown-ups were trying to soldier on as usual and were pestering me about clothes that evening after the driving lesson with Mother. Solange in particular, trying to recover from her sordid past, wanted to see me looking like a respectable young lady again.

'We ought to buy Julia some everyday things, at least. Yours are too big for her, Madame,' she told Mother.

'She has clothes!' Jamie said. 'I brought all her favourite things down from Craig Castle!'

'The Schiaparelli blouse Lord Craigie will not allow her to appear in at dinner!' Solange exclaimed. 'It is *sheer*. She has nothing to wear beneath it. *O, seigneur* … Imagine, in this house, with the workmen coming and going! And there is the Vionnet frock with the silver thread all down the front.'

'I do love that one though,' Mother said. 'It's modest, but it makes her look very grown up.'

I put in: 'It would make *her* look silly on the river path if *she* wore it to visit Mary or the McEwens.'

Really, did we need to *argue* about getting me some decent clothes? When did we become so frugal?

'I bet the McEwens could get me something to wear,' I said. 'They do a trade in old clothes.'

Mémère suddenly spoke up. 'I have made you an appointment with my seamstress in Perth, Julia.'

'You need a party frock,' Mother reminded me. 'For your birthday. Mrs Menzies has very kindly offered to hold a ceilidh for you at Glenmoredun Castle after the grouse shoot on the Twelfth. It's only a month off now. It won't be big, but your father will come down – he's going to let Davie manage the Craig Castle shoot, and I can't be in two places at once organising things – and we must do something for your sixteenth. It's always awkward your birthday falling on Opening Day.'

'Mother, whose fault is that?' Jamie teased.

It *was* awkward. I rarely got decent attention on my birthday, since everyone was always so focused on killing birds. A birthday dance at Glenmoredun Castle would be *marvellous*, especially after the gloom that had been shadowing us all summer – even if everyone was exhausted after tramping about on the moors all day. Very nice of Mrs Menzies and her husband the Laird of Moredun, though I am sure it was partly out of respect for Grandad and sympathy for Mémère. I had been looking forward to a grown-up frock without tartan ruffles on my sixteenth birthday, and sweeping my hair up in a French chignon like Mémère's, since forever.

Oh blast it, I thought, remembering. *My hair. Blast and drat.*

Well, there's many a slip 'twixt the cup and the lip, for although I was determined to be a good girl when they took me into Perth to be measured (and I was looking forward to demanding powder-blue silk), the following day again I did something I ought not have done (and it had nothing to do with Mummy's car).

That was the morning it finally stopped raining: the morning when Euan would start going to work digging on the pipeline for the new Glenfearn School swimming pool.

The sun was out for the first time in glory knows how long, and it was a stunningly and unexpectedly beautiful summer's day, everything sparkling. There was only room for two in the Magnette, so Jamie couldn't come along when I went to collect Euan. Instead, Jamie gallantly offered to help Mother escort Mémère and her entourage to Edinburgh again. I did not envy him that job.

My maiden voyage alone in my mother's car was actually so banal it is almost not worth mentioning. I crept so very carefully down the drive I never even dared shift out of low. Nor did I gather much speed on the Perth Road heading for Brig O'Fearn village. The lane to Inverfearnie Island comes off the main road and goes past Inchfort Field on its way to the library, and I passed Ellen McEwen on her way to the Boatman's Well, laden with one of the big milk cans the McEwens use to fetch water. She had to stand pressed up against the hedge to let me pass, her almost-always hostile stare full of disbelief.

I felt triumphant, but the lane was so narrow there I didn't dare let go of the driving wheel to wave. I drove all the way down to Inverfearnie Island so I could turn around in the wide gravel drive in front of the library. I wasn't sure if Mary saw me but I was still so mad at her that I didn't care.

When I parked by the field gate at Inchfort and climbed out of the car, Pinkie the dog came galloping to greet me.

'My own girl!' I cooed as she showered me with kisses.

Mrs McEwen was out in front of their big camp tent, washing breakfast cups and plates in a white enamel tin tub. The baby – which I knew now to be Ellen and Euan's very junior adopted sister, the child of a cousin who'd died giving birth to her – was chortling away in a little willow basket nearby.

'I didn't bring you a present last time,' I said. 'So I did this time.' I'd cut an armful of roses for Mrs McEwen, the reddest reds and darkest pinks I could find. Knowing that we couldn't take them with us made us rather free with the cut flowers.

'The bonny things!' Jean McEwen shook the water from her hands and buried her nose in the velvety, scented blossom. 'What beauties! Are these out of Lady Strathfearn's garden? Let me get the tea on – you'll need a cup of tea after your ride in the motor car. We can put these in to soak when Ellen gets back – she's just fetching another can of water. Euan's away to the Big House.'

'Oh! I wanted to give him a ride and spare him the long walk! Didn't Ellen tell you I was coming?'

I felt pretty sure she hadn't really believed I'd manage it.

'It's nae bother for Euan this morning – he rode in the cart with his uncle Hamish who's away to Perth peddling tin. We had a time getting the dog to stay behind, but it's no place for her among those dredgers! How kind of you to think on Euan. We've told him to meet you by the Strathfearn garages at day's end. No doubt he'd be glad of a lift home by then, and if you stop here the now you'll catch our Nell when she comes back.'

Another, separate plan hatched itself beautifully in my brain. Meanly, it didn't include Jamie. Naughtily, it did include my mother's car.

'Maybe Ellen would like to go for a drive?'

'I should think she'll like that very much!'

Shaness, Julie, you are a devious wee temptress.

Of course she wanted to go for a drive. Who can resist a cherry-red two-seater open-top sports car?

I was waiting for Ellen at the gate when she got back with the water. I was sitting in the car, ready to go.

'I went to a lot of bother to come out here for Euan this morning,' I said. 'You might have told him to wait.'

Her stony eyes glinted. 'Oh, aye?' she responded noncommittally.

'Well, as I'm here anyway, you may as well come for a ride instead.'

I could see she was ridiculously excited, and a little scared. I don't think Ellen McEwen realises how *obvious* all her emotions are.

'You can do the shifting, if you like,' I said. 'I'll put the clutch in and tell you when to move the stick.'

177

'You're a radge dilly. Horn moich.'

'I know what that means, you know.'

'Oh, aye?' she repeated.

'A pure mad girl. So I am! Do you want to do the gears or not?'

'Let me just give Mammy this can. Wait for me.'

It was a good lesson for both of us: it made me have to think even harder about getting the timing of clutch and stick right. I let her do it all the way out to the main road, slowing down and speeding up on purpose so she could practise.

Then I took over to drive carefully through Brig O'Fearn village and back to the gate lodge of Strathfearn House, and that was all I had permission to do. But …

… But Mother was in Edinburgh and I had officially finished being convalescent and I was still a little jealous of all the time that Jamie had spent with Ellen and I hadn't, and –

Suddenly all the sorrow and uncertainty that entwined our lives with Strathfearn dropped away from us both. We were nothing more than two lucky girls on a jolly holiday in a motor car.

I swung around neatly in the lodge entrance to the driveway and headed back towards Brig O'Fearn.

'Where are you going?' Ellen cried.

'Over Pitbroomie Hill to Glenmoredun Castle!'

It is only a little detour from Brig O'Fearn, only the next road over.

'Madwoman!' Ellen accused approvingly.

'I want to see what the moor looks like. They're shooting there soon. There must be grouse about – bet the car will scare the birds!'

'Do they need beaters for the shoot? Or loaders? Our men used to work the Opening Day shoot for Strathfearn.'

'I'll ask Mother.'

It occurred to me that Ellen and I must have had rather different views of Opening Day. Mine had always been: *This frenzied killing of birds interrupts my birthday but can be rather fun.* But to Ellen, it was just *work*.

And she added schemingly, but without the accusatory tone I'd come to expect from her, 'If Jamie's shooting, Euan could load for him. He's fast.'

Feeling a bit awkward now, but not wanting to admit it, I said cheerfully, 'I'll volunteer him!'

Then we came to Brig O'Fearn and I stopped talking so I could concentrate on driving carefully through the village again. But I had the hang of this now. The road to Glen-moredun Castle went haring away to the south, twisting around Pitbroomie Hill as though it couldn't decide which direction it wanted to go, but I followed it anyway, picking up speed.

'I don't believe you know where you're going,' Ellen said.

'Oh pish, there isn't any other road! How could I possibly get lost here?' (It is true I am hopeless at directions. I came down the wrong side of the mountain on that skiing holiday and had to be brought back to the chalet by a policeman. But the Pitbroomie Moor was familiar. Part of it used to belong to Strathfearn.)

We were between stone walls and hedges on the way up, thorn and bramble, and couldn't see where we were in relation to anything else. Then over cattle bars and there were no more walls. The thorn turned to gorse, still brilliant here and there with yellow blossom and heavy with bees.

The pavement disappeared suddenly and we were on gravel just as the gradient increased dramatically. I had to slow down but I forgot to shift out of high gear and, horror, three quarters of the way up, the Magnette stalled with a tremendous lurch.

Ellen made a little shrieking sound like '*Eep!*'

I tried to start the motor again and found myself in neutral, slowly bumping backward down the steep hillside and gathering speed. I yanked on the handbrake and both of us nearly went flying out of the open car like a pair of jack-in-the-boxes.

'*God pity us.*'

I could hardly blame Ellen for that.

We paused quietly in the middle of the track, catching our breath in safe and sudden stillness.

After a few moments, I said, 'Well, we can't stay here.'

'I might get out,' Ellen whispered, 'before you go anywhere else.'

'You get out then. I'll reverse back down to the pavement and turn around in the field gate just before the cattle bars.'

'You can't reverse!'

'I'm *good* at reversing.'

I couldn't get the damned thing started though, because of the slope which made me keep stalling. Eventually I had the brilliant and simple idea of freewheeling backward – very, very slowly – down to where the road widened. Ellen knelt up on the passenger seat while I did this, gripping the back of it with both hands, and bawling directions at me like a banshee:

'Stop, stop! There's a bend and a CLIFF – almost a cliff – STOP! Oh, sweet heaven. Thank you. Turn, yes, just go slowly here … Aye, you're around. Straight back a ways … Go … go … *STOP!*'

I slammed on the brakes for the thousandth time.

Ellen was doubled over laughing – out of mirth or hysterics I was not sure.

'What?' I demanded. 'Another cliff?'

'There was a …' She was gasping with hilarity. 'In the way! It was a …'

On edge with the nerve-racking task of trying to reverse my mother's car down a road about as wide as a bed and as steep as a staircase, where I wasn't supposed to be, I found Ellen's hilarity contagious.

'A rockslide? A horse and cart? Another car?' I craned my neck, trying to see as far as she could, tall Ellen riding up on the seat back like a figurehead turned around. 'Oh help, not the bus coming?'

'You just missed it!' She was doubled over with laughter.

'The *bus*? I missed the bus!'

'A *grouse*, not the bloomin' bus! There was a grouse ran under the car. Straight between the wheels and out the other side!'

'That's lucky, then.'

It took us a while to manage the journey back down to the place where the road widened at a field gate, but we did manage it eventually without hitting anything, not even one of the suicidal moor birds. I was able to turn around and park with the Magnette squeezed on to the grass verge so that it was pointing in the right direction (back down hill).

I had definitely overstretched myself, though I dared not admit it to either Ellen or Mummy. Feeling a bit limp with relief, I pulled on the handbrake and climbed up on the seat back next to Ellen.

'Golly, what a beautiful day,' I said appreciatively. 'You can see all the way to Dundee from here!'

The Tay spread between us and the Sidlaw Hills, away from Perth out to the North Sea like a widening train of blue silk. Turnips and tatties, berries and flax grew green below us.

'What a lot of ships going into Perth Harbour!' I said. 'And look, you can't see the Big House because of the wood, but there's Aberfearn Castle at the river's edge.'

'Euan and myself used to romp all over inside it when we were wee,' Ellen said.

'So did we! Playing at kings and queens! Did you climb up inside the chimneys?'

'Aye!'

We laughed in amazement at this improbable shared memory.

'What a shame we weren't ever there at the same time,' I said. 'We could have had proper battles.'

We turned around. Behind us, the hillside climbed away, clad in heather almost ready to burst into purple bloom, hiding young grouse.

'This moor used to be my grandad's,' I said.

'Aye, we used to work it for him,' Ellen said.

'He sold the family jewellery so he could go to America for treatment, and he sold the moor to keep the house going. The land joins on to the Laird of Moredun's, so now Moredun's got one big grouse moor. He and Grandad always used to manage their shoots together anyway.'

'Nice the land won't change,' Ellen said quietly.

I turned to look at her. She was gazing across the fields and woodland of the Tay Valley, her face expressionless, her eyes hot.

'Sometimes it makes me feel like I own it all, when I see it like this,' I said. 'Mine by right of me being here.'

'I ken.' She glanced at me sideways. 'By right of keeping the willows and knowing where the Bronze Age boat is hidden in the burn. By right of climbing up inside the chimneys of Aberfearn Castle!' She turned her head fully. 'You don't own any more of it than I do, do you?'

'Not one twig of willow. Not one pearl.'

Even as I said it, I remembered the pearl I'd stolen from my grandfather's empty envelope. 'Not a single thing in Strathfearn belongs to me.' Not one forgotten pearl. 'Not even the kilt I'm wearing!' I finished, and we both laughed again.

'I used to think Grandad was as rich as the King,' I said. 'But that was just me being little and ignorant. There were never bank vaults full of gold sovereigns and silver ingots.

There wasn't a family fortune; there was never much *money*. There was only Strathfearn, only the estate and its land, cows and flax and berries, grouse and salmon and a few river pearls. And now it is gone, and so is he.'

Ellen was silent – because what was there to answer to that?

'Sandy inherited the title by a complicated thing called Special Remainder,' I added. 'He's not the eldest, but he's my grandad's namesake and his most special grandchild, and our big brother Davie will get our father's title anyway. But even Sandy doesn't get a bean to go with it. Not that he cares about land. He's like an ostrich, head underground, digging up artefacts.'

'He gets that from your grandad.'

'We all do, a bit,' I said. 'Even you. Though I wouldn't want Sandy's job, stuck in a museum all day. I need complicated railroad journeys and people speaking to me in foreign languages to keep me happy. I want to see the world and write stories about everything I see.'

'Will your folk let you do that?'

'I don't know. Nobody ever mentions that I'm almost old enough to be married; but I'll bet *other people* mention it to them. And maybe my people discuss it behind my back.'

I realised I would be forced to run away from home if someone tried to arrange a marriage for me. I didn't want to think about it.

I pointed at the Sidlaw Hills across the valley. 'See King's Seat? Just in front of it is Dunsinane, where Macbeth lived. He's supposed to be one of Grandad's forebears.'

Ellen opened her mouth to speak.

I beat her to the post. 'Don't you *dare* call me Lady Macbeth.'

She laughed again. 'I wasnae going to. I was going to say: we're half the way up Pitbroomie Hill anyway, we may as well walk to the top. The motor car's all right here for a wee while, aye?'

So we got out and walked.

It was a steep hike – for the same reason that the Magnette hadn't made it up the hill, we found ourselves so out of breath we were unable to talk (I was, at any rate). But it was lovely once the hillside began to level out. Able to breathe again, I sang:

'Now the summer's in its prime
Wi' the flowers sweetly bloomin'
And the wild mountain thyme …'

'*All the moorland is perfumin'*,' Ellen joined in.

We finished the verse together, and sang the whole thing at the tops of our voices, scaring birds. We walked side by side on the track over the moor that was ours by right of our being there, singing to the sky and the wind.

I thought, just then and fleetingly, there wasn't any place I'd rather be or any person I'd rather be with. If I could have chosen one moment of my life to go on forever, just then, it would have been that one.

We came over the summit of Pitbroomie Hill and Ellen pointed towards the high mounds of East and West Lomond across the next valley. 'Those are both Iron Age hill forts,' she said. 'There's a big one on this side too, up the Knowes above Brig O'Fearn village. People have been here a long time. But now there's nothing on top but birds and gorse and wind. A glen like this always makes me think: why did folk leave the hilltops?'

'When exactly is Iron Age?' I asked.

'Well, two thousand years ago, give or take an odd few hundred either end. Hard to tell unless you dig things up. That's why your grandad's work is so important: they line up all those different blades and compare them, and then they can work out the dates. Like geological layers, but not so old.'

Frank Dunbar had said the same thing about the Murray Hoard being important. He'd quoted Hugh Housman saying it, anyway.

'I think it's easier dating rocks than arrowheads,' Ellen considered. 'But maybe geology seems easier because I learned it in school, and I've kent the rest myself.'

'Did you really learn geology in school?' I asked. 'How do you go to school when you're moving about?'

'We have to do a hundred days a year or they send Cruelty folk out after us – you ken, the Royal Society for the Prevention of Cruelty to Children. They'll take a bairn away from a family if your school attendance card isn't filled. We mostly go in the winter – we share a cottage by Aberfeldy with my cousins. I left high school last year. Euan left when he was fourteen, but I had a scholarship for science and history.'

My heart stirred with a baffling jealousy. 'Did you finish the course?'

'I didn't take the exams. They were arguing some rubbish about not being able to send the results to a proper address, but I don't believe that. Dad collects his Black Watch pension at the post office wherever he is. I know it was really three scaldy lads making a fuss at having to share workspace with a lass – and a dirty tinker lass at that – and I left.' She shrugged. 'So no, I dinnae have a pass mark. But I still know what I learned.'

We passed the upper drive to Glenmoredun Castle, with its ornate stone archway and gate lodge incongruously plumped all by itself in the middle of the moor. Below us, further down in a fold of the hillside, nestled the turrets of the castle itself.

'Ready to turn back?' I asked. 'If we go further we'll just have to march back up again to get back to the car, like the Grand Old Duke of York.'

Behind us, a pair of voices suddenly chimed: 'Hey, youse – tinkies!'

Ellen spun round at the catcalls.

I turned more slowly.

'*Tinkies, tinkies, carry bags, Go to the well and wash your rags!*'

'Got rags for us, tinks?'

It was two girls. Two working girls from Glenmoredun Castle, in service as housemaids or kitchen staff maybe, on their afternoon off. They'd come out to the gate lodge since we first passed it and were waiting for the bus.

Ellen was now one step ahead of me – and her steps were longer than mine. I could see the cords tightening in her wrists as she clenched her fists.

'Going down to Glenmoredun, aye?' asked one of the girls. She was round and rosy, with dark curls. 'What are youse peddling? Needles? Wooden pegs?'

'Or reading tea leaves?' This with a self-conscious giggle from the other girl, whose brown hair was waved and fluffed.

They both had on lipstick and little heeled sandals, and I reckoned they were younger than me – just done with school, working for the first time. The slim one with the crimped brown hair was somehow more self-assured, more worldly than her wholesome-looking friend.

'Tell my fortune!' was her next knowing suggestion.

Ellen missed a step, and flinched, as though she'd stubbed her toe. She stopped, straightened her shoulders and faced the pair across the narrow unmade road.

I drew up short at her elbow.

The two other girls bent their heads together, black hair and brown, whispering and giggling. Then they looked up, and the cheeky, crimped-haired one called out, 'What about your wee brother, would *he* tell my fortune?'

'I bet your wee brother would like to give me a kiss,' squealed the rosy one daringly.

'I'd like to give your wee brother a kiss!' squealed her more experienced friend.

In unison they broke into a cascade of giddy mirth.

Now Ellen faced me again with her back to this brace of gleeful idiots, and she looked me up and down with an expression of vexed and bewildered astonishment.

They went on as if we couldn't hear them.

'Florrie, you'd kiss anything that *moves*. You'd kiss my old grandad – you'd kiss a *sheep*.'

Florrie chastised her friend by batting her on the arm, and they both rocked with hilarity.

'Now that is how a well-bred young person speaks in polite company,' I said to Ellen in a level voice, hoping my attempt at deadpan Traveller sarcasm would cool her down. 'And aren't they optimistic about your brother!'

Ellen gave a jerk of her head in the direction of the two silly things, who were still chuckling like hens and staring at us with a kind of sideshow fascination, as if we were covered with tattoos.

'They mean you,' she answered quietly. 'Wi' your old kilt and bare legs. They think you're a boy.' She reached out and fluffed my Joan-of-Arc hair with one quick, rough hand, as if I were Pinkie. Or, indeed, as if I were her younger brother. As my older brothers have been doing to Jamie almost all his life.

'Come on over here, laddie. Florrie is *gasping* for you!' called the rosy one with the dark hair.

'So I am. I'm all yours. Come over the road, wee man ...'

I took a step forward, very deliberately, hands on my hips, and with a wide grin that I couldn't quite control. I let the girls take a good long look at me. They stared and elbowed each other in the ribs.

'I wouldn't kiss an old woman like Florrie,' I told them.

Ellen grabbed me by the back of my shirt. 'Shaness, *Davie*, let them be.'

I shook her off.

'You waiting for the bus to Perth?' I asked them.

The rosy one answered, 'Aye, we're going to the pictures. We'll –'

More elbows and titters were exchanged between them.

The bolder friend finished for the other, 'Brenda will take you along if you gie her a kiss!'

'Ooh, I willnae. I'm no paying a tinker's bus fare! It's you that's gasping for him.'

Ellen didn't try to stop me.

'Come on, then, Florrie,' I said.

I crossed the road, still grinning like the Cheshire cat. Well, I'd practised on Frank Dunbar, hadn't I? Florrie had a lot to learn from me about playing this game.

She tried to dodge me. Brenda, tipsy with laughter, held her by the shoulders so she couldn't escape. Florrie was a little bit taller than me, but not so tall I couldn't reach her mouth when I stood on tiptoe.

'You said you were gasping!' I accused, as she turned her face away.

'Go on, Florrie. He's bonny as the day.'

Florrie turned back very quickly, and gave me a peck on the lips.

I didn't move. 'Call that gasping?' I scoffed.

Bold now, challenging, she did it again, and then let her mouth hesitate over mine. For a second the tip of her tongue explored the space between my lips, intimate and secretive.

And this is so strange: it was just as nice as kissing Frank Dunbar.

But in a completely different way.

At this point the bus came rumbling over the hill.

'Oh!' Florrie cried, stepping back suddenly as if I'd stung her, and cracked me a bone-shaking wallop across the face with the flat of her hand.

'Cheeky devil,' she said primly, as I bent over one knee with my face in my hands, seeing stars.

The bus pulled up in a cloud of dust and Ellen vaulted across the road in front of it to pinion me, instinctively guessing I'd turn murderous the instant I recovered from the shock of being attacked. As I straightened up she grabbed my arms from behind and clamped them to my sides as if I were about to be shot from a cannon. That snake Florrie was escaping, hustled on to the bus by her still tittering friend Brenda. I fought Ellen in fury, quite ineffectively.

'Let me go!'

Ellen held me in a grip of iron. She murmured softly in my ear, '*Julie.*'

I stopped struggling, breathing hard.

'Whisht. Hush. Now, Julie.'

The bus pulled away, and she let me go.

I stood staring after it, raging with impotent anger, one hand pressed to my burning cheek.

'This is how it always goes,' Ellen said. 'You have to play-act. You have to bite your tongue and pretend you dinnae care. If you'd hit her back you'd have had the bus driver jump out and knock you silly. And if you ever tell my mammy or daddy I let you kiss another girl while I watched, I'll knock you silly myself.'

She gave her characteristic snort of disgust, and added, 'You should have let her gasp.'

From somewhere in her skirt Ellen pulled her tobacco pouch, the exact shape and colour of a river mussel, and her little clay pipe.

'Have a draw. Witless scaldies. Forget about them.'

She got the pipe alight and handed it to me.

She'd smoked her pipe in front of me more than once before, but she'd never let me share it.

Something had changed between us. I wasn't sure what had made it happen. The car ride, the song on the moor? Or me having to take a slap in the face as if I really were one of *her kind*?

Whatever it was, I thought, she had finally called me Julie and offered me a smoke. I thought it was probably worth it.

'Thank you,' I said, feeling dragon-like, my face still burning with the sting of Florrie's slap, my mouth full of smoke.

'All right?' Ellen asked me.

'Nae bother,' I answered, trying to be stoically Euan-like, and got a sardonic snorted laugh out of her.

We set off towards the car. I gave Ellen back her pipe.

We didn't say anything else for a while, but as we came to the wonderful view of the Tay Valley, Ellen observed in the neutral tone of a policeman making an accusation, 'You just take anything you want when you want it, aye, Lady Julia? Just take and take. Born to it. You need a gift for my mam so you pick your gran's roses. You want a motor car so you help yourself to your mother's. You were raging at those scaldy lassies and you just thought you could play them for fools.'

I didn't answer. What was I supposed to answer? Because, uncomfortably, I thought Ellen was right. I thought of how I'd tried on Solange's pearls, and that kiss I helped myself to from Frank Dunbar, and the pearl in the envelope. Even the way I'd so blithely put my taxi fare to Strathfearn on my mother's account. And I'd very gladly taken Ellen away for the morning to have her to myself when I knew she and Jamie were … Well, I didn't know what they were. If anything. But I was childishly unwilling to share her.

Ellen swept her arm towards the river and forest and fields that lay at our feet. 'You think this all belongs to you just because you're in it.'

'So do you! You agreed!'

'I don't just *take* what I want. My folk don't steal things. We don't *keep* things.'

'It's not the value of a thing that's important,' I said, trying to defend myself. 'I love the *story* of a thing. I love a thing for what it *means* a thousand times more than for what it's worth. You know the pearl bracelet in the Inverfearnie Library, the one that belonged to Mary Queen of Scots when she was a child? I don't give a *toss* what that's worth. But *Mary Queen of Scots' own bracelet*! And the Reliquary – what about that? The price you paid for your willow bank, four hundred years ago? It's *hard* to have your happiness tangled up in things you can't keep.'

'We don't mind about keeping things,' Ellen said. 'If you give a Traveller girl a ring, she'll wear it until some other girl admires it, then like as not she'll give it to her friend. For love. For the pleasure of giving. Because what's the point in just *having*? If I give a thing, I'll remember how happy we both were when I made the gift.'

She handed me her pipe.

'Here, it's yours. Keep it. It's more blessed to give than to receive.'

She never dropped her superior air of queenly command, but suddenly she was warm and fond too.

I took it. I had to.

Then she smiled at me sunnily. 'And aren't *you* happy, now I've given you something you wanted badly – something of mine?'

And I was. I really was.

She is wonderful.

9

THE APPEARANCE OF LEGS

After the thrilling excursion up Pitbroomie Hill with Ellen, the Big House felt empty without my family in it that afternoon, even though it was full of builders and painters. Feeling abandoned, I let my natural vanity take control of me, and I spent a long time in front of Mémère's dressing-table mirror checking my face for damage (there wasn't any) and trying to make my hair look a bit more feminine (impossible). Finally I took a bath and got dressed in my own frock, the rose-coloured Parisian georgette with the silver zigzags down the bodice that Jamie brought from Craig Castle, utterly useless for doing anything sensible in, BUT. But very much what I needed to make me feel myself again, cool and stylishly sophisticated. (Is that myself? I don't know if I *am*, but I like to *feel* that I am.)

And all the while my hands were occupied fussing with my face and my hair and my clothes, my mind was turning over and over again the multitude of disconnected events of the past month. My injured head. The naked man in the river. Mary's betrayal of Euan. The scholar's farewell slipped under the door. And pearls.

Scottish river pearls … there they were, like beads torn from a necklace: in Solange's jewellery box, seen through the lens of Hugh Housman's jug, lying on Jean and Ellen McEwen's palms, under glass beneath Mary Kinnaird's watchful eye in the Inverfearnie Library, hidden in a brown envelope on Francis Dunbar's desk, fixed forever in the floorboards of the tower room of Strathfearn House.

Pearls.

I thought there *must* be a way to string everything together. Only I couldn't see it yet.

It was frustrating. I didn't know what I was looking for. And the night-time intruder – Mother seemed sure it had been a legitimate estate watchman, but I wasn't convinced. I began another unproductive search, this time looking at the French doors of the morning room. I didn't have long till I was supposed to go and collect Euan to drive him back to Inchfort.

I was peering intently at the door handles, wishing I knew something about fingerprinting, when instinct caused me to straighten quickly. Someone was coming up the terrace stairs from the lawn with heavy footfalls. I turned around.

It was Francis Dunbar. I had about one second in which to straighten myself out before presenting myself as the presiding lady of the house – thank God I'd changed out of Sandy's moth-eaten kilt.

Frank Dunbar looked pale and grim. He did that same little leap backward when he saw me as he'd done on the day we met.

'I'm so sorry, Miss Beaufort-Stuart.' He frowned, wondering if he'd got it right, and obviously decided that it didn't matter. 'I'm so sorry. I'm looking for your mother. Or your grandmother, I suppose.'

'They're in Edinburgh,' I said. 'Is it urgent? I'm about to go out myself.' I didn't want to let Euan down. 'I won't be long – I could come back in an hour or so. The others won't be back till about eight.'

He hesitated, standing one step below the level of the terrace, as if he couldn't decide whether to come up or not. He swallowed, making a conscious effort to soften his expression.

'I've had some bad news.' He bit the single-syllable words off in the back of his throat as if each one were choking him and he could hardly get them out. He swallowed again.

'Oh.' I did so like Frank Dunbar, and felt sorry for him. 'Would I do, in place of my mother?'

I could see him swithering.

'I don't think …' he began.

Instead of trying to persuade him with words, I held up a formal arm for him to take.

I read him right: he couldn't refuse the polite, wordless request for physical support. I saw his face change when he made his decision.

We met halfway across the terrace. He took my arm, very politely, and escorted me through the French doors of his own side of the double room and into his private office.

He offered me a chair, but didn't sit himself. It felt very like our first meeting, except he looked so beaten. He paced back to his open terrace doors and stood staring out over the hive of activity across the grounds.

'You've had bad news,' I reminded him.

He turned around to face me, still not quite willing that I should be the one with whom he'd share whatever it was.

He winced, looking at me. It was something he thought I'd find unpleasant, something inappropriate for a young lady's sensibilities.

I guessed.

'Your men working along the river have found Hugh Housman?'

He blinked in surprise. He opened his mouth and shut it again, then nodded. '*My God.* You're a mind reader.'

'You wanted to speak to my mother. We've all been looking for him for a month. People hardly ever just *vanish*. He was bound to turn up eventually, wasn't he?'

I didn't dare ask the obvious question: alive or dead? Nothing in Dunbar's manner suggested the former, but I didn't want it to look like I *expected* the latter, even if I *did*.

I waited.

He didn't elaborate, so finally I found a neutral way to get him to go on.

'Where?'

He hesitated unhappily.

'Julie, this is so unpleasant. I don't know where to begin.'

It was like being a tennis ball getting thwacked back and forth, swapping between being Davie Balfour and Lady Julia. I needed to let Frank know I wasn't made entirely of glass. I got up and crossed the room to stand beside him.

'Is he dead?'

'Well ... yes. Well ...'

'*Yes?*' I prompted.

'*Probably ...*'

I narrowed my eyes, overwhelmed with the feeling that all adults are incompetent lunatics.

'You found Dr Housman and he's *probably* dead?' I said sharply. 'What on earth is that supposed to mean? Goodness, Mr Dunbar.'

He looked stricken. 'I'm telling this very badly. I said it was unpleasant.'

'Please sit down,' I told him. 'Just here. Have you anything to drink about? Whisky – excellent. Just a moment and I'll pour you a wee drop.'

His housekeeping was chaotic, evidence of his lonely bachelor's existence – a decanter sharing a bookshelf with half a loaf of bread and cheese wrapped in brown paper. I found a glass and wiped it with a leaf off the blotting pad.

'There you are. I'm not going to faint.' I pressed the glass into his hands and squeezed them lightly beneath my own. 'Now, Frank, just tell me what happened.'

'They found a body. They found … most of a body.'

This time it was I who winced.

I instantly regretted it. He tried to jump up and the dark gold liquid spilled over his fingers.

I pressed my lips together and held up a warning hand.

'What's missing?' I asked brazenly. Because truly, sickening though his news was, the man needed *shaking*. One of us was going to have to be brazen, or I'd never find out what had happened.

Frank Dunbar drew a sharp breath but managed to get the words out. 'The head and shoulders are missing. And one arm.' He drew another breath. 'There aren't any hands or feet, either.'

Very gently, I took the glass from him and set it on his desk.

'Go on,' I said quietly.

'The poor devil – he's been … well, quartered by one of the dredgers somehow. Terribly mutilated. We think the spade of the digger caught him across the chest.' Frank paused and looked up at me. I returned his gaze unflinchingly. He reached for my hand and held it tightly, clenching and unclenching his fingers as he continued speaking. 'The water level's been a serious difficulty for us in digging the pipeline for the swimming pool. There's a tidal change of over a metre, twice a day, where the Fearn meets the Tay, and we can't dredge at low tide because the water isn't deep enough for the barge that holds the digger. But we haven't been able to work at all because of the high flow that came with the rain. The body must have tumbled into the trench while the water was deep.'

'Goodness!' I exclaimed. 'If the McEwens had been looking for pearls further downstream they might have found him two weeks ago, when the water was so low because of the spring tide!'

'But if he hadn't got trapped in the trench we might not have found him till the *next* spring tide, which isn't till the end of July.'

'Oh! It's perfectly morbid to think about.'

I said this because I felt that I ought to sound more sympathetic towards the decapitated man on the riverbed. But I couldn't think of anything other than how upset Solange was going to be, and it made me angry with poor Dr Housman on her account.

'Did they find his clothes?' I asked.

Frank knocked back a gulp of whisky.

'No. But … the river's been so high … they may have long washed away. The workmen trawled the ditch when they found his body, and that's when they picked up his arm. And two beautiful bronze spearheads, of all things; they must have been buried in the peat. But not his clothes.' Frank emptied his glass. 'I don't understand why he took off his clothes if he was planning to drown himself … You'd think he'd have been trying to keep them dry so he could get dressed again.'

Regardless of that letter to Solange, which neither Frank nor I had seen (Mummy sent it off to the police before I could get hold of it – sometimes she is wise to me), I didn't think Frank believed Housman drowned himself on purpose. I felt that he was focusing on the drink to cover up his doubt. Did he think *someone else* did it? That someone – me? Solange? – pushed him in?

'What about the … the hands and feet?' I asked. 'Did they all get cut off by the digger?'

'The doctor who's going to examine him said they often detach after a body's been in water a few weeks.' Frank sounded defeated. 'The doctor's not seen the damage yet though.'

Ugh.

Frank didn't voice any of his own doubts. Maybe I was imagining doubt in him, but I didn't think so. Well, it wasn't up to me – the Procurator Fiscal, who deals with accidental deaths, would decide whether there needed to be an inquiry. Fair enough Frank keeping quiet.

I didn't have any idea how close Frank Dunbar and Hugh Housman might have been – it sounded as though they'd only just met this summer and shared a few meals. But I felt Frank needed a little compassion. I picked up his glass, added a dollop of water to it from the jug by the whisky decanter and passed it back to him.

'Julie, you're marvellous,' he said.

'I do try to be marvellous.'

He gazed at me as if it rested his eyes to do it, as if he were appreciating the view from a mountaintop. I let him look. I stood still in the rose silk Vionnet dress, with my face turned away a little so I didn't seem to be self-aware. When I turned back to him he gave me the ghost of a smile.

'I said I was going to drive Euan McEwen over to Inchfort,' I reminded him. 'Is it all right if I go and do that now?'

'Yes, of course. I – I'm sorry I told you any of this. I should have waited for your mother.'

'I'm not sorry at all,' I said with feeling.

Indeed, when I met poor Euan McEwen by the garages, I sent up a little private prayer of thanks that I already knew what was going on.

He was soaked and shaking. We looked each other up and down without speaking for a moment or two.

Euan broke the silence first. 'That's a bonny frock.'

My face flamed. My God, it was like being slapped again, and I don't even know why. As if I were mocking him on purpose with wealth and elegance and – yes, and my *beauty*. And he knew it. But I wasn't – I wasn't. At least, I didn't mean to.

'Whisht.' I drew a sharp breath. 'I didn't realise the work was going to be so wet.'

'I was shifting barrow-loads of peat this morning,' Euan said. 'That wasnae so bad. But this afternoon –' He stopped abruptly.

'I ken,' I told him in a low voice, so he knew he didn't have to explain to me about what the pipeline diggers had found in the trench that day.

'They asked me and the other lads who work the spades and barrows to hunt for the missing parts. They added fourpence the hour to our pay for doing it. But you had to get into the ditch.' He paused, steadying himself. 'I'd have done it for nothing … But I'm glad it wasnae me who found the arm.'

He counts his working hours in pennies. I don't think I'd realised that. I felt so *stupid*.

'Are you all right?' I asked.

'Aye, nae bother.'

I should have known I'd get 'Aye, nae bother' for an answer.

'I really can't take you in Mother's car as wet as that,' I said. 'Let me get a mackintosh or something for you to sit on. There used to be car coats in the garages here – *buckets of blood*.' There wasn't anything but paint cans and builders' ironmongery now. Everything belonging to the Murrays had been cleared out.

'Never mind,' Euan said. 'I'll walk round by Brig O'Fearn.'

'No, you will not walk. We'll find something in the house. They haven't finished painting and the whole place is covered in sheets.'

'*No.*'

He spoke quite firmly, quiet as always, but with the determination of a soldier.

'I walked across Perthshire and Angus on my own feet when I was seven. It's summer and I like walking. I'll take nothing from the Big House. I'll take nothing that belongs to the Glenfearn School, not even to borrow.' He paused for breath.

'Why is that?' I asked sharply. 'That foreman Robbie Munro doesn't trust you?'

'Not just him. All the lads on the site. I'd only been there an hour before I had to turn my pockets out and prove it wasnae me who'd lifted some gadgie's packet o' fags he thinks he left in a digger overnight!'

'Huh,' I said, narrowing my eyes. 'I bet one of them *is* pinching cigarettes, or they wouldn't be trying to blame it on you.'

'They likely would. They'd leave it on the train by accident and blame me.'

'Well, I'm not letting you walk ten miles in those wet trousers.'

'They'll dry.'

Eventually I won, thanks to the moth-eaten kilt from the nursery bathroom, which we used to line the passenger seat.

'Did you see anything?' I asked. 'Did you see any of it yourself – what they found?'

'Aye, but I'll not tell you about it.'

And I didn't try to get it out of him. After that, Euan sat in absolute silence the whole way back to Inchfort Field. The morning in the sun with Ellen seemed a very long time ago.

I pulled up in front of the field gate. It is easier to turn around in the gravel drive in front of the library than in the narrow lane that runs past Inchfort on its way to Inverfearnie, but I didn't want to risk getting Euan in trouble with Mary again just by being in the car with me as I reversed, so I dropped him off first.

He started to get out.

'Euan …'

He waited, sitting next to me with the door open and one leg out of the car.

'Euan, now that they've found Dr Housman and it's officially an accidental death, the Procurator Fiscal might decide there needs to be an inquiry. If there's blame to be found, I *know* they're going to try to blame you.'

After a moment of absolute silence I heard him swallow.

'That day you found me – that last time anyone saw Dr Housman alive,' I reminded him. 'Do you remember what you did that day?'

Euan nodded.

'I'll swear you did nothing but help me,' I said fiercely. 'I'll swear you had nothing to do with whatever happened to Hugh Housman.'

'I'll swear *you* did nothing but fall on your face at my feet,' Euan said shakily.

We sat quietly for another moment.

'Meanwhile we just go on as usual,' I said finally. 'Shall I come for you tomorrow morning? I wouldn't blame you if you never went back.'

'The work's worthwhile,' Euan said. 'And I've done *nothing wrong*. I'll be waiting for you.'

The next morning, the kilt I'd left in Mummy's car in the garages overnight had disappeared.

A good many of the lads working on the building site were more ragged than any of the McEwens, and could probably use a well-made kilt, regardless of the moth holes. I was damned if I'd be the one to cast aspersions at anyone. I just knew that the second I said something had gone missing, someone would point a finger at Euan again.

Bloody hypocrites. It made me *furious* to think that the Glenfearn School builders were blaming Euan for stolen cigarettes. But in the uproar over Hugh Housman's mutilated body, disappearing kilts and cigarettes didn't attract the attention of anyone in authority.

Still, I'd miss that kilt. Father mentioned on the 'phone that my trunk had turned up at last, but *of course*, it was sent home to Craig Castle instead of to Strathfearn. Blast it.

10

LYING ABOUT ONE'S AGE CAN BE A FORM OF ART

Three days after my outing with Ellen I acquired a DRIVING LICENCE. Quite illegally, as I was not yet seventeen (or even sixteen for another month), and it was all down to Mummy. Inspector Milne's suspicious prying appeared to have awakened her inner Bolshevik, and so I discovered my own lady mother is not above quietly circumventing the law.

'I wouldn't do this for just anyone,' she told me. 'But Jean McEwen is a good woman and we'll help her son in any way we can.'

Mummy had the driving examiner from Perth meet us at the Brig O'Fearn railway station. Then she waited on the station platform with Lisette Romilly's latest novel (in French, of course) for half an hour while I took the examiner for a sedate tour of Brig O'Fearn village. I thought Mother was probably very happy to get a quiet half-hour alone with a book.

She knew I'd pass because she'd already tested me herself. Mother was very thorough. We spent the *entire day* on the road practising on Sunday; we drove all the way home to Craig Castle and back, had a lovely lunch with Father, and – hurrah! – *collected my clothes*. Not my trunk, obviously, as it couldn't possibly go in the Magnette. But proper ordinary clothes that actually fit me. I had no excuse for being Davie Balfour any more.

Driving for twelve hours in a single day, or whatever it was in total, was shattering. I slept most soundly the night before my examination.

Thus, *mirabile dictu*, I now had documentary proof that I was 'seventeen' – apparently approaching my eighteenth birthday – in case Frank Dunbar ever had any serious doubts. I was grown up and comfortable all in an instant, a proper young lady, appropriately dressed, at the wheel of a racing car.

Sandy came up on the train that night. Mummy let *me* collect him from the railway station when he arrived on Tuesday morning.

He looked straight over my head as he tried to hail a taxi.

'*Sandy!*' I cried.

Surprised, my big brother looked down and found me sitting not ten steps away from him at the wheel of our mother's motor car.

'Julie! Great Scott! I didn't see you!'

'I'm not as insignificant as *that*!' I parried.

'I saw the car, but it wasn't Mother driving it, so I thought it couldn't be hers … Does she know you've taken it?'

'She certainly does,' I said with pride. 'She even fibbed to the examiner himself when I got my licence yesterday. For the "Age" box on the form she told him, "Put seventeen – Julia will be seventeen in August".'

Sandy burst out laughing. 'That is not technically untrue.' He bent to kiss me on top of my head. Even up close I don't think he noticed my hair at *all*. He hopped irreverently over the side of the car without opening the door, a habit all my brothers share, and rode balancing his worn leather valise on his knees.

I had hoped it would even up the sides in terms of youth and age to have another of my brothers about the place, but in truth Sandy might as well have stayed in London for all we saw of him after that. He stopped in to sleep (up in the former servant's room in the attic with Jamie), but spent every waking second organising the Murray Hoard at the Inverfearnie Library. He even took his meals there. I couldn't tell if it was the collection itself, or *Mary Kinnaird*, that he was so enchanted by. Possibly both.

I had not yet made peace with her.

On the Wednesday after Sandy arrived, the fourth day of Euan's ditch-digging work, Euan and I passed Mary on her bicycle on the Perth Road as I drove Euan the long way round from Inchfort Field to Strathfearn House. She had her head down, focused on the road ahead of her, and didn't recognise me at the wheel of Mother's car.

I didn't recognise her either; I mean, I didn't *notice*. I wasn't paying attention. But Euan noticed her right away.

'There's the librarian getting her messages.'

'She always does that on a Wednesday morning. She's early today.'

'Aye, we've seen her before. Dad and I passed her on the day we found you. We were in Brig O'Fearn that morning collecting tin.'

'You *were*?' I stared at him instead of ahead of me, thinking hard.

'*The road!*' he cried as the Magnette sashayed a bit.

'Fiddle, that was nothing.' I straightened up.

It was time to visit Mary.

I was fed up with being angry with her. Sulking wasn't mending things for anyone. I needed her help and I was going to get it.

I caught Mary in her study the next morning. Sandy was upstairs beavering away at the Murray Hoard, and Mary's face lit up unguardedly when she saw me, then fell again as she immediately remembered the disaster of our last meeting.

'I'm sorry, Mary,' I said simply.

'Oh, *darling*!' She leaped up from her desk to embrace me with fond arms. 'Julia, I have been meaning to come to see you …'

I saw that because I'd made the first move I was now playing a strong hand. By God, I was going to play it carefully.

'Sit down, sit down.' Mary fluttered. 'I want to know how you're feeling …'

She made me wait in her red leather armchair while she bustled about with tea and shortbread. I felt disloyal, between knowing that Sandy's there *all the time*, and my fury over what Mary did to the McEwens. I *knew* she hadn't many friends. But I wouldn't pretend I wasn't friends with the McEwens as well.

I needn't have worried. She was glowing. She wasn't thinking about the McEwens and she was scarcely aware of the sordid business which the *Perth Mercury* was now calling 'the Strathfearn Suicide'. All she wanted to talk about was Sandy.

'He works so hard, it's a pleasure to be able to help him,' she twittered. 'And he's so respectful of my own work. But the nicest thing for me is that it's lovely to have company after supper. We've been reading to each other in the evenings, Burns's poetry and Dickens – *Our Mutual Friend*. When Dr Housman was here, I always felt I was on my own. Isn't that strange? Yet I'm constantly aware of Sandy upstairs, even though I can't hear him. I so enjoy having him here.'

She poured tea and sat down on the footstool beside me, clasping her hands around her knees. I'd never considered what a world of difference it must be for *Mary* to have swapped Dr Housman for Sandy. I wondered if it had made her uneasy having Hugh Housman coming and going, right there near the rooms where she lived and undressed and slept all by herself.

'What was Dr Housman like?' I asked.

'He was really very patronising, you know, Julia. He was dismissive of my interest in the catalogue and didn't welcome suggestions. He made me feel a bit like a charwoman, there to bring him cups of tea and fresh pencils, rather than a trained librarian. It was the way he avoided looking at me when he spoke to me ...'

'What did you –'

She turned abruptly towards the window, so suddenly it made the gold pencil and the ear trumpet clatter together.

No, I'd better not ask that question yet. I could see she wasn't ready for it.

Of course I knew why people avoided looking at *her*. But I realised suddenly that when she avoided looking at *you* it was like she was sticking her fingers in her ears, making it so that she didn't have to know what you were going to say. Like Mémère, who has a trick of going foreign and feminine in situations requiring mental acumen, which shifts the difficult work on to other people.

I waited for Mary to turn back so she could see me speaking.

'It's good having people about you though,' I said. 'The river watcher isn't here all the time.'

Mary nodded in fervent agreement. 'I don't like the tinkers being here. Every year they make me uncomfortable, me here all alone and them up at Inchfort piping and drinking into the wee hours.'

Ah, *hurrah*, I'd got Mary to bring up the McEwens *herself*.

'You know those Traveller folk at Inchfort Field are part of Strathfearn just as much as my grandfather was,' I said, still being cautious. 'They own the willow beds at the mouth of the Fearn. They've been coming here for *hundreds* of years. Maybe longer than the library's been here. My mother and Jean McEwen used to play together when they were wee.'

Mary looked away again. I reached across to pick up the trumpet and offer it to her so she could listen to me without having to look at me. After a moment she twitched it sharply out of my hand and I thought she was angry, but she held it to her ear and let me continue.

'Mary, the McEwens *love* this place. And Ellen McEwen is a great deal like you. She helped Grandad with the typology he made for his spear tips. You must have seen those drawings – Ellen did them herself! She knows so much about the estate and its past, the land and – and the way the land has its own story. She just didn't get to learn it at university like you did.'

Mary lowered the ear trumpet and turned back to look at me once more. Her smooth face was still expressionless.

'It's true not many young women are as lucky as I was about university,' she said. 'But I shouldn't think tinker folk care for that kind of study.'

I gazed down into my teacup. I held my breath for a moment. I couldn't allow myself to get angry with her again. And truthfully, I didn't like it that the McEwens muttered superstitiously to bless themselves and make Mary feel self-conscious and peculiar.

'You set an example for everybody, Mary,' I said. 'I don't know if *my* folk care for that kind of study either – not for me. But I'm going to go to university. I *love* to read. I don't want to run shooting parties all my life until my husband dies and makes me sell everything. I want to be like you.'

'Oh, Julia.'

Her eyes were brimming. I felt cheap and manipulative, because although I'd meant it – I'd meant it with all my heart! – I had been trying to hit her hard, and I could see that I'd succeeded.

Mary said, 'Julia, mine is a very solitary existence.'

'All the more reason to let some more interesting people into it!' I added warmly, 'You let Sandy in.'

Mary stood up. She went to her desk and fiddled with the inkwell, very deliberately dropping blobs on to her big desk blotting pad.

'It's not been an easy summer for me, Julia,' she said.

And here was the other opening I'd been waiting for.

'All those police interviews! It must be dreadful for you. But they're finished with you now, aren't they?'

'I might have to act as a witness if there's an inquiry,' she said unhappily. 'I was the last to see Dr Housman alive, other than you.'

'What did you tell Inspector Milne about that day?' I asked.

She drew in a sharp breath.

'Oh, Julia, why do you want to know more about that unfortunate incident?'

I answered with a fair amount of honesty: 'I just wish I knew what happened to *me*!'

She sighed. She sipped her tea.

Finally, she said cautiously, 'I saw Dr Housman come in that morning. I ... I went out on my bicycle to shop in

Brig O'Fearn village. The library is closed to the public on Wednesdays but Dr Housman had often been on his own there and I'd left the back door on the latch for him; that's how you got in.'

'He left the back door standing open,' I remembered.

'Yes,' Mary agreed softly. 'Anyone could have got in. There are all sorts of people about.'

'Do you really believe any of the McEwens would come in here when the library was *closed*?' I asked. 'Even if the back door was open? Without me and Jamie to encourage them? Have they ever before?'

She didn't say anything for a bit. At last, being as honest and straightforward as only Mary can be, she admitted, 'No.'

Now to finish my hand.

'Were they about the place?' I asked. 'Did you see them at all that morning?'

She frowned. 'I didn't see them here. But …'

I held my breath. I cocked my head a little, gazing out of the window, feigning nonchalance. I didn't want her to know how much I cared about her answer to this question: how important it was for Euan McEwen that she answered as I hoped she was going to.

'I suppose I did see the McEwen lad that morning. In fact, he wasn't alone … He was with his father. I passed them twice, coming and going, in Brig O'Fearn village. They'd a cartload of scrap tin.'

'You passed them *twice*!' I exclaimed, unable to suppress my excitement. This was more than I'd hoped for.

'Well, they were there the whole morning,' Mary said with a small huff of irritation. 'They were going door to door along the High Street, collecting tin.'

'*Door to door along the High Street!*'

'It's what they *do*, Julia,' Mary said patiently, as if she were instructing a small child. 'Didn't you know?'

If they'd been going door to door through Brig O'Fearn, and Mary had passed them coming and going, they had a whole *village* full of witnesses to prove they hadn't been anywhere near the library or Hugh Housman that morning. Mary had arrived back at Inverfearnie *after* whatever had happened to Hugh Housman – and to me. If Euan and Alan McEwen had been in the village all that time they couldn't possibly have been involved. Even the police would have to agree.

'I do know, Mary,' I agreed rather breathlessly, trying not to give away my elation. 'Oh, I'm *so* glad we've had this talk!'

And I put down my teacup and saucer and got up so I could squeeze her warmly in my arms.

'I *hate* for us to be angry with each other. Please do agree with me that Euan and Ellen McEwen weren't trespassing before,' I said. 'I like them and I'm friends with them. I can make sure Euan won't bother you here, if only you'll let him cross over to Strathfearn by the Inverfearnie footbridge.'

Mary scowled.

'Really, Julia. You are very manipulative.'

I laughed. She didn't have any idea to what extent I'd manipulated her.

'Well, perhaps so, but it's a little thing, Mary!' I confessed. 'A little thing mended. I know you don't want to have to mix with the Travellers, but I'd so like you not to be afraid of them, either. I want *you* to feel at ease.'

'Well.' She sniffed. 'Only for you, my dear. I will try to be brave!'

'You're the bravest person in the world,' I swore.

It was some time after I left her, when I was once again alone along the river on my way back to Strathfearn, that it occurred to me I still didn't know how I'd ended up lying on the path near Inchfort Field where Euan had found me later.

When I got back to Strathfearn and started to cross the lawn up to the Big House, Frank Dunbar was pacing around the edge of the newly tiled swimming pool, sucking furiously at a cigarette and leaving behind him a trail of smoke like a steam engine. He was alone, and I was decently and girlishly attired in my own summery flower-print cotton dress; I couldn't resist a diversion in his direction.

'Hello,' he said quietly.

'Hello! How are you?' I asked.

'As miserable as I know how to be,' he answered honestly, but shrugging. 'Cigarette?'

'Not out in the open, I won't. But thank you.'

He blushed.

'I can never get it right.'

'Frank by name, Frank by nature,' I teased, which coaxed a smile out of him. 'What are you doing?'

'Just a routine inspection. Once the pump room is finished we'll enclose the pool, but I'm afraid the pipeline out to the River Tay will be delayed.'

I didn't ask why.

But I did ask, 'Is there a nightwatchman on the estate?'

'There are several,' he said. 'There have to be, with so many workmen staying in the stable apartments and servants' quarters. There's also a guard in the gate lodge who makes regular rounds, and the Water Bailiff sometimes checks the river path late in the night as well.'

'Does somebody check the doors of the Big House?'

'I expect so,' Frank responded vaguely. He took a drag on the cigarette, with that air of faint distraction which I found so inexplicably attractive. After a moment he added assertively, as if trying to excuse his initial lack of a definite answer, 'Unless I draw up a schedule they don't always coordinate their shifts.' He sighed. 'I've been scolded by the Procurator Fiscal for not having a better grip on the reins of this place.'

He took another pull on his cigarette, then bit his lip, looking away when he finally spoke.

'The doctor who examined Housman wasn't able to determine the cause of his death – his body's quite deteriorated. When we pulled the … pulled him out of the water we should have taken him straight to the mortuary that evening. But we waited till the next morning and apparently this … um, dried him out and … *accelerated* decay. And because of where the poor fellow got cut, without a proper post-mortem the examiner can't actually tell if he drowned or –'

'Good gracious, or *what?*'

'Well, that was what I said,' Frank huffed. 'Or anything else. He might have had a heart attack, or choked on a sweet. Or poisoned himself, if it really was suicide. But it's not obvious that he drowned and the doctor can't issue a death certificate in case the Procurator Fiscal tells him to conduct a post-mortem.'

'How it does drag on so horribly!'

'It does. At first I kept hoping they wouldn't find *any* of him – that he was still alive. Now I keep hoping they'll find *all* of him and lay the poor fellow to rest.' He laughed nervously and dragged at the cigarette again.

'I'm sorry,' he continued. 'What a bloody awful thing to say. His sister's had to come up on the train from somewhere in the Home Counties to identify him, and of course there isn't anything that helps. Apparently she *did* though – told the doctor, "Well, he always did have spindly legs, which is a poor excuse for not being able to swim!" She wouldn't stay in Perth but one night. "Please do send him south so I can bury him." Damned unfeeling woman, if you ask me – though I suppose it's hard on her having to wait for the Procurator Fiscal to make up his mind about an inquiry.'

That Francis Dunbar should feel intimate enough with me to share such obscenities and confidences was almost as intoxicating as sharing a cigarette, and we stood for a moment side by side with our hands not quite touching, both of us gazing down over the birch wood in the direction of the river. The ruined tower of Aberfearn Castle just cleared the treetops, looking ominous against a drab grey sky.

'Hullo, there's your foreman Mr Munro hailing you,' I said.

The engineering manager was stumping up the path at a purposeful pace with a large canvas parcel under his arm. There was a wooden rod awkwardly sticking up out of it over Mr Munro's shoulder, so that he looked almost as if he were carrying a bagpipe, and I stifled a snort of laughter.

Shaness, Julie! God pity you!

Oh heavens, it couldn't be more pieces of Hugh Housman, could it? I decided it couldn't possibly be or Mr Munro would have looked queasier. He didn't look happy though.

Frank Dunbar had gone white as a sheet.

'You've found something?' Dunbar asked shakily. 'Not another damned Bronze Age spear point.'

'Not this time.' Mr Munro nodded at me again. 'Perhaps it's not fit talk for the wee lassie.'

I deemed it best to say nothing. I took a step backward, affecting cool containment (when in reality I was *burning* with curiosity and already planning how to spy on them if they insisted on getting rid of me). I raised one hand in valedictory, as if requesting a dismissal.

'Please don't go,' Frank said to me. And to Mr Munro, 'It's all right. Miss Beaufort-Stuart is very sensible about this business.'

'What is it?' I prompted. 'If it's horrible I don't want to see. But I want to know.'

'We've found the chap's trousers,' said Mr Munro, offering the folded bundle up to Frank.

'Found his *trousers*?' Frank repeated in what sounded like sheer baffled disbelief.

'Aye, all folded tidy doon by the stone river gate to Aberfearn Castle. And his tangs and glass for pearl-fishing. It doesnae look like suicide to me though; it looks like he went for a swim and maybe got into difficulty with the tide. Why would you fold up your clothes like that if you were going to drown yourself?'

'*The bloody idiot!*' Frank burst out incredulously, and he backed away from the pathetic bundle Mr Munro was holding out to him.

I suddenly put my finger on what it was Frank kept refusing to accept: *any of it*. He was completely incapable of getting it into his head that Housman was actually dead. Every piece of proof hit him as though he were hearing the news for the first time.

'Let's see, shall we?' I offered, and took the parcel from the foreman with firm hands. I put the canvas down at our feet and unfurled it carefully.

Beneath the bulky glass-bottomed jug and the pronged stick for pearl fishing, Housman's tweed plus fours were still folded neatly, but after a month of sitting out on the riverbank they looked as though they'd just come out of a very muddy tub-load of washing without being rinsed. I didn't want to touch them. Frank, the moment he clapped eyes on them, swooped down to check the pockets. Mr Munro crouched along with us to get a better view.

Frank gingerly produced ten shillings in change, a sodden box of matches, a chewed-looking fountain pen and a silver card case which he pried open with shaking fingers. It contained no calling cards, but there was a reader's ticket to the British Library with Hugh Housman's name on it, smeared but still perfectly legible.

'The bloody *idiot*,' Frank Dunbar repeated softly. 'The bloody, blithering *idiot*.' He dropped the case back on to the muddy, sodden cloth.

I stood up because I was tired of crouching and I didn't want to get my knees wet with kneeling.

Frank stayed hunched over Housman's abandoned things, shaking his head in outraged disbelief, while the foreman grimaced at the grubby collection.

'Well, there's nae doubt that's your man,' said Mr Munro, and Frank glanced up at him angrily. He didn't say anything, just raised his eyebrows and looked back down.

'No, it doesn't really look like suicide,' he said at last, finally agreeing with Munro's prosaic deduction. 'But …'

He didn't say it, but I knew he was thinking about the letter to Solange. One of these jigsaw pieces really did not fit properly.

I stood with my hands on my hips, gazing down at the disarray we'd made of this potential evidence, considering that Frank was already in trouble over the poor horrid man's body not being treated with any kind of respect either.

'Hadn't we best take better care of this stuff?' I suggested. 'Won't the police want to look at it too?'

That made Frank back away as if he was sorry he'd touched any of it.

'Is this all you found?' I said. 'No shirt, no tie, no shoes, no socks, no jacket?'

'Perhaps the rest of it is with the rest of *him*,' Munro suggested morbidly.

Frank began to wrap the canvas folds closed again, more carefully this time.

I thought that he and Munro were both right: it was a most bizarre and haphazard way to prepare to drown yourself. It rather looked to me as though Dr Housman had been fishing for a peace offering for Solange, in haste and passion. He'd given her pearls before. Maybe what Frank said the other day was right, and Housman had taken his clothes off to keep them dry, planning to put them back on.

The two men were still on their knees by the canvas bundle, but they were both looking up at me. I suddenly felt very vulnerable. What if they asked me to describe the scene for them? After all, it was *me* who'd seen Housman in the nude, but *oh, mercy*, I couldn't imagine telling Mr Munro – still less Frank Dunbar – about *that*. There were limits to my impudence. After all, I was certifiably *intact*.

I *wished* that did not make me feel so dirty every time I thought about it. The reality of having been *examined* was somehow much nastier, in my head, than the assault that didn't happen and which I couldn't really imagine. Almost as if people were trying to blame me for what wasn't done. As if my body were rude and lewd just because it was a girl's body.

At any rate the uncomfortable feeling with Dunbar and Munro was something I couldn't quite put my finger on, but it had to do with being very attracted to one of them and having to hide it while we pawed over the dead man's clothes like the witches in *Macbeth*.

'I should go,' I said. 'I'll tell my mother what you've found.'

'Tell her I'll meet her in my office whenever it's convenient,' Frank Dunbar agreed.

And I fled up the ruined lawn and into the savaged house.

11

HOW A LAD GIVES A KISS WHEN HE MEANS IT

Mémère insisted that we make the trip to her seamstress in Perth together. It was astonishing, and a lesson in dignity, how my grandmother managed to soldier on as though nothing were out of the ordinary in a house full of builders and the poisoned atmosphere of Hugh Housman's 'suicide'. I came away from the excursion to the dressmaker's feeling that every critical thing Ellen McEwen had said about me was true. Even the blue silk I'd wanted for my party frock was too expensive and I was sorry now I'd asked for it.

Mémère and I were both fingering it in rapt admiration when she muttered wistfully to herself, 'I could if I had to' – and I *knew* then that she could not afford it.

Mummy took me aside very delicately and whispered in my ear, '*Let her choose something she can pay for.*'

And I felt rotten.

Mémère picked out a leaf-green chiffon with a gold sheen to it when it caught the light. It really was beautiful, but I was afraid it would make me look like a fairy – I could just imagine Jamie and Sandy teasing, 'Happy birthday, Tinker Bell!'

And then, my goodness, I'd never thought about that name being insulting. But it was. *She is quite a common fairy ... She is called Tinker Bell because she mends the pots and kettles.* How *much* I did take everything for granted, even the storybooks I had thought were so harmless.

Euan could have walked home the next evening, but I liked the excuse to take the car out, and I gave him a ride anyway. Euan laughed at me as I started to guide the Magnette up the drive.

'What?' I demanded.

'I like the way you start the car.'

'How's that?'

'You always look as if you think it's going to fight you. Your eyes go wee and narrow and you hunch your shoulders and lean in as if you're going to give it what for.'

'I do not *hunch*,' I told him with dignity. 'I have to sit right up on the edge of the seat so I can see out.'

I became terribly self-conscious then. Because when I was starting the *car*, I was only thinking about the car. I was not thinking about my hair or ghosts or some stupid dead man's trousers. And *that* was when Euan was watching. What could I possibly look like when I was just being me?

'I'd no' want you to look at me like that,' Euan said.

'I would *never*,' I vowed. 'I say, have the Perthshire and Kinross-shire Constabulary come out to visit you at Inchfort since they made their last find? Because Mother rang them and told them to go door to door through Brig O'Fearn asking folk if they saw you on the morning Dr Housman disappeared. And almost everybody did.'

'Aye! That Inspector Milne, the wee man with the wee beard? He talked to everyone digging on the pipeline this noontime, him and the Water Bailiff.'

'I hope he didn't make another fuss over you in particular.'

'Aye, nae bother. And we're all away the morrow so it's finished. There's new tatties we help with every year out Comrie way and it's time we were out of this mire for a bit. When the inquiry's over we'll maybe come back.'

My heart fell. I hadn't expected them to leave the second they found they were cleared of suspicion.

I could understand getting itchy staying in one place. But I didn't really *understand* the McEwens.

'They found Dr Housman's trousers yesterday,' I told Euan. 'Perhaps there won't be an inquiry.'

'Perhaps pigs might fly,' he said with resignation. Then he offered suddenly: 'Come in about and have a sup of tea with us. If we don't see you for another fortnight Ellen will miss you.'

And I could not resist even if there'd been reason to. I thought that the uncertainty of Ellen in my life must be a bit what it was like for Mémère in the months and weeks leading to Grandad's death. Eventually, you know, you are going to have to go without. But until then …

When we got to Inchfort, Euan hopped out over the side of the car (like my brothers) and opened the gate so I could pull safely into the field next to the wagons and horses and, that evening, also the van belonging to the Camerons, the McEwens' motorised cousins who were going to help whisk them all away to the headwaters of the River Fearn or wherever it was they were going.

It really was only a sup of tea to start with. Ellen was away out with her mother doing one last round of the houses in Brig O'Fearn village selling their willow baskets and heather pot scrubbers and horn spoons, so I waited. Old Auntie Bessie started frying up a mess of skirly (oatmeal and onions together), which honestly smelled so good I started pestering her to show me how to make it, thinking we could easily do it on the portable gas ring in the morning room. The kiddies were shy with me, and Euan slipped away with them to the bottom of the field to organise a game of rounders which I didn't quite dare join in.

When Ellen and Jean McEwen got back they were carrying a great sack of new potatoes between them; Ellen dumped them off and hooked my arm through hers to drag me away up the lane to Boatman's Well, taking with us a few big tin cans for water. Pinkie came prancing at our heels – she would desert Euan in favour of me any day of the week.

'You're away tomorrow,' I accused Ellen. 'And I thought things would be all right here for you now.'

'Och, at it again!' she warned. 'Fixing and managing everything. The world's supposed to stop just where you want it, aye?'

'No, of course not,' I answered in irritation. 'I meant I'd miss you. I'm not being selfish –'

She gave her little snort of scorn.

'Not *only* being selfish, at any rate! I'm trying to say something *nice* to you.'

We reached the well, but Ellen kept on walking.

'Where are you going?'

'The telephone by the Bridge Farm post office. Call your mammy and tell her you're stopping for tea with us. I've pennies for the 'phone – we sold all those baskets.'

We dropped the empty water cans outside, with Pinkie standing guard over them, and jammed ourselves into the old white concrete 'phone box so that Ellen could listen in on what I said and be in charge of making the call. Of all the people who could have picked up, I got Frank Dunbar on the other end, which flustered me. Ellen had her ear pressed against the other side of the receiver, ready to eavesdrop.

'Who's that?' she whispered.

I elbowed her in the ribs to shut her up. And made the error of saying aloud breezily, 'Oh, hello, Frank.'

Ellen leaned back against the glass and concrete frame of the telephone box, smirking, fanning herself mockingly with one hand. She mouthed at me, *FRANK!*

Bloody flipping hell, I thought, and there wasn't anything I could do to take it back that I'd called him such a familiar name, or cover it up.

'Julie?' he said. 'Where are you?'

I tried frantically to beat Ellen away from the receiver and almost instantly gave up because it was too hard to maintain dignity in the tone of my voice while I was engaged in a brawl with Ellen at such close quarters.

'I'm just up the road at the post office,' I said evenly, taking deep breaths. 'I wanted Mother to know I've been invited out to supper –'

Ellen mouthed mockingly, *Invited out to supper – oooooh!*

I paused, *forcing* myself to sound measured and cool. 'Is my brother about? I mean Jamie, not Sandy. I'd like to talk to Jamie.'

'I'll get him, but, Julie, I'm so pleased I've got you on the 'phone. I just spoke to the Procurator Fiscal. He'd like to avoid a fatal accident inquiry in court, and there won't be any further precognition. He told me he doesn't want to know any more about the habits of travelling tinkers when it's clear the unfortunate fellow couldn't swim. He was very short-tempered about it. But he's uncomfortable telling the doctor to issue a death certificate without the rest of the remains, so we're to go on searching for another two weeks and then he'll review the situation.'

Ellen was grimacing hideously at everything he said, and at this point it was necessary to stuff another penny into the telephone, giving a sense of false urgency to my call.

When he came back on the line, Frank added hastily, 'I'll just get your brother.'

Ellen gave me a little space – not much – for the simple task of telling Jamie to let Mother know I was coming home late.

When Ellen heard me insisting that the car was in a safe place she got annoyed with the waste of her pennies and snatched the receiver out of my hand. 'You come too!' she ordered Jamie. 'Then you can be sure *Lady Julia* gets home safely.'

'Tell him to bring me a sweater!' I added.

I heard Jamie's far-off voice say, 'Pardon? Speak up!'

'M'lady wants a wrap.' Ellen spoke through her nose, giving her best impression of landed gentry. 'The mink or the ermine will do –'

'Oh, *stow it*, Ellen McEwen!'

We wrestled again for control of the receiver.

Jamie was laughing down the line on the other end. 'Which sweater?' I heard him ask, and the warning pips clicked on to let us know our last penny was about to run out.

I was beset with a host of afterthoughts. 'Bring coffee! Bring roses for Mrs McEwen! Bring *Sandy*!' I cried just before the line went dead.

A mournful dirge on the pipes came skirling up the lane as we sloshed back towards Inchfort Field, laden with the cans of water from Boatman's Well.

'That's Euan,' Ellen said grimly. 'Let's see if we can change his tune.'

It wasn't a nice evening. The air was close and damp, with low cloud hanging sullenly overhead, as if it wanted to burst and had been told not to. We'd only been back a minute or so before Jamie and Sandy came lurching out of the mist down by the Salmon Stane, Sandy carrying what was obviously a workman's paraffin lamp from the estate in one hand and an armful of red roses in the other. All the kiddies came pelting up for the safety of the tents, and everyone else froze in suspicion because they couldn't tell who it was at first.

Then another thought occurred to me: I suddenly worried it might be awkward to have so many Beaufort-Stuarts from the Big House descending on the McEwens' camp. I tried to swoop in to the rescue.

'My brothers ... Ellen, you know Jamie. This is Sandy.'

'Sandy Beaufort-Stuart,' he introduced himself, distributing his burdens and shaking hands all round. 'Thought you might appreciate this last offering from the Earl of Strathfearn ...' And he produced, from inside his tweed jacket, not only a packet of French coffee but also a dusty bottle of Grandad's favourite single malt, aged well beyond the thirty-six years the label boasted.

Ellen suddenly remembered a thing I'd told her about Sandy. 'That's you, aye?' she said. 'The Earl of Strathfearn.'

Sandy looked surprised, then laughed. 'Why, yes! I suppose it is. But the drink is thanks to the late Earl.'

Sandy went round pouring a dram for anyone who had a cup, chatting amiably.

'Aye, I'm cataloguing the Murray Collection now. I understand there's quite a few fine pieces contributed by yourself, Mr McEwen? No, I don't get a penny to call my own, nor any of the land, but if I'm lucky they'll elect me as a representative peer for Scotland some day, and I'll get a vote in the House of Lords. Imagine being able to shake things up down in London! What new legislation is troubling you at the moment?'

There was a little bit of an uproar as everyone started to offer opinions at once.

Later, laughter, and Sandy drinking with Alan McEwen and the Cameron men, and Aunt Bessie scolding Euan for his mournful piping. The roses, which the McEwens would never be able to take with them when they left, got divided up by the little girls who stuck them in their hair and behind their ears. The skirly got served up along with oatcakes and sweet new boiled potatoes and a great slab of butter that Jamie had liberated from the icebox at the Big House.

In the blue-white gloom of the misty North Sea haar, one of the Camerons joined in with Euan on a fiddle, and there was a woman I didn't recognise playing an accordion, and Sandy and Jamie and Ellen and I ended up in a foursome reel, skipping and skidding over the damp grass.

'See, you didnae need your mink after all,' Ellen said in between tunes as I abandoned my sweater. 'This'll keep you warm.'

And the fiddle and pipes launched into 'Strip the Willow'. It was so damp and misty that you couldn't even see the Salmon Stane at the bottom of the field, but I wasn't chilly at all.

I think my most constant dance partner was Alan McEwen! Gallantly polite and formal, he reminded me of *Grandad*. Euan was stuck on the pipes. I'd have danced with Euan McEwen. I don't suppose he'd have been brave enough to dance with *me*. He hadn't Ellen's bold streak and there were plenty of friends and cousins to fill in the gaps, though not so many of our own age set.

Contrary to whatever those stupid small-minded women in the hospital thought, the McEwens and their folk are all incredibly modest. Skirts down, legs together, blouses done up properly. The older women were watching me closely, I noticed. I was worried the eccentric clothes I had been turning up in all summer might have caused them to peg me as dangerously wanton.

In a moment when we'd stopped for a swallow of lemon-ade and to catch our breath, I said again to Ellen, 'I really am going to miss you. It will be very dull when you are gone.'

She sang to me teasingly from Robert Burns's 'A Red, Red Rose':

'And fare thee well, my only love!
And fare thee well awhile!
And I will come again, my love,
tho' it were ten thousand mile!'

We had a good big fire going by the time it got dark, past ten o'clock still despite the cloud. The music just didn't stop, and we kept on dancing till we were falling over each other (and the excited Pinkie, who thought she knew how to dance), because we really couldn't see any more.

Someone took me by the arm and bent to murmur in my ear. It was Sandy.

'I'm going back to the Big House,' he said. 'I'll stop at the library and let Mary know there's no harm doing here. She doesn't like a ceilidh much, and it's half past eleven. Jamie said he'd like to stay a while later. But if you want to go now –'

'I don't want to go *ever*.'

Afterwards I asked Jamie if he noticed anything between Mary and Sandy, and he told me not to be ridiculous.

'What's ridiculous about it?'

'Sandy doesn't notice women.'

I felt my eyebrows leap up into what was left of my hair.

Jamie laughed. 'I mean, he doesn't notice *anybody*. He's thirty years old and I don't believe he's cast a glance of appreciation at anything under five hundred years of age since he left school. He's celibate as a monk. Probably more so.'

It was true; Sandy hadn't even seen *me* when I picked him up at the station.

And yet … part of me thinks maybe that is why he hadn't noticed what Mary looks like, and why they can get along so well – the way he gets along with the McEwens and their folk – because he just doesn't *see* people.

In the end, Jamie and I didn't go back to the Big House at all that night.

We stretched the cover over the car in case it rained, and then Jamie and Euan and Ellen and I all sallied back up the lane through the dark and the haar to the post office telephone box. The silly thing was, it was nearly as far as it would have been to walk back to Strathfearn House – but this way we didn't have to negotiate the river path, or worse, the swinging iron footbridge in the dark. You know what I mostly didn't want to have to do – pass close by those flipping standing stones! I seemed to be more afraid of ghosts during the last summer at Strathfearn than I usually was.

Mother was remarkably level-headed on the 'phone.

'Jamie and I are going to stop at Inchfort overnight,' I told her.

'Thank you for ringing, Julia. Your grandmother was worried about you driving all that way around so late at night.'

'Oh dear, she's not still awake?'

'Very much so, but she has used it as an excuse to listen to the whole of *Lucia di Lammermoor* on the wireless and it's not yet finished. Sandy warned us you might stay. Try to be polite – it's most kind of Jean McEwen.'

243

'Och, nae bother,' said Mrs McEwen, sounding like Euan, when I passed on Mother's gratitude. 'Your mammy Esmé was always in about the camps here when she was a girl. Just like her dad.'

You see … you *do* lose track of people. Because the McEwens were here every summer since our mothers were children, and so were we, but our mothers played together and we did not. Somehow Jean and Esmé went their separate ways and their paths swung so far apart that their grown children only just learned each other's names. How long does it take? How do you ever hold on to anybody?

'Where's your gran going to live when you've packed up at the Big House?' Ellen asked me as we made up the extra beds.

'Well, with us, of course. She's coming to Craig Castle. I won't be there though; I have to go back to school.'

'Will you go back there when you finish school?'

'I think I'll go to Oxford It'll be like an extension of school. I like it.'

'I thought only men went to university.'

'Lots of women go. Mary went! You could go!'

'Why would I want to?'

'You could study archaeology.'

'Huh.' She sounded sceptical. 'Would *your* folk let *you* do that?'

'I keep *telling* them I'm going to university. Two of my brothers have already gone and no one ever objects when I say I'm going too. Sometimes you just have to do what you want, even if they say no.'

She laughed. 'There you go again, taking the reins of the world.'

'Isn't it just taking the reins of *myself*?'

The bow tent was set up so that there was a bit of living space in the middle and a sleeping space at either end. Ellen and I and some of the younger cousins were at one end and the older McEwens were in the other end with the baby. The lads went out to a different tent. There wasn't quite enough bedding with me and Jamie unexpectedly there as well; I had to share with Ellen, and Jamie had to make do with a ground sheet.

Auntie Bessie and the woman with the accordion were still cracking away by the fire out front as I crawled into the cosiest, most wonderful camp nest I'd ever imagined, on a mattress stuffed with straw and heather and well protected from the wet ground by troughs dug round the edges of the canvas for drainage.

I really was tired, but my mind wouldn't turn off. I was so delighted by the snugness of the camp.

'Is this where I stayed when you brought me here after I got that dunt on the head?' I asked, staring up into the dark, aware of Ellen warm and wide awake on one side of me, and her three little cousins already snoring gently on the mattress made up next to us.

'Well, a bit. We've been and gone to Blairgowrie since then, so the camp's come down and been put back up on other greens since. And we were further across the field before, but it's muddy there now.'

After another time of quiet, listening to the little girls' trio of purring snores and sleeping sighs, I decided I was the only one still awake in our end of the tent, so I jumped when Ellen whispered suddenly at my ear, '*I like your brother.*'

'Which one?' I whispered back – to provoke her, as I knew perfectly well which one she meant.

She gave her characteristic snort. 'The one who's not old enough to be me dad! Young Jamie. He talks to me like … like I'm one of his mates. I never met a lad who does that.'

'They all do that. All my brothers do, I mean. I'm the only girl they've ever had to talk to, and the youngest, so they just treat me like another one of them.'

'You're lucky.'

I considered.

'I suppose I am. But it's like being raised by wolves – you don't realise you're not one yourself until someone points it out to you. Sometimes it makes me so mad that not every-one treats me just like another wolf.'

'Those lassies did, up on Pitbroomie Hill.'

'When you said, "I like your brother", just then, you sounded exactly like those lassies. I thought you meant you wanted Jamie to kiss you.'

She laughed softly. 'I wouldnae mind.'

We lay very quietly for a minute or two, listening to everybody around us being quiet. Then Ellen pulled the covers up over our heads so we were in a little cocoon of privacy. She lay very still. I was just about to free my own nose to avoid suffocating when she whispered in my ear, so softly it was hardly more than her lips moving and carefully shaping words, as though she were talking to Mary Kinnaird – as if she'd do that!

'*What was it like?*'

'What was what like?'

All I could hear of her answer was a click and a hiss.

'I can't hear you,' I whispered back. 'What?'

'On Pitbroomie Hill. *That kiss.*'

'Oh that.'

I put one finger against her lower jaw and tilted her head towards me. And then I pressed my lips against hers, just softly, and kissed.

'Like that.'

She snickered silently, the ghost of her scornful snort. Then she cranked her whisper up a notch, so I could hear her.

'You never. That's all? And you fooled her, just with that?'

'Why not?'

'That's not how a lad gives a kiss. Not when he means it.'

I am not entirely sure what possessed me, and that is the honest truth. It was part – yes, it was – curiosity, but partly anger at her *constantly* being so patronising, and also I wanted to call her bluff, to throw her challenge back at her. But … well, and it was excitement. I wanted to *know*.

'Go on then,' I said. 'Since you know so much about it.'

'*Hush*,' she warned.

'*Go on*.'

Just as I'd done, she used the tip of her own index finger to turn my face back towards hers. Just delicately. And then she suddenly closed her mouth over mine, and –

And there was strength in it, and hunger, and control, and it was like standing on the edge of a cliff in a gale, frightening but also marvellous.

Ellen backed off. She lay silent, waiting for my reaction.

I whispered at last, 'Golly.'

She gave her derisive snort.

'Do you like it, when a lad does that?' I asked.

'Depends on the lad,' she whispered. 'It definitely depends on the lad.'

I tried to imagine who I'd like to kiss me like that. My Swiss ski instructor seemed very amateurish all of a sudden. I wondered, feeling the blood rising to my cheeks, what Frank Dunbar thought of me for the prudish little kiss I'd given him last month. I tried to push him out of my head but I couldn't.

Yes, I could imagine Frank Dunbar kissing me like that.

I wasn't sure I'd *like* it. But I couldn't stop myself *imagining* it. I'd have to try it to find out whether I liked it or not.

I shivered.

I could feel Ellen laughing even though I couldn't hear her.

'Scared?' she whispered.

'Not of you,' I answered.

And then, to prove it, I kissed her back.

When I absolutely had to come up for air or pass out I stopped.

We lay breathless and shaking with suppressed and nervous laughter, both of us suddenly quite overcome with hilarity.

'You said you've never!' she hissed.

'I haven't!'

'Then how –'

'You showed me!'

'Copycat.'

We both shook with mirth again.

At which point we'd become careless about the noise we were making, and Ellen's mother suddenly told us from across the darkness, soft and sharp, 'Whisht, Nellie, hush up and go to sleep. You are keeping Lady Julia awake.'

'Lady Julia is keeping me awake,' Ellen complained loudly, and I thought I would *die* trying to smother myself and not burst out laughing.

She grabbed my hand and squeezed it.

And that was enough to shut me up, can you believe it? Being her conspirator like that – lying together in the dark, holding hands, not needing to talk, not needing to do anything else. Just *knowing*.

Nothing else happened. But we were still holding hands when I fell asleep.

12

ENOUGH TO PAY FOR A 'PHONE CALL

I was awake and restless less than five hours later, and Ellen chivvied me out into an exquisite pearly dawn of gleaming sun-tipped haar mist, grey at the foot of the field and rising to luminous pink overhead. It was burning off fast but still piled like cotton wool in the riverbeds. Jamie and Euan were already awake, and everyone else was stirring too, packing up to move on.

Jean McEwen was red in the face. She and Alan weren't arguing, but holding a heated discussion in undertones; she angry, he trying to calm her down.

'I thought the police were *finished* with us!' I heard her say. 'Old clothes strewn halfway down the field – they've no business searching our things without asking! And to do it while we're asleep – what cheek!'

'It might not be the hornies. Maybe one of those scaldy workers from the Big House. Maybe just a fox –'

'A fox looking for rags! Aye, that's likely.'

I'd been nonchalantly folding blankets but Alan McEwen saw me, all ears, and switched into cant.

Mrs McEwen shook her head. 'They're no' Nawkens, but the Strathfearn lad and lassie ken what you're saying.'

'Take the horses down to drink,' Alan McEwen ordered us. Or ordered his children, at any rate, knowing that Jamie and I would follow along.

Ellen and Euan shrugged off the mysterious night-time searching of the rag collection with the same stoic sufferance I'd seen in them so many times before when they met with injustice: in the hospital, in the confrontations with Sergeant Angus Henderson and with Florrie, in being denied high school exams. I tried to imagine Ellen's lifetime spent enduring such an endless string of insult and violation. You'd have to have such certainty in your own self. You'd have to be *so strong*.

'Are you stopping for breakfast?' Ellen said as we negotiated the narrow path, leading the horses and ponies down to drink. 'Or do you get poached kippers on silver platters up at the Big House?'

'Only ever bread and jam,' Jamie answered. 'The old women are all French.'

'And we don't use the kitchen,' I added. 'We make coffee on a portable gas ring in our gran's sitting room.'

'Your coffee's better than ours.'

'Also because of us being French,' I let her know. Suddenly, impossibly, I was happy – instantly, blithely, fleetingly happy. Happy for the wonderful ceilidh, for the strange and beautiful morning, for the Procurator Fiscal's crabbit dismissal of the police inspector's precognition, for Mary's unexpected defence of Euan.

'So you'll stay here and drink it with us?' Ellen said. 'You'll take anything, won't you! Pennies for the telephone. Your own gifts given.'

I shot her a look, but if she'd intended a double entendre she didn't show any sign of it. Yet she'd managed to turn her own breakfast invitation into a challenge. *Everything* she said to me was a challenge.

We stood in the chill mist at the water's edge down by the little beach where I'd been hit on the head over a month ago. The Drookit Stane was a ghostly grey shape in the middle of the burn; it seemed to shift as the mist thinned around it, as if it were hopping from foot to foot to keep warm. You could see where the story about the stones walking to meet each other came from.

I said, 'You can get a penny for a jam jar, aye?' I started to take off my shoes.

Euan knew right away what I was up to. 'You wee galoot. You're no' diving for rubbish.'

'Your dad said there was all kinds of scrap in the burn

here. I want to pay you back for the telephone.'

'Let her fish about,' Ellen said. 'It'll be a better show than a day at the pictures.'

But her natural prudishness took over when I started to unbutton my dress in front of our brothers. '*Shaness!* You wee midden! Stop that!'

Euan dodged behind one of the horses so he didn't have to look. They were both honestly and genuinely shocked.

Jamie intervened. 'You crazy little idiot,' he scolded. 'Keep your clothes on. I'll fetch your jam jars.'

I think he just likes an excuse to go swimming.

He took off his shoes and stripped efficiently down to his underwear – why is it all right for *boys*, but not for *girls*, to do this? He waded out into the stream, and I thought how many times we'd all been paddling just at this place in summers gone by. The mist made it magical. You still couldn't see much of the opposite bank, but it was clearing around the Drookit Stane now.

'I could do with one of those glass-bottomed pearl fisher's jugs,' Jamie complained over his shoulder. He was over his knees in the water already. 'I can't see anything but rocks. Wait a minute …'

The burn got deeper around the Drookit Stane, and with one false step and a splash Jamie was suddenly up to his waist.

'Oomph! COLD!' he cried. 'All right, I see now how Housman might …'

He trailed off.

'God pity us,' Euan whispered superstitiously, because we all guessed what Jamie had been going to say and hadn't said.

'*Do you see any jam jars?*' I reminded him determinedly.

'There are mussels.' Jamie stood balancing himself with one hand against the Drookit Stane, bent a little at the waist and peering into the swirling clear brown water.

Wraiths of mist crept around him. I shivered, and Ellen hooked her elbow through mine.

Euan said, 'Come out the burn.'

'I didn't know these were here!' Jamie said. 'Rows and rows of them around the base of the stone! They're as big as bricks!'

'Aye, Daddy won't touch them. Stone-grown, he calls 'em. Leave them be.'

'Actually there is a jar! It's wedged in a sort of nook, right at the foot of the stone.'

Jamie suddenly plunged into the burn, like the heron spearing a fish, and came up a few seconds later spluttering and triumphant, holding aloft a large stoneware Keiller marmalade pot. The lid was sealed with an elastic band around cotton wool gone green with algae.

My mouth dropped open.

It was my jam jar. It was the one I'd drawn so idly, a month ago, alongside Housman's broken glasses. It was the jam jar whose lid I couldn't get right.

I felt quite detached from myself, watching as Jamie came sloshing back to the bank. He held the prize out to me.

I just stared. For a moment I couldn't make myself touch it.

And then I was angry, furious to think I'd *never* know what had happened to me that day, and the anger swept over me like the heat of a bonfire. It made me able to move and act and rise to the outrageous challenge of taking that dripping mysterious thing between my hands without them shaking.

I said through clenched teeth, 'This had better be worth a penny.'

'It wasn't you who had to get all wet for it,' Jamie remarked.

He sloshed back into the water, his hands on his hips, peering about in case there were more.

Euan still hid between the drinking animals, holding their lead ropes, one hand resting on a pony's back. Pinkie was sniffing about after foxes or badgers along the overgrown path. All of Ellen's attention was on me and the jam jar.

She said, 'Och, that's a big one. That's worth twopence.'

I was like Pandora. I was mesmerised by the sealed Keiller jar in my hands, and the terrifying but irresistible compulsion to unseal it and find out what was inside.

I crossed the tiny beach to the flat rock where I'd fallen asleep guddling for trout the day I was hurt. I sat down on the rock, gripping the jar between my knees, and picked the elastic band away from the lid. The disgustingly perished slime of cotton wool came away with the elastic. I lifted the lid. There was another damp layer of cotton lining the top of the jar. I peeled it back.

'*Oh.*'

The horses were forgotten. In a moment Ellen was sitting tight against me, and Euan was crowding over my shoulder. Jamie came splashing up out of the water to see.

'Hold Pinkie. Hold her back,' Ellen commanded, and Jamie knelt on the bank with his arms full of fox-scented golden fluff so Pinkie couldn't get in our way.

The jar was full of pearls.

257

'Oh,' Euan breathed close to my ear, echoing me. 'Oh, the beauties.'

Ellen said, 'Jamie, give us your shirt.'

He tossed it to her in a ball. She spread the pale blue cotton over the flat rock, and I tipped the jar carefully out on to the soft cloth.

The pearls made a sound like rain falling in the river, pattering against one another as they slipped into the pale light of the damp morning.

They were grey and pink and salmon and buttery cream. A very few of them were as white as white, like Christmas cake icing. The biggest ones were a sort of dusty silky grey and exactly the same; there were three dozen of those at least.

Ellen picked one up and rubbed it against her nose, then held it out on her palm. Polished that little bit, just from the natural softness of her skin, the grey pearl seemed to take on a rosy sheen. It glowed like a little planet in Ellen's open hand.

'No one's sold them,' she said quietly. 'Here they are.'

'I *said* there were pearls in the Murray Hoard,' I cried in triumph. 'I *said* there were pearls in the Reliquary!'

'These need loving.' Ellen was fierce. 'Oil and cotton wool and rubbing. What a thing to do with pearls four hundred years old – chuck them back in the burn like that, all mashed together against that dirty crockery!'

Ellen and Euan were like a couple of jewellers. Unlike me and Jamie, they knew exactly what they were looking at. It made me feel ignorant to listen to them.

'These are from the upper River Fearn. Right up at the foot of the Trossachs. I ken Daddy showed me the like in MacGregor's last year, this same fawn yellow. But did you ever see any such a size!'

'And these Tay pearls, so close to white! And the big grey ones, all matched – how old can they be? There's never so many this big. It would take years to match this many.'

'It would take a lifetime.'

They touched the pearls lovingly without picking them up, rolling them against the blue cloth of Jamie's shirt beneath gentle fingertips, turning them over to see their whole shapes. Many of the pearls had tiny imperfections: a funny little bump on one end, a peculiar shape, uneven hues. But they were each individually *beautiful*. And there were *so many of them*.

It was like finding pirate treasure.

Of course after our first initial wonder and delight, it occurred to us that this was *actually treasure*.

'How much do you reckon they're worth?' Jamie asked shrewdly.

Euan shrugged and faltered, 'I dinnae ken. I truly dinnae ken. I've never seen so many.'

Ellen said, 'It's like trying to count the stars.'

'Oh come now, there's only a couple hundred,' said Jamie. 'Say five pounds apiece?'

'You cannae say that,' Euan answered. 'Because –'

Ellen held up one of the big grey ones, the size of a healthy pea. 'See the hole through it? Some of these are sets. Likely off a necklace, or more than one. It makes them more valuable.'

She gave the grey pearl to me to look at.

'Thousands,' she said. 'Thousands of pounds.'

'How in blazes did they get in that jam jar in the middle of the Fearn?' Jamie exclaimed.

I thought the answer to that was most obvious.

'Hugh Housman put them there.'

'Oh now, *Julie* –!'

'I saw him do it,' I said.

I didn't remember seeing him do it. But it was like a jigsaw in my head, and now I had all the pieces: Hugh Housman bending over in the middle of the river, the light off his glasses reflecting in the water, the jar I'd sketched, the missing pearls from Grandad's cup, the last forgotten pearl hiding unnoticed in the empty envelope. Grandad must have shifted them out of the cup and perhaps into the envelope, probably just because it was convenient – nothing to do with the original letter it had held. Then he'd added a hundred others from somewhere else – maybe some he'd found himself – and they'd gone unremembered, unnumbered, without any recorded value, until Hugh Housman found them among the intellectually valuable antiquities of the Murray Hoard.

And Hugh Housman had taken them, unnoticed, and hidden them. Presumably he'd meant to come back for them, maybe at the end of the summer when his work was finished and the Murray Collection was long gone. Then he could have gone away and sold the pearls without anyone knowing where they'd come from.

Only he'd never be able to come back for them now.

Those are pearls that were his eyes …

Euan suddenly snatched his hand back as though the pearls beneath his fingertips had burned him. He and I had the same thought at the exact same moment: dead man's hidden treasure, and stolen too. It was stained.

'Put them all back,' said Euan.

'Dinnae be daft,' said his sister.

'I'll not touch them.'

'They need loving,' Ellen repeated. 'They're … they're like the spearheads. Someone cared about them. They need proper looking after.'

'Who's going to *buy* them?'

Ellen leaned back, sitting up on her heels. 'Well, nae doubt MacGregor's in Perth would, for a start. Who's going to sell them though? There's a question.'

We'd all backed off a little.

'I suppose they ought to go to the police,' Jamie said dubiously. He'd tentatively let go of Pinkie, who was sitting with pricked-up ears and watching with interest, completely baffled by our excitement over something that smelled not interesting in the least.

'Are you going to take 'em in?' I asked scornfully. 'I'm not.'

Because truly … Why did the flipping *police* need to know? The pearls were unremarked in the Murray Estate by everyone but me.

'And they're *ours*,' I said fiercely. 'They're *all of ours*. The McEwens used them to buy the Strathfearn willow beds from the Murrays.'

There was a little awkward silence. Of course they weren't *ours*.

'I expect they're part of the Murray Estate along with everything else that's having to be sold to clear the debt,' Jamie said, puzzling over what to do with them. 'If we took them to Mémère she'd have to turn them over for auction –'

I said hotly, 'Bother the Murray Estate. They belong *here*. Like Mary Queen of Scots' bracelet. Let's hide them again.

I mean, not put them back in the burn, but let's hide them like *proper* treasure. In Aberfearn Castle –'

'*Up the Laird's chimney,*' said Euan.

'The tower room at the top!' Jamie agreed.

'In one of the dove holes,' I finished triumphantly.

Ellen said, 'I want to polish them first.'

We were … My goodness, it was like being *enchanted*. We were bewitched.

'Come on, Euan, if we take the horses back up we can get the baby oil and come back quick. Dinnae go anywhere, Julie!' Ellen jumped to her feet and whistled to the dog.

Pinkie sat giving her mistress a very silly grin. As long as I was sitting on the rock by the burn Pinkie wasn't leaving except by force.

'Oh, all *reet*, I'm coming back in a wee minute anyway.'

Euan was already away up the path to Inchfort with the horses. Ellen followed with the ponies, and Jamie and I waited.

After a moment I couldn't resist playing a little with the pearls – beautiful miniature marbles – running my fingers over their silky surfaces.

'That must have looked like the perfect crime to him,' Jamie said softly, coming to join me on the rock.

'He couldn't have sold them all at MacGregor's. Can you imagine going in there with this lot? They'd want to know where they came from. They would have suspected something. I'll bet the pearls Housman gave to Nanny were from here. He never found them himself. But I'll bet he had those earrings set at MacGregor's to see what they were worth.'

'Clever,' said Jamie. 'And careful too.'

I exclaimed suddenly, 'What was that he said in his letter to Solange – all that guff about how he couldn't give her any answers, no *measure of his worth*, only his *promise*? I'll bet that wasn't a suicide note at *all*! He was asking Solange to run away with him!'

Jamie's mouth fell open.

'All that *rot* about returning to the river! He wasn't exactly lying – he had to code it, in case she didn't come with him and she showed it to Mother, or in case someone else found it. He didn't want to tell her how he was going to get rich, but he wanted her to come along when he did! Only, if she didn't, it wasn't going to stop him – that's what he meant about the river's gifts being more eternal than flesh.'

Jamie stared at me as if he'd never seen me before.

'*I think you're right.*' He sounded as if he absolutely couldn't believe I'd worked it out, but knew it made sense. 'No wonder he was rude about Mémère managing the estate badly,' he breathed. 'Imagine everyone but him overlooking something so valuable!'

'Well, *I* didn't,' I huffed. 'I kept saying the pearls were missing.'

Jamie swore. 'Poor Mémère.'

'And, oh, poor *Nanny*.'

'Let's not tell her.'

It wasn't long before the McEwens came back. The four of us sat in the steaming mist and polished and counted three hundred and twenty-seven pearls before we put them back in the jar, packed in clean cotton wadding.

Then we all went up to Inchfort Field one last time, and Euan and Ellen went off away west with everybody else, waving wildly back at us till we couldn't see them any more, and then I drove Jamie over to the Big House in Mother's car. We hid our recovered stolen goods under my bed until we had a chance to take them to Aberfearn Castle.

I was tempted to fill the little wooden cup with the pearls again, but it would have been too dramatic. And also – there were too many. Where did they all come from? But Mémère had never missed them, and for all the thousands of pounds they might have been worth, they would not bring Grandad back nor stop the inevitable conversion of Strathfearn House to the Glenfearn School. Nothing in the Murray Estate belonged to us any more. What would Sandy have done with them if he'd found them? Labelled the jar with a number and noted it in the catalogue?

And they'd just have gone off to Sotheby's in London to be auctioned with the rest of the Murray Hoard.

Suddenly I felt rather sympathetic towards poor old Hugh Housman. He knew what he'd found. I might have tried to run off with those pearls too, if I'd been him.

WHAT HAPPENED
24TH JULY–17TH AUGUST 1938

13

SEVERAL THINGS I CAN'T HAVE

I missed the McEwens tremendously.

All that weekend the lifeboats hunted for Hugh Housman up and down the Tay, although apparently the authorities didn't think he'd have moved much from where the original bits of him were found. Even the fact that his lower half was so far downstream from where I saw him (and so were his clothes) suggested that he'd wandered down there, alive, before he drowned.

It was amazing, and not very nice, either, how much the disappearance of Hugh Housman taught us about the science of drowning. I felt like we were all holding our breath, hoping and dreading some more of him would turn up.

Hugh Housman was not in the pipeline trench. They checked and checked. They must have accidentally dug him out and tossed him aside when they were dredging. Frank Dunbar was finally given permission to lay the pipes and get on with it. The tennis courts were shaping up too; the whole estate was beginning to look properly academic.

It was possible Hugh Housman's upper half was part of the new tennis courts now.

The night after the McEwens left we had another midnight visitor – Pinkie.

The silly, wonderful creature. She abandoned Ellen and even Euan in favour of *me*. I was convinced she was very protective, and had it in her doggy head that I was naturally fragile. Indeed, I believed Pinkie was a reliable witness to whatever really had happened to me – if only she could speak. I'd called her faithless, but I thought now that was very unjust. She was *relentlessly* loyal. Only she wanted to be with the person she felt had the greatest need at any given moment.

Here's how she announced her arrival at Strathfearn House: rattling the door handles of the morning room at two thirty in the morning, *just* below my window, nearly frightening me out of my skin once again. I was the only person to awaken at first, and reminded myself sternly: *Frank sends someone round to check the doors*. But then Pinkie started howling and woke up everyone else. So of course we had to let her in.

Jamie and I took her with us on the Sunday to smuggle our stolen pearls into Aberfearn Castle.

We'd both been clever enough to wear trousers and leather shoes. The path that leads through the gate arch in the curtain wall was overgrown with nettles and bramble all in flower. Grandad's groundsmen used to keep it mowed – I remembered coming here on a very elegant picnic with Mémère, which we ate on tartan blankets on the bare stone floor of the tiny sixteenth-century stone summer house overlooking the River Fearn. In my childhood memory we crossed a wide green swathe of lawn, so truly velvet that I pulled off my sandals and ran barefoot on it; I could feel the cool, worn stone of the summer house steps beneath my feet when I thought about it.

But now Jamie and I had to trailblaze our way through a thicket that felt like the Briar Wood surrounding Sleeping Beauty's castle, except that all around us you could hear the roar of engines and the thump of diggers.

'Dunbar says they're going to fence this off from the school grounds,' Jamie said. 'If they can't keep the boys out of the castle they'll have to pull it down.'

'I hate the *ruin* of things,' I mourned. 'I like that they're *fixing* things, making the house *useful*. I can see the good in it. But why the castle has to be fenced off and Inchfort Field made private … I just hate it.'

'You sound like Ellen. She should run for Parliament.'

'That's even less likely than Sandy being elected to the House of Lords.'

'Don't,' Jamie said. 'You'll just end up cross.'

Nettles didn't seem to bother Pinkie. She bounded ahead of us up a narrow trench through the undergrowth.

'See, someone's used this path this summer,' Jamie said.

'But it's all springing back,' I pointed out. 'None of it's newly trodden. They probably came to take a look at it when they started dredging the pipeline for the swimming bath.'

'You can get in through the eastern wall too though, through the river gate. They'll have to block that off as well if they want to keep the boys out.'

'Wouldn't it be nice to have just one last summer picnic with Mémère here?' I said wistfully. 'But she's too frail to march through these weeds.'

'She could if she had to,' Jamie said, and we both laughed.

The stout medieval wooden door that I remembered was gone. It was doubly weird to think that this forlorn place was no older than our own solid and beloved Craig Castle in Aberdeenshire. The wreck of Aberfearn Castle seemed to belong to another geological age.

We left Pinkie sniffing about in the kitchen cellars and tiptoed up the grand stone spiral stair to the Great Hall. The place required silence. It was so ... so grey and still within and so green without.

The floor of the Great Hall was covered with bat and pigeon droppings and moss, but still mostly solid. We negotiated the gaps and made it across to the Earl's Chamber, without needing to speak to each other about where we'd go next, and I followed Jamie up the chimney. I could still do it. It was even *easier* than it was when I was little: all the handholds and footholds were there, but now I was taller and could use my body to brace myself between the chimney walls in places where I used to have to hold my own weight with just my fingers and toes. Jamie had more trouble than me, bumping about like a bear in a heffalump trap, but I tried not to be smug about it because he was carrying the pearls in their big stoneware jar in a leather cartridge bag over his shoulder.

We emerged through the collapsed chimney wall into the wonderful little attic dovecote under the roof where the wood pigeons still roosted. *They* had not noticed that the place was in ruins. Only me and my brothers and Ellen and hers, and possibly our mothers when they were children, had been up here in the past two hundred years. The pigeons all went rushing out in a panic of disturbed wings as we crawled out on to the solid (and rather mucky) floor.

'You could hide something here forever and no one would know,' Jamie said.

'Till the floor falls down, and then you'd never get it back.'

'*Let it fall,*' he said fiercely, and I knew he felt exactly the same way about it as I did.

Jamie climbed up on the window sill so he could reach the lowest of the nesting holes of the dovecote, and we stowed the jar of pearls deep inside. Then he jumped down and we stayed a moment looking out over our lost demesne, field and river and wood and sky, through the mullioned window of what used to be a chamber below the dovecote. The floor between these rooms was gone so it was high and narrow, a bit like a chimney itself, lit by the windows at our level and the round holes in the wall above for the pigeons to use as doors. The endless hum of building works seemed distant, like the hum of grasshoppers. They were working even on Sunday to make up their lost time.

We could hear Pinkie barking her head off somewhere far below us, so we climbed back down.

She was gambolling in the kitchen and cellars, scrambling from room to room and carrying on like a demented thing.

'What's got into you, you ridiculous dog?'

She leaped to greet me, but turned immediately and galloped into the kitchen. That was the biggest of the below-ground rooms, with barrel-vaulted windows and a fireplace the size of the ladies' waiting room at Brig O'Fearn railway station, with a baking oven built into it. Pinkie bolted straight to one of the corners of the fireplace and, after a bit of excited snuffling, came back to us producing a jute sack whose contents she had clearly been worrying for some time.

As far as we could tell from the remains, she'd eaten a Thing entirely wrapped in brown paper, possibly a loaf of bread, and another Thing that had been very greasy. Neither I nor Jamie wanted to get near enough to try to discover whether the latter had been of a Meat or Dairy nature. The bag clunked when Pinkie dragged it about the stone floor, and when we managed, gingerly, to get it away from her and dump it out, we found that the last Thing inside it was another Keiller marmalade jar – a small one. It rolled across the floor as it fell out of the jute sack, and Jamie and I jumped back as if it were a firework about to go off in our faces.

Jamie prodded it with his toe.

'Bloody coward,' I said.

'Language!'

I grabbed the jar and uncapped it in one defiant move-ment. It was half full of marmalade. We both burst out laughing.

'Someone's been camping,' Jamie said.

In the darkest, innermost corner of the bread oven, which is a nice big flat ledge raised a good four feet above the damp stone floor, we found a bucket from the building site partly filled with water, a carefully folded mackintosh and a car rug. It would be a *hard* place to sleep, but safe and dry. Not so safe as the secret room in the attic, of course.

'Maybe they're still here,' I said. 'There's no mould in the marmalade.'

'Maybe it's one of the workers from the school renovation. Anyone down from Highland Perthshire wouldn't be able to go home easily. It's never one of the McEwens' folk – they'd make themselves more comfortable than this.'

'But the Glenfearn School provides lodging,' I pointed out. 'There are lots of people staying on the estate.'

'They take it out of your pay though.'

We put the mac and rug back. The plundered jute sack was harder to replace.

'Gluttonous dog,' Jamie remarked. 'D'you think we should restock the cold provisions?'

'*No*,' I said forcefully, feeling mean. 'I think this chap's been nicking sandwiches and cigarettes from the other workmen all summer, and they've been blaming it on Euan.'

In the end good breeding overcame suspicion, and Jamie left a half-full packet of Craven "A" cigarettes and a matchbox on top of the depleted sack as an apology.

We didn't once, either of us, mention aloud the pearls we'd just hidden. It was hard not to imagine that the owner of this little stash might be listening somewhere nearby, and it was irritating to discover that Aberfearn Castle wasn't quite as abandoned as it ought to have been. But we both felt certain no one was going to climb up the chimney among the doves looking for pearls.

'Come on, let's leave by the river gate,' said Jamie. 'I want to see if that path's been used recently.'

It had. It had been used a lot more than the main path.

'Well, there are a lot of people working on the pipeline,' said Jamie.

This was the first time I'd been down to the end of the path all summer, and the mouth of the River Fearn where it meets the Tay was a busy hive of frantic activity.

Out in the Tay a Royal National Lifeboat was doggedly dragging for the rest of Hugh Housman. Along the pipeline trench they'd got hoardings and pumps working to keep the water out while they laid the pipes. The generators billowed clouds of coal smoke and made the most deafening racket I've ever heard; the men in the trenches nearest the noise were communicating with hand gestures, like mill girls. Pinkie sat down on the river path suddenly and refused to budge.

'Oh, lord. This *daft dog*,' I yelled. 'Jamie, help me move her on.'

He was staring in the same direction as Pinkie, but with intelligence and comprehension that Pinkie has not got.

'What is it?'

Jamie narrowed his eyes like a rat's – Mother's intolerance-for-stupidity glare that we have all inherited. He stalked forward a few paces, then stopped and spun on his heels to face me. He yelled, 'It's the log boat.'

'What?'

He grabbed me by my arm and pulled me forward, pointing. '*The bloody idiots!*' he gasped through clenched teeth. 'They dug up the log boat!'

'Grandad's boat? The Bronze Age boat Sandy wrote about?'

'Yes, that one, the one he got birched for poking about when he was a lad –'

'– and Grandad left it buried in the peat so he wouldn't damage it!'

'Because it's THREE THOUSAND YEARS OLD! Yes, *THAT* LOG BOAT,' Jamie cried.

It had been destroyed.

They'd chopped it out of the riverbank in pieces. They must have had no idea what it was – just an old wooden boat in the way of their work. Maybe they didn't even realise it was a boat; Sandy wrote that it had been carved out of a single log, from an oak tree the size of which hasn't existed on British soil since before the Romans.

When Jamie and I found the boat, the biggest chunks of it had been tossed up all anyhow on a pile in the brambles on the other side of the river path to get them out of the way of the pipeline. I don't know if I'd have recognised that dried-up heap of mud and mould as the River Fearn log boat on my own, but once Jamie identified it, I knew without a doubt that he was right.

I remembered something that Frank had said about Housman's legs: once they dried out they decayed faster. I made my way into the briars and rubbed my fingertips over the topmost layer of millennia-old wood. It came away on my fingers like shoe polish, browny black as the peat it had been buried in.

'The air's disintegrating it,' I said. 'It's damp now, but that's because it rained last night. It's been drying out.'

I tried unwisely to shift the top piece of boat, and a chunk of it broke off in my hand. It was crumbly and brittle as fudge.

'Bother. *Bother!*'

'Don't touch it again!'

'I'm not going to!'

Jamie gave me his hand to help me back out of the brambles.

I said angrily, '*Now* I feel violated.'

'I know,' he agreed. 'It's … it's like someone's vandalised Grandad's grave.' He looked around for Pinkie. 'What the devil is the matter with that dog?'

Pinkie had flattened herself on the path again, cringing and making pathetic little whining sobs.

'*Whisht. All right*, lass,' Jamie said, long-suffering, and allowed Pinkie to bundle herself over his shoulder so he could carry her past the wreck of the Bronze Age boat. It made him look like he was wearing a lion's-mane hood, like the warriors in the pictures of the Abyssinian Emperor's coronation.

'You are a hero,' I told him.

'I wouldn't do it for any old dog. Only this one reminds me of you.'

'I'm not afraid of *boats*.'

'You are of ghosts.'

'Ha-ha.'

Jamie put Pinkie down again after thirty yards or so. We were all a bit bedraggled after the safari through the Aberfearn Castle jungle and climbing in chimneys and adventures with greasy Things in dungeons.

'What I'm really scared of now,' I said ominously, 'is Sandy.'

With good reason, as it happens. I have never seen him so volcanic with rage. I never realised he *could* be.

It was all over the dailies the following day; in his outrage Sandy rashly rang both the *Glasgow Herald* and the *Scotsman*, but of course it was the *Perth Mercury* who got there first.

They sent a lady photographer, Catriona Lennox, and I was distracted by her brisk skill and competence from the outrage of this 'rape of a national treasure' (Sandy's *exact words* to the reporters – he has never reminded me *so much* of Grandad). I envied Miss Lennox, not for what she was doing, but because she was able to do it so well. A bit like my envy of Ellen's pipe-smoking! Incidentally she was the only one of the photographers who *didn't* try to move about the pieces of the boat so she might get a more 'boatlike' picture.

It was no longer very boatlike, poor thing.

And then my loyalties were torn to shreds, for Sandy and Frank Dunbar had a terrific row. Right in the reception hall of the Big House with half a dozen workmen and me and Jamie and Colette all gaping at them.

'You have no control whatsoever over this project!' Sandy raged at the harassed site manager. 'You don't know who's working out there. You don't know where they are or where they're staying. When they disappear you don't think to follow up until they've been gone for a solid week. When you find –'

'I know what I *haven't done!*' Dunbar interrupted in fury. 'Do you think I *don't know* what I've failed to do?'

They faced each other like boxers, shoulders squared and heaving as they fought to control their breathing. Sandy was a good deal shorter than Francis Dunbar. But Sandy was sturdier, they were about the same weight, and they must have been near each other in age, though the silver showed in Frank's brown hair and not in Sandy's strawberry blond.

'You've been here *one week*,' Dunbar accused Sandy. 'You've been here *one single week*, sitting cosy and quiet on that island making lists and being served cups of tea by the librarian –'

This made Jamie and I both suddenly aware that Colette was manfully maintaining the burden of steaming china she'd been carrying through to Mémère. Jamie quietly took the tea tray from her.

'How can you have *any idea* of what I've had to cope with in the past month?' Frank cried. 'What gives you any kind of authority to accuse me of negligence?'

With fearsome loyalty, and freed of the servitude of carrying the tea tray, Colette sallied into the battle. She said frostily, 'He is the Earl of Strathfearn.'

It was a moment of extraordinary awkwardness.

Sandy held up one hand, flapping it back and forth in a deprecatory way as if to clear the air of his inheritance.

Dunbar recovered first.

'With all due respect to your hereditary title, Lord Strathfearn …' He paused, raised his chin with that direct

282

and winning confidentiality and added apologetically, 'It is Lord Strathfearn, isn't it? With all due respect, the house and grounds of this estate belong to neither one of us. But I have the burden of maintaining them in trust. I understand why you'd feel I've failed that trust, but how was I to know – how were any of us to know –?'

Sandy brandished at him his Exhibit A, last year's *Proceedings of the Society of Antiquaries of Scotland*, in speechless agony.

'It's not exactly the *Perth Mercury*,' said Francis Dunbar. 'I don't get a copy delivered to my door.'

I let out a choked and hysterical squeak of laughter.

All of us watching had withdrawn into sides. Jamie and Colette and I stood in a huddle behind Alexander Lawson Murray Wallace Beaufort-Stuart, Earl of Strathfearn, and the six painters and paper-hangers stood uncomfortably lined up across from us behind Francis Dunbar, the project manager for the Glenfearn School renovation. It was like the Battle of the Clans on the North Inch in Perth, and I was Hal o' the Wynd, not sure which side I was fighting for.

Everyone glared at me when I giggled.

And I caught Frank's eye. He was silently imploring me to switch sides, to defend him.

I pitched my voice as low and level as it would go, trying to sound like Marlene Dietrich, and said slowly, 'Wouldn't the Glenfearn School itself want to save what's there of the log boat if it can be saved? Can't you ask the trustees if they'll help? Perhaps let Sandy direct a few men from the site, and see if any of the boat can be salvaged?'

Sandy slammed the *Proceedings* flat on the table where the post gets left, a metaphoric gauntlet.

'Yes, I can do that,' Frank said gratefully. 'I'll ring tomorrow morning.'

Sandy didn't move.

'I'll ask if they'll pay for any outside expertise you might need.'

Sandy didn't say anything. He nodded, turned on his heel and stalked back out through the front door, which stood open as usual; we could see him heading for the river.

Heading, I felt sure, for Mary, who would understand, and who would never tell a soul if he wept over it.

'Come, Colette, Mémère will be waiting for this and it's getting cold.' Jamie beckoned with his head, and Colette followed him away from the reception hall towards the morning room.

The little audience of workmen slunk back to whatever it was they'd been doing, and – without expecting it – Frank and I were left on our own.

'Thank you,' he said softly. 'It *is* my fault, I suppose …'

I took the three long steps that brought me next to him, snatched his hand in mine and stood on tiptoe to kiss him on the chin – it was as high as I could reach.

'How can it possibly be your fault?'

He tilted his face carefully away from mine, but didn't let go of my hand. God. I felt traitorously disloyal to my Murray bloodline. Dunbar's palm was cold and dry. *Mine*, I thought, *must feel like a quiet flame against his. Better not try to kiss him again.*

After a moment he turned back to look down at me, his eyebrows lowered in a faint frown of baffled unhappiness, and said, 'If nothing had happened – nothing at all, none of this –'

'Something would have.'

He changed course so fast it was dizzying.

'There's a variety playing at the City Hall in Perth. The trustees gave me a pair of tickets – worrying now that I never stop working. I thought ...'

He paused to let me fill in the blank. To let me *choose*.

Oh, glory, I was tempted. Because why not – *why not*? If I was a decent, ordinary girl working in a hat shop – if we'd been introduced at a dance or a shoot or a village-hall concert, if we'd played golf at the same club – wouldn't it have been perfectly all right for him to ask me out? It wouldn't have to end in marriage, for goodness' sake. I wouldn't have *minded* going to a music-hall variety show in Perth with Francis Dunbar.

But I knew I couldn't. It wasn't the age difference, or my being the daughter of an earl, or the fact that I hadn't yet finished school, though Mother and Father might have pointed to any of those as reasons. It was more … the way the summer had started. Solange's sad affair shadowing everything. My virtue being in question behind my back. I had to walk the tightrope without drink.

I think he knew it too.

At any rate I was damned if I'd give away my game by finishing his sentence. If he wanted to take me to a show he could jolly well ask me himself.

He sighed. He didn't let go of my hand; I got the impression he'd forgotten it was there, or felt so comfortable holding it in his that it didn't occur to him he shouldn't really be doing it.

He said, 'I thought you and Jamie might like to go.'

'But they're yours!'

'I'd like to give them to you,' he said quietly. 'I owe you *something*.'

And remembering what Ellen had said about giving, I had to take them.

14

THOSE ARE PEARLS THAT WERE HIS EYES

Sandy press-ganged me and Jamie out to the riverbank with him at dawn the next morning armed with trowels loaned us by Francis Dunbar, so we could try to salvage pieces of boat. Mother brought us breakfast – bread and jam and a flask of coffee – in a willow basket that I'm sure she bought from Jean McEwen.

The work was messy and dispiriting. Being the one with the smallest hands and the lightest touch, I was supposed to move the clammy slabs of decaying wood at Sandy's direction; Jamie was required to draw pictures. But everything I touched seemed to crumble. Pinkie lurked some distance away panting and sulking on her belly, unwilling to come anywhere near this project.

By about nine o'clock the sun was high and a few reporters had turned up again, along with a small crowd of intrigued citizens from Perth and Brig O'Fearn village who'd seen last night's papers. I spotted the photographer from the *Mercury* whom I'd admired, and waved her over.

'Can you take close photographs of these bits and pieces? Can you do a lot of them – not for publication but to record it before it falls apart?'

She looked surprised. 'Do you really –?'

She glanced at Sandy, mud-streaked and carrying with him an air of weary gloom as though he'd already been on his feet for a solid day. 'Show me what you need.'

There was also more than one terrifically annoying urchin who wanted very much to nick bits of archaeological treasure. I tried to keep a wary eye on the crowd. There was someone at the back trying awkwardly to get a bicycle past everyone else standing gawping on the river path; the bicycle had a wide basket attached to the front handlebars and a great tin washtub strapped over the rear wheel. Pinkie suddenly exploded in joy like a demonic buttery rocket and launched herself at the bicycle.

I mean, at the person in charge of the bicycle.

It was Ellen.

I recognised her myself a moment later. Jamie said I looked just as excited and silly as Pinkie as we leaped to greet her. Perhaps he was jealous that I got there first.

Ellen had to lower the laden bicycle into the undergrowth so she had her hands free to manage both me and the dog.

She'd only been gone three days, I realised later – it felt like I hadn't seen her for a *month*.

'Pinkie, ye're tiresome. All right, Jamie? Julie –'

Her stormcloud-blue eyes danced.

'I had to come back for the dog,' she said.

'You never,' I accused. 'You came back for the log boat!'

'Daddy might have mentioned it to me. He was in the pub in Comrie last night and heard the men talking. And I did want Pinkie back, so I borrowed my uncle's pushbike and came out here this morning.'

'It's thirty miles!'

'It's mostly flat. Well, for Perthshire. Straight along the Fearn Valley.'

She got Pinkie subdued, left the bicycle where it lay and we all worked our way past the bystanders back to Sandy.

I told him, 'This is Ellen McEwen. She's the one who did the spear-tip drawings for Grandad two years ago, when his eyesight got so bad.'

He pushed back his cap, rubbed at his muddy forehead, and gave Ellen the ghost of a smile. 'So it is. Of course, we were dancing at the weekend, weren't we, Ellen, lass?'

How could it be possible that so little time had passed since the ceilidh at Inchfort Field? It felt like …

Sandy took advantage of Ellen's archaeological drawing experience and put her to work immediately. He gave her the sketching block and pencils that he'd assigned to Jamie, freeing up Jamie to help lift away the crumbling slabs of prehistoric oak. You wouldn't have thought it would be back-breaking work, but it was, squatting and bending and lifting. The closer we got to the bottom of the woodpile the damper, and consequently the more intact, the slabs became.

We kept working. Catriona Lennox, the photographer, either felt that she was on to something or else was genuinely interested in the hopeless project, and she stuck with us stalwartly, changing films occasionally and asking Sandy lots of questions.

We'd have forgotten to stop to eat, except that Mother conspired with Mary Kinnaird to bring us sandwiches while the library was closed for the midday dinner break. And it was brave of Mary too, knowing how many people were about – reporters and photographers and the pipeline workmen and the general summer holiday rabble, all of them staring (or trying not to stare) at her smooth, unfinished features, and her shining ear trumpet and her fearful determination not to acknowledge anybody as she passed.

She pulled up short, then took a step backward, when she saw Ellen sitting there drawing, perched on a shooting stick with a leather seat, straight-backed and glorious with her long coppery hair falling down her back like licks of flame. Sandy was leaning over her, murmuring something in her ear with one hand on her shoulder, stabbing the forefinger of his other hand with emphasis at the shapeless block of wood Jamie was holding.

I saw panic and hatred cross Mary's face. It wasn't intolerance this time. It was pure green jealousy. Sandy was *hers*.

'Mary!' I called.

She was carrying a net bag of provisions in each hand. I took one from her and reminded her, 'I told you about Ellen.'

'Yes.' The look in Mary's eyes was wintry.

'She only just arrived this morning. She came back to collect her dog. But we knew she'd done the other drawings, so …'

I spoke without speaking aloud, moving my lips so that only Mary could hear me with her eyes. *Sandy's in love with the Bronze Age log boat and I think maybe with you, so please just be nice to Ellen because she is my friend.*

Mary stared at me. 'You said … ?'

I nodded silently.

Then suddenly Mary pealed with laughter.

'Whisht, away wi' you, Julia. You were aye a wee sook!'

I took one of her bags. 'You'll not be cross with her?'

'If Sandy's to work with her, I suppose I must as well,' said Mary bravely.

It is possible there are some things you want *so badly* that you will change your life to make them happen.

★

291

It was at exactly that moment that Jamie prised up what looked like the last slab of the pile. Beneath it was mud.

'Sandy, I think they've buried a bit of it under this.'

He scraped away damp earth with a trowel, his touch light and delicate as a musician's. 'Julie, give me a hand.'

There was a catch in his voice that was excitement.

I gave the net bag back to Mary and knelt down to join him. In five minutes we'd unearthed a smooth, flat plane of darkly polished oak that wasn't in the least bit damaged.

'Put it back!' Sandy cried. 'Don't uncover any more – slap all the mud back on, keep it in the peat! No, wait, what's that? Careful, Jamie, lad, give her a bit of room, don't use your fingers.'

I picked at the mud with the trowel tip. I was black with peat up to my elbows. (Jean McEwen's words echoed in my head: *Och, peat never hurt anyone.*) Ellen was leaning over my shoulder now, sketching as fast as she could.

What we'd found was a bit like the stern end of a punt – the corner of a flat ledge with six inches of rope still attached to a loophole bored through the wood. We'd found six inches of *three-thousand-year-old rope*.

Sandy identified it. I uncovered it. Ellen drew it. Catriona Lennox photographed it, and Jamie covered it up again.

When we turned to Sandy he was grey as a Tay pearl and sweating. He is in love with that boat – tragically in love.

292

'Leave it,' he said. 'Leave it. I'll ring the director of the National Museum. My God.'

'Sandwiches,' Mary told him firmly, and he laughed.

'Oh, Mary!'

He stood up and kissed her on the mouth, in full view of everyone and as naturally as if she were already his wife. 'Yes, thank you!'

After that we had to send Mary back to the library to telephone the Water Bailiff so he could come and chase away the crowd. He tried to chase Ellen away too, no doubt because he knows how much Mary dislikes the McEwens; but of course we wouldn't let him. Then when he spotted all the gear Ellen had with her, he made up some non-existent rule about how only Alan McEwen is allowed to camp at Inchfort Field. Sandy coolly set him straight. Sandy's blood was up and he was on fine form. I think he was ready to take on anyone.

We went back the next day, and the next, as if we were criminals revisiting the scene of a robbery.

The expert from the National Museum of Antiquities came out on the train and we had to show him to the site. Of course when we got to the boat there wasn't much to see. Neither Sandy nor the chap from the museum dared to uncover the wonderful thing ('Stern of Bronze Age log boat with tow line in situ'), but they talked and talked about it, planning how they'd uncover and preserve it and what the proposed schedule would be like and how they might get the Glenfearn School to cooperate with them, and Jamie and Ellen and I got bored.

We were kicking our heels along the mouth of the Fearn where it meets the Tay, and the tide was down. The workers from the pipeline had disappeared overnight. There was one steam digger still parked in the water meadow, but the rest had vanished, and we took this to mean that they'd finished their work.

'They've run that pipeline straight through the reed beds,' Jamie said. 'I bet we could walk along the line they've cut and cross to your willow banks on the other side of the Tay. I've never seen the tide this low.'

'It's a spring tide,' Ellen told him. 'That's why.'

Frank Dunbar had told me the same thing. He'd said that the river would be especially low at the end of July.

'Well, what are we waiting for?' I said.

So we set off along the course that the pipes for the new pool were going to take.

The silt and mudflats in the Tay just beyond the mouth of the Fearn were all exposed, like a distant sandbar, and the water of the Fearn lapped in shallow waves against it. There was a delightful little breeze keeping off the midges. There was no one about but us and the birds.

This summer the ground had been dug up and replaced and pipes laid down and hoardings put in and taken away, and Hugh Housman's body had got cut in half somehow during all the activity. But it was all smoothed over now: finished.

Jamie was critical.

'Stupid how they did all the work underwater. If they'd just waited until today, or this week at any rate, it would have saved them a load of trouble.'

'Well, remember that when you're in charge!'

We walked along the edge of the reed beds which rose like a jungle of giant grass, with blue sky and scudding clouds overhead. Reed buntings flashed and chattered. On the other side of the Fearn, the willows made a low smear of whitish green against the greener fields and the Lomond Hills rising behind them.

Between us and the willows lay a strange riverine land-scape of round humpy sandbars, mostly exposed, gleaming darkly in the sun like the backs of a shoal of wet seals. A heron stood motionless at the water's edge, intent on fish.

And the tide was still going out.

Among the smooth humps, sections of the riverbed had been disturbed by the digging of the pipeline; great chunks of it had been lifted out and dumped back in by the diggers and dredgers.

'We can't walk across that mud,' I objected. 'We'll sink!'

'Don't you do geography in whatever posh school they ship you off to?' Ellen said scornfully. (They bloody don't. We are made to take *elocution* lessons. The German language is the closest I can get to anything scientific.) 'That's peat,' Ellen told me. 'It doesn't drift like sand or mud.' She pointed to another mucky lump so we could see the difference. 'That's mud.'

Pinkie started to whine.

'*Shaness*, you daft dog,' Ellen scolded. 'What are you greeting for? It's just tree stumps.' She pointed again.

The heron spread leisurely wings and flapped away from us, low over the drained riverbed, and disappeared among the reeds.

Before us, where Ellen was directing us, one of the islands of peat erupted in twisted, curving tentacles, like half-buried dead branches. The strange smooth coils were the same colour as the uncovered river bottom. Another tangled eruption lay beyond the first, and then another. They seemed to be growing from the tidal flats, growing *through* them, the worn roots and stumps of a forest we'd never seen. They were the skeletons of trees.

But no trees as large as once these were could have grown and died and disappeared in any living person's memory. They were part of the Tay's thousands of years of ebb and flow and drought and flood.

Pinkie stopped whining, but slunk close about my legs, spooked.

'How old are they?' I asked. I had no doubt now that Ellen would know.

'The peat's maybe three thousand years old. Or older … or not so old. Anything stuck *through* it like that is older than the peat – the peat got laid down over it. Like the boat. The peat *preserved* these stumps.'

'It's *amazing*.'

'You're saying those tree stumps are all *three thousand years old*?' Jamie asked incredulously.

'More or less,' she agreed. 'But now they're uncovered, the air and tide will eat them away. They need to be wet and covered up. Every time the tide goes out this far it'll wear them down some more.'

Pinkie cowered, silently hugging my legs. Then she lay down beside me.

She knew. The stubborn, beautiful yellow dog suddenly refused to go forward another inch.

Flat on her belly on the wet silt, Pinkie was focused on the disturbed mud pile just to our right, on the side of us that was the River Fearn as we crossed its mouth. She simply wouldn't budge, and eventually I went to give the offending pile of mud a kick.

It came to pieces beneath the toe of my tennis shoe and Ellen suddenly dragged me backward, away from it, holding me tightly from behind with her arms across my chest, and then Jamie clutched at one of my arms as well.

For a moment the three of us stood staring in appalled horror at what we'd found: the top half of Hugh Housman.

It wasn't really a whole *half* of him. It was his head and neck and shoulder, and a bit of the other arm that hadn't turned up before.

It was indescribably awful.

You wanted and wanted to look away, but for the longest time you just couldn't. The only thing recognisable in the blackened, shredded face was the wire scrubbing brush of his whiskers. But the most truly horrific thing was the rope coiled close and tight around his neck.

Jamie whispered, 'That wasn't suicide. You can't strangle yourself and then go and jump in a river.'

We all glanced at each other at last, released.

'What do we do?' I whispered back. 'The water will cover it up again and there won't be another spring tide for a month. It'll fall apart. No one will be able to find it.'

'The water preserves it,' Jamie reminded me. 'Remember how the doctor complained about them leaving his legs to dry out?'

'It's like the log boat,' Ellen said. 'We should cover it with mud again to protect it. And mark the spot so the lifeboats know where to look.'

The thing was so far from being human it didn't actually seem *foul* – it didn't make me feel sick, not like the time we took the dead deer to the abattoir to see how they cut up the venison. This was different – it felt horrific but faintly unreal, the way you sometimes feel in a nightmare when you think you're drowning or being buried alive. Your brain keeps insisting: *THIS CAN'T BE REAL.*

'I'll do the mud,' I said through my teeth. Because I was very ready to hide it. 'I'll put the mud back on.'

'Ellen, have you a knife?' Jamie asked.

'Aye,' she choked.

'Can you cross over to the willow bank and cut four or five withy wands? Stout and tall as you can get, and we can drive them into the riverbed here around it so they'll stand above the water when the tide comes in and the police will know where to look for it.'

'Aye.'

'Julie, let me do that,' Jamie said, but I wasn't going to be babied by him.

We reburied the corpse together, trying to treat the hellish thing as if it were as fragile and exquisite as Sandy's boat.

Not one of us had the stomach to go and gape at the exhumation that followed.

Not so the rest of humanity. There had been no interest

in an English antiquities scholar supposedly suffering an accidental drowning, and a *little* public interest in the discovery that part of our glorious Scottish past was under threat and might or might not be salvageable; but the press announcement that someone working on the Glenfearn School renovation had been garrotted and shoved in the Tay to decompose brought out the whole of Eastern Scotland.

My brothers and I took refuge in the library from the ghoulish onlookers, and so did Ellen.

It was Sandy who threw together the opposing forces of Ellen and Mary. He wanted Ellen to make clean copies of the boat sketches she'd done earlier in the week, and poor Mary – so resentful, but of stalwart conscience – was too enamoured of my big brother to do anything other than allow his gentle requests to be accommodated.

I met Ellen and Pinkie in front of the library on the first morning of this assignment; Pinkie, realising Ellen was without the rest of her family, now stuck to her like glue. Ellen looked most unlike herself, dressed in a respectable tweed skirt and an almost-new navy wool cardigan. She'd put her hair up in *exact* imitation of Mary.

'You look like a proper countrywoman!' I said.

'Not a librarian?' Ellen prompted gently.

It took me a moment to realise she meant the question in earnest.

'Or a librarian,' I agreed.

'Miss Kinnaird won't be able to fault my manners,' Ellen said, with the faintest hint of defiance. 'But I'll maybe have to leave the dog with you while I go in to see her the first time.'

'Don't you want me to come along?'

She cocked her head, gazing at me fondly.

'I *do*,' she said. 'But I think I should go alone. Just this once, to set myself right with Miss Kinnaird, without the Lady of the Manor about the place arranging things for us.'

Ellen smiled at me, waiting for me to back down.

'All right, Lady Julia?'

'Oh, *all right.*'

I let her go alone.

I felt very proud of her, and of Mary, and a little ashamed of myself for considering their uneasy truce to be any of my business.

Now the Procurator Fiscal was forced to demand an inquiry after all, since as a murder the case would have to go to the High Court in Edinburgh rather than the local Sheriff Court. Everyone had to be interviewed all over again – including Ellen, who was with us when we found Housman's head and shoulders (which had been whisked away to the mortuary to join his legs).

The same dreadful trio of driver, Water Bailiff and Inspector Duncan Milne turned up at the library to question Mary and Ellen. After grilling Mary in her own study for half an hour, they sent her back upstairs and the inspector dragged Ellen down.

As had happened over at the Big House, Inspector Milne posted bulldogs at the door and window to stop us listening in. *Thank God* Mary had established that alibi for Euan, but now I found myself panicking lest they try to pin something on Ellen instead.

Sandy and Jamie and Mary and I waited in the Upper Reading Room, where we couldn't hear a thing. Jamie, just as fearful as I was, slumped miserably in one of the library chairs, drumming his fingers against his thigh.

After a minute or so I said, 'Mary, can I borrow your horn?'

She'd been flustered enough by her own interrogation that she handed the trumpet over without arguing.

I lay on the smooth floor over her study with the bell of the horn pressed flat on the old dark wood.

'Anything?' Jamie asked.

'Not a whisper,' I said in annoyance. 'It's seventeenth-century solid.'

'You need a conduit for the sound,' Jamie began. Then he continued excitedly, 'Oh, I say, try listening at the fire. The chimney downstairs probably has a flue that joins up with this one.'

Mary cried, 'Darling, *be careful* with my trumpet!'

All four of us (Sandy too) knelt with our heads practically in the grate, eavesdropping on Ellen's precognition.

Inspector Milne pestered her about where she was living. Of course she was staying by herself at Inchfort Field, where her family always camped when they were there, with one small bow tent just big enough to sit up in. Everything she had with her came on the bicycle. Milne asked her question after question about who might visit her there, and for how long, until she began to get angry.

She finally exclaimed heatedly, so loudly that Jamie and Sandy heard it too, even without the aid of Mary's horn, '*Naebody* is in about wi' me! *Nae man* is in about with me! And if there were a man wi' me, what would be the wrong in it – or the business of yours?'

'I must be aware of anyone who might have had river access at the time of Dr Housman's disappearance. Or who might have reason to return there. We need to be aware of anything that might have motivated this act of violence – a secret shared? A debt left unpaid? A fight over a woman?'

'Well, nae man I'd have about me is a hangman!' Ellen snarled.

She didn't have anything to tell them. She didn't know a

thing about Hugh Housman – she'd never even *seen* him. And for all their bullying, even I could tell they didn't have anything to pin on her.

That didn't stop Sergeant Angus Henderson from giving her bicycle a good seeing-to on their way out, prodding its tyres with his cromach and testing the brakes. The bicycle, which was leaning against the stone bridge as if it were embarrassed, suffered these indignities in silence.

Ellen joined us at the upstairs casement window to watch the policemen leave. They were supposed to come back to the Big House the next day to have a go at me again, and Jamie too.

'I swear that gadgie thinks I'm here after the salmon,' Ellen said as Inspector Milne's car bumped over the stone bridge. 'He's treating me like a poacher.'

'Maybe he thinks you're after pearls,' I said.

'There's no law against me taking pearls –' She stopped abruptly.

We had the same thought. We, and we alone, knew what Hugh Housman might have been murdered for: a Keiller jam pot full of treasure.

'*A secret shared*,' Jamie quoted softly, under his breath as though he were swearing.

We knew now we had to turn in the pearls we'd found.

But there in front of the library, on our own, Ellen and

Jamie and I made a vow to get them out of the dovecote first. We weren't going to share the chimneys of Aberfearn Castle with the Perthshire and Kinross-shire Constabulary.

I did not at all like the thought of *someone coming back for them.*

Nor of Ellen being up at Inchfort by herself.

15

EATING PEOPLE UP

Another interview with Inspector Milne. He didn't ask about the pearls so I put off mentioning them. I felt I was getting good at this.

And I accepted the tickets offered to me by Frank Dunbar, and I took – not Jamie – I took *Ellen* to the variety show.

I wanted to do something for her. I wanted to distract her from the horror that infected us all now – and to distract me too. Frank had given me two tickets and I couldn't go with *him*, of course; but if I went with Jamie, Ellen would be spending Saturday night alone up at Inchfort Field with the Salmon Stane and Hugh Housman's most unnatural ghost, and nobody but the cowardly Pinkie for company.

There wasn't even a moon; it was new, and would set early. So we left Pinkie-dog at the Big House for the evening, and Mummy let me have the car after I swore we wouldn't drink anything at the interval, and we sailed off to Perth for a night on the town.

The show was *wonderful*. I'd never have seen anything like that if it hadn't been for Frank. Mémère had only ever taken me to the opera, and that not often. At home it was amateur Gilbert and Sullivan or the pantomime. Once, in a moment of blazing and astonishing good fortune, Sandy met me in London on my way home from school at Christmas and we saw a new play by J.M. Barrie, *The Boy David*, with original orchestral music in the background like in a moving picture. But good old-fashioned vulgar music-hall entertainment? Not a chance.

The featured star of the variety was a person who went by the stage name Le Sphinx. Ellen was fooled, or possibly just distracted, by the fact that in addition to peppering the audience with French clichés in an American drawl, and as well as singing jazz in a sonorous deep contralto that made you want to take off your clothes and bathe in it, Le Sphinx had skin that was easily as dark as the peat we had been digging in two days ago. The singer stood in long satin gloves and a simple evening gown of bridal white that was constantly shifting to blue and lavender under the lights, with bare thin muscular shoulders and sleek waved hair glittering with diamanté clips. That incredible voice seemed to be whispering to you in *particular* (*you, you, you*) as if you were alone together in an empty Parisian nightclub – just you at a table alone with that voice and no one else.

But I was not fooled.

I glanced at Ellen, just once, and she was watching with her mouth open.

At the interval she turned to me and said simply, 'Thank you. It's the barriest show I've ever seen. Better than a month at the pictures. She's pure magic.'

'She's a man,' I said.

Ellen burst out laughing.

I said, 'I swear it.'

'She's never a man! You can see down her dress! And in front – you'd see if she was a man, in that tight dress! She never is!'

'She is. You can hide anything if you want to badly enough.'

Ellen tilted her head, looking at me quizzically. 'But not from you – why's that?'

'I don't know,' I said, thinking about it. 'I love looking for things that other people haven't noticed and then trying to fit them together, like jigsaw pieces. You know what a sphinx is – a creature with a lion's body and a woman's head? You'd call it "she" in English. But "Le Sphinx" is masculine, so you have to say "he" in French.'

'Och, away wi' you, Davie Balfour,' Ellen teased. 'You dinnae ken your ain he from she.'

'Also, it's the answer to the Sphinx's riddle.'

'What is?'

'A man. The Sphinx goes around eating people up because they don't know the answer to her riddle, and the answer is "a man".'

Le Sphinx wasn't in the second act, but during the interval stood with an elbow propped against the bar, sipping a cocktail that glowed green as a starboard light, and autographing programmes.

I linked my arm through Ellen's to give me courage and stood in the queue to get my ticket stub signed.

'Vionnet,' Le Sphinx observed approvingly in that voice like melted chocolate, casting a connoisseur's eye over my frock. 'Been shopping in Paris, *chérie*?'

'It's last year's and you know it,' I said.

She gave a low and delighted chuckle. Her eyes were black as a moonless December night and reflected the electric lights like stars. 'A sophisticate,' she said. 'Here's me thinking I was playing a hick town.'

'*Je suis française*,' I said. '*Et vous? Un citoyen de Paris?*'

I could feel Ellen smouldering beneath my own arm, ill at ease as if she were at sea in this place. We must have looked a very odd pair, me in the shimmering rose and silver Vionnet dress with a little gold velvet evening jacket I'd borrowed from Mummy dangling over my shoulders, and Ellen in her tweed skirt and navy cardigan. She looked perfectly nice, but she wasn't dressed for the theatre. Her glorious loose hair kept buying her slanted and disapproving looks from the other theatregoers. If I hadn't been hanging on to her with such schoolgirl–chum determination she could have easily passed as my secretary.

Or my maid. I didn't want people to think she was my maid. I didn't want her to feel like people thought she was my maid, so I hung on to her arm as if I were propping her up.

Le Sphinx eyed our partnership with curiosity, then chuckled again and boldly answered my very cheeky question. '*Oui, chérie, aujourd'hui je suis français.*'

I'd used the masculine form when I called her a 'citizen' and she'd done the same when she called herself 'French'.

She said in English, for Ellen's benefit, 'You've guessed my riddle. Some people can tell; it's not a secret. I'm a more exciting performer as a woman, so why not?'

'You're the most exciting performer I've ever seen,' I said honestly.

She grinned at me. 'You're glowing, *ma petite*. You think you know men? Did you win the argument about me?'

'Yes, I won the argument, but not because I know men,' I said. 'It's because – I love to fool people. So I see through them too. You do it for a living and you get it right. And it must take so much courage, to be *so different* and not be afraid of how people might react. And I …' I laughed also, at myself. 'I don't think I could do what you do. But I am a sphinx too.'

'Chameleon, maybe. There's only one sphinx.' Le Sphinx sipped at the green cocktail, then turned, catlike, on Ellen.

'And what do you think of me?'

'I think,' Ellen said, 'you must be always lonely.'

'One of a kind is how I see it.' She reached for Ellen's ticket stub and scrawled her stage name across it theatrically, not getting a single drop of green ink on the white silk gloves. 'Are you afraid of me?' she asked.

'A wee bit, aye,' Ellen admitted with ill-concealed resentment and fascination. She took back the ticket stub as though she expected it to bite her, avoiding touching the gloved hands.

'What about you, Vionnet? Afraid of me?'

'I wouldn't tell you if I was,' I said.

'Give me a kiss, *ma petite*,' said Le Sphinx, leaning down and offering her cheek. She smelled of powder and hair oil and stage paint and Chanel N° 5.

I tilted her smooth chin towards mine with the tip of a finger and lightly touched our lips together. They were just like all the other lips I'd lightly touched this summer: warm and soft and full of human hope and fear and cruelty and kindness.

Ellen laughed. A handful of people at the bar applauded, and a woman in a hat flounced away.

311

'I like a daring girl,' said Le Sphinx.

'I do try to be daring.'

She laughed. Then she warned quietly, 'Do try to be careful too. You can be both.'

After the show I drove Ellen back to Inchfort Field and we didn't say much on the way; the slender moon had set by the time we were heading out of Perth.

As I pulled up at the field gate she said, 'Thank you, Julie. It was braw. All of it, even the silly bits. The performing budgies!'

I snickered. 'They were hilarious.'

'But that Sphinx …'

She paused, then climbed up on the back of the car and lit her pipe (a new one, I supposed).

'That singer frighted me half to death. How you cheeked her! But she was wonderful – it was all *wonderful.*'

Ellen passed me the pipe. I climbed up next to her and we sat on the back of the Magnette with our feet on the seats, looking up at the stars and smoking in silence.

'I'd better go,' I said at last. 'It's past midnight.'

'Aye,' Ellen said. She swung her legs around, slid off the car and hopped over the field gate, sure-footed and at home in the dark.

'Thank you!' she called again.

Brig O'Fearn village was pitch-black. I drove cautiously. I'd never driven at night before, except coming home from Perth half an hour earlier. But Ellen had been with me then, full of smouldering warmth and wonder, and though I'd been driving carefully I hadn't been nervous. Now the road felt cool and lonely, and something new was eating at me.

As I rounded the corner to take the humpbacked bridge in Brig O'Fearn, the headlamps of the Magnette splashed light over a dark, looming figure in the process of wheeling a bicycle by the handlebars down on to the river path below the bridge. The bicycle's own headlamp was only a dim pinpoint of baleful yellow without speed to generate enough power to keep it alight.

Probably the Water Bailiff going to check on the Glenfearn School, I thought; and yet the cold nagging in my stomach wouldn't go away. I kept thinking about the legend of the standing stones walking about to swim with the salmon on Lammas Night. It was only two nights off.

Only when I'd pulled the Magnette up to the Strathfearn House garages and a squealing bundle of doggy fluff half my size came bounding into my arms and knocked the wind out of me did I realise what was really bothering me.

Pinkie was *here* and Ellen was by herself in Inchfort Field, alone with the standing stones and the stars and the murdered ghost of Hugh Housman.

My prudent mother keeps a torch in her car. I took it with me to find my way along the river path so I could deliver Pinkie to her proper mistress; it would be faster to walk that way than to drive the long way round again.

The birch wood by the river, so alive with birdsong and the constant activity of the Glenfearn School by day, mostly has only one voice at night: the sound of running water. It is beautiful, but it is *so old*. It is the sound the long-dead pearl fishermen heard, the sound the Bronze Age people heard when they launched the log boat into the prehistoric River Fearn, the sound they heard when they raised the Drookit Stane – the river has a voice that doesn't die. It is as inhuman and ancient as starlight.

The Inverfearnie Library was slumbering calmly with Mary tucked safe inside as I passed.

Even so I managed to work myself into a funk of nerves well before I got to Inchfort.

There was a light and more than one human voice by the Salmon Stane in Inchfort Field.

I switched off my own torch to save the batteries. I could see the standing stone from the bottom of the field, a pure black silhouette against a less black and star-salted sky, and there was another lit electric torch burning in the long grass at the base of the stone to show me the way. Pinkie pressed close against my legs, keeping quiet and sensible, which made me think she knew who was up there. She was subdued and submissive, but she wasn't paralysed with fear.

Presumably Ellen wasn't either.

When I got closer I could see that there were two people there, faintly foot-lit by the torch on the ground as if they were on stage. One was Ellen, with her back against the stone like Joan of Arc tied to the stake. The man she was facing held her prisoner with a stick like a spear shaft, pinning her arms and chest against the stone. She was struggling like a salmon and spitting protests.

Pinkie dropped and cowered silently.

'I didnae!' Ellen swore.

'The librarian's seen ye,' said the other. 'And I've seen ye. Bold as brass, beneath her door, on the footbridge, on the path. Do you not bring your young man here the night?'

'I never had a man here – never, day or night. Never! I said so to the inspector – you heard – it was he as said I did that, not I! I'm working at the library with the Earl of Strathfearn. I don't – No, I *won't* – *Oh!*' She gasped, and twisted at the waist, and I could not see what his free hand was doing to her.

The man said in a low, clear voice, 'Aye, but ye will, ye teasing tinkie hussy, ye will. Or I'll have your brother

315

arrested for the murder of yon Dr Housman. Ye ken? He'll hang for it.'

He could, I suddenly realised with horror. *He could.* Mary's alibi for Euan only made sense if Housman had committed suicide – if he'd waded away into the river right after I saw him. It wouldn't work if Housman had been murdered later.

'*No!*' Ellen's entire body made another wrenching bid for freedom, and she suddenly let out a squealing, outraged sob. 'O, God, I'll have you down Sheriff Court mysel', I swear, you filthy scaldy bastard!'

'And whose word will they take, lassie, yours or mine?'

There was no way in the world I was ever again going to stand frozen, frightened and cowed and passive, and watch this man launch a violent attack on any McEwen.

I lit my own electric torch and shone it at his head.

'Angus Henderson,' I said coldly, 'what the bloody hell are you doing?'

He turned swiftly, and got a faceful of light. I knew he couldn't see a thing.

Instinctively he raised his cromach, freeing Ellen, and hit out at me. The staff caught me a thudding thump on the shoulder that knocked me sideways on to one knee.

I dropped the torch with a shrieking gasp.

Pinkie, surely in desperation, did the bravest thing she's probably ever done in her life and leaped at Henderson with a snarl.

'Pinkie! Down! No!' Ellen yelled. 'Down!' She wrestled the dog to the ground.

My arm was numb. I scrabbled for the torch with shaking, unsteady fingers.

'Let her go, Ellen!'

'No,' Ellen said, crouched, holding the dog tight against her. 'One dunt o' that cromach will break her skull.'

'*Oh.*'

Suddenly I felt sure I knew how I'd got that dunt on the head.

The river watcher was towering over me, a dark shadow like the standing stone. My frantic fingers found the torch at last, cold and solid metal, and I aimed its beam into his craggy face, trying to blind him. I could hear my own breath coming harsh and fast, and swallowed bile.

'Oh, Angus Henderson,' I articulated carefully, getting to my feet. I licked my lips. 'You want to dally with a lassie in the dark? Come *kiss me*. Come here …'

He was frozen in the beam of my torch like a hare, baffled by this turn of events. 'Why –'

I stepped closer, bringing myself toe to toe with him. 'Come along, big man.'

I hooked my hand around the base of his skull and pulled his face down to mine. My shoulder felt like it was in flames. I found his mouth and kissed him like I meant it, hard and deep.

And I did mean it – but not as a kiss. I meant it as a threat, and a warning, and a *curse*.

He pulled our mouths apart and backed away from me. I'd spooked him. Tangled up with the hysterical dog and the blinding beam of the light and the two conspiring girls, he was no longer so sure of either his strength or his authority.

'Do I know you? You're no' one of them travelling folk.'

He could hear that in the dripping sarcasm of my exaggeratedly aristocratic voice.

'You know me in the day,' I said. I held up the torch and poured light down my body, over the borrowed gold velvet bolero jacket and the flimsy rose georgette and all the curves and corners that lay barely hidden beneath. 'I'm Julia Beaufort-Stuart.'

'Och, *Lady Julia*,' he breathed, and took another step back.

'You can kiss me if you like,' I said. 'I don't mind. You can stand here and have me up against the stone like you were going to –'

'You know I never would, Lady Julia!'

'*I don't know that,*' I said. 'You took me for a dirty tinker once before, didn't you, when you thought you'd found me poaching Strathfearn's trout by the Drookit Stane? What did you do then? Thumped me on the head for fun!'

'I didnae! I didnae touch you!'

I didn't believe a word of this denial.

'You carried me up the path to Inchfort Field so you could make it look like some McEwen lad had done the damage,' I accused.

'Aye, I did that, but I didnae *touch you,*' Henderson elaborated meaningfully – if you can call changing the meaning of your words by changing your tone 'elaboration'.

'*You can now,*' I said. 'Come on, big man, I'm *gasping* for you! Maybe I'll like it and not tell anyone. But maybe I'll say you forced me, here in the dark when I was bringing Ellen home from the theatre. *And whose word will they take, Angus, yours or mine?*'

He stood frozen and silent for a long moment.

'Speak one false word against Euan McEwen,' I warned coolly, 'and I'll tell my lady mother that you raped me.'

He dropped a few cold, angry words at my feet.

'You filthy wee bitch.'

Then he picked up his own fallen torch, and took his cromach, and strode away down the field to wherever it was he'd left his bicycle.

We heard him rattling away and, for a few seconds, watched the light of his headlamp bobbing like a will-o'-the-wisp through the birch wood. Then he was gone.

Ellen gasped, 'He could –'

'*He won't dare.*'

'O, God pity me, Julie, I cannae stay here alone the night,' she sobbed.

I was still trembling. I felt like I'd been dropped down one of the Aberfearn Castle chimneys.

'Of course you can't,' I said. 'Come back with me.'

There wasn't any place to put Ellen in the Big House except in my narrow bed, so that's where we both collapsed, with our arms tight around each other so we wouldn't fall out. Ellen fell asleep almost straight away. But I lay awake with my heart full of hatred and love so evenly distributed I felt like my chest was going to explode, and my head full of the deathless, chill voice of the river and the living, volcanic voice of Le Sphinx, winding me in night and day and 'Night and Day'.

16

AN' WHA DARE MEDDLE WI' ME?

Getting dressed the next morning I had a scrap with Mother, who grabbed me by the arm so suddenly it shocked me into a howl of pain.

'Julia, how on *earth* did you get that black mark across your shoulder? You look as if you've been hit by a train! You can't wear your birthday frock with that – it has no sleeves!'

'That's where Sergeant Henderson hit me with his cromach.'

I told her about what had happened at Inchfort Field last night.

'Hanging's too good for him. That man ought to be *horsewhipped* first,' Mother said furiously.

'Mary thinks he is a dear.'

Mother went raging down to the hall telephone to ring the police.

Ellen spent all of Sunday morning sulking and scaffing Mémère's French coffee in a corner of the morning room, with Jamie waiting on her like a knight's squire. Much the way he waits on me. Watching him sitting on the floor at her feet, pouring her another cup and stirring in sugar without even having to ask how many she wanted, I realised whom the river watcher had meant when he'd said he'd *seen* her with someone, *bold as brass*.

And why wouldn't she and Jamie have kissed on the footbridge to the library as bold as brass, if they wanted to? They were the same age. They weren't married to other people. No one told them not to. It wasn't like me and Frank Dunbar.

Sly old Jamie! He didn't kiss her any time *I* might have seen it.

He looked up at me just as I was putting this together, saw that I had twigged him and blushed.

I didn't think Ellen could be any more serious with Jamie than she was with me. She was enjoying herself, testing the peaty water. Probably he was too.

But my heart twisted a little enviously that they could do it in daylight.

'Are you thinking of challenging Angus Henderson to a duel?' I asked. 'Because don't forget he strangled a German officer with his bare hands and you are not a lot bigger than me.'

'What stupid sort of fox challenges a hound?' Jamie parried. 'I've a better idea. Let's get Ellen out of the Strathfearn estate at night.'

He glanced up at her. 'There's a good train to Comrie from Brig O'Fearn every two hours. I'll take you and Pinkie tomorrow and show you how to change at Perth. You can stay with your own folk and take the train to work, like a banker!'

That was Sunday; it was August bank holiday on Monday and the building works were quiet and the police did not get back to us.

Then while Mother and I were in Perth on Tuesday, having my fairy dress altered to be made more modest, representatives of the Perthshire and Kinross-shire Constabulary arrived at the Big House and arrested Solange on a charge of murder for the death of Dr Hugh Housman.

Unbelievable, unbearable gloom descended on Strathfearn House.

Mother was hardly ever there that week. She launched a one-woman assault on His Majesty's Prison in Perth, seeing to it that Solange was supplied with every comfort a prisoner was allowed, even attempting to send her armfuls of roses (they had to sit in the prison office). Many telephone calls were made to Father in Craig Castle, and to Mémère's sister in France, concerning lawyers. Mémère kept up her stoic folding of hankies with Colette in attendance, and Jamie and I worked with Sandy and Ellen to pull together the catalogue for the Murray Collection. We weren't allowed to visit Solange and the catalogue had to be completed regardless of the Murray and Beaufort-Stuart household's emotional state.

'The Strathfearn Murder' (it was officially murder now) was shouted in all the papers *every day*. For a few days it was relegated to the inside pages, but the inevitable post-mortem revealed that the killing was utterly horrific. The poor fellow wasn't *just* garrotted. Perhaps he was like Rasputin and simply *wouldn't die*? He was so battered that now 'the examining doctor has not been able to determine the actual cause of death'.

There was a great hole in the back of his head where his skull was bashed in and also – ugh – his throat had been cut.

How could they *possibly* believe it was Solange! Surely the Water Bailiff was the most likely suspect when it came to brutal violence?

But even I could see that he had no motive. If he'd known about the pearls, he'd have taken them away weeks ago and we'd never have found them. And Solange had admitted to striking Dr Housman. She'd admitted to a fight. She'd admitted to *winning*. And no one had seen either one of them that afternoon except me, and everything I'd seen suggested that she *could* have come along to finish the job. She was even intimate enough with him that she could have hidden his clothes.

Eventually the papers printed pictures of all the wounds. Not photographs, which I suppose would have been too lurid even for the *Mercury*. They were just pencil drawings.

'They're not as good as yours,' I told Ellen when I showed her.

'That's not what the rope looked like at all. They've made it look like something you'd lead a pony with. It was bonnier than that.'

'*Bonnier!* What, you mean, *prettier*?'

She scowled. She had been fearsomely crabbit, even for Ellen, since Henderson smeared her with his mucky paws.

'Aye, *prettier* than that, all right, Lady Julia? Like a … a dressing-gown cord.'

'Decorative, you mean?'

'Stop telling me what I mean!'

I thought she was angry that I had had to come to her rescue. Not that I *did* – she'd been glad to be rescued – but that *I had to*. She couldn't have saved herself and we both knew it. And it was the good fortune of my being 'Lady Julia' that let me do it. It was embarrassing to both of us.

I also had an argument with Sandy. Of all people.

It was my own stupid fault, especially as I'd already remarked that he was ready to take on *anyone*. It started innocently enough, when we were all having rare drinks on the terrace on the Thursday after Mother came home from visiting Solange. We were just all so tired of being miserable that Mémère started pouring sherry.

'And, Jamie, take one to Monsieur Dunbar,' she said magnanimously. 'It is awkward him always sitting at work there with his terrace doors standing open.'

I sat quiet, pointedly pretending I hadn't heard and didn't care. I had been very cautious all summer long about not letting Mother or Solange know about my crush on Frank Dunbar. But it was not a secret that Frank was so at home in his office adjoining the morning room that it had become a little den.

Jamie disappeared next door with a sherry glass and came back a minute or so later commenting, 'That man is in desperate need of a housekeeper. There's cheese parings and a half-eaten loaf of bread going stale among his blueprints.'

'Am I going to be remembered for leaving a legacy of mice to this house!' Mémère exclaimed.

I bit my lip. I couldn't possibly leap to Frank's defence without giving myself away.

Mother sighed. 'We really ought to have been more thoughtful of him since this trouble started. He could have certainly joined us for soup or cold meats from time to time. I suppose we should ask Mary to join us more often too.'

'I do ask her.' Sandy, who'd been standing at the stone railing gazing out over the grounds of his lost realm, joined in the conversation unexpectedly. 'I asked her to come round tonight. But there's a lecture at the library – "Victorian Angling" – and she has to be there to serve sandwiches.'

Sandy paused, then turned around deliberately to face us all. 'And I've asked her to come along to the shoot with me on Opening Day,' he announced a little defiantly. 'Perhaps I'll even let her take the gun a time or two. She shoots rather well.'

He sat down on the railing. I went and sat down next to him.

Sandy turned to me. He looked as tired as Mother. He said to me in a low voice, 'I didn't ask her to the Menzies' party after the shoot because I thought you should do that yourself, Julie. It being your birthday.'

'Oh!' I hadn't thought about it. 'Am I allowed to ask people? But Mary never goes to parties.'

'She might if she were asked. She's a great deal more of an explorer than you might think. She's giving Miss Ellen McEwen a good second thought.'

'Yes, she is.' I had to admit she was doing that. I wondered if I could ask Ellen to the party too. But I didn't quite dare. It wasn't *really* my party. I didn't want to offend or upset Mrs Menzies, or indeed Mémère herself.

I sulked, feeling cowardly and Victorian.

'I want Mary to get out more,' Sandy confessed. 'She'll have to, if I marry her.'

'Sandy!' I teased. 'Would you really?'

'Well, why not?'

'But what if she wants children?'

He stared at me as uncomprehendingly as if I'd spoken in cant. 'What if she does?'

'They might be like her. Isn't it risky?'

'They might all be as beautiful as you,' he said coldly, 'which would be riskier.'

I felt truly slapped.

Sandy took a swallow of his sherry.

'They'd be your nieces and nephews, in any case,' he added. 'So get used to the idea.'

I thought about it and felt so ashamed of myself I wanted to weep.

O brave new world that has such people in't!

I lay awake trying to find some cast-iron way to prove Solange's innocence, of which we were all convinced. The only piece of hard evidence I had to offer were the pearls in the jam pot. I still didn't understand the connection, but I felt certain it existed. It would be worth giving up our priceless, pointless heritage to save Solange's life.

And at exactly the right time, the McEwens came back. They were getting ready to work with their cousins the Camerons on the shoot at Glenmoredun Castle on Opening Day – loading guns, beating the grouse out of the heather on the moor and collecting the dead birds afterwards. In the meantime they were harvesting flax at Bridge Farm, except Ellen who was now being reimbursed for her time by the Murray Estate itself at considerably higher wages than Euan was ever paid for *his* time digging on the pipeline for the Glenfearn School swimming bath.

So it wasn't just Jamie and I who went to collect the pearls from hiding, but the full reconnaissance party who had found them in the first place. We all wanted to see them again, Ellen and Euan just as much as we Beaufort-Stuarts, and we knew the only place to do it safely was right there in the dovecote under the last roofed room of Aberfearn Castle.

I dressed for mountaineering in proper shoes and trousers, but did not take into account the sore shoulder until I was halfway up the chimney.

The going got harder and harder. Euan came up last, behind me, and I grew aware of him having to wait for me.

'I'm going to stop for a minute,' I told him, pressing my back against one wall of the chimney shaft with my feet braced against the other wall and my legs across the empty air so I could take the weight off my arms. 'I think you can squeeze past.'

He climbed up to where I was and wedged himself alongside me.

'I'll bide wi' you.'

'I don't suppose you've got a pipe? This is the *perfect* place for a smoke.'

Euan laughed, but answered ruefully, 'No, Ellen's got it.' His long legs seemed awfully bunched up next to me.

'You'd make a terrible chimney sweep,' I said.

It wasn't as though he could carry me down, or catch me if I fell. But being packed so tight actually did make me feel safer.

We heard the rush of wings as Jamie and Ellen emerged in the attic above us and startled the wood pigeons away.

After a minute or two Ellen called down the murky shaft after her brother, '*Sproul kinchen!*'

I laughed. 'Wee brother?'

Euan laughed too. 'Or wee sister.' He cried back, 'Sproul kinchen yourself! Our Davie's having a rest.'

'Our Jamie's getting worried,' she told us. 'Have a rest at the top.'

I gritted my teeth and fought my way up. Jamie reached through the broken chimney wall to help pull me out on to the solid floor of the lost room.

'What's wrong?'

'My shoulder hurts. Bother.'

'It's easier going down.'

'I know.'

As a consolation for my being pathetic they let me be the one to free the pearls.

Ellen had brought along polishing equipment in her fisherman's creel: soft puffs of cotton wool and a jar of baby oil and a swathe of elegant fabric to tip the treasure out on. 'Mam says pearls look best on black velvet,' she said.

They looked marvellous on black velvet – all their subtle hues more vivid. We played with them as if we were babies playing with alphabet blocks.

'These aren't just the Reliquary pearls,' Ellen said. 'There's too many.'

'I know. Grandad must have collected some of them himself,' I said.

'It's a shame they've been mixed. We'll never know which are the oldest.'

Ellen lined up the big grey Tay pearl beads, the ones that matched. Against the black velvet they seemed to glow silvery white as moonlight. Against the black velvet they looked like …

Ellen and I gave a unified shriek of excitement and disbelief.

'The library pearls!'

'*They're the same as Mary Queen of Scots' bracelet.*'

We had to explain it to our baffled brothers.

'They're a match with the pearls on display in the Inverfearnie Library –'

'*An exact match!*'

'They're from –'

'*The same set!*'

'It must have been –'

'A *necklace*. A necklace *to match the bracelet.*'

Jamie let out a soft and fervent oath.

Euan breathed quietly, '*Mary Queen o' Scots'* own necklace? *How?*'

'The ones in the library were a gift to the Murrays,' I reminded him.

Half the birds had come back to roost grudgingly in the top dove holes. They settled into their soft chirruping murmur, a sound as timeless as the river, yet alive and warm. They warbled in the background as I enthusiastically constructed a plausible history for Mary Stuart's lost pearls. 'Maybe she gave the Murrays the necklace and bracelet together, but then the necklace broke and someone put the pearls in the Reliquary with the other pearls, and they forgot about them, and a hundred and fifty years later when the donation was made to the library only the bracelet was left –'

Ellen interrupted suddenly, 'I smell smoke.'

We had our backs to the hole in the wall we'd come in by. Ellen turned around. She said, 'The chimney's smoking!'

We all spun round to look.

A soft roll of cloud was spilling out of the broken chimney wall and over the old wooden floor like haar mist. It was opaque, a pale and milky grey, the same colour as the Tay pearls in the shadow of a fold of cloth.

'That's torn it,' Jamie said. 'We're stuck here!'

We couldn't get back down a chimney filled with smoke.

All of us started to chatter at once, like the wood pigeons, trying to keep our voices low.

'If this place catches fire we are cooked,' I hissed.

'It's a chimney,' Jamie pointed out. 'It's supposed to smoke!'

Ellen said through her teeth, 'But who set the fire? Sergeant Henderson, trying to smoke us out?'

We stared at each other with drained faces.

'We might be able to climb down holding our breath,' I said. 'Or breathe through handkerchiefs. If we did it quickly –'

'*Could you?*' Ellen asked sharply.

'I'd try,' I said. 'I could if I had to.'

'We could have boiled a can of tea in the time it took you to get up. You cannae hold your breath so long.'

'I don't think it's Henderson, and I don't think he's trying to kill us,' Jamie said in a low voice. 'Not by building a fire in a fireplace, even if it is five hundred years old. I think it's the fellow who's been camping here. I think he heard our voices and now he's trying to trap us for a little while so he can clear off. He's been here a long time without getting caught.'

'So we bide until the fire burns out?' Ellen asked.

'Aye, we could bide …' Jamie stuck his head out of the door to the empty stairwell where the stone spiral had long ago collapsed, knowing there wasn't a chance of getting down there. Then he moved to the mullioned window. 'I wonder though …' He leaned out, then turned around to look at us. He stood silhouetted against grey sky.

'Sandy said that he and Davie and Archie had a race once. Before you and I and Grant were born, Julie. Up this tower, along the wall of the keep and down the kitchen chimney. You have to do this first bit like you're rock climbing, just hanging on with hands and feet. There's no ledge till you get to the wall of the keep.'

'We've climbed the kitchen chimney,' said Euan. 'But it's not so narrow as this one. You have to climb it the whole way using hands and feet as you said. And it slopes in the way at the top. It's no' easy.' He nodded towards me. 'She couldnae.'

'She doesn't need to,' Jamie said. 'If I go, I can put out the fire.'

'Or we could bide,' I said.

Jamie said forcefully, '*I want to catch him at it.*'

Euan stood up. 'I'll go along wi' you.'

'Jamie Stuart,' Ellen told him, 'take my knife.'

Euan went first. Ellen and I watched our brothers crawl one at a time through the mullioned window, cling like spiders to the stone wall as they inched their way from our window to the roofless wall of the ruined castle's central keep, and begin the precarious journey across that wall, five flights up and with a sheer drop on either side.

Then they had to scale the outside of the huge kitchen chimney. First Euan lowered himself inside, long-limbed but lithe and efficient, while Jamie sat perched on the topmost surviving stone of Aberfearn Castle, waiting his turn with his legs dangling down the chimney; then he, too, was gone.

Now there wasn't anything for me and Ellen to do but wait.

I hugged myself, still reeling with the discovery we'd made. 'We're the Aberfearn Castle guardians,' I said. 'We're the guardians of —'

'Mary Queen o' Scots' jewels!' Ellen finished.

The smoke continued to billow blue and foul across the attic floor. It was coming out here and using the whole dovecote as a chimney because of the broken wall.

Ellen added soberly, 'Let's be proper guardians. We'd best get those pearls away.'

In the time it took to scoop the pearls back into the jam jar we were both choking and weeping. The air of the little room was quickly turning poisonous. Ellen tore the black velvet swatch in half; I had to hold the cloth over her face and mine while she stowed the jar in her creel basket. Now my eyes and throat were burning and we were both wheezing, overwhelmed with the acrid smoke. The wood pigeons took off again.

'Bloody hell,' I spluttered, as we stuck our heads back out of the window, gulping in fresh air, one of us on each side of the stone mullion.

Smoke wreathed around us as it, too, found its way out of the broken room into the sky, so that there was no way for us to avoid it. My eyes were streaming as if I'd been rubbing them with pepper; I tied the velvet cloth fast over my nose and mouth.

We squinted at the narrow stone parapet that led across the ruin to the kitchen chimney.

'Could you?' Ellen suggested dubiously, her voice harsh and grating. Euan said she'd climbed the kitchen chimney before.

But I didn't think I could. My shoulder wouldn't support me.

Ellen just seemed like her usual naturally grim self, so I didn't want to show her that I'd never felt so frightened in my life.

'We could climb out of this window and sit on the wall, I suppose,' I choked, although I didn't really believe I could manage to spider across to the wall of the keep without splattering myself among the stones and nettles five floors beneath us, either.

A cascade of happy barks came pealing up from somewhere far below.

'Well, they've found my dog,' said Ellen.

'Nell,' I said, and took her hand.

'Don't fret, lass,' she told me through her own soft black mask.

'I'm not fretting. I just want to hold on to you.'

'You look like a train robber!'

'So do you.'

Her defiant determination braced me a little.

She sang softly:

'*My castle is aye my ain,*

An' harried it never shall be,

For I'll fall ere it's ta'en …'

'*… An' wha dare meddle wi' me?*' I joined in.

Our voices nearly twined together once more, but she broke off in a spasm of choking coughs.

'Don't sing for me,' I told her. 'Just breathe.'

She let go of my hand so she could wreathe her arm around my waist from behind. When I wove my own arm beneath hers, she clasped my hand against her ribs on the other side. We clung to each other as if we were drowning.

We were drowning.

After what seemed like another very long time we heard Euan calling up the chimney to his sister, just as Ellen had called down earlier.

'*Sproul!*'

We glanced around quickly, and we couldn't see a thing through the smoke that was still hanging in the tower room.

It took us a long moment to realise Jamie and Euan must have put the fire out.

I'm sure neither Ellen nor I noticed how tightly we were holding on to each other until we both went limp with relief. Then, after one last tearful hug, we tried to get back to the chimney.

But the smoke hadn't yet cleared enough for us even to turn around for more than a second or two, let alone cross the room, so we had to wait before we were able to hoarsely answer Euan's call. Jamie said later that it was the most fearsome part of the whole afternoon, that silent ten minutes before the smoke cleared, when they called and called until their own throats were raw and got no answer from us.

I am very glad that wasn't something I had to do. If it were the other way around – me wondering if Jamie were alive or dead … Not knowing. At any rate …

At any rate, we weren't dead.

It seemed *ages* before the chimney was sufficiently smokeless that we could climb back down. But we managed it at last, Ellen with the pearls stowed safely in her creel basket. The climb itself was easier than going up – gravity helps when you're on your way down. Pinkie, yapping her encouraging love from below us, helped too.

Jamie caught Ellen, then me, in the hearth of the Earl's Chamber at the bottom. The entire floor was a mess of damp, half-burned scraps of reed and gorse and heather and birch, slippery and deceptively awash with what must have been a tiny amount of water from the stolen builder's bucket Jamie had brought with him from the kitchen fireplace.

We three knelt on the old hearth in a clinging, grateful huddle, like a bundle of kittens for a moment, with the frantic dog bouncing around us. Then Jamie untangled himself, stood up and pointed.

'He says he's not a killer. I rather believe him. He's too scared to say anything else. We had to bully him a bit so he'd help us stamp out the fire though. *He didn't want to ruin his shoes.*'

The man they'd caught was cowering in a corner of the empty room with Euan standing casual guard nearby, and oh, this was surely Euan McEwen's finest hour: he stood straight and impassive, making use of his full six-foot-two-inches or whatever it is, holding Ellen's knife half-raised as if he were ready to toss it like a dart straight between the creeping villain's eyes the second he made a false move.

'Who is he?' Ellen asked.

'He won't say.'

'Oh, will he not?' she murmured in her best Lady Macbeth.

He was the very model of a tramp, with a full but badly barbered beard, wearing an unravelling tweed jacket, a stained shirt and an ill-fitting faded kilt with half the pleats let out of it to make it bigger.

It was Sandy's kilt; my kilt.

It was the kilt that had disappeared from the Magnette the night they found Housman's legs.

'He's the one who's been nicking everything,' I said.

'He nicked Housman's spectacles,' Jamie told us. 'Remember the broken spectacles? He had the rest. We nicked them back.'

Jamie patted his cartridge bag, and the craven person in the corner suddenly protested, 'Do be careful with those specs – I'm blind as a bat without them.'

His voice was cultured and *English*.

'Jamie,' I said, 'Give him back his specs.'

'It's quite useful keeping him blind as a bat,' Jamie said. 'He stopped fighting when we got them off him.'

'Give them back. I want to see what he looks like when he has them on.'

Jamie opened his bag and gracelessly passed the broken wire-rimmed glasses back to the prisoner, who sulkingly put them on.

'Look down,' I told him.

Very cowed by whatever his encounter with Jamie and Euan had been, he obeyed.

I took a step towards him.

'Bend over.'

With a frightened little gulp, again he obeyed.

'Now look up. *Look at me.*'

He raised his head, blinking at me over the top of the battered gold spectacles, and met my eyes.

'You're *Hugh Housman.*'

Not dead.

Not a ghost.

Alive and cringing and criminal and bewildered.

'*Solange!* What about *Solange?*' I cried out in fury. 'Waiting for trial like Mary Queen of Scots! You weasel! All those professions of love and you skulk here hiding while she's been accused of your *murder?*'

I could see by his expression that he wasn't aware of this turn of events, but I couldn't stop – the accusations and outrage came pouring out of me.

'Someone's dead! My God, who in blazes is that poor man they fished out of the river? Solange didn't kill *him* – did *you*? Did Angus Henderson have anything to do with it?' I stopped to breathe. 'I say, did you see Henderson? *Did you see Henderson hit me?*' Then I began to cough again.

The man was now nodding his head tremulously, but it was impossible to know to which of my battery of questions he was responding.

Euan had backed away, gaping.

None of the rest of us would have known Housman – I was the only one who'd seen him before.

I turned to Jamie, who was also gaping. 'Can he walk?' I demanded.

'Aye.'

'Let's take him to the Big House and call the police.'

The miserable Dr Housman suddenly leaped into life.

'I've done nothing – at least I don't think I have –'

'Well, we have to call the police, because *Solange is in prison*,' I snarled.

'Because of *me*? But all I did was leave my post,' he said plaintively. 'I-I needed some time alone. I knew she'd be

upset, but I thought she'd understand my message ...
I never thought ...'

Now we *all* gaped at him. I realised he was taking a
gamble, guessing we didn't know about the stolen pearls.

'I left my post,' he admitted again. 'I've lost my position.
I beg your pardon, young lady, but I think I did witness
your ... your accident last month.'

'You saw the Water Bailiff hit me! You actually saw him
hit me? You know! What happened? You know!'

I'd advanced on Housman, which scared him back into
confused and sullen silence. Jamie was right: the man was
far too much of a coward to have killed anyone. Not on
purpose, anyway. My God, I was ready to twist the details
out of him with a corkscrew.

But no – I could see that wouldn't work. He'd been lurk-
ing here for over a month waiting for the dust to clear and
a quiet opportunity to get those pearls back, and hadn't
once been brazen enough or devious enough to manage it.

Maybe he hadn't even thought it was possible to change
his original plan to collect them at the end of the summer.
There'd been too many builders and newspapermen and us
coming and going, and the river watcher patrolling the
path, and Sandy camped at the Inverfearnie Library and
the McEwens camped in Inchfort Field, and the high water
in the Fearn after all that rain.

Hugh Housman was a scholar. He wasn't a natural thug and he wasn't naturally bold. He needed babying. I wouldn't get anything out of him if the police whisked him away.

'Och, Euan, give Ellen back her knife,' I said. 'What this Sassenach needs is a cup of tea. Let's take him to the Big House and turn him over to Francis Dunbar.'

'Aye, maybe it'll give Dunbar a chance to do something right for a change,' Jamie said.

'Oh, yes, Dunbar!' Dr Housman agreed with hangdog haste. 'I expect he's had a rough time of it. My fault as well – he never should have had to answer for me –' He shut up guiltily.

Ellen put her knife back in her creel.

Mild-mannered Euan, enjoying his first taste of authority, told Dr Housman, 'Stop quaking, man. The daft dog's more likely to hurt you than I am. Come away.'

'I can't wait to see the headline in the *Mercury*,' Jamie said cruelly. '"Narrow Escape for Drowned Man."'

I chummed Dr Housman along as we made our way back to the Big House, with Pinkie at our heels being very forgiving now that we were all heading in the same direction.

'Lovely creature,' Housman said. 'Tan Border collie? What's she called?'

'Pinkie. She's not mine. She belongs to her.' I pointed towards Ellen. 'A gift from the late Earl of Strathfearn.'

'Oh,' he said, surprised at the combination of tinker lass and purebred hound.

'Perhaps you'd prefer brandy to tea!' I suggested winningly, at my most devious. 'You must have had a rough time of it too. I don't understand why you've been hiding! If you saw the Water Bailiff knock me out, why didn't you just tell someone right away? Francis Dunbar, or Mary Kinnaird, for example? I was off my head for three days and nobody knew who I was!'

'I … well … I was fishing for pearls when the – what did you call him?'

'The Water Bailiff.'

'Yes. No.' Housman added hastily, 'I *didn't* see him hit you. But I saw him carrying you. And he saw me. He threatened that if I gave him away he'd haul *me* in for assaulting you. And it could have easily been me. I couldn't prove … I was afraid …'

Irritatingly, he let that sentence go unfinished.

I forced myself to be patient with him.

'That's why you didn't tell anyone,' I said. 'But I still don't understand why you hid.'

'I'm sorry.'

He was panting a little; we were walking at a youthful pace and he was not young. And of course, he'd been living on stolen sandwiches for a month.

'I'm sorry,' he repeated sheepishly. 'Who are the others with you?'

I thought, *Oh, don't you try to change the subject, you wee weasel of a man.*

I answered his question, but I wasn't going to be so familiar as to give him our names. Let him wonder.

'The short fair one is my brother; the tall ginger ones are friends of ours who stay here in the summer. They took me to the hospital after the Water Bailiff hit me.'

'I–I'm sorry,' he stammered for the third time. 'I didn't see him hit you.'

It was almost as though he was trying to tell me Henderson *hadn't* hit me.

Fleetingly, I wondered if Housman could possibly have hit me himself.

But as he rabbited on, I couldn't believe he was remotely capable of committing an act of violence against *anyone*.

'When Henderson left me there with you, I realised I truly might get blamed for the attack,' Housman said. 'I thought you were going to die. And then it would look like I'd killed you. And I panicked. So I hid. I didn't really know what to do when the lifeboats first started searching for me … I hoped it would all blow over if I didn't turn up.'

'You perfect coward,' I sympathised patronisingly. 'Please don't tell me again that you're sorry. Scavenging sandwiches and newspapers from the workers at the Big House! And was that also you pawing through the McEwens' things while they slept? You're a disgrace to academia.'

It took every fibre of my being not to scream at him: WHAT ABOUT MARY QUEEN OF SCOTS' PEARLS, YOU SNEAKING WEASEL?

'Why didn't you just run away back to England and make up some scholarly excuse?' I asked. 'To stop everyone thinking you'd drowned yourself?'

He fell abruptly silent. The rest of what he'd told me was probably true – it fit the jigsaw properly. But the answer to this particular question was: 'I wanted to go back for those three hundred and twenty-seven pearls I hid in the river', and he wasn't going to tell me that.

He hadn't given up on going back for them.

And with Solange still in prison …

Greedy, treacherous little coward! I thought. *Go and see if you can find them now. Good luck to you.*

17

THE GLORIOUS TWELFTH

The morning after we discovered Hugh Housman hiding in Aberfearn Castle, Ellen telephoned me from the Inverfearnie Library to tell me I must come to see her at once.

I did not go rushing out there in a blaze of curiosity. The events of the past fortnight had left me wary and cautious of strangers. It *sounded* like Ellen on the 'phone, but it could have been *anyone*. I thought irrelevantly of Housman's 'damned unfeeling' sister. After I hung up I sat on the bottom step in the hall swithering for ten minutes, and then rang back just to prove the call *had* come from the library.

Mary answered. Yes, she'd let Miss McEwen use the telephone. Miss McEwen had paid her twopence to put the call through.

'Do you think I should come?' I asked, irrationally cautious.

'What is the matter with you, Julia? Why wouldn't you come to see her if she wants you to? I thought she was your friend.'

★

Ellen met me by the iron footbridge. She was carrying a large brown envelope.

I thought of pearls.

'What is going on?' I asked.

'I want to show you something.'

'Where's Pinkie?'

The envelope was flat. It couldn't be pearls.

'In Miss Kinnaird's kitchen. Pinkie's not let through to the other rooms, but Miss Kinnaird has fallen in love with that dog.'

'She's pure magic, our Pinkie.'

'Come along,' Ellen said, and strode ahead of me across the circular drive of the library, the gravel crunching beneath her feet. She moved with force and purpose and I had to keep making uneven little skips to keep up with her, because her legs are so much longer than mine.

'Where are we going?'

'That flat rock by the Drookit Stane – I want to show this to you before I show Strathfearn.'

She meant Sandy.

'I want to see what you think,' she added.

When we reached the flat rock at the beachy place, she sat down and slid a sheaf of glossy paper from the envelope.

'Come and look.'

I sat beside her.

'The photographer from the *Mercury*, that Catriona Lennox, sent us these this morning,' Ellen said. 'It just says "Strathfearn Log Boat Excavation Project" in the address, so I opened it because I took in the post. No one else has seen it.'

They were the photographs Miss Lennox had taken during the morning we'd first begun our salvage operation. Ellen shuffled through them rapidly; I watched over her shoulder.

'You ken what you're looking at?' she asked.

'Aye.'

'What's this one, then?'

'That's looking close at the bit of cord tied to the boat.'

'So what's this?'

'That's it again.'

'Is it?'

I frowned. 'Well, yes, or another angle – it's the same bit of rope.'

'Why?' She held the two photographs up before me.

The camera must have been very close, but it made the detail perfectly clear. 'You can see that criss-cross woven pattern in it, there and there,' I said. 'This bit's mostly crushed or decayed, but you can see they're the same, can't you?'

'Aye,' she said in an expressionless voice. 'I can see that. I wanted to know if you could too.'

She didn't lower her hands, but held the pictures up, waiting.

'But that's not the boat,' I whispered. 'The rope's the same, but that picture –'

'*The rope's the same,*' Ellen echoed.

The photographer had accidentally included a picture of the rope that had strangled the murdered man. She'd shot it so close that his decayed skin beneath it was as dark and cakey as the wood of the Bronze Age boat.

But the rope was the same.

'He can't have been killed with anything that old!' I said. 'You saw how fragile it was.'

Ellen said softly, 'Maybe it wasnae sae old when he was killed.'

She let that sink in. She'd had a bit longer than me to get used to the idea. For me, it was as if a half-completed jigsaw had been flipped upside down and now I was looking at a completely unfamiliar picture.

'You're saying the dead man is *as old as the log boat*?'

'All I'm saying is it's the same rope.'

I shook my head.

'Two ends of the same rope,' Ellen suggested. 'Maybe even one end tied to the boat, one end tied round his neck.'

I had a wild vision of a person being dragged to death by a boat. No, of course not. 'He was buried in the boat,' I said slowly.

'Maybe.'

'Did people *do* that?'

'Not in the Bronze Age. They're mostly buried in wee chests, crouching. But the Vikings did it. People have found ship burials in Norway, and in England. And deep water was sacred to the Picts, who were here before the Christians …'

'The burn's not very deep at the mouth of the Fearn!'

'They buried him in the peat, below the riverbed. Places where rivers meet are sacred too. He was beneath the crossing of two rivers, downstream of the Drookit Stane. And that killing – the triple death – that's a sacrifice.'

'How d'you know all *that*?' I exclaimed in disbelief. 'Old Travellers' tales passed down from Auntie Bessie?'

Ellen gave her snort of scorn and answered coldly, '*Proceedings of the Society of Antiquaries of Scotland*. But true enough, Auntie Bessie likely has a thing or two to say about it.'

'I'm sorry.'

She put the photographs back in the envelope and got out her pipe and tobacco pouch.

'Have a draw.'

She gave me the matches. When she'd filled the bowl she let me light it myself, laughing at my incompetence. 'Why have you no' been practising?'

'I don't want to break the one you gave me. I want to take it to school to rag the other girls.'

We smoked in silence for a couple of minutes, listening to the timeless voice of the burn as it chuckled past the Drookit Stane, thinking about our ancestors.

'Those spear points,' I asked suddenly, 'the ones they keep finding in the pipeline trench. Are they part of it?'

'Likely buried with him. I looked them up. They weren't all bronze; the newest is iron, maybe fifteen hundred years old, not more than two thousand. Perhaps they buried him just before the Christians came in to Scotland.'

'So the boat's not as old as we thought.'

'Well, I think the body's *older* than anyone guessed. I dinnae think it's as old as two thousand years, but there's nae telling. The boat could be older – the folk who buried him could have kent it was there, like we did, and put him in.'

'There's no way *ever* to tell,' I said. 'Because we dug it up and chopped it in pieces and tossed them about as if it didn't matter.'

'*We* didnae do that,' Ellen pointed out.

'No one can ever prove any of what you just said.'

'Yon mystified doctor will help. If Strathfearn asks him to consider whether the body's ancient – well, then it's a matter for the Society of Antiquaries instead of the High Court.'

'It is,' I breathed in agreement.

'So you dinnae think it's mad? You think I should tell Strathfearn?'

'It'll be the most wonderful, astonishing discovery of his entire *life*,' I said. 'Even if he lives to be a hundred! Of course you should tell Sandy. But all that digging about for a murderer – all for nothing!'

'Best that way though, aye, Julie?' she teased. 'Look, I've made you a birthday present.'

She drew it from her pocket in a fold of black velvet. 'Of course you must gie it back after, but you can wear it to your ceilidh dance wi' your new gown. You'll be the first one to wear it since Mary Queen o' Scots.'

She'd strung together Mary Stuart's matched Tay pearls to make a necklace. It was like a little strand of moonlight.

'*Crikey!*' I laughed hilariously, and for so long that Ellen started giggling too. 'I can't wear these. Do you know what a necklace like this would cost? Even if it weren't … *what it is*?'

'I ken better than you!'

'Everyone will *notice*.'

'But no one will recognise them. Jamie didn't. Tell a story! You're good at that. Say they're on loan from the Murray Estate. That's *true*. Hold still … turn around …'

With cool, smooth-tipped fingers she tied the pearls around my neck.

'I told you my folk don't care much about keeping things. But it's pleasure to give.'

She rested her hands on my shoulders for a moment.

'Let me see.'

I turned to face her, feeling radiant.

She laughed. 'Och, they suit you, Queenie! Promise me you'll wear them.'

'I absolutely will.'

I thought then that I'd give her my own pearl, the one I found in the envelope, the only one that didn't get stolen. I'd give it to her whether she kept it or not. Because she's right: it's pleasure to give. I wanted to give her something that *mattered*. And I didn't think she'd take anything else.

With tragic dark rings around her beautiful dark eyes, holding her proud head high, Solange was released into our flood of embraces and floral offerings, which she accepted with grace and tears.

She did not put fresh roses in Dr Housman's bedroom, nor greet him with forgiveness.

Housman himself seemed none the worse for his misadventures. He slept them off upstairs in the room he'd been given when he first arrived here, avoiding Solange. He'd been immediately sacked by the Murray Estate, but as he hadn't done any work for them since June anyway, it hardly mattered. His sister was supposed to fetch him back to England sometime soon.

We did not treat the prodigal scholar kindly. Jamie, at Solange's bidding, took the pearl earrings Housman had given her and used the box to wedge open the door to Housman's room (I liberated the pearls first; we considered they were probably part of the Murray Hoard, but Solange didn't need to know they were stolen). I delivered to Housman a copy of the *Mercury* each evening, carefully folded open to choice stories: the most recent update on the log boat, or on the ancient body discovered on the Murray Estate, or even just an occasional gossipy tale of domestic bliss gone sour. Housman was too much of a coward ever to complain about us to Mother.

Frank Dunbar would not speak to him – they met once on the staircase while I was coming in the house, and Frank actually turned his back on Housman halfway down the stairs to avoid an encounter with him.

Jamie and I took it in turns to be constantly in Housman's way when he tried to get out of the house, thwarting his pathetic attempts to go after his stolen treasure, which he presumably thought was still hidden in the river at the foot of the Drookit Stane.

It wasn't, of course. We'd got Ellen to plant the pearls in their jar quietly back in the Murray Collection, where Sandy would discover them eventually and report them to the National Museum of Antiquities or the Murray Estate. He hadn't noticed them yet and I couldn't help thinking of them as our secret wedding present to him. I knew that just the discovering of them would make him joyful, even if he had to give them away in the end. It was *true* what Ellen had said about giving; and nothing of Strathfearn's was ours any more except in spirit.

Because now the Glenfearn School was ready to finish and furnish the Big House, and the other dormitories and the new classrooms, before the school term began. The grounds were not ready but the house was nearly complete – as was the catalogue – and the plan was for the Murray/ Beaufort-Stuart party to clear out north to Craig Castle in the week following the Laird of Moredun's Opening Day shoot. I had only a fortnight of my holiday left anyway.

The day before the shooting party (and my birthday), Father arrived in the landaulet from Craig Castle, so as to be able to transport those of us who didn't fit in the Magnette. Sandy would stay on to finish the log boat excavation, but for the rest of us it was going to be goodbye to Strathfearn House for good.

The day of the shoot was warm and bright.

That was a blessing and a curse. I started out feeling brisk and happy but by mid-morning my blouse was sticking to my back and when I took off my tweed jacket Jamie grumbled at me, even if he was my favourite brother, because the white stood out against the heather; notwithstanding I was well hidden behind the sheltering wall of the butt and the birds couldn't *possibly* care what I was wearing. And I couldn't get my hair out of my eyes because of that vindictive nurse chopping it all different lengths so that it wouldn't stay pinned. And I hadn't held a gun since December, so I had to be womanly and be satisfied picking up other people's dead birds with the dogs and beaters after each drive. And it was my birthday but *even Euan and Jamie* were too focused on loading guns and killing birds to remember to say anything about it. And when they were kind and offered me a gun during one of the drives, I couldn't hit a single bird.

I would have started to feel sorry for myself had not Mummy and Mrs Menzies arrived with the lunch at midday. They were accompanied by Jean McEwen leading ponies loaded with baskets stuffed to bursting. A couple of housemaids from the castle ran back and forth spreading white tablecloths over picnic rugs and laying out cold meats and Dundee cake, and, oh, lord, *one of the maids was Florrie.*

My legs were decently clad in stockings and wellington boots, and I was in a proper tweed skirt of my own and not Sandy's hitched-up kilt, but in a sweaty blouse with sleeves rolled up and hair standing in spikes in the Pitbroomie wind, the only things keeping Florrie from recognising me were my collection of useless hairpins and the fact that this time I was supposed to be a girl.

I didn't think I could count on the hairpins to disguise me, so I threw all my soul into Being A Girl.

I snatched up a couple of cold beef sandwiches and two bottles of ginger beer and made a beeline for Francis Dunbar, standing awkwardly a little apart from everybody else, looking a little lost, with one hand deep in his pocket and a cigarette in the other. Father and Jamie were chatting to Moredun about moorland maintenance; Euan had vanished discreetly into the gorse with the rest of the beaters; Sandy was being solicitous of Mary; Jean McEwen was organising the emptying of the ponies' baskets; and Mother was helping Mrs Menzies be hostess to a party of about twenty-five local people who all knew each other. Frank was a clear outsider.

'Here you are, Mr Dunbar,' I said, holding up a sandwich and a bottle. He came out of his dream, smiled with pleasure and crushed his cigarette underfoot.

'Thank you, Miss Beaufort-Stuart,' he said. 'Have you had a good morning? Oh, and many happy returns!'

I looked up at him archly (*so stupid* – perfectly embarrassing behaviour on my part, but of course I was trying to avoid being recognised by Florrie). He took the bottle and sandwich and watched me wrestle ineffectively – on purpose – to get my own bottle open.

'Let me,' he said, predictably.

This allowed our hands to brush against each other's, and me to laugh as the fizzy drink popped and bubbled over the neck of the bottle, and when he gave it back to me we had to wipe our hands on the edge of a tablecloth. And we ended up sitting together.

'I missed everything I shot at,' I admitted. 'How about you?'

'Not too bad. I'm out of practice, but I've been satisfied this morning. I was a soldier for ten years; I did a lot of game hunting in India.'

'That's right – you're a veteran of the Black Watch, like Sergeant Henderson and Alan McEwen! You'll wear your kilt tonight?'

'Of course!'

Embarrassing.

But I was enjoying it too; and when he noticed my birthday present from Mummy, it was an excuse to give him my hand and let him hold it and admire it – my hand, I mean, though the ring was the excuse.

It is a square-cut ruby in rose gold, set between wee triangles of tiny pearls.

I told him, 'It was my great-grandmother's. My grand-mother gave it to Mother for *her* eighteenth birthday.' (See how I slipped that in? Quite true, but perpetuating the illu-sion that today was *my* eighteenth.)

'Are they Fearn river pearls?'

'All but one of them is. There's a story about it. The setting is French, and my grandmother lost one of the pearls right after she was married, and the jeweller in Perth couldn't match it. So my grandfather replaced them all with Fearn pearls that he'd found himself. After *my* mother was married, she lost another! So my father replaced it with a Dee pearl *he'd* found in the river on our estate at Craig Castle in Aberdeenshire. They don't quite match now, if you look closely.'

'Would you believe that after all the time I've been at Strathfearn, I still can't tell a Fearn river pearl when I see one?' Frank said.

He raised my fingers and bent his head to look at the ring, then prudently let go, flushing a little.

'Can't you see the difference?' I asked.

'One's almost gold-hued!'

'That's the one from the Dee. The pinker ones are from the Fearn.'

'Pearls from two of your rivers. I like that.'

I said honestly, 'I do too. I love it fiercely for just that. Because it is a little bit of Strathfearn and a little bit of Craigie and a little bit of France, and of my mother and father and grandmother and grandfather, and I will have it with me always. It is all of ours and they are part of me.'

We caught each other's eyes. I turned away demurely.

'Have you met my father?' I asked, recognising the moment when our tête-à-tête was beginning to look too intimate. 'Come along and be introduced.'

And that gave me the excuse to be tucked into Father's side with his arm around my waist, receiving a kiss on the head instead of the dreadful birthday bumps we used to get as small children. By this time I was fairly sure my diversion was successful and Florrie wasn't gasping for me today.

When the afternoon was over, one of the big guest bedrooms at Glenmoredun Castle was relegated to the girls to change in; and we got to use the bathrooms, which was delightful (if rushed). The castle is as old as the one at Aberfearn, bits of it fourteenth century, but in good nick.

Their hot-water boiler was installed five years ago, modern and efficient, unlike ours which is Victorian.

By the time the ceilidh was to start I'd been fully transformed not just by the green-gold dancing frock and long white gloves and priceless necklace that wasn't mine, but also by my fairy godmother Solange's incredible magic wrought with hot curling tongs and sugar-water. I swear it took a full hour for her to wave my hair and, if it was not as swift a transformation as Cinderella's, it was certainly as complete. Not a single hairpin was used and I ended up looking like I was ready to be photographed for Vogue.

Solange indeed looked beautiful too, in a dress of asymmetric black and white panels that she bought the last time we were all in France. The other girls were rather in awe of her recent brush with injustice; I found myself feeling protective and proud.

The party was bittersweet, knowing we'd probably not be here next year. Also, as I found myself whirling and stamping to the same tunes that Euan had piped us three weeks ago, I grew melancholy about the McEwens.

I had a moment of glory during one of the breaks as everyone sang 'For She's a Jolly Good Fellow', and Father made a speech in which he teased me about my aim but praised my fortitude, in light of my not-so-recent accident. I did not sit out one single dance. This, of course, was because I was being cunning about whom I danced with. And Francis Dunbar looked splendid in his Black Watch kilt and black Prince Charlie jacket twinkling with silver. It took careful planning to end up across from him.

Ellen's necklace was a source of much probing curiosity.

The other ladies, to Mother: 'My dear Esmé, *where* do Julia's pearls come from? That's surely not a birthday gift?'

'They're part of the Murray Estate. She says Sandy found them among the objects he's cataloguing for the Murray Collection.'

'Really, they ought to be locked up.'

'She's to return them the second she takes her clothes off, I can assure you. And they *will* be locked up, or more likely put on display in a museum, but don't you think it's lovely that they're being *worn*?'

And the Menzies girls, my own age, to me: 'Are those *your* pearls, Julie?'

'They're on loan from the Murray Estate.'

'I'd be terrified to touch them, let alone dance in them!'

'Go on, touch. They don't bite!'

And Francis Dunbar, mid-waltz: 'Are those Fearn pearls too?'

'No, they're Tay pearls. They're not mine. They're part of the Murray Estate.'

'Part of the Murray Estate,' he echoed, staring down at me with that air of perpetual bafflement that makes him seem faintly vulnerable and which I find so appealing. 'I thought those pearls were sold.'

'Sandy found 'em in the Hoard,' I said. 'They have to go back tonight.'

'How disappointing for you!'

'No, I'm happy I get to wear them for my birthday party. They make me sensational.'

He laughed. 'You'd still be sensational without them.'

And because Mary had given me the key to her kitchen door to allow me to return the pearls to the Murray Collection straight away, Mummy let me have the Magnette so I could stop at the Inverfearnie Library on my way back to Strathfearn House. And because Frank was going back to Strathfearn House too and there was an extra seat in the car, I asked him to come along with me.

Oh, that was probably an error. My own error. I should have at least *told* someone he was coming with me. But I was no longer being watched over like a Russian princess and it was late, and I was feeling adult and elegant and sure of myself – dressed for *Vogue*, old enough to be married – *and* I thought I was being responsible.

18

AS FAIR ART THOU, MY BONNIE LASS

The moon was one single night past full, the light flooding and shadowing the birch wood and the River Fearn. It was stunningly, ethereally beautiful. The little library on Inverfearnie Island had two yellow lights left welcomingly glowing, one in the kitchen and one upstairs.

'Mary went straight home after the shoot. She said she'd go to bed about nine,' I said, as I drew the car up on the gravel in the circular drive in front of the old building and shut off the motor.

The undying night voice of the Fearn was suddenly interrupted by a sharp, warning bark. Frank started.

'Is that the Travellers' dog?'

'It's the heron. They sometimes hunt at night. Listen …'

The heron cried again, wild and strange in the dark.

'I'm glad you know what it is!' Frank told me.

'Me too,' I laughed. 'I don't like ghosts!'

I got out. Frank had a harder time extracting his long body from the confines of the little Magnette. I laughed again, and went round the front of the car to hold the door for him.

'I'm supposed to do that for you!' he objected.

'Never mind, I know you can be chivalrous when you try.'

The night air was still warm; even in the evening wind of the open motor car I hadn't wanted a wrap. I got out Mary's key. Frank offered me his arm as we made our way around the back. He held the door open for me, and followed me inside.

'Have you been here before?' I asked softly. Silly, I know, to keep our voices low, as Mary couldn't possibly have heard us. But knowing she might be sleeping made me want to be quiet.

'I've not been inside.'

'How ridiculous! It's a national treasure. It's one of the oldest public lending libraries in Scotland, opened in the seventeenth century. Mostly just useful stuff for farmers and landowners, but there's a rather wonderful display of first editions of Robert Burns, and …'

It was too dark to see the display cases downstairs. I didn't want to switch on lights.

'I can't show you in the dark, but there's a pearl bracelet that belonged to Mary Queen of Scots as a child. She gave it to the Murrays and they gave it to the library.'

He drew in a breath, then exclaimed, 'How wonderful!'

I led the way upstairs.

'This is the Upper Reading Room. This is where they've been cataloguing the Murray Collection.'

The casement window was propped open to the silver night. The Keiller jar of stolen pearls (minus the ones I was wearing) was *still* sitting on the big table in the middle, unopened, undiscovered.

There was one electric standing lamp which Mary had left alight by the stairs. I glanced over my shoulder at Dunbar, a pace or two behind me; his face was shadowed, but the light behind him caught on his silver cuff buttons.

'Can you help me with the necklace?' I asked. 'It's not got a proper clasp – the pearls are strung on a thread that ties at the back. I can't see to untie it.'

I turned around and bent my head. His fingertips at the nape of my neck were hard and gentle. I turned again when he'd finished and held out my hand for the pearls; they slid like running water from his palm into mine.

Again I turned around, and dropped the pearls into the small round wooden cup, cracked and black with age, where I'd first seen them, and they piled up in its dark globe like a little celestial host of moons.

That's where you belong, I told them silently, and spun on one heel back to Dunbar.

'Oh, Julie, stop there a moment,' he begged. 'You never stop moving. Let me *look* at you. Just for a moment.'

I did stop. It was startlement – the longing in his voice was so genuine, and unexpected. I froze and I tried to imagine what he saw: Tinker Bell in a cloud of spring-green chiffon, my mouth and eyelids dark with grown-up paint, lamplight glinting on the glossy artificial waves of my hair.

'*Julie,*' he repeated hoarsely.

No, he didn't see a dusted fairy. He saw clear hazel eyes like Cairngorm amber in the lamplight, and defiant hair like ripe wheat, and smooth skin like new milk. He saw through the coloured powder and the floating silk. He saw a woman.

I took a step backward and found myself trapped against the library table. I grabbed the edge for support; the polished chestnut was slippery beneath my gloves. *Here it comes if you want it*, I thought, *that kiss*.

And suddenly I wasn't sure I did. I wasn't … well … I didn't know if I was ready.

But he was more beautiful than ever in the black coat and silver buttons and Black Watch tartan, and I thought, *Shame on me if I don't* try.

So I stood still and let him look at me. I had to turn my face aside a little so that the lamp behind him didn't blind me. After a long, hushed moment he stepped across the space between us. He leaned down towards my face and kissed me very chastely on the lips. Just briefly, but so intimate.

'You are …'

'What am I?' It came out as a whisper, half-caught in my throat.

'I don't exactly know,' he laughed.

And then he took me by the shoulders and suddenly it wasn't chaste any more; suddenly another kiss came slamming into me like a rolling wave and I was caught in it like an empty shell dashed against shingle.

And I realised I *wasn't* ready. It really is that simple.

It wasn't that I didn't enjoy it. It was that I knew I was about to lose control. Ellen had let me choose. Even the Water Bailiff had let me choose. Francis Dunbar wasn't going to.

Our mouths were glued together and I was gripping the edge of the table behind me with both hands. I let go with one hand and reached up to grab him by the back of his neck, trying to dig my nails in to get his attention, trying to hurt him enough that he let go for a moment. The gloves foiled me. My nails were blunted and he mistook my grip for returned passion. I changed my tactic and got my fingers hooked between his collar and his throat, and pulled until he had to come up for air.

'What?' he gasped.

'I lied to you!' I babbled wildly. 'I'm sorry, I shouldn't have, but it was so easy! I'm not eighteen.'

'It's not your birthday?'

'*I'm not eighteen!*'

Oh, heaven help us, does passion make all men so *stupid*? He still didn't understand that I was trying to turn him away.

'It doesn't matter, Julie,' he said. 'You needn't lie to me. No matter when. You're unbelievably lovely –'

'*I'm sixteen,*' I rasped at him. '*Sixteen today.* It's my sixteenth birthday today.'

He looked baffled for a moment, then showered me with his slow and melting film-star smile. He shifted his grip on my shoulders and murmured enticingly, 'Many happy returns of the day.'

I heard myself make a sound that could as easily have been a gasp of laughter as a sob of frustration. O God, I was being terribly cack-handed. I didn't want to hurt his feelings.

He moved his hands across my shoulders. He'd been a soldier and a hunter in India; his touch was firm and experienced, and his fingers were large and strong and restless. They slipped lightly a little down my torso and hesitated, tautening, over my breasts. He explored the lines of my body through the silk. I could tell he was doing it on purpose, touching me. It made me feel entirely naked.

'Don't,' I said sharply. 'Stop.'

He paused. He was so much taller than me.

'You vixen,' he said quietly, moving his hands back up to grip my shoulders, and bent his mouth to mine for another plunging kiss.

I was wholly out of my depth.

I tore my face away from his; it hurt to do it.

'Mary!' I screamed desperately, '*Mary!*'

Of course she couldn't hear me.

But Francis Dunbar could, and he took a baby step backwards, though he was still holding tight to my shoulders.

'Why, Julie!'

He was shocked, amazed to discover I didn't want this. No, not amazed – *disbelieving*. Because he wasn't toying with me. He was serious. *This is how a lad gives a kiss when he means it.*

'I'm not … I'm not ready!'

'Let me show you.'

'I know how. I'm not ready for you. It's not right.'

Oh, if it *had* been right, he'd have *listened to me*.

'Julie,' he said gently, relentless as a roadroller, 'it's easy. Don't be afraid. You are *so beautiful*. I won't hurt you again.'

And it was true – he wasn't hurting me now. He was … *worshipful*, almost. But fearfully intimate. Now he'd somehow got his thumbs worked into the low neckline of my frock, and beneath the fabric he rubbed them gently across the bare skin of the sides of my breasts – and … *God*. It made the fine down stand up on my spine, like a cat's.

Mary wasn't going to come. I was on my own. I had to do something to wake him up – something he'd notice, something he'd *mind*.

I was arched backward now, cringing away from him, but still trapped by the table's edge. One of my gloved hands slipped again and I thought fleetingly of throwing myself across the table, except it would make chaos of the Murray Collection, just when Sandy had finished sorting most of it out – and worse than that, I'd risk Francis Dunbar throwing his hot and heavy body over mine. He didn't care about the blinking flint arrowheads and bronze blades.

My hand, sliding backward, stopped abruptly against the baize table cover and knocked over the wooden cup with the necklace in it. I heard the pearls' watery cascade as they slid out on to the table.

And a jigsaw hole tore open.

'How do you know there are pearls in the Murray Collection?' I whispered.

He sucked in air. For a moment he wore his look of bewildered worry, then regained his composure with that foolish, winning smile.

'I didn't, till I saw these.'

'When I told you they were part of the Murray Estate you said you thought they'd been sold. Even my mother didn't remember those pearls. *How did you know about them?*'

He hesitated for half a second. 'Dr Housman told me, of course.'

'Why would he have told you *anything about them?*'

This time his hesitation was damningly long.

At last Dunbar answered with even care, 'He talked about the collection all the time. I'd helped him move it from the Big House to the library; he knew I was interested –'

'Yes, but he wouldn't have said *anything* to you about the pearls because *he was going to steal them.*'

Dunbar's invading hands tightened, involuntarily gripping me in a new way.

He whispered, '*You know.*'

'Of course I know – I found them! We *all* know, me and Jamie and Ellen and Euan! We found the Murray pearls where Housman left them, all three hundred and twenty-seven of them – we counted them on the riverbank!'

'You don't … you don't remember?'

'Remember what?'

He shook his head just once, his face serious. 'Julie, it doesn't matter.'

Just like it didn't matter how old I was, except this time he was bluffing. His voice was hollow; his grip still tense and harsh. He wasn't worshipping me any more. He was still bent on seduction, but for a different reason now, and in a different way. I had woken him up.

'You knew! You were in on it!' I accused. 'You were going to share those pearls with him! You found them when you were moving the things to the library, and you must have hidden them together …'

I'd overheard Dunbar talking to Housman on my first day in the house; I remembered how Dunbar's voice had brightened. The words came tumbling out almost faster than I could throw them at him.

'That telephone call – Housman rang to call you out to help him! He'd found the perfect hiding place – he'd been talking to Alan McEwen, and he knew the McEwens would never go near the foot of the Drookit Stane. You must have gone to the library just after I did – you knew the Water Bailiff would be busy with the McEwens, and Mary was away, and you thought no one would notice you hiding the pearls. And afterwards *you knew Housman wasn't dead –*'

The pieces were clicking into place in my head as if by clockwork.

'That ancient body was a godsend for you both! It made it look as if Hugh Housman really had drowned! And when he stole my kilt and left his trousers by the river to make people think it was him they'd found, you knew – you *knew* he'd done it! You were angry about it! You were helping him –'

'Julie, *don't*. Please stop.'

'You helped him hide! I'll bet you slipped that dreadful suicide note under our carpet for him. You let him creep into your study at night – you left food for him! I *saw* him trying to get in. What a *flipping bungler* he is – he came to the wrong door! And now you've let him hang about the house for the past week because you both think you're going to go back there at the end of the summer, when the rest of us are gone, and get the pearls back –'

Francis Dunbar pulled me tight against his body, crushing our ribs together, and I could do nothing to separate my mouth from his, and the suffocating kiss was meant to silence me.

But my arm was free and I could see the jar with the rest of the pearls in it out of the corner of my eye. I reached for it and grabbed.

And in a flashing instant I knew where I'd seen that jar in the first place. I'd seen it out of the corner of my eye on that first morning at Strathfearn. Sitting on the flat stone where I'd been guddling for trout, laughing at Hugh Housman splashing about in the river with no clothes on, I'd heard the bramble and elder rustling behind me; and I'd turned my head a fraction just in time to catch, in the corner of my eye, a glimpse of that stoneware Keiller jar descending at speed towards the back of my skull.

The blasted thing was too heavy and smooth to pick up with one hand gloved in slippery silk. I shoved the jar off the table and it landed on the floor with a clunk. Dunbar raised his head and glanced over his shoulder.

'My God, is that −?'

'*You hit me!*' I gasped. 'It wasn't the river watcher with his cromach. *You hit me with that jar full of pearls!*'

'They're *here*?' he gasped in return.

'You *snake!*'

He was holding on to me so tightly it was making my ribs ache.

'Yes, they're here! Not just that necklace but all the rest of them too, all three hundred and twenty-seven of them − so what? *What about my head?*'

He relaxed his grip on me a little, and I managed to wrench myself sideways and dive under the table. I bowled the jar across the floor like a football and emerged on the other side of the table. I picked up the jar in both hands and scrambled to my feet.

'You recognise it, *don't you*? This jar full of pearls. They're all still here in this jam pot, except the ones I was wearing −'

'Julie, I didn't mean to … I thought you were one of the tinkers, and you'd seen Housman –'

'You *ran away*! At least Housman stuck around for a minute wondering if I was dead or alive. Anyway, couldn't you just have gone off without hitting me and come back later to hide your stupid jar? I didn't know what was in it or what you were up to! You didn't need to smash my head in – even if I *had* been a tinker, you didn't need to smash my head in!'

'I *panicked.*'

'*So am I panicking!*'

I flung the jar at the window. The casement was propped halfway, and the jar went straight through the leaded panes with a satisfying crash.

Dunbar cried out, 'You – you *didn't!*'

He came tearing around the table.

I bolted. I ducked under the table again, hurled myself across the room and vaulted pell-mell down the stairs, screeching Mary's name – but she'd heard the glass breaking right above her room, and the jar smashing on the gravel outside her window. She came running with her shotgun just the way she'd done when I first broke one of her library windows three years earlier. For a moment we were wedged breast to breast on the narrow spiral stair: Mary on the way up in her nightgown and bare feet; I on the way down in an evening frock of chartreuse-coloured silk and long gloves, like Cinderella at midnight.

'Julia! What's happened?'

'Francis Dunbar. Still there,' I gasped, pointing her upward.

She didn't hesitate. We squeezed past each other and I skidded and bumped the rest of the way down on my silk-clad bottom.

I picked myself up, gathered the stupid dress around my waist and tore outside.

The open-topped Magnette stood waiting for me. I vaulted in over the door the way my brothers do; the blessed motor, still warm, started right away. Over the engine I heard people yelling a selection of my names as Dunbar and Mary called out to me, side by side in the smashed window of the Upper Reading Room.

'You damned seductive Bluebeard,' I gasped – to myself; he couldn't hear me. 'You *rat*. You greedy *rat*. *Those. Aren't. Your. Pearls.*'

I threw the car into reverse and screeched backward across the drive, spraying gravel against the nearest library windows. If anyone was calling to me still, I couldn't hear. I tried to shift into low and ground the gears terribly, so that the poor car shrieked in protest. I tried again, jammed the stick into the right place, and roared forward ten feet across the gravel. My glove slipped on the stick and I stalled trying to get into reverse again.

I struggled to pull off the damned gloves. It took ages. I got my left hand free.

Clutch in, engine on – the Magnette roared backward. I drove it like a roadroller, ten feet backward and forward, up and down and up and down across the drive. Beneath the motor car's screeching wheels, pearls and broken shards of jam jar ground against gravel, ground into powder, into stony dust.

Suddenly Francis Dunbar was practically on top of me again; he'd run out after me and somehow leaped on to the car. He now had one leg over the door frame, as he tried to climb into the passenger seat and grab at the handbrake.

'*Get out!*' I snarled.

I lashed at him blindly. To my horror and satisfaction, my fingernails connected with skin. He howled. The Magnette stalled again.

I cowered with my face against the driving wheel and my arms over my head as Mary, close behind him, fired rather a lot of birdshot into the back of Francis Dunbar's Black Watch kilt.

Mary was merciless.

Together, one of us on each side of him, we helped the moaning Francis Dunbar into her bedroom where she made him stand upright, leaning against her chest of drawers, while she laid out a multitude of protective towels before allowing him to collapse on his stomach on the bed.

'Now, Julia, you're not needed here. Go and telephone the police, and an ambulance, and I'll get him some brandy. You know where the 'phone is.'

So I did, rather dreading that they'd send Sergeant Angus Henderson. (They didn't.)

After I'd hung up the receiver I thought I'd better put a call through to Glenmoredun Castle and Strathfearn House.

At last Mary left her victim groaning in her bedroom, waiting for proper medical assistance. I heard her close the door and step out into the corridor. I was still sitting, like a stunned bird, in the telephone cupboard.

'Come along, Julia. Come and sit in my study. I'll get us both a cup of tea. Or you'd like brandy too, perhaps?'

'Tea's fine.'

She settled me in the red leather chair and bustled about in her dressing gown with her ear trumpet hanging triumphantly on its gold chain around her neck.

'You're my knight in shining armour, Mary,' I said, when she was facing me.

'What did he *do* to you?'

'He's the one who gave me that dunt on the head.'

'Then I'm *glad* I shot him,' she said fiercely.

The cup and saucer she'd been holding clattered as she set it back on her desk. She came and sat on the footstool by my side and suddenly buried her face against my knee, weeping into the leaf-green chiffon.

I had to fiddle with the chain around her neck to free the trumpet. I held it to her ear and bent over her, with one hand resting gently on her shoulder.

I said, 'Great Scott, Mary. Don't cry!'

'It's a crime to shoot a man,' she sobbed. 'Your grand-father had to appear in Perth Sheriff Court that time he shot the poacher. They put Mademoiselle Lavergne in prison just because they *thought* she'd killed Dr Housman, even though she hadn't. What will happen to me? I'll lose my position! What in the world will I do?'

I was pretty sure what I'd just done to the Murray Estate pearls wasn't legal either. I wasn't in the least afraid of what would happen to *me* and it seemed unbearably unjust that Mary should fear for her life's work because she'd defended me when I was being attacked.

'Sandy will make sure you're all right,' I assured her, certain of this. 'And I will too. I'll defend you in court if I have to! So will my mother!'

'I never do the right thing,' she wept.

'What *tosh*! You do better than that. You are able to *see* when you've done wrong. Most people just try to make excuses.'

She scrubbed at her eyes, still weeping.

'I want to *be* like you, Mary –'

'Oh, Julia, how *could* you!'

'I do! Oh, I do. You are so – so clever and independent and brave. *So* brave! I feel I could never be as brave as you – to have so much of the world pitched against you all the time, and to face it and face it and face it.'

I leaned down to kiss her smooth, tear-stained cheek. 'I have always wanted to be like you.'

She didn't show any signs of stopping and for a while I just let her cry, leaning over her with my arms around her shoulders. Probably, if I'd just spent an evening at home in a lonely old house by myself, too self-conscious to go dancing with my intended at his little sister's birthday party, and then had to shoot a man in said little sister's defence, I'd have collapsed in tears at the end of it too.

When her sobs began to subside a little, I squeezed her in my arms again.

'Do buck up, Mary. I want my tea.'

She gave a choking little laugh.

'I'd better find a handkerchief first,' she said.

She extricated herself from my clinging arms. I realised I'd been holding on to her rather desperately.

She looked up at me with fond, red-rimmed eyes.

'You are quite like me in some ways,' she said, and stood up with determination, and went to get the kettle.

The Murray Estate initiated charges of theft against both Housman and Dunbar – of the necklace Ellen made me! Which was all that was left of the Murray pearls after that night at the library. MacGregor's hadn't valued it by the time we were ready to depart Strathfearn but the whispers I heard *began* at the staggeringly preposterous sum of *seventy thousand pounds*. Father said it would likely raise more than that at auction; the British Museum and the Ashmolean had already both expressed interest, not to mention the National Museum in Edinburgh. Father thought it was even possible some of the amount would come back to Sandy if it completely cleared Grandad's debt.

Housman and Dunbar were expected to plead guilty to try to mitigate the sentence; and Housman was also going to act as a witness to Angus Henderson trying to get the McEwens in trouble by dumping my senseless body on the path near Inchfort Field. A prank against Travellers wouldn't be considered much of a crime, but accessory to an assault against the Earl of Strathfearn's granddaughter was a serious accusation against the Water Bailiff. I like the idea that *even unconscious* I may have helped to put a stop to Angus Henderson ever again battering Euan McEwen.

In the meantime Francis Dunbar was still in hospital on his stomach, and there was a new project manager taking over for the final phase of the Glenfearn School renovation. This young man delivered a letter without an envelope to Mother as she passed him in the corridor on her way into the morning room.

'For the Earl of Strathfearn, I believe,' the man told her briefly. 'I'm still sorting through Mr Dunbar's desk drawers next door.' He disappeared back into his own office.

Mother found herself looking down at yet another sheet of Housman's engraved writing paper, frowning. I jumped up to read over her shoulder.

My dear Sandy, As you requested, I'm returning the samples you supplied ...

Mother lowered her hand with the letter in it.

'This isn't for Sandy,' she said. 'It's two years old. It's from Dr Housman to my father. But why would it be among Francis Dunbar's correspondence?'

'*It's the letter that went in the empty envelope!*' I cried. 'Dunbar must have got it out of Housman's bedroom – he was up there right after Housman disappeared, before the police got to it. He said he was looking for Housman's address! Don't you see? Housman took it when he took the pearls. Maybe he even told Dunbar where to find it after he went into hiding! Oh, Mummy, it will explain why Grandad didn't sell the pearls! *Let me see!*'

I couldn't be good. I snatched it from her.

'*Julia!*'

'*Let me read it!*'

She let me.

My dear Sandy, As you requested, I'm returning the samples you supplied and am writing to confirm the values I suggested in our earlier discussion by telephone. As I said then, I do not feel you would benefit by selling these at this time …

I looked up. Suddenly my heart was breaking.

Mummy could see that in my face.

'What's wrong, darling?'

'I don't know why those snakes didn't burn this piece of paper,' I said furiously. 'Or, I do – they kept it because there's a little inventory list of pearls at the end of the letter. But –'

'Julia, I will expire right on this spot if you don't tell me what's in it,' Mother scolded. She sounded very much like me all of a sudden.

I wanted to cry.

'Grandad tried to sell the pearls to save the Reliquary,' I told her. 'And Housman lied to him and said his museum didn't want them.'

The pearls may be of historical significance but without proof the Ashmolean is not willing to make a financial offer.

Now I *was* crying. Tears dropped on to the page, smearing the treacherous ink.

'I bet Housman never even *showed* them those pearls! They're jolly well interested *now*, aren't they? He was already scheming to get hold of them, even while Grandad was alive! And you know what else –?'

Mother prised the damp letter from my hand so she could read it herself.

'You know what else? I'll bet Grandad never opened this. Ellen said he never opened post after he'd asked someone to confirm a telephone call in writing.' I had to stop and take a breath, choking on little sobs. 'Except that this envelope had a few pearls in it that Housman was returning to him. I'll bet Grandad just put the whole packet back with the rest of the Murray Collection pearls when it arrived. Housman probably opened it himself when he found it.'

Mother looked up at me, and now her face was tear-stained too.

'I'm not crying over the *pearls*,' I wept. 'I'm not even *sorry* about them. Just – *Grandad*.'

I took another gasping breath.

'Oh, Grandad.'

'My dad,' Mummy breathed. 'Yes.'

She took me in her arms and we sobbed together.

The pearls *would* save the Reliquary. The necklace was so valuable that it would pay for the Reliquary to stay in the

Inverfearnie Library, alongside Mary Stuart's bracelet.

Feeling triumphant and proprietorial, Jamie and I managed to dig up a couple of the rose bushes to take with us, though most of them were too old to move.

Mémère was scornful of our efforts. 'The same ones are already growing at Craig Castle. They all come from my sister's garden in France.'

I wished I could be like that, and like the McEwens: able to let things go without looking back.

But I was determined to look forward too.

Jamie and I went to Inchfort Field for the last time early in the morning before we left Strathfearn.

'It's been almost like a Shakespearean comedy, hasn't it?' Jamie said as we crossed the iron footbridge. 'One of the darker ones where someone has to be saved from execution or from being eaten by a bear. Everyone romping in the wood and bumping into the wrong people. You, for example, should have been wandering the bonny banks of the Fearn kissing Euan McEwen all summer, not throwing yourself at Francis Dunbar.'

'Kissing Euan McEwen, gracious!' I exclaimed. 'I never even thought about kissing Euan.'

'He thinks of you,' Jamie said.

I caught Euan on the path from the field to the river, almost exactly where we'd met two months ago, though I do not remember that meeting. He was carrying a milk can down to the burn to fill with water for washing.

Jamie gave me a quiet wink as he went on past us up to Inchfort.

I took Euan by the arm and made him put down the can.

'You're up early, Davie Balfour,' he said.

'We're away now,' I answered. 'I came to say goodbye.'

The melancholy of the end of the summer holidays, which I expect never goes away no matter how old you are, hit me suddenly in the chest.

'I have to go back to school,' I explained mournfully.

He laughed.

'Also,' I said, 'I have never properly thanked you for picking me up off the path and taking me to the hospital, so …'

So I kissed him, in the dappled light of the birches by the running sunny waters of the River Fearn, full of peat and secrets, and he kissed me back very gently and easily, and we both meant it.

But –

But I thought of Ellen while I was doing it.

Was it better kissing Euan or Ellen? Euan's kiss was honest; the only honest kiss I've helped myself to all summer. But Ellen – goodness …

I can't decide.

I don't understand the difference between my passion for Francis Dunbar and my passion for Ellen McEwen. They were both, in their way, impossible to act on, impossible for either one to end well. And that means I just have to live forever a little aching and incomplete. But –

There's something else.

It's nothing to do with the kissing. Or – not just to do with the kissing. I could stay with Ellen for the rest of my life, kisses or no kisses. I could never put up with Francis Dunbar indefinitely. Even if he hadn't nearly killed me, I'd have wanted to throttle him eventually for being so wet.

But Ellen McEwen, seeing through me and accepting what she finds – *showing me myself* …

When I found her at Inchfort that morning I gave her my pearl. I didn't need to tell her where it came from and she didn't have to ask. She closed her fingers around it and smiled.

'Pinkie will miss you,' she said.

'Oh, *Nell*.' I wanted to cry.

'I suppose I might miss you too,' she admitted softly.

I was damned if I'd cry.

'There's pearls in the Dee up at Craig Castle,' I said, rather desperately. 'And the oats and tattie harvest when the summer's done. You'd be welcome.'

'Your dad invited mine already.'

'But I'll be in school,' I mourned.

'Not *always*,' she pointed out. 'And I might find another lad like your brother and forget about you.'

She said that. As if I might, in her imagination, be an alternative to finding a lad.

'You think so?' I challenged.

'Would you mind?'

'I want you to be happy.'

'Och, away wi' you, Queenie.'

'I *do*,' I said stubbornly.

She cocked her head, and gave that little appraising *hnnph*.

'Well,' she said at last, 'you're better at giving than you were.'

Then softly she sang a part of the song she'd sung to me at the ceilidh at Inchfort, Burns's 'A Red, Red Rose':

'Till a' the seas gang dry, my dear,
and the rocks melt wi' the sun:
I will love thee still, my dear,
while the sands o' life shall run.'

She stopped. She was waiting for an answer.

I started to sing the rest, and she joined in.

I *so loved* singing with her.

'And fare thee well, my only love!
And fare thee well awhile!

And I will come again, my love,
tho' it were ten thousand mile.'

She opened her hand. The pearl gleamed for a moment on her open palm. And then she put it in her mouth and swallowed it.

She met my eyes, waiting for my reaction.

For a moment I was stung and blinded by tears.

Then we both burst out laughing.

The kisses don't matter.

AUTHOR'S NOTE

Living with Uncertainty: Travellers and Pearls

The 2011 census records about 4200 people living in Scotland today who identify themselves as Travellers. That's probably a low estimate; there may be four times that many. The Scottish Government recognises 'Gypsies' or 'Travellers' as an ethnic group, and is taking a stance against the ingrained prejudices and active discrimination which is launched against them to this day. Scottish Travellers include several distinct nomadic identities, some with Romani (Gypsy) connections; the cultural groups loosely termed Highland Travellers are native to Scotland, sometimes tracing their heritage as far back as the twelfth century. Like the McEwen family, many take their names from Scottish clans. For generations, folk outside their way of life have disparagingly referred to them as 'tinkers' because of their trade in tin and metal.

I am an outsider to the Traveller way of life, which is partly why I chose to tell this story from Julie's outsider's point of view. The small portrait of the Highland

Travellers represented by the McEwen family in these pages does not reflect the full spectrum of local names, folkways, beliefs, bloodlines and customs associated with Travellers from different parts of Scotland, nor does it deal with the complexities of their relationship with authority and the law, nor does it actually show them *on the move*. It's a glimpse into their lifestyle *during one summer* in the 1930s, but tells you little about their long history or how their communities have been scattered and disrupted in the past hundred years.

Scottish Travellers, like other nomadic ethnic groups throughout Europe, have long been treated as pariahs. But for hundreds of years Travellers made an intricate and intrinsic contribution to agricultural and village life throughout Scotland, as they assisted with seasonal work and provided an assortment of essential goods and services to Scots living in fixed dwellings. The sweeping changes of the twentieth century have caused cataclysmic upsets to their lifestyle, and indeed, to their cultural heritage.

Ironically, the automobile – that revolutionary mode of individual transport – appears to be responsible for some of the most negative recent impacts on Scottish Travellers. With cars came road improvements and laws that shut down ancient camping greens, closed well worn paths and byways, and enabled remote settled communities independent access to the myriad goods and services that Travellers had once provided for them. Many Travellers were respected horse dealers, and the petrol engine put an end to the horse trade. Scottish river pearls, found in freshwater pearl mussels, were another traditional source of Traveller income; the pearl mussel's decline in Scotland is probably also due in no small part to the automobile.

The freshwater pearl mussel *(Margaritifera margaritifera)* is now considered by some to be the *most endangered species in the world*. Though pollution and destruction of habitat also played their part in the decline of the pearl mussel, the discovery of the enormous Abernethy pearl in the River Tay in 1967 created a media sensation and started a sort of Scottish 'pearl rush'. There was then no law against taking pearls; cars made it easy for day trippers who knew nothing about pearl fishing, except that they were eager to get rich quick, to access remote stretches of riverbank and leave them stripped.

Within thirty years the pearl mussel population in Scotland had been utterly decimated. In 1998 the freshwater pearl mussel officially became a fully protected species and it is now a criminal offence to disturb them. The pearl mussel is so close to extinction that there is no retail trade in new Scottish river pearls *at all*. If you sell Scottish river pearls, you must have a licence from the Scottish Government to do so, even if the pearls you are selling belonged to your grandmother and you want to sell them privately. They must be known to have been taken before 1998 to be legal. On its webpage dedicated to the freshwater pearl mussel, Scottish Natural Heritage urges people to report to the police any suspicious activity seen in or around rivers that may contain mussels. Scotland's protected rivers are now the last fragile breeding ground for a species that was once widespread throughout Europe.

Until about thirty years ago, there was an intrinsic connection between Scottish Travellers and freshwater pearl mussels. Now, with the Traveller lifestyle and the pearl mussel's habitat both under threat, their futures will take distinctly separate courses. I am cautiously hopeful for both.

We don't ken half what's buried in the peat

Part of the joy of writing this book was that it is set *where I live*. I've never done that before. Everything I wanted to look at was right at my fingertips. Cairncross of Perth, one of two retailers in Scotland who are licensed to sell Scottish river pearls, is within walking distance of my house. Cairncross were very generous and enthusiastic about showing me their stock, even though they knew perfectly well I wasn't going to buy anything; without getting up close and personal with Scottish river pearls, I'd never have become aware of the subtleties of colour and lustre that make these jewels so exquisite. The Scottish Crown Jewels on display in Edinburgh Castle are set with Scottish river pearls, too, but those are locked behind glass.

Cairncross is not the only local organisation who let me get close to my subject matter. I experienced a wonderful insider's view into Iron Age Perthshire by volunteering on the Moredun Top hillfort excavations in 2015 and 2016, sponsored by the Tay Landscape Partnership and led by David Strachan. Strachan also led the Carpow Logboat excavation in 2006. The Carpow Logboat dates to 1130–970 BC and was discovered in Carpow Bank at the confluence of the River Earn and the River Tay, the setting for my imaginary Strathfearn. I saw the logboat on display in the Perth Museum in 2012. Needless to say, it provided the initial inspiration for this book. While *The Pearl Thief* was in progress, the Carpow Logboat was being scrutinised at the Glasgow Museums Resource Centre and wasn't on public view, but David Strachan kindly pointed me to a newer Tay logboat (485 AD) in the MacManus Gallery in Dundee.

Look away now if you're reading this before you've finished reading the novel, because there are spoilers ahead.

There is no evidence that the Carpow Logboat had any ritual use, but nor has such a use been discounted, for the exact reason Ellen McEwen cites in the novel: river crossings are strange and sacred places. However, no bog bodies have ever been discovered in mainland Scotland. This thread of the story comes from Wilmslow in Cheshire, England, where I lived when I was just starting school, and from the discovery there of a two-thousand-year-old body in Lindow Common in 1984. This murdered man, now on display in the British Museum, may well have been the victim of ritual sacrifice. As a four-year-old living not far from Lindow Common I was *terrified* of the place because of the eerie role it played in Alan Garner's *The Weirdstone of Brisingamen*. The discovery of the ancient body there in my twentieth year seemed like a complete vindication of my earlier anxiety.

But this is what authors do: we make up stuff that might be true. We populate the concrete landscape of the real world with the spirits and atmosphere of the landscape of our imagination. Sometimes the difference is very nebulous. Strathfearn does not exist; but Perthshire does, and so does the River Tay, and the River Fearn is closely related to the River Earn. The geology and geography of the imaginary landscape where I have situated the Strathfearn Estate is a sort of artist's impression of the Tay valley. Elcho Castle stands where Aberfearn Castle might have stood, the village of Bridge of Earn is more or less in the same place as Brig

O'Fearn, and the concrete telephone box (one of two survivors of its 1929 design) is in Rhynd, near Perth. Strathfearn House, renovated to become the Glenfearn School, could quite easily be mistaken for Freeland House, now home to the Strathallan School. I imagine Glenmoredun Castle in the same place as Balvaird Castle, though in better condition; I've deforested Dunbarrow Hill to turn it into the Pitbroomie grouse moor. And everything is a bit closer together in my fictional Perthshire landscape.

The Inverfearnie Library is the most uprooted location in the book. It's a tribute to the Innerpeffray Library on the River Earn near Crieff in Perthshire. The Innerpeffray Library was founded in 1680 by David Drummond, Third Lord Madertie; it was the first free public lending library in Scotland and is now the oldest. In 1680, making books available to the public for free was more or less unprecedented. Originally the library was housed in the Innerpeffray Chapel, which dates to 1507, with the current structure purpose-built for the collection in 1762. The library is funded to this day through a trust set up by its founder, alarmingly styled 'The Innerpeffray Mortification'. The Mortification is now a Scottish Charity (SC013847) and is supplemented with visitor donations. The current Library Manager and Keeper of Books is a young woman with a degree in English and Theatre.

And thank you

I tend to be shy and sneaky about my research. I did tell Cairncross of Perth that I was working on a book when I visited them, but I didn't give them any details, and I didn't have the courage to tell the Keeper of Books at Innerpeffray what I was doing when I visited the library, either. There is, however, one person who was let in on the project in detail: Jess Smith, storyteller, author and outstanding advocate for the Traveller community in Perthshire and beyond. She was my consultant in the art and culture of pearl fishing, advised me on the use of cant within the text of *The Pearl Thief*, and spent a painstaking amount of time annotating the original draft of my book. It was her suggestion that the Murray pearls be a gift from Mary Queen of Scots, which changed the course of the story. And her own writing provided me with a wealth of resources for the Traveller background for *The Pearl Thief*. I alone take full responsibility for any errors I've made in my portrayal of Scotland's Traveller community, but Jess Smith has been hugely supportive to me in this project and I hope that it helps to give her own life's work a wider voice. Her website is www.jesssmith.co.uk.

A novel is a much more collaborative project than readers may realise. This one had no less than five editors working on it: Amy Black, Kate Egan, Ellen Holgate, Emily Meehan, and Julie Rosenberg all helped to craft it into the thing of beauty that it has become. Amanda Banks, Miriam Roberts and Tori Tyrrell were my usual trio of first readers and I now don't know what I'd do without them, as they are always *so fast* with their feedback. Kathryn Davie, knowing nothing about the story except where it was supposed to take place, insisted I include Elcho Castle in it: so Aberfearn Castle was born. I am also grateful to Iona O'Connor, my 'Scotland' consultant – she also helped me with *Code Name Verity* – and to Sally Poynton and her father, who provided background information on early twentieth century farm equipment. And of course I would never get anywhere without the staunch and steadfast support of my agent, Ginger Clark, who I happen to know wears Scottish river pearls from Cairncross in her ears.

Some invaluable references and links of interest
Books

Christian Miller. *A Childhood in Scotland*. London: John Murray, 1981.

Timothy Neat. *The Summer Walkers: Travelling People and Pearl-Fishers in the Highlands of Scotland*. Edinburgh: Birlinn, 2002 (1996).

Graham Ogilvy. *The River Tay and Its People*. Edinburgh and London: Mainstream Publishing, 1993.

Ewan MacColl and Peggy Seeger. *Till Doomsday in the Afternoon: The Folklore of a Family of Scots Travellers, The Stewarts of Blairgowrie.* Manchester: Manchester University Press, 1986.

Jess Smith. *Jessie's Journey: Autobiography of a Traveller Girl.* Edinburgh: Birlinn, 2002.

David Strachan. *Carpow in Context: A Late Bronze Age Logboat from the Tay.* Edinburgh: Society of Antiquaries of Scotland, 2010.

Betsy Whyte. *The Yellow on the Broom: The Early Days of a Traveller Woman.* Edinburgh: Birlinn, 2001 (1979).

Websites

The Scottish Government's Equality statement on Gypsies and Travellers:

http://beta.gov.scot/policies/equality/gypsy-travellers/

Shelter Scotland maintains a sympathetic website offering information and advice on accommodation-related issues for Scottish Travellers:

http://scotland.shelter.org.uk/get_advice/advice_ topics/finding_a_place_to_live/gypsiestravellers

British Pathé newsreel video, released 5 June 1961, showing Bill Abernethy fishing for pearls in the River South Esk:

http://www.britishpathe.com/video/pearl-fishing

Scottish Natural Heritage's webpage on the freshwater pearl mussel:

http://www.snh.gov.uk/about-scotlands-nature/species/invertebrates/freshwater-invertebrates/freshwater-pearl-mussel/

The Scottish Government's statement regarding the freshwater pearl mussel:

http://www.gov.scot/Topics/Environment/Wildlife-Habitats/paw-scotland/types-of-crime/fresh-water-pearl-mussels

Perth and Kinross Heritage Trust's webpage for the Carpow Logboat excavation:

http://www.pkht.org.uk/index.php/projects/carpow-logboat/

Innerpeffray Library Website:

http://www.innerpeffraylibrary.co.uk/

QUESTIONS FOR DISCUSSION

1. Julie admires Ellen for 'being herself', unconstrained by the social pressures Julie feels. Do you think Ellen is freer than Julie?
2. Ellen accuses Julie of thoughtlessly taking everything she wants from life. Is that a fair accusation? Does Julie's attitude to giving and taking change during the story? Does Ellen's?
3. How do you think Ellen feels about Julie?
4. How does the appearance of the singer Le Sphinx contribute to the overall story?
5. Do you think Julie means it when she tells Mary Kinnaird she wants to be like her? What about Mary might Julie admire?
6. Some of the characters can 'switch on' a heavy Scottish accent. How do they use this ability in different social situations?
7. The Travellers face terrible discrimination from a number of characters in the novel, but are accepted by others. Who accepts them and who doesn't? Why do you think this might be?

8. Julie bonds with a number of people in the novel who are 'outsiders' – Ellen and Euan McEwen, Frank Dunbar, Mary Kinnaird and Le Sphinx. Do you think Julie is an outsider in some ways?

9. How did you feel about Frank Dunbar at the end of the novel?

10. The idea of violation comes up many times in the story: violation of privacy, of bodies, of land, of history and of law. What are the weapons that the women in the book can use to fight back against these trespasses? Are they different to those available to men?

11. How are some of the issues experienced by *The Pearl Thief's* characters in 1938 relevant to us today?